The Witch entered the temple as the men met. She gasped, unable to believe even now that she saw it. How had the man gotten through the citadel's defenses? What man could have earned such great power?

Clouds of light and shadow contended. Larger than life, figures turned in an almost formal, elegant dance around the slice and dart of flashing mystic blades.

The shadow was overpowering the light slowly, consuming it, but she did not see that in her fear for the man she loved. She saw only that an enemy was trying to kill him and that enemy was a great enough wizard to have penetrated the citadel's impenetrable defenses. She screamed, all reason fled before the prospect of loss. "Nakar!"

Startled, the shadow turned her way.

The light struck its blow.

. . . and so begins a tale of doom and wizardry that brings us all, in the end, to

The Tower of Fear

TOR BOOKS BY GLEN COOK

THE
TOWER
OF
FEAR

GLEN
COOK

TOR
fantasy

A TOM DOHERTY ASSOCIATES BOOK
NEW YORK

This is a work of fiction. All the characters and events portrayed in this book are fictitious, and any resemblance to real people or events is purely coincidental.

THE TOWER OF FEAR

A Tor Book
Published by Tom Doherty Associates, Inc.
49 West 24th Street
New York, N.Y. 10010

Cover art by Gary Ruddell

ISBN: 0-812-51933-7

First edition: August 1989
First mass market printing: October 1990

Printed in the United States of America

0 9 8 7 6 5 4 3 2

THE PLAYERS IN
THE MANY-FACED GAME

Qushmarrah—The conquered city where events take place

THE QUSHMARRAHANS—
Called *veydeen* by the Dartar tribesmen, the literal meaning of
the word being stone-sitters. Applicable to any city dwellers
Aaron Habid—A carpenter and war veteran
Laella—Aaron's wife
Arif—Aaron's older son
Stafa—Aaron's younger son
Raheb Sayed—Aaron's mother-in-law
Tamisa ("Mish")—Aaron's sister-in-law
Taidiki—Aaron's brother-in-law, now dead
Billygoat—Aaron's friend and co-worker, who caulks the seams
in ships

Naszif bar bel-Abek—a metalworker and war veteran
Reyha—Naszif's wife, Laella's best friend
Zouki—Naszif's son

Nakar the Abomination—a sorcerer, now dead, who ruled
Qushmarrah in the name of the god Gorloch
The Witch—Nakar's wife
Torgo—a eunuch serving the Witch

1

Azel—a professional killer, talented and deadly. A man of many
    faces
Muma—innkeeper and associate of Azel
Ishabel bel-Shaduk—professional criminal and child-taker

The General—Leader of the Living, the Qushmarrahan resis-
    tance to the Herodian occupation; khadifa (colonel or
    chieftain) in the quarter called the Shu
General Hanno bel-Karba—the Qushmarrahan national hero
Colonel Sisu bel-Sidek—the General's adjutant and heir, khadifa
    of the waterfront
Meryel—woman shipping magnate, supporter of the Living, and
    bel-Sidek's lover
Colonel Salom Edgit—khadifa of the Tro quarter, caught be-
    tween greed and honor
Colonel "King" Dabdahd—khadifa of the Astan quarter, a
    bootlicker
Colonel Ortbal Sagdet—khadifa of the Hahr quarter, more
    gangster than patriot
Colonel Carza—khadifa of the Minisia quarter, a fanatic
Colonel Zenobel—khadifa of the Shen quarter, a fanatic
Hadribel—second-in-command in the Shu quarter

THE DARTARS
Desert nomads, mercenaries acting as auxillaries to Herod's
    occupation forces
Yoseh—a young warrior just in from the desert
Nogah—Yoseh's older brother, leader of his band
Medjhah—Yoseh's older brother
Mahdah—member of Yoseh's band, a cousin
Kosuth—member of Yoseh's band, a cousin
Juba—member of Yoseh's band, an adoptive cousin
Faruk—member of Yoseh's band, a cousin
Melchesheydek—Yoseh's father, something of a rogue

Fa'tad al-Akla—called the Eagle, commander of the Dartar
    mercenaries

Joab—captain of Yoseh's company and an old friend of Fa'tad

Mo'atabar—sergeant of Yoseh's company, related to Joab

THE HERODIANS

Called *ferrenghi* by the Dartar tribesmen, the literal meaning of the word being outsider, stranger, enemy. In contemporary usage specifically someone whose allegiance lies with the imperial city, Herod.

General Lentello Cado—conqueror of Qushmarrah, now military governor and commander of occupying forces

Taliga—General Cado's brother-in-law and batman

Colonel Bruda—Herodian intelligence chief in Qushmarrah

Marteo Sullo—civil governor of Qushmarrah

Annalaya—a witch brought to Qushmarrah by Sullo

Cullo—Aaron Habid's supervisor at work

Ala-eh-din Beyh—a wizard, antecedents unknown, whose successful attack upon Nakar the Abomination made possible the Herodian conquest of Qushmarrah

OTHERS

Chorhkni, Suldan of Aquira—permanent threat on the eastern boundary of the Herodian empire

THE GODS

Gorloch—an ancient, ferocious deity long abandoned by most Qushmarrahans

Nakar—an angel in Gorloch's pantheon, associated with death, from whom the sorcerer Nakar adopted his name

Azel—a messenger demon associated with the angel Nakar

Aram the Flame—a gentle, compassionate deity whose cult supplanted that of Gorloch

God—the Herodian deity, ferocious, jealous, contradictory. Extension of his cult is the excuse for Herodian conquests

Prolog

The smoke was oppressive. It crept south into the Shu from the Shen, where sorcery had birthed fires when the invaders breached the Gate of Winter. It brought chaos. Within it combatants recognized neither friend, foe, nor fleeing civilian. Men struck now and wept later. Animals careened around in panic. The heavy overcast turned back the light of day and worsened seeing.

Qushmarrahan, Dartar, and Herodian alike prayed for rain. Rain might quench the fires and cool the killing insanity.

Qushmarrah was lost but its men fought on. While Nakar lived they dared not surrender.

The surrounding horizons were clear. It seemed the city was circumvallated by walls of light. The clouds grew rapidly darker nearer the heart of the city. Above the acropolis, over the citadel of Nakar the Abomination, those were black as the breath of Hell. The citadel's tower pierced their low bellies.

Lightning shattered darkness. Thunder crushed the uproar in the streets. A hundred thousand smoke-teared eyes looked toward the sorcerer's stronghold. Clouds above began to swirl, to stream inward, forming a whirlpool in the sky, a celestial maelstrom.

4

An end-of-the-world flash and crash rattled the city to its foundations.

The rains came. They fell in torrents like none before witnessed by man.

The sorcerer sat on his dark throne, amused. He would wait a while longer before he crushed the invaders. They would perish in agony, every one, Herodian and Dartar traitor . . .

Something moved in the shadows at the far end of that last temple of Gorloch. He sprang up, robes flying, eyes wide. He did not recognize the man but knew what he must be. "You!"

"Yes, High Priest." There was soft mockery in the voice. The man wore peasant garb. He was too tall to be Herodian, too dark to be Qushmarrahan. The breath of the desert informed his voice but he was no Dartar. "Another has come."

Nakar relaxed. They came and they came but he devoured them all. "I should have suspected." He chuckled. "Cado has been unnaturally lucky."

"Not my doing, wizard. Cado's genius, your failings, and human frailty."

The sorcerer sneered. "The fire is come. It will scour away the weakness of Aram. Herod's triumph will turn in her hands, like an adder. Gorloch will stand forth in his glory again. Come. I grow impatient. I will destroy them after I finish you." He laughed. "Come, little dog of the desert. Let it be done between me and yours. You are the last."

"No." The man's slow advance did not falter. "There is another training already. Always there will be another somewhere, hidden from your eye, till you are driven from the world and torment it no more." A dagger flashed in his hand. It radiated power.

Fear touched the sorcerer for an instant. Then the rage came. He *would* sweep them out of the path of destiny. "Gorloch, attend me!" He hurled himself toward his challenger. They met before the great idol, beside the altar where thousands had screamed their last that Gorloch might be pleased and his apostle Nakar might live forever.

* * *

The Witch entered the temple as the men met. She gasped, unable to believe even now that she saw it. How had the man gotten through the citadel's defenses? What man could have earned such great power?

Clouds of light and shadow contended. Larger than life, figures turned in an almost formal, elegant dance around the slice and dart of flashing mystic blades.

The shadow was overpowering the light slowly, consuming it, but she did not see that in her fear for the man she loved. She saw only that an enemy was trying to kill him and that enemy was a great enough wizard to have penetrated the citadel's impenetrable defenses. She screamed, all reason fled before the prospect of loss. "Nakar!"

Startled, the shadow turned her way.

The light struck its blow.

Nakar's bellow shook the fortress. He lurched into his enemy, clawing at his attacker's throat. Their struggle flung them against the altar.

The Witch wailed. She had killed him with her interruption. While they yet fought, before death claimed its prize, she wove her greatest spell ever, binding them in timelessness. Someday she would bring back the man she loved, when she found the way.

She finished. In pain, as she collapsed, she cried, "AZEL!" The summons rolled through the citadel but there was no answer. Nakar had sent his right hand far away, to work his will in another land. There would be no help.

It was too late. For now.

The avalanche of rain faded as fast as it had come. The clouds blew away from Qushmarrah like the souls of men newly dead. Throughout the city men began to lay down their arms. Nakar was gone.

* * *

In the Shu the stillness yielded to the cry of a newborn. And a moment later its cries were joined by those of another entrant into the lists of life.

The war ended. The wheel turned. A new story began.

1

The boys came up Char Street in a mouthy pack. The hazy turquoise of the bay backed them. There were twenty of them, ranging from three to eight years old. The pretend they were playing reflected their parents' private rejection of history. They were soldiers returning victorious from Dak-es-Souetta.

Their rowdiness caught the old woman's ear. She looked up from her mending. A scowl deepened the wrinkles webbing her dark leather face. She thought their parents ought to whip some sense into them.

One of the boys kicked something the size of a melon. Another raced forward, snatched it up out of the dust, shook it overhead, and shouted.

The old woman's frown deepened. Wrinkles became gullies of shadow. Where had they gotten a skull?

The boy dropped the headbone and booted it. It ricocheted off a man's leg. Another man kicked it past the old woman. It vanished in a canebreak of legs. That was a busy street.

The old woman saw char marks on the skull before it disappeared.

Of course. They were razing the ruins near the Gate of Winter, where, after breaching the wall, several hundred invaders had perished in a fire touched off by errant sorceries. The area would be rich in treasures for small boys.

The pack raced after their plaything, disrupting commerce and generating curses both good-natured and otherwise. One boy, about six, stopped in front of the old woman. He was very formal as he said, "Good afternoon, Grandmother Sayhed."

The old woman smiled. She had teeth missing. With equal formality, she replied, "Good day, young Zouki. You've been exploring where they're tearing the old buildings down?"

Zouki nodded and grinned. He was missing teeth, too.

At the beginning and at the end, toothless, the old woman reflected. Like Qushmarrah.

The boy asked, "Can Arif come out?"

"No."

Zouki looked startled. "How come?"

"It wouldn't be safe. You boys will be in big trouble in a few minutes." The old woman put her mending down. She pointed in the direction of the bay.

The boy looked, saw the eight black riders swaying like the masts of ships above the turbulent human sea. The leader rated a horse. The others rode camels. They came straight up the hill, leaving it to the mob to get out of their way. Dartar mercenaries.

They were in no hurry to get anywhere. They were after no one. Just a routine patrol. But if they saw the boys abusing the skull . . .

Zouki gawked.

The old woman said, "Get along now, Zouki. Don't bring the heathen to our door."

The boy spun and plunged after his friends, throwing a shout ahead. The old woman continued to stare at the riders. They were close now.

They were young. The leader was the eldest. He might be twenty-three. None of the others had reached twenty. They wore black veils to mask their features, but those were not heavy. One could not have been more than sixteen.

As the Dartar riders came abreast of her, that youngest's eye met the old woman's. Her stare was hot and sharp, accusing. The youth blushed and looked away. The old woman muttered, "Well you might be ashamed, turncoat."

"Oh, Mother. He's not responsible. He was a child when the Dartar tribes betrayed us."

"Dak-es-Souetta," the old woman hissed as she looked up at her daughter, who had come from the house with a child on her hip. "Never forgiven, never forgotten, Laella. Herod is a passing wind. Qushmarrah is eternal. Qushmarrah will stand when the invader is dust. Qushmarrah will remember the Dartar treachery." She spat toward the mercenaries.

"Why don't you go burn a memorial tusk at the gate of the citadel of Nakar the Abomination, Mother? I'm sure the Witch will appreciate the gesture."

Laella retreated into the house. The old woman sputtered curses under her breath. Another symptom of the conquest. Children showing no respect for their parents.

She glanced uphill. The citadel of Nakar the Abomination could not be seen from her vantage. Even so, chills tramped her spine.

Some good had come of the occupation. Even she would admit that much. Even she thought Ala-eh-din Beyh a hero. Before his sacrifice no one would have dared call Nakar "the Abomination" in any voice but the most breathless whisper.

The old woman pointed and Zouki's gaze followed the spearthrust of her withered arm.

The Dartar riders were like something out of the nighttime monster stories the older boys told to scare their little brothers. All in black, with nothing but hard eyes and a bit of dark, tattooed cheek showing.

He spun and ran into the crowd, alternately yelling, "Yahoud!" and apologizing to the adults he jostled. With everyone taller, and the dust so thick at his level, it was impossible to see his friends. He thought he heard his name.

Bam! He ran into Yahoud, who had just lifted the skull from the dust. "You dope!" Yahoud said. "Look out where you're going."

"Yahoud. Dartars."

"What?"

"Dartars are coming. Right back there."

"Really?"

"Yes."

Yahoud looked at the skull a moment. "Here, Zouki. Go throw it into that alley."

Zouki held the skull in both hands and wove through the press. The alley was not far away. Before he reached it several boys were following him, alerted by Yahoud.

He was about to step into the alley when he saw the vague shape back in the shadows. He paused.

A voice just loud enough to be heard said, "Bring it here, boy. Give it to me."

Zouki took three steps, paused. He did not like this.

"Will you hurry it up?"

Zouki responded to the authority in the voice, taking another three steps. That was one too many. The man leaped. A hand slammed down on his shoulder, a clamp of agony. "Yahoud!"

"Are you Zouki, son of Naszif?"

"Yahoud!"

"Answer me, brat!"

"Yes! Yahoud!"

Children crowded the alley mouth, shouting. The man shifted his grip to Zouki's arm and dragged him deeper into the shadows. Zouki screamed and kicked and struck out with the skull he still clenched.

Yoseh fought the awe that threatened to overwhelm him whenever he left the Dartar compound. So many people. So many *thousands* of people, more than he could have conceived of as inhabiting the whole world a year ago. And the bay? Who cold conceive such a sprawl of water, vast as an arm of the Takes, but the blue of heavenstone? With far vaster expanses of sea beyond the Brothers, the headlands flanking the strait that led into the bay.

And the buildings! He did not believe he would get used to the buildings, ever. In his native mountains there were no builded things at all, except ancient fortresses that had begun their fall to ruin centuries ago.

There was an eddy and swirl in the mass of humanity ahead. An exuberant cry went up.

"Medjhah," Yoseh said. "That's the mudha-el-bal." Though that battle cry was still heard in the canyons of the Khadatqa Mountains, here even Dartars were denied it.

"And we should go cut them down, Yoseh?" his brother asked. Medjhah was an old Qushmarrah hand after a year in service. "Eight of us meting out capital punishment to kids amongst a couple thousand of their relatives? If the ferrenghi want them punished, let them see to it themselves. Let them bear the hatred."

Their elder brother Nogah, who was the captain of their little company, turned in his saddle, said, "Well spoken, Medjhah. Yoseh, we're not here to die for the ferrenghi. We're here to take their wages."

Yoseh grunted. Ahead, one of the children had gone to the side of the street to talk to a crone seated on a mat. Old people lined the street on both sides, some on mats, some seated on steps, some trying to hawk, some just watching the parade of life. It was a miracle they did not get trampled.

The crone pointed. The boy looked, saw Yoseh and his companions. His eyes bugged. He yipped and dashed into the crowd.

"You see?" Medjhah said. "The streets of Qushmarrah are free of heresy and sedition."

The others laughed. Yoseh did not. As the youngest he was always the brunt of their humor. He looked at the old woman. She looked back, her face as empty as a statue's. But he could sense the angry hatred within, like the lakes of molten rock simmering deep within the holy mountain Khared Dun. Sometimes the god in the mountain became angry enough to spew fiery destruction upon anyone unfortunate enough to be nearby. The crone reminded him of the holy mountain.

That old woman had lost somebody at Dak-es-Souetta.

He felt the heat climb his cheeks. He tore his gaze from the old woman and called up all his Dartar contempt for city dwellers. But the embarrassment continued to mount. He had forgotten what he was. Now all these sessile goat flops would see a Dartar betraying his feelings.

Yoseh was very conscious of his youth, of his inexperience, of the unfaded newness of the manhood tattoos upon his face, and of the lance across his lap. Medjhah assured him that the self-consciousness would pass, that none of these city veydeen even noticed.

Yoseh knew that. But knowing with the head and knowing with the heart could be separated by the journey of the hundred nights.

Someone shouted. Yoseh saw the children rush to the side of the street. Adults followed after more shouts. The children seemed distressed.

Nogah yelled. He begun swinging the butt of his lance, urging his horse through the press. Yoseh did not understand. He had difficulties with the cants and dialects of Qushmarrah. But something was happening that Nogah considered to be within their venue. He kicked his mount. The camel promptly tried to take a bite out of the nearest citizen.

The crowd was thickest around the mouth of an alley about four feet wide. The children clustered and raised a repetitive wailing chant that sounded like, *"Bedija gha! Bedija gha!"*

Nogah shouted at Faruk. Faruk sounded the horn that would summon any Dartar or ferrenghi troops within hearing. The crowd began to thin immediately. Nogah said, "Yoseh, Medjhah, Kosuth, go in there after them. The rest of us will try to get around and cut them off. You. Boy. Hold these animals."

The Dartars dismounted in a clatter. Still baffled, Yoseh followed his brother and cousin into the dark, dank, stinking alleyway. His lance was unwieldy in that narrow passage.

Fifty feet in they heard a cry. It sounded like an echoing call for help.

Twenty feet onward the alley split at right angles. They paused, listened. Medjhah shrugged, said, "This way," and turned to his right.

Ten steps. That cry again, from behind. The Dartars turned and ran the other direction, Yoseh now in the lead and more bewildered than ever. He kept his lancehead extended before him.

Fifty yards. A hundred. All upslope, tiring. "Slow down," Medjhah said. "Let's be careful. It could be a trap." The veydeen were not all passive about the occupation.

A whisper of scuffling came from up ahead.

The alley bent to the right. Yoseh dashed around the angle and sensed a presence. It resolved into vague shapes struggling. A man trying to drag a boy. Panic swept the man's face momentarily. Then he flung a hand toward Yoseh.

The alley filled with a blinding light and heat and a child's cry of despair. Yoseh went down as Medjhah and Kosuth stumbled into him from behind. The fire burned like the furnaces of hell.

"Gorloch, thou art merciful," Azel murmured as he watched the target take something from an older boy and hurry toward the alley whence he watched. He had anticipated a long and difficult stalk. They had become wary. But this bird was flying to the snare like it wanted to be caught.

What the hell was the kid lugging? A goddamned skull. Where the hell did he get that?

Azel fell back a few steps, hoping the kid's eyes would be used to the glare off the bay and he would come into the alley blind.

No such luck. The kid was not seeing good, but he was seeing good enough. He stopped a dozen feet too soon.

"Bring it here, boy. Give it to me." The kid moved some. Not enough. He wasn't completely unwary. "Will you hurry it up?"

That got the brat close enough. Azel leaped, grabbed. The kid started yelling. Azel made him give his name. Taking the wrong brat would be worse than doing nothing.

The kid kicked and yelled and flailed around with the skull. Azel ignored that, backed up, watched the brats at the alley's mouth, yelling themselves.

Then figures in black appeared, their weapons glittering.

Azel cursed. "Dartars. Where the hell did they come from?" Fear snapped at him. He spent a part of it by yanking the boy violently. He would lose those whoreson turncoats in the maze webbing the Shu quarter south of Char Street. No one alive knew that one better.

Only the brat wouldn't let him get the head start he needed. He kept on fighting and kicking, yelling and tripping. Azel smacked him around as much as he dared, but not as much as he wanted. There would be no tolerance shown if he delivered damaged goods.

Then they were there in the labyrinth with him, the mercenary betrayers, with absolute terror coursing before them, and for the first time ever Azel found himself compelled to employ his penultimate recourse.

The ultimate recourse fluttered blackly behind his lids as he clung to the brat with one hand while flinging the contents of the envelope, his eyes sealed.

Heat drove him back.

The Dartars cursed and clattered into one another. The kid squealed and quit struggling. Azel opened his eyes. "That's more like it, you little bastard." He glared at the Dartars. If he didn't have to keep the kid in hand he would stick them with their own spears.

He grabbed up the by now passive boy and draped him over his shoulder. The boy clung to the skull as though it was a protective talisman.

This time it was hard. This time it took all his knowledge of the labyrinth to lose the hunters. Dartars and Herodians and angry citizens were everywhere. Azel zigged and dodged and at times even crouched in hiding, the kid clamped helpless and silent in his arms. Of all the damnable luck, those black-clothed camel jockeys turning up when they did.

There was a warning in what had happened. The easy times

were over. And they were barely past halfway down the list. With Gorloch knew how many more yet to be discovered.

There was going to be some serious talk after he made this delivery. No way was he going out again with nothing but a pack of flash to cover his ass.

He reached the outlet from the maze that lay nearest his destination. The brat started to struggle again, but that did not last. And he finally turned loose of the damned skull.

Azel scanned the square he had to cross. He saw no sign of excitement. He had distanced the hunt but probably not the news that a child had been snatched. Should he try it now, in the long shadows of afternoon, or await the friendly darkness?

The square was almost empty. The kid was out of fight again. Gorloch knew what might creep out of the labyrinth behind him if he sat on his hands.

He grabbed the brat's paw and headed out, fast, like an angry parent. The kid stumbled and whimpered, and that fed the illusion.

As he tramped across the square Azel lifted his gaze and rehearsed and nurtured the rage he was going to vent.

And that fed the illusion, too.

Aaron pressed up the hill, the black fear gnawing his heart. He was a man kept strong and trim by his labors, but emotion had driven him to a violent storm up the long climb from the waterfront. His legs were billets of lead, as they were in his nightmares.

It was over now. Long over. But some of the spectators remained, still telling one another what had happened. Beyond them were a handful of Herodian soldiers and several Dartar horsemen. Ranking Dartar, Aaron realized after a second look. Startled, he found himself exchanging momentary glances with a fierce-eyed old man who had the face of a raptor and a savage grey beard.

Fa'tad al-Akla himself! Fa'tad the Eagle, commander of all the Dartar mercenaries, bloodthirsty as a vampire, merciless as a hungry snake. What was he doing? Making himself a target for the Living?

Of course not. Was he not supposed to know as little of fear as the desert windstorms that brewed over the Takes and raged north over the Khadatqa Mountains and beyond, to inundate Qush-marrah with dust and torment it with a ferocious dry heat? Fa'tad al-Akla held the Living in contempt.

Aaron thought them quixotic at best. But he also believed they were going to kill Fa'tad, and he did not think it would be long before the dark angel brushed the Eagle with the shadow of his wing.

Ahead, in front of the house, he saw Laella and her mother. They were not bereaved. His heart spread white wings. Then it soared as he spied Arif.

His son was all right! The nightmare had not come true!

Arif saw him coming and ran to meet him. He snatched the boy up and surrounded him in a hug almost brutal in its intensity. Arif squealed, surprised. People stared. It was not a culture that encouraged emotional display.

Arif wanted to tell him all the news but he had squeezed the breath out of the boy.

Aaron joined Laella and her mother. His wife had Stafa, their younger son, seated upon her left hip. Stafa was midway between his second and third birthdays, and on his better days he was happy mischief incarnate. Arif was, by contrast, a quiet child, often seeming sad.

The younger boy reached out. "I want some Daddy hugs."

Aaron reached and let him monkey over to sit on the hip opposite Arif, grinning. Aaron told Laella, "I heard. I was afraid it was Arif."

There was pain and relief and guilt in Laella's eyes as she said, "No. It was Zouki. Reyha's Zouki."

"Oh."

Laella's mother watched Fa'tad with the fixity and dispassionate intensity of a vulture waiting for a corpse to cool out. "They went after him."

Aaron turned. "What?"

"The Dartar patrol. They were right here when Zouki was taken. Not much more than boys themselves. The children screamed '*Bedija gha!*' and the Dartars went after the taker."

She sounded amazed. As if so human a thing was beyond comprehension if done by the villains of Dak-es-Souetta.

"And?"

Laella said, "Three went in Tosh Alley. And they caught him." She did not sound joyful.

"Something bad happened?"

"They were all burned when they brought them out. Not dead. Not really bad hurt. But one of them's clothes was smoldering."

Aaron grunted.

"Aaron, something has to be done."

He grunted again. He agreed. But he did not know *what* could be done. There had been talk among the men, but it never went beyond that. One could do nothing when one did not know which way to strike.

The old woman muttered something.

"Mother?" Aaron asked.

"The Dartars think the Living did it."

So. No wonder she was in shock. For her the Dartars had become the wellspring of all evil. And here they had tried to rescue a child, and thought the last ragtag remnants of Qushmarrahan partisans had done the grabbing.

"The children yelled '*Bedija gha!*' Could that be it? Are the old gods stirring?"

Bedija gha sprang from an older form of the language. Today it meant "child-stealer." In Qushmarrah, as in all cities in all times and lands, there were people who wanted to buy children. For whatever reason. So there were others willing to harvest and sell. But before "child-stealer" or "kidnapper," in the old days *bedija gha* had had a more sinister and specific meaning, "collector of sacrifices."

That had been in the time of Gorloch, cast down and banished by Aram long since. The god's followers had been dispersed, his temples demolished, and his priests forbidden human sacrifice.

He had not gone quickly or quietly, though. Superseded gods never do.

Aram the Flame had brought light to Qushmarrah but Gorloch had clung to the shadows and it was not till the coming of the Herodians, with their strange, nameless, omnipotent god, that Gorloch's last High Priest's time had ended.

Aaron shivered and glanced uphill. Nakar the Abomination. How he had deserved that name, that dark sorcerer-priest-king unassailable in his citadel. Bless Ala-eh-din Beyh and the Herodians for having laid that terror to rest.

Laella said, "No, it couldn't be Gorloch. They say Nakar was the last priest who knew the rites." Her mother nodded agreement without taking her eyes off the Eagle. "And the Witch never was a believer."

"There must be manuscripts that tell about the rituals."

"You're trying to talk yourself into something again, Aaron." Laella smiled to take the sting out of the admonition.

She was right. He wanted conspiracies to explain away his fear of something he did not understand. Chances were there was no more child-stealing going on now than there had been at any other time. He was just more aware of it because he and his contemporaries were of an age to have children of an age to be at risk. That and the fact that there had been a rash of kidnappings in the area, some as broad-daylight-brazen as this latest. A thing like that caused a lot of talk that led to more talk that maybe magnified the problem out of all proportion.

If it were not for the nightmares . . .

He realized his arms were aching with the weight of the children. "All right, Stafa. Back to Mom. Arif, down you go. Daddy's arms are tired."

Stafa flashed his little white teeth and shook his head "Can't," he said.

"Yes, you can," Laella told him. "Come here. Your father's been working hard all day."

"Can't. My dad."

Aaron bent and let Arif down. Arif's feelings were hurt, of course, but he hid that as he always did. He was convinced everyone loved his brother more than him, and no logical argument could reach his heart and convince it that a smaller child always needed more attention.

The firstborn are always the sad ones, Aaron thought, and felt vaguely guilty. He always seemed to expect more of Arif.

He leaned toward Laella, who tried to pry Stafa off him. Stafa laughed and declared, "Can't! Daddy's Stafa!" He grabbed two fistfuls of Aaron's hair. Aaron suppressed the usual flash of anger and impatience and played the game out.

Laella finally peeled the boy off. The battle shifted ground. She wanted to put him down and he did not want to be put. Laella won. Stafa went into a pout, declared, "I hate you, Mom!" He ran and clung to Nana's leg. But the old woman had no attention to spare.

Aaron grabbed Arif up and set him on his left hip, ignoring the ache in his arm and shoulders. "Come on, big guy. Let's see what's going on." His relief at finding Arif safe persisted. It left him feeling select and immune and more daring than was his nature. He even managed to meet the Eagle's eye without flinching.

Bel-Sidek dragged his log of a bad leg up the slope of Char Street. It got worse every day. His pride was under ever more severe strain. How long before it broke, he surrendered, and he became just another crippled veteran begging at street side?

As it did every time, the thought sparked white-hot rage. He would not surrender! He would not become a vegetable patch beside the thoroughfare, watered by the charity of Herodian conquerors whose generosity consisted of tossing back fragments of the ghosts of plunder ripped from the heart of Qushmarrah.

Bel-Sidek sometimes tended toward a dramatic turn of mind.

The leg did not hurt as badly, nor drag nearly so much, when the thought of a commander of a thousand begging at street side drove him into a fury. Dartar and Herodian had humiliated him and reduced him by strength of arms and right of conquest. But he would not finish what they had begun. He would not degrade himself.

"They have not won," he muttered. "They have not beaten me. I am one of the living."

For the true believer the formula was as potent as a magical cantrip.

There was something wrong with his surroundings. He stopped instantly, coming out of himself to look around suspiciously. Yes! Dartars and Herodians everywhere. How had they . . . ?

Wait. Maybe not. Whatever had happened, it was over long since. And the enemy did not have that grim look he got when his own had been hurt. Someone would have gotten hurt had they found the General.

Still . . .

Still, it had been something that interested them a great deal. A great deal. That was Fa'tad al-Akla himself. The Eagle would not be out here for trivia.

Was he at risk here? Had they been found out? Was it a search? No. Hardly. How would the old man know them in their present circumstances, after ten years, when he and the General had been but faces in the background when last they had crossed paths?

There was Raheb Sayhed and her daughter. Raheb spent her life planted on her mat there. Nothing escaped her. He limped over to the two women.

A smiling face peeped around Raheb's skirt. Bel-Sidek grinned. "Ola, Stafa." He liked the child. "Ola, Raheb. Laella."

The older woman replied, "Ola, Khadifa." She inclined her head almost imperceptibly, to show that *she* still honored him. She continued to stare at Fa'tad.

Bel-Sidek frowned his question at the daughter.

Laella said, "The foundations of her world took a shaking this afternoon."

"What happened?"

"A child-stealing. Reyha's son, Zouki. A Dartar patrol was right in front of the house when it happened. They tried to rescue Zouki. Three of them got hurt."

"That explains Fa'tad."

"Maybe. But I don't think so. They weren't hurt bad. I hear he's here because they think the Living had something to do with it."

"That's absurd."

"Is it?"

"Why would they take a six-year-old kid?"

"Why would they beat up shopkeepers and steal from artisans and leave their own people floating in the bay while never, *ever*, laying a finger on the people they're supposed to be fighting?"

"You're exaggerating."

"Am I? Let me tell you something, Khadifa. There are ordinary, everyday, loyal people in Qushmarrah—people who hate Herod and Dartars as much as you do—who're so fed up with the Living they've talked about maybe letting Fa'tad find out some names."

"Laella."

Bel-Sidek turned. "Aaron. How are you?"

"Upset. I have small children. It disturbs me that the Dartars seem more interested in their safety than do those of my own people who might say they have some claim on my sympathy. People who, by their nature, ought to have some insight into the problem if there's a racket behind the child-stealing."

Bel-Sidek understood. He did not like it. "I hear what you're saying, Aaron. Here. Come. Walk with me to my house." He began dragging the leg uphill.

The man turned his son over to his wife and followed. It did not take him long to catch up. Bel-Sidek asked, "Is it true, what she said?"

"You know how women are when they're scared or mad. Say any damned thing that pops into their head."

"Yes." He glanced back at Raheb, still frozen in place. There was an omen as sinister as her daughter's threat. "I know some people who know some people. I'll say something to someone."

"Thank you. How is your father doing?"

"He sleeps a lot now. The pain doesn't bother him as much as it did."

"Good."

"I'll tell him you asked about him."

The old man wakened when the door slammed. It had to be slammed or it would not close all the way. "Bel-Sidek?" He winced as the pain shot down his side.

"Yes, General."

The old man composed himself before the khadifa entered the dimness of his room. Only a part of the dimness was due to a lack of lighting. His eyes were growing feeble. He could make out few details of bel-Sidek when he appeared. "Was it a good day, Khadifa?"

"It began well. Three ships came with the morning tide. There was work. We needn't worry about where our meals will come from for a few days."

"But?"

"I encountered an unpleasant situation coming home. It was illuminating."

"Political?"

"Yes."

"Report."

He listened carefully, with a feeling for nuance. His hearing was excellent. Time had been that kind. He heard not only objective substance but the implication that the khadifa was troubled in heart.

"The woman—Raheb?—bothers you. Why?"

"She had one son. Taidiki. Her sunrise. Her full moon. He went to Dak-es-Souetta with my Thousand. A brave lad. He held his ground till the end. He was one of the forty-eight of mine who came home. He came back in worse shape than I did. A lot worse. But he was a proud kid. He thought he'd done something. His mother cried for him, but she was proud of him, too. And of everyone who fought the odds at Dak-es-Souetta. Fanatically so."

"Is there a punch line to this story, Khadifa?"

"A year ago Taidiki went into the street and started telling anyone who would listen the same things his sister said today, only he spoke more straightforwardly. He said hard things about our class and the Living. He said the Dartar tribes were not the traitors of Dak-es-Souetta, that Qushmarrah had betrayed them first by ignoring them in their need. They had done only what they had to do so their children could eat. When one of the Living tried to hush him, he denounced the man. When the man resorted to threats, Taidiki's neighbors—our neighbors— beat him senseless."

"I'm still waiting for the punch line."

"Taidiki took his own life afterward, as a protest. He said Qushmarrah had murdered him already and he hadn't had sense enough to lie down."

"The point?"

"That was the moment I first realized there were people of Qushmarrah who were less than enchanted with our efforts."

"And?"

"A more dramatic incident occurred in the Hahr day before yesterday. The Dartars rounded up eighteen ground-level members. They had been denounced anonymously. The Dartars did not bother interrogating them. They just executed them there in the street. Some of the onlookers cheered."

"I see."

"Do you? Some of the brethren have been feathering . . ."

"I said I see." The General reflected for several minutes. "Khadifa, your father has just had another of his spells and thinks he's dying again. You round up your brother and cousins and have them here later tonight so they can be given their legacies."

"Yes sir."

"Fa'tad is in the street out there?"

"Yes sir."

"Help me to the door. I want to see him."

"Is it worth the risk, sir?"

"Is he going to recognize a man who's been dead for six years?"

He did not get his fuzzy glimpse of the enemy. Fa'tad al-Akla and his tribesmen, and the Herodian infantrymen, had gone. Char Street had become its normal twilight self.

2

"What's this?" Aaron asked, looking at the concoction Laella had set before him. He shifted on his cushion. The aches of work and the terror of the afternoon were fading. His question was one of honest inquiry, not complaint.

"What does it look like?"

"Half a yellow squash with stuff baked inside it."

"Can't put anything past you when you put your mind to it, can I?"

Arif said, "I don't like this stuff, Mom." Stafa echoed him immediately. The younger boy was just into that stage.

"You haven't tried it yet."

Aaron didn't think he would like it, either, but it turned out to be good. The boys did right by their portions, too.

Laella had filled the partially baked squash halves with a mix of chopped and sliced vegetables, and slivers of mutton, in a heavy, spicy brown sauce. There were mushrooms and nut meats in there, too. And dates promised for afterward for boys who ate their supper.

Old Raheb worked on her meal without speaking. Hers had been cooked longer so meat and vegetables would be easier prey for toothless gums. Tonight she worked every mouthful twice as long as usual. Aaron pretended not to notice. Nobody could get quite as fixated as Laella's mother. If one of her fixations won an audience it could turn into years of high drama.

Look at Taidiki. She had been mourning Taidiki since Dak-es-Souetta. He might not have broken had she not been there wailing all the time.

Aaron needed distracting himself. "What do you think of it, Mish?"

Tamisa, Laella's fourteen-year-old sister, completed the household. For a time after Dak-es-Souetta there had been other sisters. They had gotten married one by one. The latest had gone just before Taidiki's mad gesture.

Maybe that had contributed to Taidiki's despair. All those sisters to dowry and no other relatives to soften the blows to his patrimony.

Raheb did not mourn her husband, did she? He had fallen at Dak-es-Souetta, hadn't he? But she hadn't so much as mentioned his name since moving in here.

Tamisa said, "It's all right." Howling praise. About as definite a statement as anyone could get out of her these days. She had changed over the eight years Aaron had known her. Sometimes he felt vaguely guilty about that, though he did not see how he could be responsible. Too much time spent close to her mother, he thought.

He worried endlessly that Arif and Stafa would drift down the same pathway to a life of quiet despair. He worried about his sons too much, he knew. Children survived childhood. He had. It was being grown-up that was lethal.

Laella said, "When we're done I want to go see if I can do anything for Reyha."

"I thought you might."

"Mish can clean up."

"Of course."

"We've known each other a long time. We went through labor together. There was still fighting in the streets."

"I know."

"We lay there holding hands and listening to people killing

each other outside, not sure that somebody wouldn't break in and do something to us."

"I know." There was a part of Laella that could not forgive him for having been a prisoner of the Herodians on that critical day, unreasonable as she knew that to be.

"Zouki came only a minute after Arif. It was the last day of the war. The day Ala-eh-din Beyh broke the barrier and killed Nakar the Abomination."

"I know." He knew the preamble was all because he would have to take her if she was to go see Reyha. And he loathed Reyha's husband, Naszif.

Naszif was an ironwright and prosperous. The Herodians had plenty of work for metalworkers and gave Naszif all he could handle. Aaron and Naszif had been in the same artillery engineers troop. Aaron was convinced that Naszif had betrayed them during the siege of the Seven Towers in Harak Pass.

Three of the towers had been reduced already. There was never a doubt that the Herodians would break through. The defenders were supposed to buy time until the defeated of Dak-es-Souetta, the new levies, and the allies could gather on the Plain of Chordan. The lords of Marek, Tuhn, and Caldera were sending seventy thousand men.

But someone heeded either cowardice or the Herodian offer of rewards and unsealed the tower's postern. The treachery advanced the Herodian cause sufficiently that they were able to reach the Plain of Chordan in time to keep it all from coming together.

"When we heard, we both had the same crazy idea. Name our sons Peace," Laella said.

"I know."

"Why don't you like Naszif? You were in everything together."

"That's why. I know him." He had told no one what he believed about Naszif. Not even Laella.

"But . . ."

"I was there and you weren't. The subject is closed. Get yourself ready if you're going to go. Arif, Stafa, one story from Nana, then go to bed."

In one year the coast as far as Caldera had fallen to Herod. Not, Aaron was convinced, because of the great and so close thing at Dak-es-Souetta, but because of one traitor in one tower in Harak Pass.

When he started brooding about it he got himself out of the mood by mocking himself for thinking someone as insignificant as he could have been so near the heart of any crucial historical event.

Yoseh lay on his cot with his hands behind his head, staring into the darkness between the ceiling beams. The burn on his face hurt. The ointment didn't do much to help.

"Why so thoughtful tonight?"

Yoseh looked up at Nogah. He replied with complete honesty. "That man in that alley. He could have killed us if he'd wanted. All of us. Easy."

"Probably. But he didn't."

"But he did want to. I could see it in his face, behind the fear and surprise. He hated us and wanted to kill us but it was more important to keep that little boy under control."

Nogah looked at him a moment, then nodded. "Come on. Fa'tad wants to ask you about it."

The muscles across Yoseh's stomach tightened till he felt like he was having cramps. His eyes began blinking. He could not stop. "No. I can't."

"Come on, Yoseh. He's only a man."

"He's only Fa'tad al-Akla. He scares the Demon out of me."

Nogah smiled. "It's about time somebody did that, little brother. You've always had too much brass for your own good. Come on."

Yoseh rose. He followed Nogah, wondering if this was how men felt as they went to the gallows.

The Dartar compound was outside Qushmarrah proper, beyond the Gate of Autumn, on a field where the city's soldiers once trained. A thin curtain wall twelve feet high surrounded it. All the buildings within abutted against this, their roofs forming a platform for defenders. Everything was crudely constructed of mud brick painted to protect it from the rain. The wall enclosed about three acres.

Yoseh and Nogah had to cross the enclosure to reach Fa'tad. Stars had come out. The air overhead was unusually clear. Camels and horses, goats and cattle mumbled to one another. The smell of hay and crowded animals was strong. "It must be about time to send a herd south," Yoseh said.

"Any day now. There are enough men whose time is up to take them."

"You've been here five years, Nogah. Why do you stay?"

"I don't know."

"Foo. I'm your brother, Nogah. I've known you all my life. You would've thought about it a lot each time before you signed on again."

"Maybe I can do more good here, earning the ferrenghi silver that buys the herds. Down there I'd be just another mouth."

"Not to mention that while you're up here you don't have to keep butting heads with Father."

Nogah snorted. Then he chuckled. "No. Up here I have Fa'tad al-Akla, with whom there is no arguing. Father you can wear down sometimes."

"Before I left he almost broke down and became human. 'Four sons I send to Fa'tad now. And none of them come back. You come back when your time is done, little Yoseh. You come home.'"

"That sounds like him. And I'm sure he sent some blustery message to his prodigals."

He had, of course, but Yoseh hadn't bothered to report it. "Yes."

They walked a few steps. Nogah said, "So?"

"He said, 'Tell my Nogah, my firstborn, to come home. Tell him I am one step ahead of the dark angel and beginning to limp. An heir's place is beside his father in his last hour.'"

"His last hour, eh? One step ahead of old Death?"

"He said it. I didn't."

"And he just took another wife."

"Yes."

"That's the third one since I came north."

"There are a lot of women who can't find husbands because so many of the young men don't come back from duty in Qush-marrah."

"So Father is easing the shortage."

"His duty to the tribe, he told me. If he hadn't taken the poor girls in, their fathers might have put them out of their tents. They might have starved."

"No doubt these foundling waifs come without dowries, too."

"Are you kidding? He'll take ugly but he won't take poor."

"And they always call him that charming old rogue Mel-chesheydek." They reached the opposite side of the compound. Nogah said, "Nogah, Yahada. We're here."

"I'll tell him." The guard posted outside Fa'tad's quarters stepped inside.

"It's a serious problem, Nogah," Yoseh said. "The old men are talking about making it so nobody can join Fa'tad who hasn't already taken a wife and at least gotten her with child."

"Those sour old bellies must be full, then."

"What?"

"They didn't talk that way when they were starving. Then it was send the boys whether they want to go or not."

Yahada opened the door. "Come in."

Yoseh preceded his brother, his knees starting to shake. His first glimpse of Fa'tad did nothing to reassure him. Those eyes . . . Grey as iron and cold as the bottom of a well. There was no anger in them, but still he felt like a clumsy child.

Fa'tad nodded infinitesimally, "Nogah." The old man sat cross-legged on a small cushion. He had filled the room with the appurtenances of a cave shelter. They did not hide the truth. "This is your brother Yoseh?"

"Yes sir."

"I overheard what you said a moment ago. Is it true, Yoseh, that they intend to meddle with me down there?"

Yoseh did not know how to answer. The question sounded like one with a snare built into it. He chose his words carefully. "They want to encourage the young men to return home more quickly."

A specter of a smile twitched Fa'tad's lips. "Oh, yes. As they so quickly did when they were young auxiliaries scouting for Qushmarrah's armies. You were right, Nogah. Their bellies are full, and sour with memories of what they lost with their youth. Yahada, find Barok. Tell him he needn't worry about how he's going to get all that livestock safely to the mountain." Fa'tad smiled a genuine smile. He looked at Yoseh as if he were speaking to him alone. "They need to be reminded that the drought is still with us." His face clouded, then lost all expression.

Eight years of drought. There was nothing to match it in Dartar history.

"Your brother told me what happened this afternoon, Yoseh. Now I want to hear your part of it from you."

Yoseh fumbled the story out.

"Would you recognize the man again?"

"Yes sir."

"Describe him."

"He was short, even for the veydeen. And very wide. Very muscular. Not a young man. Middle thirties to early forties. Dark for veydeen. Very quick, and I think very strong. His nose was flattened, like somebody smashed it in. Wide mouth and heavy lips."

"Beard?"

"No sir."

"Obvious scars?"

"Well . . . I can't be sure. His lip curled up, like this, a little. There was a man back home with a lip like that from a knife wound."

"Uhm."

Nogah asked, "You know the man, sir?"

"No. But I'd like to meet him. Yoseh, how did he make the fire?"

"He just reached down and got something out of his belt . . ."

"An envelope? A packet? A sachet?"

Yoseh glanced at Nogah, back. "Yes sir. One of those."

"Hunh! Do what he did, as closely as you can ape it. Slowly."

Yoseh did so, puzzled by Fa'tad's interest and cowed by the intensity of his scrutiny.

"He reached across his body with his left hand and emptied the packet at you backhanded?"

"Yes sir."

"And the stuff he threw. Did you get a good look at it before it caught fire?"

"It was dust, sir. Yellow, I think. Yes. Almost saffron."

Nogah asked, "Sir, is this important?"

"The gestures probably not. He had one hand busy holding a child. But I'm very interested in the powder. What sort of powder is inert in an envelope open to the air but bursts into flames when it's thrown?"

"Sorcery?" Nogah suggested softly.

"Certainly a possibility. I'm *very* interested in such a dust."

"Yes sir."

"I'm also interested in that maze of passages in the Shu. We have more trouble with the Shu than any other quarter. Because the villains can use that maze to come and go as they please."

Yoseh had a feeling Fa'tad was leading up to something. His suspicion was confirmed immediately.

"I want you to go up there tomorrow, Nogah. Start exploring. Start mapping. There is no map of that area. Even people who live there don't know what's going on out their back doors. Starting tomorrow everyone not on duty for the ferrenghi will be up there exploring. We'll go in there and stay. We'll take the maze away from Qushmarrah's bad men."

Nogah said, "Yes sir." Yoseh echoed him hastily.

"That will be all for now. Yoseh, if you recall anything significant, I want to know right away."

"Yes sir." Yoseh got out as fast as youthful dignity would allow. His legs almost betrayed him returning across the compound.

Zouki sat inside the door of the cage, leaning against the cold iron bars, motionless, for a long time. He was so scared he had wet himself.

There were thirty other kids in the cage. They were scared, too. They seemed to have spaced themselves out. Only two, who looked like twins, were close to each other. The kids all seemed to be about his age. They all stared at him.

They did not seem starved or abused. They were clean and clothed. But they were scared and Zouki thought they must cry a lot.

He wanted to cry. He wanted his mother.

He looked at all those kids looking back at him and didn't know what else to do. So he did cry.

Azel had just finished a meal for which the cook ought to be convicted. He could not guess what he had eaten.

Torgo walked in. "She's ready for you now." He sounded like a man talking to a cockroach.

"Yeah? Good. Who cooks this slop? They ought to be staked out on an anthill. The brats get fed better."

"The children are valuable. Come."

Following Torgo, staring at the eunuch's huge, broad back, Azel said, "Torgo, I like your attitude so much I think I'm going to kill you. You ball-less wonder. Maybe pretty soon now." He looked at the eunuch's bare feet and knew just how he would start.

Torgo glanced back, for a moment the expression on his big round flabby face more puzzled than anything. Then a slow smile spread. "You're welcome to try. But you'll be disappointed."

"You bad, Torgo? You think you're bad? You ain't never been out of this dump. You ain't never seen the real world. Out there is where the bad boys play. You don't know bad from dog turds. You ain't bad. You ain't even hard. You're just pig-stupid and mean."

And pretty good at keeping his temper, Azel reflected.

Few who lived in the citadel went in or out. The Herodians knew who they were. If any got recognized those bastards would realize there was a way through the barrier, after all. Only Azel

and a few other trusted agents came and went through what the
barrier's creator had nicknamed the Postern of Fate.

Two of those agents were women who busted their butts doing
the grocery shopping and whatnot.

Azel wondered if he really would get aggravated enough with
Torgo to take him out. Maybe. If the eunuch kept on with his
airs.

Well, whatever. He shut the eunuch out of mind and scanned
his surroundings. An ordinary hallway. Except that it was decked
out in enough treasure to ransom a platoon of princes. The
whole damned citadel was like that. But old Nakar, he was the
boss wazoo around Qushmarrah for a long time. And when they
knocked down the temples and busted up the idols he was the
kind of guy who made them pay for the privilege of replacing
Gorloch with their candy-ass Aram the Flame. When they had
done that he started taking any damned thing he pleased.

Azel could not figure out why the old boy had let them get
away with dumping Gorloch. He knew Nakar had claimed there
was no point imposing on jerks who refused to believe. But he
never quite figured out why that mattered.

He had been around, up and down the coast, and even across
the sea, out where the gods were really bizarre, and he thought
he knew one thing about religion: the fact of actual belief did not
matter. You had to know how to go through the motions and you
had to be able to say, "How much?" whenever a priest stuck out
his hand and said, "Gimme." That was all.

Azel did not know if he was a believer or not. He had been
doing all the right things for so long it was all habit. He did know
he found the ferocious Gorloch a more satisfying deity than
Aram with his softhearted, softheaded, otherworldly love and
forgive-thy-neighbor crap.

He irked Torgo by chuckling. If he wanted a stand-up, he-man
god he ought to go with the Herodian's anonymous deity, who
had no other name but God. That one was all thunder and
lightning and kicking ass. But a goddamned psycho, too. His
doctrine was all do what I tell you or die, sucker, and the hell

with it's something stupid, or it conflicts with something you've already been told to do.

Herod had not pressed religious issues in Qushmarrah. Yet. The Herodians were spread thin. If ever they felt secure enough to dispense with the unpredictable Dartar mercs it would be Granny bar the door, Qushmarrah you're going to get the One True Faith. Or burn.

Azel chuckled again, remembering a scheme he'd bounced off the General three, four years back. It involved having kids—so small any Herodian laying a hand on them would get torn apart—go around giving the occupiers chunks of stone with lots of points and sharp edges.

It would have worked. They would have laughed Herod out of town. But the old man had said it was undignified to attack a man through his toilet habits. Crap. You went after your enemies any way you could, and you kicked them when they were down.

Azel chuckled again, because that irritated the eunuch. But he cut it off as they approached the guard at the door of the audience chamber. Time to work himself up.

A hundred years ago she had been the greatest beauty on the coast, and for that alone suitors had come to Caldera from as far west as Deoro Etrain, where Ocean hammered and raged against bleak and rocky shores. They had come from the east, from far Aquira, Karen, and Bokhar. They had come from over the sea, on ships with sails purple and scarlet and blue the color of heavenstone, from Cathede and Nargon and Barthea. Those princes and lords could have swooned when they saw the reality. They would have taken her with her beauty alone for dowry.

But there was more. Much more. It made them bring great treasures with which to gift Caldera.

She had been that one girl child in a generation born with a talent for sorcery. That one in a generation whose talent could become a tool more potent than the genius of any general.

She had had the world at her feet then. And young as she had been, already they had begun to call her the Witch—more because of the way she had toyed with them than because of her talent. She had led them around, taunting them into escalating their offers, with no real intention of selling herself off, or of allowing the lords of Caldera to auction her . . .

That had been their plan and wish. Gold, power, alliances. Her father himself had been one of those she had made excruciatingly uncomfortable, with a cruel case of boils, when the attempt to sell her was made.

Then the Archimage of Qushmarrah, Nakar, had come to Caldera.

He had not come in style or state. He had brought no gifts or promises. Already his dread god had been shorn of significance by the fickle Qushmarrahan mob. He had only his unassailable citadel and his ruthless deathgrip on the political power in Qushmarrah.

He had been half as old as the world even then, though he had looked a fit, lean, virile forty. He had been a darkly handsome man with wavy black hair spotted by a hen's egg of silver above his right eye, an inch and a half behind his hairline. His eyes had been dark and magnetic and afire with intrigue.

She had known the moment she met his smoldering gaze.

Dark tales clustered around him like moths fluttering around a lamp. They said this. They said that. They said he lived on, young, not because of his sorcery, nor because he was first acolyte to, and favored of, his god, but because he had become one of the undead, the devourers of blood and souls.

None of that mattered after that first meeting of eye with eye. None of that mattered now.

She had aged, but not her hundred years. She looked a well-preserved thirty-five. Little of the impact of her beauty had faded. It remained her most potent tool.

It was a tool without a handle or edge when she dealt with Azel. Azel seemed blind or just plain indifferent.

He pushed inside behind Torgo. Torgo's jaw was tight. Azel's taunting had begun to reach him.

She steeled herself. Azel would be brash and crude and raw in an effort to put her on the defensive. He would succeed, probably. Because of that absolute, deadly confidence with which he faced everyone—even those able to swat him like a fly.

She did not know his true name. Her husband had called him Azel, after Gorloch's demonic messenger. Nakar had trusted Azel. Azel was, she believed, the only living being Nakar had trusted without reservation. And even he, majestic and dauntless as a storm in his power, had been a little afraid of Azel.

The trouble was, Azel never failed to accomplish what he set out to do. That made you uncomfortable when you tried to push him a direction he did not want to go.

"Good evening, Azel. I understand you have a problem."

"We all got a problem, woman. They're closing in. I had to use my flash packet to get a gang of Dartars off my back today."

She knew where he was going. He'd hinted before that he thought she was pushing the project too hard, that gathering too many subjects too fast would catch the eye of the Herodian commander. "Tell me the circumstances, Azel." She wanted to stall.

But she had had time to think already, since Torgo had told her Azel insisted on an audience. She had not gotten her mind ordered.

Why did he rattle her so?

Azel told it in his clipped, raw way.

"It was a coincidence, then. Not something to worry about, after all."

"You missed the point, woman."

"Torgo!" Offended by the man's tone, the eunuch had started to move. Azel grinned. "If I'm blind, Azel, open my eyes. Show me the point I missed."

"I *had* to use *flash* to give *Dartars* the slip. If I wanted to hang on to the kid. I should've killed them. But I couldn't do that without letting go of the brat."

"I still don't see . . ."

"Flash, woman. Flash. You think every guy that hangs out in alleys has got a pocket full of flash to throw when the heat closes in?"

"Oh."

"Yeah. It's going to start them wondering. Maybe even wondering why it was so damned important to hang on to the kid. They're going to start asking questions. If they get any honest answers they might start seeing patterns. There's plenty of clues if they pay attention."

"So what would you suggest?"

"Back off awhile. Don't give them anything more to check out. You got thirty kids down there and don't have a notion if one of them isn't the one you want. Let it ride till you find out."

"No. There are nineteen more on the list, Azel. And it's mathematically certain that between five and ten remain unidentified. That's almost as big a group. Another third of the whole. Every hour we delay is an hour of risk. It's been a lucky group of children. Only six have died between birth and the present. But if the one we want is one that had died or will die before we get hold of him, we end up starting all over with a new group. A group, in fact, for every one that died. How much greater the risks, then, with groups of younger children? The thing grows monstrous, Azel."

"How much chance you got of pulling it off if the Herodians figure it out? If you keep us on the street and one of us gets caught? Zippo, woman. Zero. Zilch. They figure out what's happening they're going to be on you like a snake on shit."

"That terror is less fearsome than the mathematical horrors that come of each additional death, Azel. We will continue the current program."

"The hell we will. I'm not getting myself torn apart by the mob or put to the question by Herod. I'm off the case until *I* decide it's safe to work it again."

"You've said you believe in the project."

"I do. It's Qushmarrah's last hope. But what does believing in something have to do with walking off a cliff to hear the splat when you hit bottom? Back off. Take it easy. Let it cool down. And when you go on, give us better tools."

The anger, born of frustration, grew in her. She fought it. Argument would do no good. Azel never did anything he did not want to do. "Very well. I'll go on without you. When you're ready to continue your work Torgo will give you your next assignment."

Azel stared at her till it was impossible to meet his gaze. Then he shook his head in disgust and walked out.

Torgo stepped closer. "Did you watch us as we came to the chamber, my lady?"

"I caught part of it, Torgo. You have to ignore it. Don't let him get to you."

"He made threats."

"That's his nature. Forget it."

"Then you don't want anything done about him?"

"Not yet. He could be useful still. We have a long way to go."

"But . . ."

"If it becomes necessary to remove him I'll let you know."

Torgo bowed, satisfied for the moment.

She would not send Torgo after Azel. Not unless it was Torgo she wanted dead.

Azel stepped into the vast dark hall that was Gorloch's last bastion in the world. Rites continued to be held there—attended only by the few believers who lived in the citadel. Last rites. A wake for a lost, majestic fury.

The appropriate candles were burning but, it seemed, they could not beat back the darkness as they had in earlier times. The only real light glowed around the great altar where the sacrifices had been given up to Gorloch. But even that light had faded. It had not been fed for six years. The glow no longer beat back the night enough to reveal the great idol that looked down upon all.

Azel stirred himself, strode forward. His heels clicked upon the basalt floor. Echoes bounded and rebounded and mixed till they sounded like the noise made by the wings of a flight of bats.

Azel paused beyond the glow, considered the tableau frozen before him.

Nakar still lay arched backward over the altar, Ala-eh-din Beyh's enchanted dagger in his heart. One hand gripped the altar for leverage. The other was a claw at the end of an extended arm, now clamped upon air as once it had been clamped upon the

Herodian sorcerer-hero's throat. Ala-eh-din Beyh lay on his side at Nakar's feet, still locked in the stance of a man using both hands to drive a blade into an enemy's heart while trying to lean back from a hand tearing at his throat.

All the Witch's power had been able to do only that much to separate them. The enchantment into which she had put them at death was that powerful.

Azel came to view the tableau each time he visited the citadel. Each time he came the darkness seemed to have closed in a little more.

If it devoured the glow entirely would it be too late for the project? Too late for Qushmarrah?

Was the Witch so driven because she was racing against the darkness?

As he did each time he came, Azel genuflected slightly—but whether to Nakar, the altar, or to the god in the darkness beyond, even he could not have said. Then he turned and left that place, and went out through the Postern of Fate into the real world of a Qushmarrah sprawled helpless at the feet of her conquerors.

Bel-Sidek got the General seated at his table only moments before the first of the "nephews" arrived. The old man had called forth surprising reserves of will and had banished the appearance of ill health. He almost looked like the General of old.

That first to arrive was "King" Dabdahd, who ran the Astan quarter. King was the least important of the guests expected. No trouble came out of the Astan. King was the General's man.

Qushmarrah within the wall was divided into seven "quarters": the Shu, the Shen, the Tro, and the Hahr (the original four quarters of the "Old City"), the Astan, the Minisia, and the waterfront. Bel-Sidek and the General ran the waterfront and the Shu. The troublesome quarter, the Hahr, belonged to one Ortbal Sagdet.

There were other quarters beyond the wall but they weren't even considered New City. They did not interest bel-Sidek or the General. The General's authority extended only to the wall.

Bel-Sidek posted himself at the door, to greet the General's heirs as they arrived.

"Good evening, King," the General said. "Make yourself comfortable. You're several minutes early." His tone said he understood that meant King had something to say before the others arrived—and he did not approve.

King always arrived early. King always had something to say about the others. He was a petty, spiteful, back-stabbing, exasperating man working on getting himself designated heir apparent to a sick old man.

He had his good side, his uses, his talents, not the least of which was his ability to swim in the social waters inhabited by the big fish of the Herodian occupation. His courage he had proven at Dak-es-Souetta.

Dabdahd said, "I saw Sagdet on my way here. He said he wouldn't be coming."

"Indeed? And why not?"

King did look chagrined as he said, "You know I've never been shy about expressing my opinion of Sagdet, nor reluctant to report his shortcomings and pecadillos, but tonight I'll restrict myself to the observation that Ortbal Sagdet no longer feels he is bound by your authority. Maybe Salom Edgit will state it for him."

Dabdahd talked that way. Like he was making speeches he had rehearsed. Bel-Sidek thought he probably had.

Salom Edgit ran the Tro and was Sagdet's crony. His record at Dak-es-Souetta was a match for the best, but he had changed since then. Bel-Sidek thought of him as an onion rotting slowly from the heart outward, layer by layer.

Salom Edgit arrived only moments after King finished. He looked at the man from the Astan and seemed disappointed. Bel-Sidek suspected he'd had something he'd wanted to say before the others arrived, too.

Bel-Sidek considered the two. Dabdahd was a tall man but slim, courageous enough but small at heart. Edgit was a slight man, short, still tough and gutsy, but somehow he had lost the vision that had breathed life into the Living. His autonomy had died. He seemed to have become a chameleon, changing to look more and more like Ortbal Sagdet.

Carza and Zenobel arrived together. Bel-Sidek was sure that was significant. Those two had no use for one another. The only thing they had in common was their dedication to the cause. Each bordered on being a fanatic. But they disagreed fundamentally on strategy.

Zenobel wanted to build a strong secret army of patriots that could be wielded in one furious hammer stroke. In the Shen he was doing things his way. The Shen was as quiet and trustworthy as the Astan.

Carza's vision was apocalyptic. He wanted to bring down the fire. He wanted to temper Qushmarrah in a holocaust that would rid the city of human dross and consume the invaders. He did not expect to survive the fire himself.

He was willing to pay the price.

The General was not.

Carza was always a moment of frustration short of breaking away and raising the standard of holy war.

The General made a sign indicating that bel-Sidek should remain where he was. When the newcomers had settled, he said, "Disturbing events in the Hahr two days ago, khadifas." The strength of his voice surprised everyone. "Eighteen soldiers identified by citizens and executed by the Dartars."

Salom Edgit said, "The traitors will be rooted out and slaughtered."

"No. They will not. They were driven to it. When a man's supposed guardian becomes more savage and rapacious than his avowed enemies, what is he to do? I have investigated, Salom. The people of the Hahr have been provoked beyond endurance. There will be no reprisals."

Edgit snapped, "We let a bunch of shopkeepers and artisans get away with betraying us? The policy from the beginning has been . . ."

"There will be no reprisals, Salom. None. The Living have heard what those people were saying. There will be no more extortion. Those who fail to heed this directive will be replaced. Am I clear?"

Edgit fumed. Twice he started to speak, thought better of it.

After a half minute of silence, during which bel-Sidek tortured himself trying to understand how the old man could have probed events in the Hahr, the General said, "Let us consider al-Akla's motives for doing what he did. Eighteen soldiers taken and executed without questioning. The first implication is obvious. He wishes to place his men in a favorable light while sparing the consciences of those who denounced them.

"But the Eagle flies high and far. His vision isn't that simple. His action could suggest that he had no need to question those men because he already knew everything they could have told him. An unpleasant supposition but plausible considering the way things are run in the Hahr.

"Be still, Salom. This senile old man, who doesn't have the grace to die and leave you to the spoils, isn't finished."

Bel-Sidek watched carefully as Edgit fought the temper for which he was well known. Bel-Sidek wondered, and expected Salom was wondering, if the old man wasn't trying to provoke an outburst.

The General continued, "What message was Fa'tad sending us when he killed our men? What else is in his mind? The Eagle soars on the high wind, above everyone and everything, but he is also like the sea. He has dark deeps, and many secrets lie hidden within them. We don't know what surprises might surface from them."

No one said a word, though the General let silence expand till it became a rushing cold wind pouring through the nighted and frightened hollows in every heart.

"Carza. Have you surrendered? Have we lost Qushmarrah forever? Have we come to the day of every man for himself?"

"No sir."

"Bel-Sidek?"

"I have a leg and two arms left. Sir."

"Zenobal?"

"There is no defeat, General."

"King?"

"I am among the living."

"Yes. As am I, to the despair of some. But I will not last much longer. I do not need to last. We are close to an event that will make this the year of Qushmarrah's delivery. We in the active organization need only buy time."

For the first time since the meet's commencement the General suffered a spasm that was too much for will to control. Bel-Sidek straightened, poised to help if summoned.

But it passed.

One day it would not.

"These are my commands. No member shall extort anything—whether monies, goods, or anything else—from any citizen of Qushmarrah. None of the Living shall participate in gangsterism or hooliganism in any form. Anyone guilty will discover that while the lion is old he has a tooth or two left. That is all for tonight. Tomorrow night we will meet again. The khadifa of the Hahr will join us."

Salom Edgit concealed surprise ineffectually. Bel-Sidek watched his mouth twitch with words aching to be free, that dared not be spoken.

The General had asserted his primacy successfully. For the moment.

As Edgit approached the door, the General said, "Salom, I'll want your answer tomorrow night."

"Answer, sir?"

"To the question 'Is Salom Edgit a thief or a soldier?'"

The old man could barely discern movement as bel-Sidek shut the door. "How did I do, Khadifa?"

"Superbly, sir. But I'm concerned about the physical price you paid. We'd better get you to bed."

The body wanted nothing more. But, "The work isn't finished. Bring writing materials."

Bel-Sidek did as he was instructed, started to settle to take dictation.

"No. I will do this myself. Put the things here before me."

Bel-Sidek obliged again, retreated to the far end of the room. He understood.

The old man inscribed his message with painstaking effort,

making no mistakes. He amazed himself, what with his shaking hands and aching flesh. He sanded the ink, folded the paper, inscribed a solitary character on the outside.

"Now you can put me to bed. Then take that to Muma's hostelry. Give it to Muma himself. No one else. Insist. Then go spend the night with your widowed friend." He did not have to caution bel-Sidek against prying. The khadifa would deliver the message unopened.

"Should we risk having you stay here alone after so much exertion?"

"We'll risk it, Khadifa. And I won't be alone long."

That was as much as bel-Sidek needed to know.

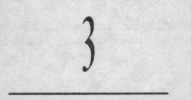

Aaron sat there looking at Naszif, mind void of conversation. Across the room Reyha burbled in Laella's arms. Naszif's face was pallid and wooden. He had gotten through the amenities by rote. Aaron doubted that he knew who his guests were.

A part of Aaron insisted that Naszif deserved any misfortune Aram handed him. Another part—the part that so loved Arif and Stafa—empathized. Zouki was Naszif's only son. The only one he would ever have by Reyha. And under Herodian law he could not put her aside, nor could he take a second wife.

Under *Herodian* law, which would not have been in place had the Seven Towers held a few more days.

"Thus do the Fates conspire to render justice," Aaron muttered. Naszif's eyes unglazed for a moment, but he just looked puzzled, like a man who had heard an inexplicable sound. Then he slipped away into silent torment.

Laella sped him a look of appeal. It said, *Do something! Say something!*

Say what? That he was glad it was Naszif who had the pain? Reyha was *her* friend. He had brought her so she could do what she could do. More she had no right to ask.

For all Naszif was a traitor and a bootlicker, though, Aaron had to admit that he cared for his wife and son. Strongly. And in that care, perhaps, the seeds of treason might have found root. Aaron recalled Naszif's growing distress as Reyha's day had approached. Maybe he had convinced himself that the Herodians would let him run to Reyha if he opened the tower before her time.

Men had done meaner things for reasons less exalted than love.

Aaron swallowed. His throat had gone dry. Through that aridity he forced, "They found two children that were stolen. Last week. In the Hahr. Where Goat Creek runs out of that boggy ground they're always talking about filling but never get around to doing anything about."

Naszif began to show signs of interest. Laella sped Aaron a look of gratitude.

He continued, "The kids were all right. Healthy. Well fed. Decently clothed. They just didn't remember anything."

"Where did you hear that, Aaron? When?" Suddenly, Naszif was all attention. "If there was news like that I think I would have heard."

"I heard it yesterday at work. From this old man they call Billygoat. He's a caulker. He lives across from where they found the kids."

Naszif's intensity disturbed Aaron. He had tossed the incident out as a crumb of hope, not because he felt it meant anything. Concerned though he was about Arif, he had given the story no weight. In a city the size of Qushmarrah children would be stolen and a few would turn up again.

"How could something as important as that happen and the news not be all over the city, Aaron?"

"Be reasonable. Because it isn't news. You and me, we got a reason to care. Most people don't. Only reason Billygoat told me was I was fussing about Arif and he wanted to cheer me up."

"But if there were two, maybe there were more. Maybe a lot. And nobody ever said anything."

"That's possible. Good news don't travel like bad news does." Aaron noted that Reyha had stopped sobbing and was listening, face alight with irrational hope.

Naszif said, "I'm going to look into it. I'm going to ask around. Maybe there's something going on."

Aaron wondered what he had started. All he'd wanted was to lend a little support.

Laella said, "Those Dartars that tried to get Zouki back. They seemed to think the Living did it."

Aaron sighed. He had known that would come. Sooner or later. When Laella got an idea in her head she could hang on as long as her mother.

"That's absurd," Naszif said.

"How do you know?"

Aaron had not repeated bel-Sidek's assurances for Laella, though she, like everyone in the neighborhood, suspected that the cripple was connected with the Living and might even be important. She did not need more ammunition to be cast into the volleys of gossip flying around the neighborhood.

"I just know," Naszif said, and there was a smugness to his declaration that set Aaron's teeth on edge, that hurled a moral dilemma into his face like a bucket of lava.

Naszif among the Living? Naszif, who might have been a tool of Herod once before . . .

Suddenly, like lightning's strike, there were a thousand questions to be debated between himself and the ceiling beams. It was going to be a long and sleepless night.

His abrupt withdrawal excited no interest. Naszif was preoccupied.

Laella did look at him oddly, though. She would have questions. Whether to answer would be the first decision. If so, then he would have to decide how much he dared reveal . . .

Zouki managed to cry himself into a shallow, fitful, whimpering sleep, interrupted often by the outbreak of nightmare from one of the other children in the cage.

Azel strode into Muma's Place with no thoughts beyond getting a decent meal and a hot bath, not necessarily in that order. The bath was overdue. Then a long sleep. Tomorrow was

soon enough to decide what he'd do with the week or so he would
let the Witch stew.

Ride up to the Elephant Rocks country and do some hunting?
Too much like work. Maybe to al-Quarda territory to fish in the
sinkholes there. Whatever, wherever, someplace alone. He
needed to get away from people and all the chains of duty, honor,
loyalty, with which they tried to bind him, trying to jerk him this
way and that. He needed to go somewhere where every step was
not a step on a tightrope.

He picked a table out of the way. It was late enough for the
place to be quiet and offer him a choice of seating.

Maybe he ought to let her roast for two weeks. Or even a
month. She needed dead time to make her think, time to
understand that she was not letting reason be her guide.

Azel grew wary the instant he spotted Muma. Muma no longer
waited tables. Muma no longer stayed awake till this unholy
hour. He glanced around carefully, looking for that odd late
patron who took special notice of Muma's remarkable behavior.

Anyone paying special attention did so with superbly feigned
indifference.

Muma came to Azel's table.

"Muma."

"Azel." The proprietor invited himself to sit.

"You're up late."

"Got dragged out of a warm bed."

"I never have liked dropping in here late and finding you up.
It's like coming home and finding vultures perched on the roof
trees. You know the news ain't going to be good."

"Uhm."

"What is it this time?"

"What would it be? A message." Palm flat on the table, Muma
pushed something across. "You know the sign."

That was not a question.

"Yeah. How old is it?"

"Half an hour, tops. Not stinking yet at all."

"Hmph! Time to get some food down, then."

"You know the sign."

"I got to take time to read the damned thing, don't I?"

"I suppose. What do you want?"

"Something portable. This is bound to tell me to go somewhere and do something two hours before it was written."

"Be right back with something." Muma hoisted himself up and
waddled away.

Azel read the message.

Come to me as soon as you receive this.

There was no signature.

Elegantly simple. Nothing there to tell Herodian or Dartar a
thing. Even the sign on the outside, a crudely drawn palm
sparrow, had no obvious or suspect meaning or symbolism. If it
fell into enemy hands it was unlikely to excite any interest, unless
by circumstance.

Muma came back with a loaf and a lump of a vigorous
goat's-milk cheese. Azel muttered, "It must be my day for
gourmet dining."

"You're going out?"

"Of course. What else? Are your sons awake? I don't see any
trouble around, but it's the kind you don't see that catches you
up."

"They're awake. I told them. They'll cover you." Meaning
anyone who tried to follow him would be in for some major
distress.

Azel stood, handed a coin across, collected his provender.
"Later, Muma."

"Good luck."

"With him I may need it."

The night had grown cool and clammy. Dew had started to
form. Down nearer the harbor it would be getting foggy. The air
was still as death. His heels sent echoes frolicking through the
night. He did not sense anyone following him. He saw no sign of
Muma's sons. But they were good. They would not be seen,
unless by a watcher a moment before the risks of his trade caught
up.

Nevertheless, Azel took his usual detour through the Shu
maze, where the only way a follower could stay on him would be

by sorcery. He knew the maze well enough to walk it eyes closed at midnight.

In places it was just as dark at noon.

He left the maze for Char Street through the same alleyway he had used that afternoon. Fog had gotten that far up the hill already. He turned right.

And three steps later nearly collided with a man and woman coming downhill. He muttered an apology as, startled, they dodged around him. His own damned fault, walking on cat feet, listening for footsteps behind him and paying no attention at all to the path ahead. He followed their hasty footsteps and urgent, whispered reassurances without turning his head. He let his heels fall like those of an honest man so they would know he hadn't doubled back on them.

He walked a hundred yards past his destination, then crossed Char Street and returned downhill on quiet feet. A hundred yards below his destination he crossed again and walked uphill. There was no sign of the couple he had startled. Nor were there any of the watchers against whom his maneuver was directed. He had not expected any, but when you had an al-Akla and a Cado finagling on the occupier's side you took precautions.

He glided to the door and inside with serpentine grace.

Salom Edgit had not gone home after leaving the General, though his lieutenants were there awaiting his report. Instead, he had gone a half mile out of his way, to an upthrust of rock called the Parrot's Beak by most but remembered as the Kraken's Beak by a few of the old folks. It was supposed to be haunted by the shades of eight brothers who had been murdered there in the year of the city's founding.

Salom had been fleeing to the Parrot's Beak for time out to think for as long as he could remember. If ghosts there were, they accepted him. He'd never been discommoded by a supernatural intervention.

He perched on the tip of the Beak and without focusing on anything, stared out at what could be seen of Qushmarrah by starlight. A tide of mist was rising from the harbor.

He spent an hour there, then went off down into the Hahr.

Salom hammered till Ortbal's man opened up. "Yes, Khad-ifa?"

"I need to see Ortbal."

"His Lordship is sleeping, sir."

"*His Lordship?* You go tell Ortbal to get his fat royal butt up before . . . Never mind. I'll tell him myself. His Lordship. Aram have mercy on fools." He pushed past the protesting batman, stamped through the house. It had several storeys but Ortbal, being lazy, seldom left the ground floor. He noted that the house, like Ortbal himself, had begun to take on airs. He kicked open Sagdet's bedroom door.

There was light aplenty inside. Ortbal was at his pleasures.

"You! Out!" Salom snapped at the woman.

She fled like a whipped dog.

Ortbal reddened, but he restrained his anger. Salom Edgit was not the kind of man who busted in on people. And he was mad as hell. You were careful with Salom when his temper was up. He was unpredictable. Dangerous. Ortbal Sagdet was not the sort to put himself at risk. "You're upset, Salom."

"Damned right, I'm upset. Look at you! . . . Yes. I'm upset. I'm overreacting. I know it and I can't stop."

"Rough meeting?" The slightest concern edged Sagdet's voice.

"You should have been there."

"I was making a statement by staying away."

"Your statement was heard, understood, and dismissed as trivial. That wasn't a blind, senile, dying old man, Ortbal. That was the General and he was in charge every second. He did the talking. Not a word got spoken that he didn't ask for. He didn't ask, he didn't argue, he just told. And he knew about everything that's been going on."

"King."

"No. More than King."

"You'd better give me the details." Sagdet's concern was plain now.

Salom told it. Sagdet interjected questions as he progressed.

"No reprisals at all?"

"Those were his orders."

"My people are going to be real irritated about that."

"I don't think he cares, Ortbal. You know that? I don't think he's concerned about your . . ."

"Stuff the moralizing and get on with it." And a minute later, "Did he say how I'm supposed to raise operating funds?"

"If the old man was here he'd just look at this bordello and tell you *he* lives where he lives."

"He would. The old bastard expects us all to live like vermin."

And later, Sagdet exploded with incredulity. "He said I'd be there tomorrow night?"

"He did. And you'd better show. You miscalculated your time and started your break too early. You'd better back off. Let time finish its work."

"Time, huh?"

Ortbal asked several questions. Then, "What did he hit *you* with, old friend?"

"He told me I had to decide if I was a thief or a soldier."

"And you've made up your mind, haven't you? You still buy this foolishness called the Living. After six years of Herodian occupation you still think that crazy old man can do what armies couldn't."

"That isn't the question, Ortbal. I don't know if he can do it or not. Probably not. That doesn't matter. He told me to decide if I'm a thief or a soldier. I'm not a thief. I came here because I owe you the debts of friendship. I had to caution you. I've acquitted my obligation."

"Probably expected you to run straight here, too. Twisted your tail just so and here you came."

"Maybe."

"So we come to a parting of roads. If I don't show up tomorrow night. What will he do if I don't show?"

"I don't know."

"What *can* he do?"

"You take that attitude you might find out. He for sure won't sit still."

"So I'd better do some thinking."

"Will you be there?"

"You'll find that out when you walk in the door, Salom."
Sagdet smiled. That only made his pudgy face look malicious.
Edgit knew he had no intention of showing.

Azel paused to lengthen the wick in the little lamp inside the
door. A voice croaked, "I'm in bed."

Azel stepped into the bedroom. The old man looked terrible.
He set the lamp down. "You were waiting? You were that
confident I would get your message right away?"

"No. I sleep a lot but I'm a very light sleeper. You woke me
when you opened the door."

Azel felt he had not made enough noise to disturb a mouse.
"I'll have to lighten my step."

"I have very good ears. Was that you with the boy in the alley
today?"

"It was. It was a close thing."

"The Dartars were so interested Fa'tad himself came out to
poke around."

Azel was astonished. "Really?"

"Yes. You be careful. That man has a nose better than my ears.
Lay off for a while. You don't have to round up the whole
population overnight."

"Tell it to the Witch. I tried. She's got a thirty-brat backlog and
it takes three days to make sure each one isn't the one she's
looking for. But she won't slow down. She's gotten obsessed with
the idea that she's got to get all the kids rounded up before any of
them kick off. Like she's sure that if even one of them croaks
that'll be the one she wants and she'll have to do the whole
damned thing over again."

"Behind another five- or six-year wait. I can understand her
anxiety. I share it. I won't live that long and I'd like to see results
before I go. But not negative results, which is what we'll get if
Cado or Fa'tad catches on. Fa'tad's behavior today indicates that
caution is necessary. Would it do any good if I were to admonish
her myself?"

"No. Her deal with us is a marriage of convenience. She's only interested in getting what she wants."

"Any suggestions?"

Azel answered with an uncharacteristic shrug. "I walked out. For the time being. That'll slow her down."

"But she has other help."

"Yeah. Two other guys."

"Are they any good? Who are they?"

"They're good. Not as good as me, but good. One is named Sadat Agmed. He's in it for the money. The other is Ishabal bel-Shaduk."

"Comes of religious stock, no doubt."

"Very. He's the fanatic."

"The other sounds Dartar."

"His father was. He hates them."

"Could you persuade them to lay off for a while, too?"

"I doubt it. I'm not supposed to know who they are."

"I'll think about the problem. Anything else? Anything from Cado's direction?"

"He's expecting a new civil governor any day now."

The General smiled. A rare event. "That would be what? The eighth since the conquest?"

"Ninth. They just send people they'd rather not have around but don't dare kill in Herod."

"And the Living take the blame."

"Or harvest the credit. Was there some reason you sent for me?"

"The problem in the Hahr has become critical. As I feared. Quick action now appears to be the only long-term solution."

"Ah?"

"This is a difficult thing."

"Is it? How soon do you need it?"

"Sunset tomorrow at the latest. But the sooner the better."

"That's tight."

"It will become difficult after that time. I thought you were going to scout the terrain should action become necessary."

"I did."

"Can you manage?"

"If I must."

"You must. Will you need help?"

"No."

"Let me know when it's done."

"Right." Azel walked away from the old man. He tapped the lamp wick down and put it back where he had found it. Then he went out into the fog. He did a careful circuit to make sure no watcher had taken station while he was inside.

He believed in being careful.

Bel-Sidek stood staring out at the fog that covered most of Qushmarrah. He could not see much. On a night with a moon, that fog would have stretched like a sprawl of silvery carpet from which parts of buildings grew. To his right, on a slightly higher elevation, the blot of the citadel of Nakar the Abomination masked the stars. Funny. Six years and still a black odor leaked out of the place.

The Witch and her crew were still in there, still holding out, untouchable behind the barrier only Ala-eh-din Beyh had been able to penetrate. How the hell did they survive in there?

One popular theory held that they hadn't. It contended that the Witch and all of Nakar's people had killed themselves after their master's fall.

Bel-Sidek did not believe that, though he had no evidence to the contrary.

From behind him Meryel asked, "Is it the old man?"

Without turning, he replied, "How did you know?"

"You only brood when you're troubled by someone you love. I think you've made your peace with yourself about your son and your wife."

Bel-Sidek's son, Hastra, was another of those who had not come home from Dak-es-Souetta. As Meryel's husband had not. Hastra, his only child, the star of his heart. For years he had brooded the what-ifs. What if there had been no Dartar treachery at Dak-es-Souetta? Win or lose, would the poisonous hatred still blacken his blood? Was he, like so many men he knew, hanging everything on the horns of the Dartar demon, so to evade taking any responsibility that was his own? He'd never worked that out, only come to realize that the brooding was as pathetic and pointless as the howling of a dog over the still form of a fallen master.

The wife was another story. The wife had nothing to do with win or lose or Dartar treachery. The woman, whose very name he strove to drive from his mind, had deserted him almost before his wounds had healed. With the connivance and blessing of her family. Almost unheard-of in Qushmarrah, a dowry abandoned.

But they'd had an eye for the main chance. And who wanted a cripple in the family? Political or physical?

"There's you," bel-Sidek said.

"I never give you cause to brood."

True. Quite true.

The wife had run to one of the new breed of Qushmarrahans, that the Herodians were making over in their own image. The man had adopted all the approved dress and manners and had taken the conquering god for his own. And he had prospered, collaborating with the army of occupation. And then he had died of an inability to breathe, for which bel-Sidek had had no responsibility at all. He suspected the General had given the order. He had not asked, and never would.

"Is it something you want to talk about?"

"I don't think so." Out there, beneath that fog, men were moving. Some were villains and some were soldiers of the Living. There would be bodies in the morning. And who would know which had been slain by whom? The General, perhaps.

Let Fa'tad play his transparent games and take away the day. The night belonged to the old order, and would come out of the shadows someday soon.

"Maybe I do want to talk," he said. He closed the filigreed doors to the balcony, turned to face his companion.

Meryel was seven years older than he. Her skin was too dark and her features too coarse for her ever to have been thought beautiful. Or even pretty. A generous dowry had helped her marry well.

She was too short and too fat and dressed with the eye for style of a goatherd. She drank rivers of date wine, proscribed by both Aram and the Herodians' tempestuous god. She was, invariably, inevitably, an embarrassment in public. She said the wrong things at the wrong times and burst into giggles in the wrong places.

She was his best friend.

"He's shutting me out. More and more, he's hiding things from me. He didn't used to send me away when he wanted to meet with somebody. But the last six months . . ."

"You distrust his reasons?"

"No."

"Does he distrust you?"

"No. Of course not. How could he and live with me?"

"You don't think it's the normal course of security?"

"No."

"You do talk where you shouldn't."

Bel-Sidek looked at her sharply.

"Here. To me."

"I'm sure you've been checked every way he can imagine." He knew she had, knew the General trusted her almost as much as he trusted her himself.

"Should I be flattered? Is it just that your feelings are hurt, then?"

"No. Maybe. I guess that's part of it. But I'm worried for him, too."

"And have you considered the chance that his ego is involved, too?"

"How so?"

"I don't know. I don't know what he's up to. I do know he thinks enough of you to have made you his adjutant. Of all those who would have taken it. To me that says he values your opinion. Maybe that's why he's shutting you out."

"I don't follow that."

"He's a sick old man. He doesn't have much time. He knows that. He's desperate for results before he goes. Maybe he has a scheme he knows you wouldn't approve."

"That's possible."

She really was quite a remarkable woman, so inept in some ways and so damnably competent in others. In a culture wholly dominated by males she had established her independence, if not equality. She had managed that because she understood money, power, and the power of money.

The one truly daring thing she had done was, on hearing the first grim whispers from Dak-es-Souetta, to assume that her husband was among the dead. She had moved instantly to assume an iron grip on both his fortune and her dowry, and had not been the slightest bit hesitant to use force and terror to stay the claims of both families. They said she had had her own father beaten.

And yet . . . she could not cope in the society into which her wealth had propelled her.

Nor did she care, apparently. Apparently all she wanted was the power to make half the human race leave her alone.

Amazing contradictions these days, bel-Sidek reflected. Meryel was a boil on the face of all the old man held holy, yet he must approve of her, if not for bel-Sidek's sake, then for the sake of the coffers of the Living. She was one of the movement's strongest supporters.

What a tangle of ethics and traditions had come out of one day's dying.

"That could explain it," bel-Sidek admitted. "But I don't like it."

"Of course you don't. If you were going to like it you'd know everything there was to know already. Wouldn't you?"

"I suppose." He opened the filigreed doors and stepped out onto the balcony. Qushmarrah had not changed in his absence. The tide of fog had risen a little higher, that was all. The air was so damnably still that the boundary between fog and not-fog was as sharp as a saber's edge. As he watched, a man came striding up out of it like some thing of dark legend marching out of the mists of nightmare.

What a turn of mind tonight, he thought. The man was probably a baker on his way to work.

Meryel said, "Since you aren't in a mood for anything else, why not talk business? I have two ships coming in from Benagra. I'll need reliable men to unload them."

It was how they had come to meet. He was khadifa of the waterfront. She had strong interests in shipping, gently helped to grow by the gentlemen of the Living. Her captains imported the arms that dared not be smithed anywhere in Qushmarrah.

As Azel strode up out of the fog he was thinking that there was still a chance he could get some sleep tonight, but he'd have to forget about getting away for any fishing or hunting. He had been out of touch in several directions and it looked like things were going to happen. A week away and he might return to a chaos he could not unravel.

He glanced at the hulking blot of the citadel, wondered if the Witch was getting any sleep tonight. Probably. She thought she was like the citadel itself: above the dirt and turmoil of Qushmarrah.

She might end up learning the hard way.

He crested the hill, putting the harbor side behind him. Ahead lay the Hahr, the most prosperous quarter of the Old City. Behind lay the Shu, the poorest and most densely populated quarter, where sons had stacked homes beside and atop those of their fathers till half the quarter was like some enormous mad mud daubers' nest where anyone who lived off the thoroughfares first had to climb up to the sunlight and cross the rooftops in order to reach a street. The labyrinth underlay it all, sometimes open all the way to the sky, more often built over and now with old doorways sealed lest doom slip up by that route. The maze was so deadly that even the most desperate homeless seldom stole in for shelter. That territory belonged to the boldest of the bad boys.

Azel had met people in there who made *him* nervous. Weird people. Crazy people. People you had to deal with harshly to get your message across. And some who just could not learn.

Azel had grown up in the Shu. At seven he had been orphaned and left homeless. He did not remember much about his parents except that his mother had cried all the time and his father had yelled almost as much and had beaten them all a lot. He had a notion that it might have been he who had set the fire that consumed them—except that he had an equally fuzzy recollection of his brother giving the old man fifteen or twenty good ones to the head with a hammer before the fire.

He hadn't seen his brother since.

There was nothing he wanted to remember from those days, no little heirloom he carried around and treasured.

At fourteen he had gone to sea and had gotten to know most of the ports around the rim of the sea. He had survived them all and most of them had survived him. At twenty-one he had returned to Qushmarrah.

It had not been long before he had fallen in with the remnants of the Gorloch cult. Its grim philosophy appealed to him, though he took from it only what suited him and discarded the rest. He was not weak. He had no higher god than himself.

Soon he caught the eye of the High Priest, Nakar. The sorcerer gave him odd jobs. He handled them swiftly, efficiently, no matter how difficult or cruel. In a moment of humor Nakar had begun calling him Azel after the demon who carried Gorloch's messages to the living world. Azel the Destroyer.

Never did he commit himself to the god or to the man. Not entirely. Azel could not give himself wholly to anyone but Azel.

He had missed Dak-es-Souetta. He hadn't been trapped in any of the towers at Harak Pass. He hadn't participated in the rout on the Plain of Chordan nor had he been there for the hopeless defense of Qushmarrah after the pride of her youth and manhood had been slaughtered or scattered, chaff driven by the hot breath of Death.

His absence did not shame him. It would not have shamed him had he done nothing for the city that had done nothing for him. He knew nothing about shame. But he had in fact been doing something. He had been in Agadar, west along the coast, where the Herodian armies had landed. His few carefully struck blows against Herodian commanders had—unfortunately, as it had developed—delayed the invading armies the month necessary for Fa'tad al-Akla to gather his tribal warriors and race to Dak-es-Souetta.

Thus do the Fates conspire.

Azel paused across the street from the house that was his destination. Almost the instant his feet stopped moving the door opened over there. Azel eased back into deeper shadow.

Could it be?

Of course not. The Fates neither loved him so well nor hated Sagdet so much. He sank down onto his heels, tucked his hands in, turned his face down, and watched under his brows. The man passed within ten feet without seeing him.

It was the one called Edgit. Perhaps the old man would want to know that he had been here.

Azel moved almost before Edgit was out of sight. He had scouted the house. The best way in was through the front door. If he got there quickly whoever had let Edgit out might think the guest had returned for something.

He knocked. In seconds the door opened. An irritated voice started to say, "His Lordship . . ."

Azel shot his left hand to the man's throat, gripped. He brought his right around in a hook to the temple. A brass knuckleduster took the impact. The man sagged.

Azel lowered him to the floor, easing him out of the way of the door, which he closed but did not latch. Quickly, but with care because he did not know the interior layout, he passed through the house to the back, then to the east side, to unlatch the doors there and open alternate avenues of retreat. Only then did he approach the one room from which sounds of life could be heard.

The door was not latched. And the sounds were what he'd suspected them to be: those of a man and woman rutting.

Gorloch be praised! Or the Fates, if it be deserved. The woman was astride, facing away, and the man had his eyes closed. Azel slipped into the room. He picked up a discarded sash as he crossed the room, wrapped one end around his left hand, let the other fall free.

The woman sensed his approach in the last step, started to

turn. His blow stilled her curiosity before she caught a glimpse of him

No stopping the man from seeing him and loosing a startled, squeaking, "You! What the hell are you doing?" as he thrashed out of his entanglement with the woman and started to flee on all fours. "Who sent you? The General? Is he trying to scare me? I don't have to put up with this!"

Fat jiggled olive skin. Absurd broad buttocks humped and swayed. He gained ground. He reached the corner where Azel wanted him, scrabbled at the walls to get to his feet, spun with a mouth full of bluster and threats.

None of which got spoken.

"Oh, Aram! You mean it! Damn it, man. . . . I'll back down. Tell him! I'll do it his way. You don't have to do this! We can deal!" He raised pudgy hands, pushed at the air. "Don't! What do you want? I've got money. . . . Please?"

Azel was close enough. Leaving one imaginary opening to his right, he feinted with the sash in his left hand.

Sagdet darted for the perceived opening.

Azel's fist smashed into the side of his head. He spun against the wall. Before Sagdet could recover his wits Azel had the sash around his neck and a knee in the middle of his back.

Sagdet struggled, as any dying thing must, but his efforts only served to put him facedown on the floor, where his assailant had a greater advantage. Once there he could do nothing but paw and claw and pound the stolen carpet against which he was being crushed.

Azel felt the body shudder, smelled the stench as sphincters relaxed. Sagdet must have had an abominable diet. He held on for a count of another twenty, then knotted the sash in place.

He went to the woman, touched her throat. Her pulse was strong and regular. Good. None should be hurt who had not earned it.

He walked a reverse course through the house, leaving the side and back doors open wide. He checked the pulse of the man he had left inside the front door, found it a little ragged but not dangerously so. He looked outside carefully before he departed. Leaving the front door standing open, too.

It would not be long before thieves accepted the invitation and swept to the plunder, obliterating completely the reality of what had happened.

The General wakened to the whisper of the street door. The light of the lamp moved across the outer room. "Is that you?"

"Yes."

"Back already?"

"Yes."

"It's done?"

"It's done. The man Edgit was leaving as I arrived."

Something stirred in the old man's innards, settled in the pit of his gut like ten pounds of hot, poisonous sand. He could not become accustomed to ordering executions. "Good, then."

The lamp moved away, back toward the street door. "He promised that he'd mend his ways. That he'd never do it again."

The old man listened to the door close, perhaps shutting him off from half a thought. What the hell had the man meant?

That had not been a taunt, nor an accusation, nor even a bald statement of fact. It had had an odor of admonition about it, a smell of the cautionary parable.

The mass in his gut grew heavier.

He drifted off to sleep without having figured it out.

4

Aaron tore chunks off a sheet of unleavened bread and used them to dip bites of whatever it was that Mish had made for breakfast. He did not notice that the bread had been burned on one side or that the rest of the meal could not be identified even by someone paying close attention. He barely noticed what Mish was doing while Laella still slept.

After the late night with Reyha and Naszif they had come home to find Stafa restless and whiny with a mild fever and stubbornly insisting that he had not been weaned.

Aaron thought Laella had made a mistake nursing the boy as long as she had but that was not on his mind. Nor was he preoccupied with the task that faced him at work. He had not built and set a mast step before, but it was just a job of carpentry and he had faith in his skills as a carpenter.

No. His preoccupation remained Naszif and what, if anything, to do about him. And he knew he had come to an impasse because he was unable to remove himself from the situation far enough to view it dispassionately. He could not discern, much less untangle, his chains of personal and moral and patriotic obligation. If such existed. He was not sure they did.

It all depended, first, upon the depth of his conviction that

Naszif had opened that hidden postern. If the accusation was mere prejudice, if there was doubt about the guilt, if someone else had been the malefactor, then there was no problem. Naszif could be ignored.

But if Naszif *was* guilty, then the Living *might* be clutching an asp to its bosom.

Was it his place to be concerned? He had a sentimental, romantic attachment to the Living, but no commitment. He wasn't sure he really wanted them to *do* anything about the occupation. Some out-of-the-dark, miraculous triumph by the diehards might hurt him more than it helped.

Before the coming of Herod his life had been good. But it was better now. He got paid more. And there was as much work as he wanted, so that he could take home as much money as he wanted. And the Herodian operators never tried to cheat a man of his wages.

He had prospered under the Herodian occupation. He had been lucky. To balance the extra mouths in his household Aram in his kindness had given him no daughters to dowry. He had almost enough saved to get his family out of the Shu, over the hill, and into the Astan, where they could have a decent life. If Laella did not become pregnant in the next year . . .

He could work for himself in the Astan, doing work he enjoyed. Building ships required craftsmanship but allowed no scope for individual vision or artistry.

Among the few concrete certainties in Aaron's world was his conviction that Naszif had opened that postern in that tower.

Coming home last night he had asked Laella who she considered to be her best friend. He had gotten the expected answer without hesitation or reflection: Reyha. Then he had asked who she considered her worst enemy, or who she most hated. Consciously he had anticipated hearing the name of a neighbor with whom she had been feuding for years. But unconsciously, maybe, he had expected something akin to the answer he did get after several minutes of reflection. "The people who made Taidiki kill himself."

And that was ambiguous enough to include almost everyone.

He had wanted to narrow it a little, maybe get a hint of how she would feel if he told her about Naszif and the postern, but just then the man had come out of the fog like a specter, startling and frightening them, and had gained reality only after he had passed them and his feet had begun hitting the ground. After that they were too nervous to do anything but hurry for home and a door that could lock out the frights of the night.

Aaron wanted to talk. To Laella preferably, but to anyone who might show him a path out of his quandary. The situation had led him to a shocking realization. He had no friends. He did not know anyone he trusted enough to ask advice. His ties beyond his family were tenuous and transitory, involving men with whom he worked. Men who, for the most part, he never saw again after a job was over.

What had become of the close friends of youth?

Dak-es-Souetta, mostly.

Mish asked, "Are you working today, Aaron?"

The boys started in before he could answer. "Don't go to work today, Dad. Stay home, Dad."

It was a minor Herodian religious holiday and he could take the day off. If he did, though, tomorrow he would have to present his Herodian employers with an attendance token from one of the Herodian temples. A price he did not care to pay. Not to mention not wanting to lose the income. And maybe get a bad reputation. That mast step had to go in today.

"Yes. I'm working."

"Oh, Dad!"

Mish scowled. That meant she had to manage the household at least till Laella rose.

The Herodians did not take off for minor holidays.

Aaron said nothing to Mish, but he added her to his mental agenda. He was fed up with her sulks and pouts and shirkings. If she thought she had it so bad here, let her go out *there* and try to whine her way through the real world.

"Dad! Stafa's got to pee."

"No, I don't!" Stafa stood slightly hunched, one hand gripping his crotch.

"Go pee in the pot, Stafa."

"No."

"Stafa, go pee in the pot."

"No!"

The boy had reached that stage of housebreaking where he was aware of what he had to do but still fervently opposed having to do it for himself. "I'll spank your butt."

"Carry me, Dad."

"Carry you? You get over there."

"No. Carry me."

"Come here, you argumentative little rat."

All trust, Stafa came to him. He grabbed the boy's right foot, lifted it while Stafa clung to his shoulder for balance. "You see this, Stafa? What's this?"

"That's my foot."

Aaron shifted to Stafa's left foot. "And what's this?"

"That's my other foot."

"And why do you think the Good Lord Aram put feet on the ends of your legs?"

Stafa did not pause to think. He just said it. "To keep my toes pointing out."

Everyone laughed but Arif. Even Mish. Stafa grinned, though he understood no better than Arif. Aaron rose. "All right, brat. You win." He grabbed Stafa under the arms and carried him to the chamber pot. The boy wiggled and kicked happily.

It was a story to tell at work.

It took his mind off his troubles. Mish handed him his usual lunch of bread, cheese, and sausage and he took off.

The sun had not yet risen.

Glop! Plop! Slop! In quick succession the Qushmarrahan cooks filled Yoseh's bowl with a three-ounce chunk of blubbery flesh cooked forever and an hour, six ounces of some mushy stuff that might have started life in a grain field, and half a small loaf that was meant to be broken into pieces and used to dip the mush.

"Oh, boy," Yoseh said. "I was hoping we'd have this stuff again

this morning." They
he had come to the cr

Mo'atabar, whose dut
commander of a hundred n
is feast day in Qushmarrah,
gold."

That came every morning, too
of Mo'atabar's daily rituals, like h
barracks each morning, while daw   ......rtain
impulse in the councils of the god.   ....ine, my
children. Rise and shine. It's another gle.......y in service in
the city of lead and gold."

The men always laughed when Mo'atabar did one of his
things. Yoseh knew he was being sarcastic and making mock of
tribal ideas about Qushmarrah, but he did not see the humor.

He and his brothers and cousins settled to eat. Nobody said
much. Nogah was in a grim mood. What last night had looked
like an opportunity to do something unusual and maybe make a
splash had turned on him. This morning the word was that the
whole troop was going in to work on the Shu maze. One hundred
eighteen men, not eight. Mo'atabar and his uncle Joab, the
captain, would bask in the warmth of Fa'tad's approval if the
operation uncovered something al-Akla wanted to find.

Yoseh suspected Fa'tad had had one of his visions, or intui-
tions, or inspirations, or whatever they were, and had decided
that the Shu maze was sufficiently important to rate more
manpower and the watchful eye of one of his oldest cronies.

Joab was one of those half dozen men who had flown
wingtip-to-wingtip with the Eagle for forty years.

Nogah ought to think about that and not about his hurt
feelings.

The sun was still just an imminent threat when the troop rode
out of the compound and turned toward the Gate of Autumn.
Yoseh and his companions rode point. An honor, of sorts, but
one Yoseh was willing to forgo if things should look like they were
getting sticky.

marrah to become the hero of epic
dead.

ot yet open. Other traffic was arriving, too,
the small square the gate towers commanded. Joab
ward and began cursing the sleepy Herodian gatemen in
their own language, calling them the sons of whores, feeders on
the dung of camels, and suppurating pustules upon the manhood
of their god. Joab did not like Herodians. He insulted Herodian
soldiers every chance he got, in repayment for the insult implicit
in the fact that the Herodian military commander required the
tribesmen to be out of the city and in their compound by nightfall
every evening.

Yoseh said, "He's provoking them. Deliberately. Someday
somebody is going to get mad and try to kill him."

"No," Nogah said. "He scares the shit out of them. They think
he's crazy."

"So do I."

"It's all an act. Something Fa'tad put him up to, to make them
think we're all crazy. I think."

"You think?"

"You never know with Fa'tad."

Joab's fulminations had their effect. The gate groaned open.
Arrogantly, Joab led his troop through before the merchants. The
regular patrols were arriving. They attached themselves to the
column. The merchants had to wait while a thousand tribesmen
entered the city.

Yoseh hadn't been north a week before he had realized there
was a very complicated and subtle game going on between Fa'tad
and Cado, the Herodian military governor. Herodian troops held
all the key points of the city, and what had been the palace of the
city's impotent figurehead prince was now called Government
House and was occupied by Cado and his captains. Cado kept his
men out of sight as much as possible. Their standards were
seldom seen in public. The hand, the mailed fist, of the
occupation was always Dartar.

Fa'tad had responded by making his men work as a police force
of sorts, meting out instant and ferocious retribution to the city's

human predators whenever and
They settled disputes impartially.
needed workers and people wh
together. Where it was within the
suffering of the poor.

"So we end up helping old women cross the
the young ones' babies," Nogah grumped. "An
Answer me that, kid. So we can win the sympathy
classes? They don't have any power and their sympathy
send one head of livestock down south."

"I think Fa'tad's mind encompasses more than the chore of
keeping the tribes from starving."

"That's the problem. He's so busy scheming he can't keep his
mind on the business that brought us here."

The patrols dispersed into the city but Joab's troop kept on
westward, down one of the broad avenues of the Astan, across
Goat Creek, a hundred fifty yards along the foot of the tumbled
and brushy remnants of the Old Wall. One of the older men
behind Yoseh began reminiscing about how the damned stubborn veydeen had tried to make a stand along here and the
damned fool ferrenghi had wanted Fa'tad to make a mounted
charge across the boggy ground and creek and up the rubble to
dislodge them.

"Al-Akla told them what to do with their charge. So they sent
in their own men. And they got murdered just like Fa'tad said
they would."

The column passed through a gap in the rubble flanked by
broken columns, a onetime gateway. It entered the narrow streets
of the Hahr, climbed the hill to the wide-open plazas around the
citadel. Yoseh could not look at that place without shuddering,
though he knew Ala-eh-din Beyh had rendered it powerless.
Still . . .

Still, the Herodians persisted in trying to figure out how to
break in. Maybe just to recover the body of their hero, but maybe
for something more. Maybe for the fabled treasure.

Yoseh half suspected that Fa'tad had his eyes on the treasure,
too.

...ssed through the spaciousness of the acropolis ... Shu, nudging the head of Char Street tentatively ... snake checking the mouth of a gopher hole. Then ...orward.

...Street was aboil with humanity already. Like a flyblown ...ss, Yoseh thought, feeling the weight of their numbers ...ssing in on him. They parted before the pressure of the ...column, then stood at the street sides gawking. How long since they had seen such a force of Dartars in the Shu? Since the days of Qushmarrah's fall? Maybe not even then. There wasn't much in the Shu worth fighting for.

Men began dropping off the column's tail in sixes and eights each time an entryway to the labyrinth appeared. Yoseh soon realized that a hundred eighteen men were not enough to cover just the rat holes on Char Street, let alone all the others around the periphery.

Nogah told Mo'atabar, "This is the place."

"Go ahead. Peel off."

Nogah beckoned the rest of them to the side of the street, jostling Qushmarrahans who took that in silence. Yoseh looked into the mouth of that alley and shivered. Superstitious dread, he told himself. That dangerous, wide little man was long gone.

The column moved on. They watched, waiting to dismount. Yoseh glanced down toward the heavenstone blue of the bay. His eyes met those of the same old woman he had seen yesterday afternoon. This morning the iron was missing from her expression. She looked a little puzzled, a little lost.

A girl came to the door behind her. Yoseh's gaze was drawn to her unveiled face. His eyes bugged. Their gazes met.

The old woman snarled something at the girl.

She retreated, but only a step or two. Just far enough not to be seen from the corner of the crone's eye. She continued to stare. And so did Yoseh, which gave her away.

Mahdah struck him in the thigh. "Yoseh, you want to come down from there?" And he realized it was the third time he had been told to dismount. Cheeks hot, he made the camel kneel, slid off.

Nogah said, "You ___
Yoseh had the feeling ___
Nogah punched Maho ___
together to go into the alley ___
we stay in Qushmarrah."

Bel-Sidek watched the Dartar ___
groups dropping off at each alley, a ___
gaping. "What the *hell* is going on: ___ never
seen anything like it. He counted bodies. Over a hundred of the
bastards. What the hell was Fa'tad up to now?

The man was like that wild hare they had out along the marges
of the Takes, always zigging just when the wild dogs expected it
to zag. It showed a little wiggle of the tail like it was going to go
right and when the dogs were set for the move it bounded to the
left and gained thirty yards while they were getting their legs
untangled.

The Dartars just kept coming. The teams that dropped off
began preparing ropes and shields and weapons and torches.

They were serious about invading the labyrinth.

Why? It was an exercise in futility.

Another of Fa'tad's efforts to please the mob? Another symbolic
gesture?

Bel-Sidek was anxious to get across and check on the old man,
but there was no pushing through the Dartars. Not without
attracting unwanted attention.

"What are they doing, sir?"

Bel-Sidek glanced sideways at the man who had spoken. He
was one of the assistants to one of the old man's lieutenants here
in the Shu. Naszif something, a slimy little man bel-Sidek did
not like. Almost by chance the man knew he was involved with
the movement and more important than he. He had a subtly
ingratiating manner that repelled bel-Sidek more than did King's
open ass-kissing.

"I was just wondering that myself. I don't think I missed
anything about what happened here yesterday. It certainly doesn't
deserve this kind of response."

It was my son that was taken. That was what

I'm sorry. Have you had any news?"

None, sir. Though a man I knew in the army told me about a couple of missing children turning up again. I've been checking around this morning and I've heard about several others that turned up, too, so I'm hopeful."

"You have my prayers," bel-Sidek said. He wished he could get away. But there was no walking off.

"Thank you, sir. Did you hear about the murder, sir?"

Bel-Sidek groaned inwardly. "No. I didn't."

"Over in the Hahr. A very rich man. There're rumors that he was the head of the Living in the Hahr."

Bel-Sidek became alert and interested. He tried to feign mild curiosity. "What happened?"

"Thieves, the way I heard it. His house was stripped clean. He'd been strangled."

Bel-Sidek thought he covered well. The end of the Dartar column was past. "Interesting. Excuse me. I have to check on my father. He's been alone for several hours." He pushed across the street.

Sagdet strangled and his house cleaned out by thieves? That sounded remarkably like the doom that had befallen half a dozen prominent men in recent years, among them three civil governors and his own wife's second husband. It hadn't occurred to him to see a pattern before. He'd believed that the passing of the governors had been engineered in Government House, with Cado's connivance, though the Living had not refused to take the blame. The instances not involving governors, though, definitely bore the smell of punitive deathstrokes by the Living.

Bel-Sidek was in a contemplative mood when he entered the house.

"That you, Khadifa?"

"Yes sir."

"I had begun to fear I was going to have to live off my own fat."

The old man's chi... bel-Sidek was vexed. ...

"I was delayed."

"So I see. What is that ...

Bel-Sidek listened. The s... usual, but not enough for him ... of the Shu asking the other half ... to." He stared down at the frail figu... old man's only concession to the p... ...b and better than a hundred men are out there. Looks ... ...ey're going to invade the labyrinth. They brought the necessary weapons and tools."

The General's husk of a face wrinkled in perplexity. "Why would they do that?"

What sort of viper's nest seethed behind those cataracted eyes? "I don't have the foggiest idea. Because Fa'tad told him to. You're the expert on the mind of Fa'tad al-Akla."

"Do I detect a note of something sour, Khadifa? Do you have a grievance?"

"Last night you told us the khadifa of the Hahr would be with us for a general policy meeting tonight."

"So I did. You object?"

"Not at all. But this morning a man on the street—that slimy Naszif creature of Hadribel's—told me that Sagdet was murdered during the night. By thieves, perhaps. His house had been stripped of everything of value. But the timing strikes me as remarkable and the nature of the death as unusually similar to several that have been claimed as executions by the movement."

The old man did not respond for a long time. Bel-Sidek waited him out, half his mind listening for a change in the street noise. There would be no getting out if Joab was up to some elaborate ploy meant to net them. If he was alert there would be time to silence the General and maybe himself while they were breaking down the door and rushing the bedroom.

Morbid thoughts. These days, always the morbid thoughts, always the flexing the muscles in anticipation of the worst.

"There is an operation already begun, Khadifa, that could

vement. Right now it is young and
ly hatched chick. It must be nurtured.
advertent exposure, through the privateering of
brethren, could bring on the destruction of the entire
ment."

A blatant grab for his sense of the dramatic. Bel-Sidek allowed
himself a deprecatory snort.

"We have been drifting underground for months, to give Fa'tad
and Cado the idea we're fraying around the edges and starting to
fall apart. Except in the Hahr, where Ortbal Sagdet decided to go
ripping off on adventures of his own."

Essentially true, bel-Sidek admitted to himself.

"This is a crucial time, Khadifa. Every minute of the next six
months will be critical. Ortbal Sagdet was never much of an
asset, and lately had become a deadly liability. He was trying to
spread the infection."

He spread it to Salom Edgit, of course. "But to have him
killed . . ."

"Could make of him an asset in death. You analyze the
situation, Khadifa. Armed only with the knowledge you possess
as khadifa of the harbor. You're very good at analyses. When you
arrive at a superior solution, please inform me."

"You said he would be here tonight."

"I said the khadifa of the Hahr would be here. I said nothing
about Ortbal Sagdet. See what's happening out there. Then fix
breakfast."

The old man closed his eyes. Bel-Sidek knew he had been
dismissed.

Before he reached the street door bel-Sidek understood that
there had been no options with Ortbal. Not if they wanted
Sagdet's organization intact and tame and doing what it was
supposed to do.

Sagdet's death, with its signature, ought to have a salutorily
instructional effect throughout the organization.

Necessary or not politically, bel-Sidek did not like them slaying
their own.

taller case and exchanged it for its twin. This one contained fresh drinking water.

The women had finished passing out food. They stepped away from the children and waited. The four men got shovels and bags and went back into the foliage, apparently to clean up after the rock apes. None of the adults said a word.

Some of the children finished quickly. What they did then seemed to depend on the child. Some took their dishes to the women, who scraped the remains of their meals onto one of several metal trays sitting atop their cart. When one of those was full one of the men took it into the foliage for the rock apes. He brought a dirty pan back.

Most of the children were not bold enough to approach the women. They just left their plates where they were and moved away. The men collected them for the women.

The giant man never left the entrance.

The adults all went away.

Zouki spent a long time in a bubble of fear, homesickness, and longing for his mother. But curiosity about the apes slowly intruded upon his misery. He finally went to see what could be seen.

Before he got to the foliage the men and women appeared again, pushing carts that were not the same as those they had brought before. Once more the giant stood guard after the carts had come into the cage.

Each of the women selected a child that she led to a cart. The kids went docilely. The women stripped them naked and lifted them into the carts and began to wash and scrub them.

The carts were tubs on wheels. Part of them, anyway.

Zouki did not like baths. He asked the girl who had spoken to him earlier, "Do we all have to take a bath?"

"You do. You're new."

Holy Aram! They were even washing their hair! He hated having his hair washed more than he hated anything else in the world. He thought about running to hide with the apes, but he could not move.

The women removed their victims from the tubs, toweled

them off, and dressed them in clean clothing taken from a hamper on the end of the cart. Then they went after more kids.

One headed straight for Zouki!

His muscles refused to act. He could do nothing but shake and start to leak tears.

The woman was not unkind as she took his hand, hoisted him, and led him unresisting to her cart.

He did not fight back till he saw the pitcher rising to dump water over his head. He squealed and batted at it, missed. The water gushed down over his head while a firm hand held him still. He shrieked then, and started pumping his legs up and down, running in place, splashing.

Firm hands sat him down in the water and forced him to lean forward. Water cascaded over him, leaving him sputtering. Hands began rubbing soap into his scalp. But after the indignity of the wash and rinse there was more, something that smelled vile and burned his head.

A woman's voice asked, "Is this the new one?"

"Yes, ma'am." Another woman. The one torturing him.

"Is he in good shape?"

"Except for head and body lice, which they all have when they come in, he appears to be in good health and excellent physical condition."

"Good. Are you about ready to pull him out of there?"

"One more rinse, ma'am."

Water splashed over Zouki's head. Then hands hoisted him out of the tub, set him on the floor, began drying his hair with a towel. He opened his eyes.

Facing him was the most beautiful woman he'd ever seen.

She reached out and took his face between her hands, her palms against his cheeks, and made him look into her eyes. "Don't be afraid. Nobody's going to hurt you."

"I want mom!"

"I know." She patted his cheek.

The woman toweling Zouki asked, "Is he the one, ma'am?"

"I don't think so. Not obviously."

Zouki thought she looked very sad.

* * *

Arif considered the tactical situation. Mom was trying to get dressed while Stafa was trying to climb on her and Mish was complaining about something Nana had said to her. None of them were watching the door. It was a good time to go see what was happening.

He just walked out the door like it was something he was allowed to do anytime he wanted.

As children will, he had forgotten to take into account all facets of the situation. His grandmother grabbed hold of his clothing and with one yank sat him down beside her. "Where do you think you're going, Arif?"

"I was just . . ."

"Just what, Arif?"

"Just going to see what the Dartars are doing." He stuck out his lower lip.

"A bird is going to nest there." Nana pinched his lip. "You know the rule. You and Stafa can't go out unless a grown-up goes with you."

"I was just going right up there."

"Right up there is where the bad man grabbed Zouki yesterday. Remember?"

"Well, he wouldn't grab me! If he did I'd punch him in the nose! I'd punch him so hard . . ."

"Arif!" Nana glared at him. Her face was starkly serious. "This isn't a game. It isn't play. It's real. How are you going to get away from the bad men when you can't even get away from your old Nana?" She reiterated, "It's not a game, Arif. Now tell me the rules. What are you supposed to do?"

Lip out farther, Arif began reciting the litany of responses he was to make if somebody tried to kidnap him.

Mish rushed out of the house. "Mom, did you see Arif? He . . ." She saw him sitting there. Almost instantly, her eye strayed to the Dartars up the street. She did not hear a word Nana said. She always got deaf whenever Mom or Nana started yelling at her.

*   *   *

Azel strolled all the way around Government House twice, looking to see who was watching, if anyone was. He did not spot anyone. If someone was around he was good enough not to give himself away. That would be unusual for the ground-level men of the Living and impossible for the Dartars, who could not—and probably would not—disguise themselves as anything but what they were. There were jokes and parables about the Dartar inability to adapt. "Stubborn as a Dartar," was a maxim as old as Qushmarrah itself.

Azel strolled to a tradesman's entrance, knocked. A soldier opened a peekhole. "What you want?" he demanded.

"I got to see Colonel Bruda about the cut flowers he ordered." He grinned. The guy wouldn't know what the hell was going on, but he'd have a damned good idea, what with all the guys coming around about flowers for the Colonel. He could not be unique, could he? What the hell would a Colonel do with a ton of posies?

The Herodian bolted up behind Azel. In his own language he told his partner, "I'm going to take this gink up to Bruda. Hold the fort."

The partner grunted. He had not bothered to look up from his lap. Too long in garrison, Azel figured.

His guide led him through dusty, seldom-used passages. He amused himself trying to estimate Government House's back-door traffic from the disturbances in the dust. He played the same game every time.

The guide turned into the long north-south hall. Azel glanced back. Nobody behind them. Nobody up ahead. There never was, but you had to check. You didn't let up.

Should he do it?

Why the hell not? There wasn't a damned thing they could do. He grinned.

He got his weight behind the punch and buried it in the soldier's left kidney. The man folded around the blow, then crumpled. Azel leaned against the wall and waited. When the soldier finally began to get himself together and looked up, there were tears in his eyes.

"Gink, eh? You gotta learn not to let your asshole overload your brain." He said it in Herodian vulgate, not the formal, upper-class Herodian most outsiders learned.

He saw something stir behind the soldier's eyes. "Don't even think about it. I'd tie your ears in a bowknot." He extended a helping hand. "Let's go see the Messenger of the Faith." Though most everyone, including the common Herodian soldiers, used old-fashioned designations, among themselves the true believers used ranks that were religious.

The man let Azel help. He started off unsteadily, bent slightly, head hanging.

"I don't reckon I hit you that hard, but if you start pissing blood you better see your regimental doc."

The soldier said nothing. He took Azel up several floors and into a room where a Herodian ensign, still looking forward to his first shave, jumped up and opened another door, said something to someone on the other side. Then he told Azel, "He'll see you in a minute."

The soldier shuffled out.

"What was the matter with him?"

"Made a mistake. Made an ethnic slur."

The boy did not meet his eye. Azel grinned, moved to a window, looked out at the bay. Hell of a view of the harbor. He wondered if he'd ever go to sea again. Not likely. That was a young man's game. A young, stupid, blind man's game. If you saw or figured out what you were walking into you didn't walk.

"Rose?"

Azel turned. Colonel Bruda beckoned him. Azel followed him into the other room, grinning. He was not a tall man himself but he could see the top of Bruda's shiny head. "I figured out how you guys can win every battle from here on in."

Bruda faced him, frowning.

"You just pick a sunny day for the fight, put all your officers out front, and have them bow to the enemy."

Bruda's frown deepened. He did not get it.

"I never seen a one of you guys that was over twenty-five that wasn't bald as a lizard's egg. You'd blind them with the reflections. Then you could just go finish them off."

"Your sense of humor is something we don't need, Rose."

"You need some of my talents, you take them all."

"Consider the possibility that you may not be as indispensable as you'd like to think, Rose."

Azel grinned. Bruda was as predictable as sundown. "Hell. You know, Governor Straba said something just like that when he still thought I worked for him and not for Cado."

Bruda lost some color.

These Herodians were something. Hell on a six-legged camel in a gang, with their vaunted discipline and religious fervor. But catch them solo with a crack like that and they drizzled down their legs.

Of course, Bruda was the investigator of record in the hard, messy death of Governor Straba. Not a very good investigator, Colonel Bruda. He hadn't caught a whiff of the truth. He had no idea that Azel wasn't the killer.

Let him think whatever he wanted if it kept his knees knocking.

Azel had traced the murderer but had kept that to himself. It might be useful someday.

"You'll have to wait a few minutes, Rose. He's with someone. But he knows you're here."

"All right." Azel went to the window and contemplated the harbor. For the serenity of the sea . . . The serenity that masked the darknesses moving in the deeps, beneath the turquoise surface. Heavenstone, the Dartars called it. Ha. Nothing to do with heaven. Gorloch knew.

Gorloch knew that behind every facade there was nothing but shadow. Ultimately, there was nothing but The Shadow.

Gorloch knew.

Bruda made little noises behind him as he tried to work but could not concentrate. Azel heard his sigh of relief when the room's second door opened.

"Rose?"

Azel turned. "Ah. My favorite courtier."

The man's name was Taliga. Like all the Herodian aristocracy he was short and bald. Azel made no secret of the fact that he thought Taliga an incompetent asshole who would starve to death quickly if ever Cado—his brother-in-law—got an attack of smarts and planted a boot in his butt.

On some level Taliga was aware that he was a parasite. He hated Azel for waving it in front of him, in public. He was Azel's deadliest living enemy.

Azel knew that. He had created Taliga deliberately. Someday the Herodians would deem him a greater liability than an asset. When that decision was made he wanted the sanction handed to an incompetent first. Taliga was his alarm.

He did not bait the man today, beyond the initial crack. He attempted small talk, grinning all the time. Friendliness, too, would set Taliga's teeth on edge. It was a Herodian maxim that your enemies were at their friendliest and most solicitous just before they sank the knife in your back.

The military governor awaited them in a small, spartan room on the highest level of Government House. His own quarters. He took the admonitions of his faith personally. He said, "Thank you, Taliga. Good morning, Rose. It's been a while."

Azel waited till Taliga was out of the room. "Hasn't been anything worth coming in about."

"What did you do to Taliga this time? He was severely distressed."

"Nothing, General. I was the soul of civility. I asked about his wife and daughters. I commiserated properly when he reported that your sister has been suffering from a recurring flux."

"You're a dangerous man, Rose. You know us entirely too well."

"Sir?"

"And you dissemble altogether too convincingly. But I suppose that's why you're so good at what you do and I should be thankful you work for me and not for my enemies."

"There's truth in that, sir."

"You're also altogether too blunt. It makes you needless enemies. Someday Taliga will try to kill you."

"To carry bluntness a step further, sir, if he tries that they'll find pieces of him in every quarter of Qushmarrah."

"He's not much, Rose, but he's family."

Azel restrained a smile. Something had given unflappable, pudgy, but tough-as-shield-leather Cado a sour stomach and he wanted to work it off with some verbal fencing. "I like working for you, sir. But I like being alive even better. I ain't let nobody push me since I was seven years old. Ain't likely I'd start now. It's like, anybody who ever leaned on me and had to pay the price belonged to somebody's family."

"So. Let's stop being bull apes pounding our chests. You're here after a long drought. Does this mean there's finally something worth reporting?"

"Not much. The Living are either falling apart or going underground completely. Probably both. And mostly falling apart in the Hahr."

"That's where al-Akla executed those men."

"One sign of an impending collapse."

"Al-Akla's little scheme is beginning to work, then."

"Those guys made it work. The thing that brought me in, it ain't much more than a rumor, but if it's true it's sure the Living is coming apart, at least in the Hahr."

"What's the rumor?"

"A guy named Ortbal Sagdet got himself killed down there last night. That's a fact. I checked. The rumor is, he was the Living's number one boy down there. Thieves got him, looks like. Thieves usually know enough not to mess around where there's gonna be comebacks that'll get them dead."

"How soon can you get a confirmation on whether or not this Sagdet was what rumor says?" Cado's piggy little eyes were sparkling.

"Never."

"Eh?"

"How am I supposed to get your confirmation?"

"You belong to the Living."

"I'm what they call a ground-level soldier. The bottom of the heap. And I'm never going to be anything more."

"Why not?"

"The Living is an Old Boys outfit. I got three marks against me. The big one is, I wasn't out there to get my butt kicked at Dak-es-Souetta. The other two are I didn't get it kicked at the Seven Towers or on the Plain of Chordan, either. So it won't ever matter who I am or what I could do for them, I'll never be anything but a spear carrier."

Cado got up and went to a window. Physically he fit the stereotype of the Herodian ruling class. He was short, bald, and plump. He could posture, be pompous, and was vulnerable to flattery. Like the rest. Unlike most, though, there was a razor-sharp mind under his shiny pate. "Where were you in those days, Rose?"

"Out of town."

"You did say you used to be a sailor, didn't you? That that was how you learned Herodian. And there's little room on the seas these days for Qushmarrahan ships. Well, no matter. We're here, and it's now. If there is a way to identify Sagdet positively as a high officer of the Living, I'd be generously grateful."

"If there's a way I'll find it, sir."

"I know you will. And what of our friend the Eagle? Anything to report there?"

"I screwed up. I got me a job grooming horses for them but the first day, one of them got to mouthing off about city people and I broke both his legs for him. I didn't figure it would be smart to hang around after that."

"You're a man of great violence, aren't you?"

"Sometimes that's the only way to get a message across. I never saw you guys sending out missionaries to spread the One True Faith."

"A point. I . . ." Cado went red with anger.

Azel faced the window as an ensign invaded the room, so excited he hadn't bothered to knock, so young he still had hair. "Sir!" he exploded. "Signal from the South Light. The new governor's galley is in sight."

"Damn! The bastard would have good winds coming across, wouldn't he?" Cado kicked a stool across the room. "Machio, don't you ever bust in here like this again. If it's the end of the world in five seconds you knock and wait. Understand?"

"Yes sir."

"All right. Thank you. Get out."

The ensign went, tail between his legs.

"Our troubles redouble when we're least prepared to handle what we already have. Rose, I want you to stick with me today. I want you studying this Sullo pig from the beginning. He's the first one they've sent who could be genuinely dangerous."

"Stay with you? For the public reception and everything?"

"Yes."

"Too dangerous. There are people who would recognize me. I'll have no value if anyone suspects I work for you. Not to mention it might shorten my life expectancy."

"I want to explore your thoughts about what al-Akla might be up to in the Shu. I'll have you outfitted as a soldier in my personal bodyguard. You'll pass. Nobody looks at the men behind the commander."

"In the Shu? He isn't up to anything in the Shu that I've heard, sir."

"He sent Joab and more than a hundred men into the maze down there this morning. You hadn't heard?"

"No sir. I was working the Sagdet angle." Azel was disturbed. This was not good. He did have to find out what it meant. Soon. But it looked like Cado was going to keep him tied up all day. Damn!

He should not have come.

5

Aaron removed the last of the clamping straps that had held the parts of the mast step motionless while the adhesive between joins and around the holding pegs had set. He waved to the men working the hoist. They began lowering the harness that would lift the mast step so they could swing it over and drop it into the ship's half-completed hull.

The new Herodian foreman, Cullo, who had not yet been on the job two weeks, came to inspect the finished product. "Perfect," he pronounced it. "I've never seen more perfect joins, Aaron. They're cabinetry quality."

"That's the sort of work I was taught, sir. And what I'd be doing if I was well off enough to do whatever I wanted."

"Forget that. Stay with us. In five years you'd be a master shipwright."

"Yes sir." The way the Herodians were stripping the little forest on the hills south of Qushmarrah there would be no timber left in five years. Under the old regime every tree taken had had to be justified and every ounce of it put to some use. If he could find no other reason to dislike Herodians, Aaron could dislike them because they were locusts, stripping resources and wealth wherever their armies were successful. He suspected greed moved them more than did religious fervor.

He helped secure the harness, then stepped back. There would be nothing to do till the laborers had the mast step ready to drop into the hull. Cullo was on to someone else, so he went and found Billygoat where he was pounding and tamping caulking rope into laps of clinker planks with a wooden mallet and wedge. The old man was quick and deft. He was ten feet ahead of his assistant, who was sealing the laps with hot pitch.

"That stuff stinks," Aaron told the old man.

"Pitch? You get used to it. Gets to smell damned good if you're out of work for a while. You dogging it?"

"Hoisting the step."

"Uhm."

"They decided what to name her yet?" Billygoat knew everything before the foremen did. There was a battle going on at the top over the name of the ship. A struggle between zealots and practical merchants who knew she would be entering ports where the Herodian god would not find a warm welcome.

"Nope. Something on your mind, Aaron?"

"Yeah." He did not know how to broach it without sounding like an old woman, so he just had at it. "Remember when you told me about they found those lost kids out by Goat Creek?"

"Uhm." The older man's hands never stopped moving.

"You ever heard about them finding any other ones?"

"Worried again?"

"Some. Not for me this time. Friend of my wife had her little boy taken yesterday. An only child."

"Uhm." Billygoat paused to look at him directly. "You got one hell of a big determination to let this business fuss you, don't you, Aaron?"

What could he say? He couldn't mention the dreams and the nightmare certainty that something would happen to Arif. After all your precautions? they would ask. You have to be crazy.

Maybe he was.

"Now you bring it up, though, Aaron, yeah, it seems I do remember hearing about two, three other kids that turned up the same way. Good clothes, good health, short on memories of what happened to them while they was missing." Billygoat's hands were busy again.

"They knew their families?"

"I never heard anything said otherwise."

Aaron sighed a sigh that started right down in the roots of his soul. There was something to hang on to and nurture.

"Good, then," Billygoat said. "And what else do you have on your mind this morning, young man?" Part of Billygoat's charm was his assumption of the old man's role, though he was far from elderly.

Aaron was startled. Was he that obvious when he was troubled?

"Yep. The old man's a mind reader. What the hell did you expect, Aaron, moping around here all morning? Nobody pays attention? Come on. Spit it out."

"It isn't that easy, Billygoat. It's one of those things where you've got to make a choice, and even ignoring it is a choice, and no matter what you choose somebody is going to get hurt. So what you have to do is pick who gets it."

"Yeah. Those kind are a blue-assed baboon bitch, ain't they? Homar, it's time you broke. You're getting tired and sloppy trying to keep up. I see a couple places you're going to have to do over."

Aaron couldn't see anything wrong with Homar's work. Neither could Homar, he suspected, but Billygoat's assistant cleaned his tools, put more charcoal on, broke up a couple of pitch billets and put them in to melt, then went away.

"So, Aaron. Let's talk about it."

"What do you know about the Living?"

Billygoat's eyes got wary. "As little as I can. Knowing too much could get you a chance to swim across the bay with a hundred pounds of rocks tied to your toes."

"Yeah." He hadn't thought of that angle. "What I meant was, are they something worthwhile, or are they just a bunch of diehards making it rougher for the rest of us?"

Billygoat smiled. "You don't get me that easy, Aaron. It's in the eye of the beholder. Why don't you lay out the problem and if I see something I'll say so and if I don't I'll forget you even asked."

Aaron thought about it a minute, but there was not much going on inside his head. All he wanted to do was puke it up, get it out of his gut before it poisoned him.

"Say there was a guy who betrayed Qushmarrah in a way that was just as important as what Fa'tad did, only hardly anybody noticed, and only one guy knew, and the traitor didn't know he knew, and one day years later suddenly it looked like the traitor was now somebody real important in the Living. If he worked for the Herodians before . . ."

"I see." Billygoat raised a hand for silence. He had stopped working. "Say no more." He turned inward for several minutes. Then, "With the years intervening there would have grown up knots of personal considerations and complications, not so? The fight for Qushmarrah is over and lost. The traitor probably has a family now, all completely innocent, who would suffer terribly from any belated justice. Yet if he were indeed high in the councils of the Living, and still a tool of Herod, and the Living are a worthy group of men with a real chance of restoring Qushmarrah's independence and glory . . . Yes sir, Aaron, truly a blue-assed bitch baboon of a problem."

Someone up top yelled at Aaron to come on. The men on the hoist were ready to lower the mast step.

"I'll think about this, Aaron. For every no-win situation I've ever seen there's always been an extra way out if you could just back off and look at the whole map from a skewed angle. Talk to me later. Get up there before they get pissed."

"Thanks, Billygoat." Aaron trotted to the nearest scaffolding, clambered up, crossed the ship on a work deck of loose planks, checked that everything he had brought up earlier was still handy. His helpers were ready. "Lower away!"

The step assembly came down slowly. The men helping turned it, aligned it, guided it into place. Aaron beckoned the foreman. "It looks like a good fit. But let's check the join points to make sure."

Ten minutes later he was puffed with pride. Only one place did he need to plane a bit off a beam end. Cullo told him, "You have to stay in this business, Aaron. We'd get the contracts filled in half the time."

Aaron shrugged, went to the side, had the men on the hoist lift the assembly a foot and a half. His helpers started brushing all the join points with adhesive. He let it set up a little, then had the assembly dropped into place again. His helpers started driving adhesive-soaked pegs immediately, four to the join, of which there were twelve: four at deck level, two to the side; four halfway down a pair of the midships ribs, two to the side again; and four on the keel itself.

"A successful experiment," the foreman told Aaron. "It's saved us a week over putting it together in place, piece by piece. I'm sure you'll get a fat bonus. How soon can you start on the steps for the cargo booms?"

"I still have to finish this. After the glue seasons I have to cut the pegging flush, sand the joins smooth, layer on some more glue, then cover everything with lacquer."

"All stuff that could be done by somebody else, under your supervision, while you're getting the other steps. What the hell is going on?"

Men were gathering in the bow of the unfinished ship, chattering and pointing toward the harbor. Aaron followed the foreman forward to see what was up.

A huge galley was working her way in. She wore the gaudiest sail Aaron had ever seen. "Who is it?"

"Must be the new civil governor. Early. And now everything goes to hell while we fake up celebrations to show him how overjoyed Qushmarrah is that he's finally come."

Aaron leaned on the rail, watching the Herodian galley, and smiled slightly, remembering how cynical his father had been about government and those who governed.

Bel-Sidek was hard at it, holystoning the foredeck of a tubby merchantman out of Pella, a Herodian tributary where friends of the Living worked the docks. Behind him, stevedores shuffled to the dock and back aboard, loading and unloading at the same time.

Sacks of something were going off and sacks of something else were coming on and bel-Sidek could not quite see the point because he could not distinguish one group of sacks from the other. But inside a few of those coming off there would be lethal tools for the Living.

Someone hailed him from the dock. The voice was breathless. For a moment he feared it was going to be a warning that the customs goons were coming and he would have to get his men scattered before they could be identified. But when he got to the rail he saw one of that very select group of men entrusted with carrying messages between the khadifas. The man pointed toward the bay and shouted, "The new governor's ship is coming in."

Bel-Sidek cursed and signaled his understanding. "Early. The bald-headed little bastard would get here early." He tried to look for the ship but all he could see in that direction was the tips of the lighthouses atop the Brothers. The Pellans had taken the cheapest commercial wharfage available. That put them behind a jungle of masts and spars belonging to Qushmarrah's fishermen and sponge and pearl divers. And small-time smugglers. If there was any distinction between the bunch.

He limped off the ship and got himself to the nearest height where he could see the harbor. After a minute he began to chuckle. Other gawkers looked him askance. He controlled himself.

The governor's ship and two fast war galleys escorting her had bulled their way past commercial traffic beyond the Brothers and now several delayed vessels were coming in behind them. Including Meryel's two ships with the arms down in their holds. There would be no trouble getting them off-loaded and safely away. The whole Herodian colony would be going crazy and would cease to function for a few days.

Would the old man take the opportunity to welcome the new tyrant? He had before. But if Meryel was right and there was some special operation shaping . . . Could it have something to do with the new governor? Doubtful. The General had talked in terms of months.

Might as well go back to work. The governor's arrival would make no difference in his life, at least today.

As he was passing the new shipyards, put up where the old public baths had stood till they had been demolished because they offended Herodian morality, a man fell into step beside him. "So. Billygoat. Haven't seen you in a while. What's up? What're you doing these days?"

"Working in the shipyard. As if you didn't know."

Bel-Sidek did know. He kept track of those few of his men who had come home from Dak-es-Souetta. "What is it?"

"The younger men there, they bring me their problems. I had a beauty turn up today. You were the only one I could think of who could maybe help solve it. And like a gift from Aram, here you are. I saw you, it was like a command from the gods."

"I don't follow."

"Wait till I explain. I don't know if you're connected or not, but you're the only one I could think of who might know somebody involved with the Living."

Bel-Sidek did not respond.

"One of the guys—certainly not connected in any way—has convinced himself he knows the identity of a Qushmarrahan who was as guilty of treason during the war as al-Akla. He kept it to himself. But now he's stumbled across something to make him think the traitor is in a high place in the Living. He fears that once in Herodian pay, always bought."

"Eh!" Bel-Sidek rolled it around in his mind, a small part of him hoping he wasn't sweating, blanching, or otherwise giving himself away. "Exactly what do you want, Sergeant?"

"Mainly, I want to figure out if the guy is imagining things. He believes it, but people believe impossible things every day. I never heard of any traitor but al-Akla. I sure as hell ain't heard of one that was as important as him in how things came out."

"I know of no such man myself but that doesn't mean one didn't exist. Come. I'll buy you a lunch while we let reason gnaw at this." Bel-Sidek suspected he had given himself away but had a feeling the risk would be worthwhile.

"I won't name you any names, Colonel."

You will, my friend. You will if we want you to. He glanced at the man. And maybe you wouldn't. You were always a stubborn bastard.

"We'll set the hounds of reason loose first, eh?"

They went into a place that served good *bheghase*, a thick and spicy fish and vegetable soup into which the fish was introduced two minutes before serving. It was an indulgence bel-Sidek allowed himself too seldom.

He savored a few mouthfuls before saying, "Granting that no names need be named, I'll have to have a clue or two with which to work. Is your friend a veteran?"

"Who isn't?"

"A point. Not many. Dak-es-Souetta?"

"No."

"Ah. Now we're getting somewhere. A vet, but not of Dak-es-Souetta. Works in a shipyard. Must be a building tradesman. Most of those were in the field engineer outfits assigned to the Seven Towers. I presume he knows about whatever because he saw it happen. If it happened." He looked at Billygoat.

"You fishing for an opinion?"

"Yes."

"He believes it, like I said. If he hadn't sounded like a man trying to carry an unbearable load I wouldn't be here."

"The Seven Towers. I'll have to research it. The Herodians had me in chains while that was happening."

"I can suggest what to look for."

"Uhm?"

"The Seven Towers were supposed to hold out long enough for the allies, the reserves, and the survivors of Dak-es-Souetta to assemble on the Plain of Chordan. But they didn't."

"Could one traitor have been the reason the strategy didn't work?"

Billygoat shrugged. "I was five men down the chain from you."

"I'll find out. I'll ask someone who was there. Thank you, Sergeant. Enjoy the *bheghase*." Bel-Sidek limped away hurriedly, headed for the Pellan merchantman. Two of the men on his stevedore crew had fought at the Seven Towers. One had been an officer, a military engineer.

He rounded the two up. "Take an early lunch."

One man, bel-Pedra, depended entirely upon his income from stevedoring. "We're liable to get fired." There were limits to the sacrifices you could ask.

"I'll take care of it."

"What's going on, sir?"

"I've just discovered that I need some background about the Seven Towers and what happened there. Something's come up where it could be important for me to know. Malachi?"

Malachi was the man who had not yet spoken. He got off the bale where he had been seated, settled on the battered timber decking of the pier. "You've been through the pass, sir?"

"Never. We went out along the coast road."

"Yes. Demolishing the bridges behind you so the enemy, if victorious, had to come to Qushmarrah through the hills."

"Do I detect a critical note?"

"Call it a disgruntled note, sir. For five generations that was the strategy. But when it was put to the test it didn't work."

"It should have."

"In theory." Malachi used a finger to sketch an imaginary chart. "The road runs into the pass heading due east but when it gets to the crest it elbows sixty degrees south. There are four towers on the outside of this curve, two on either side of the summit. Three on the inside curve, with the middle perched on the crest. No names, just numbers, with the odds to the outside, evens in, counting from the far end. Number Four is the keystone piece. It's three times as big and defensible as the others.

"Note the angular relationships between the towers. When all seven are intact only One and Seven have much of a shadow where they don't get supporting fire from the other towers. That isn't big enough to exploit well. Four has no shadow at all.

"Interesting from your professional viewpoint, I'm sure," bel-Sidek said. "What went wrong?"

"I don't know. We took away every option but reducing the towers in series."

"Sounds like the hard way."

"Hard, but the cheapest way for them. Also the slowest, which is why we wanted them to do it that way. Their sappers and engineers were good, but we made them pay dear to take One, Two, and Three. What happened later I don't know. I was in Three."

"Bel-Pedra?" bel-Sidek asked.

"I was in Five, sir. I don't think I can help much. They went after Four like lions for three days and didn't get nothing but bloody noses. Then the sun comes up on the fourth morning and there's the Herodian standard showing up top and heralds down front telling us they'd make us rich if we'd just open up. We dumped the toilet pails on them and they went away. Five minutes later we were taking fire from the heavy engines on top of Four. Whatever happened, the guys there never had time to destroy those."

Bel-Sidek pursued that tale a little, not because he was interested but because he did not want his next question to sound especially important. He got the two men to discuss Herodian tactics in the assaults on the various towers. Then he asked Malachi, "Did they try to get Three to surrender before they attacked?"

"Oh, they tried that with everybody. A matter of form. They have some kind of law. They got the same answer every time, and they expected it."

"Uhm. Bel-Pedra, you'd better get back to work. Malachi, I have a chore for you." He let bel-Pedra depart. "Go over to the new Herodian shipyard and find Bhani Sytef. You want a list of all employees who were at the Seven Towers. You want to know which tower they served in. He's supposed to know things like that, but with so many working there I'd be astonished if he actually did. Just get a list of those he does know about. If it isn't enough I'll get back to him."

Malachi rose. He looked puzzled. "What's going on?"

"I don't know. But the big boys are trying to connect some people up with some other people and the only lead they've got is that maybe these guys were all in the same outfit at the Seven Towers."

Bel-Sidek was well known to the Living in his quarter, but very few knew him to be khadifa of the waterfront. At every level he appeared as the agent of the men a step or two up the chain of command. There were risks. Bel-Sidek felt having access to all his men all the time was worth those risks. The harbor quarter was the busiest for the Living and needed the most direct attention.

"They want to ask people from outside the movement first?"

Bel-Sidek shrugged. "I don't decide how things get done, I just do the job."

"Nothing ever changes, does it?"

"Not in the army."

Malachi left. And he returned much sooner than bel-Sidek expected.

"You were wrong, sir. He knew them well. There were only three men he couldn't pin down for sure." He proffered a piece of paper.

"I'll see that he gets a commendation. Back to work. I fixed you with the Pellans."

Bel-Sidek settled and ran a finger down the list. His finger jerked. "I should've guessed." And it all fell into place, right along with the solution. He wanted to run to the General immediately. But he still had to assemble the gangs to work Meryel's ships.

The new governor's galley was trying to warp into its pier and having a hell of a time even with help from several tugs. Bel-Sidek smiled and murmured, "I hope that breeze is an omen."

Medjhah shaded his eyes and peered at the harbor. "Ships coming in. Fancy ones."

Yoseh yanked his attention away from the girl's house. Medjhah pointed.

Three ships were crossing the slice of harbor visible from Char Street. "Warships?"

"The two on the outside. Must be somebody important."

"Ferrenghi, probably."

It took Medjhah a few seconds to get it. "Yeah. They all think they're big stuff, don't they?"

Yoseh's attention drifted back to that doorway. The girl was there again. And the old woman was giving him a truly ferocious look.

He felt puckish. He winked at her.

She was astonished. She was scandalized. Then, for an instant, a smile threatened to crack the dried mud of her face. Then she became more the basilisk than ever.

"Now what the hell?" Medjhah grumbled.

A dozen Dartar horsemen were hastening down the hill, speaking to the men at each entrance of the maze. Each pause caused an immediate stir. Yoseh guessed, "Fa'tad is calling us in for some reason."

Soon he was proven right. A man told them to call everybody out of the labyrinth and get ready to move out.

"I'll go get them," Medjhah said. He had grown bored watching the animals and the traffic in Char Street. "Give her a good-bye kiss for me, too." He laughed as he went into the alley.

Yoseh began checking and tightening the animals' tack. At least they did not have prisoners to worry them, like some of the other groups.

They had become part of the scenery quickly and the curious crowds had thinned. But now people began coming out again, to see the Dartars packing up as hastily as they had arrived.

Yoseh glanced down the street. The girl was watching and the crone was glaring. The three ships were out of sight.

Medjhah was taking a long time. Should he go see? No. These veydeen would steal the animals, or scatter them at the least, just for meanness.

He realized he was alone in a street with hundreds who hated him. He drew himself up and tried to look older and tougher and a lot more fearless than he felt.

He was worried.

Then he heard Nogah cursing Joab and Fa'tad, the veydeen

and ferrenghi, Cado and the gods, and anyone else who occurred to him. Yoseh felt better immediately.

A couple of disgusting, frightened veydeen stumbled out ahead of Yoseh's brothers and cousins. Their hands were bound behind them. One tried to run. Somebody stuck a spear between his legs. He pitched forward. Nogah jumped on him and kicked him viciously three or four times. Yoseh was astonished and appalled.

Then he noticed the cut and stain on Nogah's left sleeve. Blood did not show well against the black, so the wound had not been obvious. Which was why they all wore black.

Nogah growled, "Are the animals ready?"

"Yes. Is that bad?"

"No. But it hurts like hell." He yelled at the others, telling them to get the prisoners coffled up and get themselves mounted.

"It's still bleeding some, Nogah."

"That'll keep it clean."

"You want me to look at it?"

"Here? In the damned street?"

"Oh." Of course. Not in front of the veydeen.

"Thanks anyway, kid. The ache will remind me that even things that live under rocks can hurt you if you aren't careful."

Yoseh glanced at the prisoners. They did have a texture that reminded him of grubs.

It was not long before Joab came up the hill, the column re-forming behind him. As Yoseh turned his camel into line some impulse caused him to wave to the girl in the doorway. Though not blatantly. No.

For a wonder the crone wasn't looking.

For a double wonder the girl returned his wave shyly. Then she fled into the darkness inside her home.

He did not wake up till they reached the compound and everyone started telling him he had to get changed into his best apparel. A new civil governor was arriving from Herod and everyone had to turn out for the welcoming parade.

He was still bemused when they formed up on the plazas of the acropolis, five thousand men in black, perfectly motionless on their mounts. Opposite them, across an aisle a hundred feet wide, were the Herodian infantry in their white and red, only their officers mounted, twelve thousand strong.

With this driblet in the tide Herod held Qushmarrah. Yoseh thought it a vain and foolish thing to parade the weakness of the occupying forces.

The new governor was a long time coming. When he did, Yoseh was not impressed, despite the Moretian guards before and behind, the chariots, the gaudy trappings and people. No one else was impressed, either. The governor was a morbidly fat man on a litter. He did not look like he would be able to get up without help. There were snickers and titters till Fa'tad turned his scowl upon the formation.

The Herodians had the same problem.

The Qushmarrahan youths who were perched on the monuments and rooftops behind the formations had no superiors to silence them. They were loud with their mockery and abuse.

Yoseh was almost embarrassed for the fat man. Sullo? Sullo, yes.

General Cado and his staff emerged from Government House, clad in spartan contrast to the new governor's opulence. More show for the veydeen? Of course.

Yoseh was in a good position to observe, thirty yards from Fa'tad and only in the second rank. Sullo's Moretians spread out. The governor reached the foot of the Government House steps a moment before General Cado did so. Yes, it took the help of two men to set Sullo upright.

The veydeen hooligans howled.

General Cado stepped down and threw his arms around Sullo. Sullo reciprocated. They embraced like brothers who had been separated for years.

If Yoseh understood the way Herodians operated, that meant a hatred between them deeper than the pits of Khorglot. There were ghost knives in their back-thumping hands.

Yoseh's eyes bugged. "Nogah."

Nogah ignored him.

"Nogah!"

"Quiet in ranks," Nogah hissed. Medjhah scowled at him.

"All right. But you'll regret it."

Nogah looked over his shoulder, eyes baleful. Yoseh ignored him, kept his gaze fixed on the man he had picked out of General Cado's bodyguard.

Zouki was so bored he forgot to be scared. Till the big man came. Then all the kids got quiet and shaky. Some started to whimper. One of the girls skittered into the foliage to hide with the rock apes.

The big man came in and scooped up a boy who went into hysterics immediately. The giant went out and locked the door to the cage. Zouki stared at the bone-white nuts of his fists while the boy's screams faded and knew he'd never see that kid again.

6

Raheb said nothing as Aaron came to the house. She just nodded and began the slow, painful chore of getting herself upright. Aaron did not offer to help. Any effort to help would be spurned.

The woman believed she was a curse and a burden upon her daughter's house and she was not going to accept any help of any kind that was not absolutely forced upon her. Aaron accepted that.

His feelings toward Raheb were mixed. Always there were eddies and crosscurrents and dangerous undertows when the mother of the wife lived in the household of the wife. Still, he could have done worse for a mother-in-law. He knew men who got more grief with their wives' mothers living all the way across town.

Arif spied him first. "Daddy's home!" He charged, a flurry of clumsy limbs. Aaron caught him and lifted him up and squeezed him. Stafa roared in at knee level and wrapped both arms and legs around his shin and grinned up at him.

Laella's question was in her eyes. She was always troubled when he arrived home off schedule. "They dismissed us early. Because of the new governor coming in. Only have to work a half day tomorrow. They expect the whole Herodian colony to have to assemble for speeches by General Cado and the new governor. His name is Sullo, I think."

"Why do they waste the time?" Raheb wanted to know.

"What?"

"Somebody's just going to kill him. They always do."

Startled, Aaron realized she was right. Eight civil governors in six years. They killed them off within a few months every time. Qushmarrah spent more time awaiting the arrival of new civil governors than she did being ruled by them.

He shrugged. That was a trouble for the Herodians. He squeezed Arif. The boy squealed. Aaron took a few steps. Stafa clung to his leg and giggled and proclaimed, "We've got you now, long-legged demon!"

"Decorum!" Aaron laughed. "What we need around this house is a little decorum and discipline."

Arif laughed and hugged his neck. Stafa repeated, "We got you now, long-legged demon." But Aaron's remark did not go over well elsewhere. Raheb grumbled sarcastic agreement. Mish's eyes sparked with rebellion. She muttered to herself. Laella looked put upon.

"Problem?"

Mish surprised him by answering. "Mother thinks I was flirting with a Dartar soldier." She spoke each word almost as a separate sentence and loaded every one with the infinite, weary exasperation of the very young.

"That's enough of that, Mish," Laella said. "Mother! We've been through it already."

"Dartar?" Aaron asked.

"You should've seen, Dad," Arif said. "There were hundreds of them. Thousands. With camels and everything."

Stafa said, "Forty-three," which was his favorite number of the week and meant a lot instead of any specific number.

"Dartars? What is this?"

"They came this morning," Laella said. "A hundred. Maybe a few more. They put men outside all the entrances to the maze and then they went in. They took prisoners."

Raheb said, "And about time that cesspit was cleaned, too. Maybe those Dartar maggots are good for something, after all."

Which led Mish to a caustic remark. Her mother responded. Laella snapped, "That's enough of that! You're both old enough to know better." She pinched her temples between thumb and forefinger. "I'm yelling at my mother and sister like they were kids squabbling."

"You need to get out. Let's go for a walk. Up to the Parrot's Beak."

"I haven't done the marketing yet. It was too rowdy out there while the Dartars were here."

"Never mind. We'll manage. What happened to the Dartars?"

"After they were here a few hours messengers came and they all went away again."

"Probably because of the new governor. Come on. Let's go walk."

She saw it was important to him, so she collected her shawl.

"I want to go, Dad."

"Me, too." Stafa still clung to his leg, grinning, stubborn as a barnacle. He deposited Arif on the floor.

"You boys stay with Nana."

"Aw, that's not fair. You don't never let me . . ."

"Yeah, you long-legged creep. I hate you."

Aaron rolled his eyes toward heaven. "Let's sell them both to the Turoks." The Turoks were nomads who ranged south of the Takes, reputedly so ferocious even the Dartars feared them. Turoks seldom visited Qushmarrah. The only Turoks Aaron had seen he'd been unable to distinguish from Dartars.

Selling the children to the Turoks was a family joke. Laella completed the ritual. "The Turoks wouldn't take them. They're too mean. You boys behave for Nana. Mish, you can make mountain bread. There're beans soaking in the crock. There's cheese. There're odds and ends. Put something together."

Mish put on her martyr's disguise, filled the house with her agonized adolescent sighs.

Raheb shook her head in disgust and took herself back outside to abort a squabble provoked by proximity.

"Are you going?" Laella asked, Aaron suspected more sharply than she intended.

"I still have this grinning goiter on my shin."

Stafa giggled.

Laella peeled him off amidst a one-child chorus of hate-you-moms and deposited him amongst blocks Aaron had made from scraps from the shipyard. Arif observed sourly. Aaron hugged him. Laella twisted her shawl around her head and across her face and followed Aaron into the street. She said, "Give me time to relax. Mom and Mish have been at it all morning."

He grunted. He had no intention of saying anything till he had relaxed himself. In some way.

They did not exchange a word all the way to the Parrot's Beak.

The acropolis was crowded. The parade for the new governor was still breaking up, with soldiers moving back to their barracks or garrisons or duty stations. They moved through the traffic and found a place in the shade of the Beak. They settled. They remained silent. The breeze tugged at their hair and clothing. Clouds banking beyond the Brothers suggested some rain moving in later.

Laella waited.

"I want to tell you about something. I don't really want to *talk* about it. I don't want to answer a lot of questions." The trouble with talking with Laella was that she always asked a thousand questions that had nothing to do with anything, about half of them vaguely accusatory. Interposed would be two or three questions that were too much to the point.

"It's about what's been bothering you?"

"Yes." That was one. "Just let me tell it."

She bit down angrily.

"This has been eating at me for six years. Last night it came to a head. I have to make a move. But I don't know what." Before he finished that his hand was moving. He laid a finger across her lips as she started to open her mouth.

"Six years ago one of the men in my company opened a secret postern gate and let the Herodians into the tower we were holding at the Seven Towers. He almost got me killed. He did get half the men in the outfit killed. He almost got me sold across the sea as a slave. They were going to do that with all the prisoners that had trades. Till they decided that would cause more hate in Qush-marrah than it was worth. He got a lot more people killed here in the city."

He lapsed into several minutes of silence. Laella bemused him by keeping her peace. It was not like her to recognize a time for quiet.

"Do you know that if we'd held the pass for two more days the allies and the new levies would have had time to assemble on the Plain of Chordan?"

Laella nodded. "Everyone says."

"We could've held out for another week. We knew it and they knew it. They were so desperate they started trying to run cavalry past us at night. Not the Dartars. Fa'tad is too smart to let his men get massacred the way we massacred them."

Laella was frowning. "Is there a point to this?"

"Maybe I'm straying. But I want you to know that the Herodians knew they couldn't win if they didn't get to the Plain of Chordan first. Even with Fa'tad to help. People who were on our side forget that part and just jabber about Dak-es-Souetta. Maybe because everybody who ever thought they were anybody in Qushmarrah was there and they don't want their defeat to be less important than one man opening a postern gate. I mean, how could all those tens of thousands of men getting killed be less significant?"

"You think you know who did it."

"I don't *think* I know. I'm not guessing. I *know*."

"Naszif."

He was startled into open-mouthed silence.

"It explains so much, doesn't it? Why you've always been the way you are about him. How he's managed to do so well without working very hard at it. You should hear how Reyha worries about his making so much. And you kept this bottled up all this time."

"There's Reyha. And Zouki. And the war is over and lost."

"And no bitterness? No urge to get even?"

"Hell, yes, there is! I got a father and two brothers under the ground on the Plain of Chordan. Pop was too old to go to Dak-es-Souetta. Tuddo and Rani were too young . . . Yeah. I'm bitter. Yeah. I hate. But what happens to Reyha and Zouki if you take Naszif away? The war didn't leave them anyone else at all."

Almost shyly, like the first time they had been allowed to be together alone, she touched his hand. "You're a good man, Aaron. Thank you for telling me."

"I'm not done yet."

"There's more?"

"You didn't pay a lot of attention to Naszif last night, did you?"

"I ignore him as much as I can." She smiled. "I don't like him, either. Even Reyha doesn't like him very much. But a woman has to live with what she has to live with. What about Naszif last night?"

"He made me have to make my decision all over again. And it was hard enough the first time, and living with it."

"Why again?" Straight to the point today. None of the usual nonsense.

"Because at the end last night Naszif was practically bragging that he's a big man in the Living."

"But what does that . . . Oh."

"Yes. Maybe he's still getting Qushmarrahans killed."

Bel-Sidek waited patiently while the old man considered what he had said. When the General spoke, he observed, "I note that you haven't named a single name."

"I wasn't told any names."

"But you wouldn't be telling me if you didn't think you knew the man."

"Yes."

"So?"

"Your solutions tend to be abrupt and permanent. You see a threat, you extinguish it. But in this I see a great opportunity to stick it to Cado big. If the whole thing doesn't turn out to be somebody's pipe dream."

The General reflected. He said, "You're right on all counts, Khadifa. It is an opportunity. And rightfully yours to exploit—if, as you say, it isn't a pipe dream."

"Thank you, sir."

"But you have to know you have game afoot, for certain. Then you have to decide if you let him know you know or not. If you just feed him select lies he'll continue hurting us elsewhere. If you try to turn him you run the risk of losing him if he panics. Either way, it's likely that Cado or Bruda will sense a change in the texture of the information he supplies. Unless you're very careful."

"That much I know."

"What first?"

"Find out for sure."

"I have a suggestion. I have a man to do the finding out. He's the best the movement has. He'll do the job right."

Bel-Sidek smiled.

"True, you'd have to give me the name. But I've said he's yours. I think this is important enough to give to someone who won't screw it up. We have too many amateurs at the ground level. Or he might recognize someone."

"I'll trade you a name for a name."

The old man thought about it. "No. I can't. His rules. You find out when I go."

Bel-Sidek considered that and the General's previous remarks. "All right. You watch your man Naszif."

The General remained still for a long time. His pallor deepened. "You're sure?"

"He's the one."

"We praise the gods, who are merciful, and smile upon us."

"Sir?"

"I was going to send Hadribel to take charge of the Hahr and add Naszif to the command staff of the Shu. Even if he did not recognize me himself chances are Cado would once he described the khadifa of the Shu."

"Promote him, anyway, sir. You don't have to reveal yourself.

If he's running with the Herodian pack it'll give him something he'll want to report to his masters."

"Yes. Bring writing materials."

Bel-Sidek waited a long time while the old man wrote. The General's efforts seemed weaker and more painful than they had been the evening before. Bel-Sidek worried silently. The old man wrote three notes.

"Take this one to the same place you went last night. Then take the others to Hadribel. This one is for him. He's to deliver the other to Naszif himself after he has supper. You go to your friend's house. Stay there till time for tonight's meeting."

"Yes, sir." Bel-Sidek went, his leg aching so badly he began mumbling, "I will not yield. I am not beaten. I am among the living."

Azel rambled in and dumped himself into a chair at the only open table in Muma's Place. Muma himself came right away, settled opposite him. "Bad day?"

"Just rough. You got any of that Narbonian beer hidden in the cellar still? I feel like swilling a pail full."

"There's still a little down there. You can't drink it out here."

"I know."

"You may not have time for it," Muma said, rising.

Azel watched Muma cross to the kitchen doorway. A limping man arrived there moments later. The limping man was deft of hand. Azel almost missed the passing of the message.

Muma summoned one of his sons. The youngest went out with the crippled man. After a while, Muma returned to Azel's table.

"For me?"

"For you. A sparrow."

"Let's go find that beer."

Muma grinned. A few teeth were absent. "You're not going to jump on it?"

"I'm going to relax and have something to drink and eat. The pot will simmer along as nicely without me to watch."

"No doubt. You serve too many masters."

"I serve only one. Myself."

"Perhaps that one is too exacting."

"Maybe." Azel thought about a couple of weeks in the silence and solitude of the sinkhole country. Qushmarrah *could* simmer without benefit of his watchful eye. Surely.

Maybe in another week or two. Times were too interesting right now.

"A wonderful change of pace tonight," Medjhah said, staring into his bowl in feigned despair. "Raw instead of charred."

"Is it wiggling?" Nogah asked.

"Too ashamed."

"Are the worms playing tag through it?"

"They're embarrassed to show themselves in this glop."

"Eat up, then. You'll grow up big and strong and brave and fierce and smart like our beloved . . ."

Some glint of mirth in the eyes of those opposite him warned Nogah. He glanced over his shoulder. "Mo'atabar. We were just talking about you."

"I heard the fierce and smart part, which touches on the truth as heavily as a maiden's blush. Meantime, your beloved leader wants to see you and the kid. No hurry! No hurry! I'm nothing if not civilized and compassionate. I'd be worse than a Turok savage if I denied men the once-in-a-lifetime chance to fill themselves with delicacies such as these. Eat up, Nogah. Eat hearty. Enjoy while you can. Shall I have the cooks bring you more? They probably have a taste or two left."

"No. No. Wonderful as it is, I'll have to restrain myself. Have to set an example for the men. Gluttony is an unforgivable and disgusting vice."

Mo'atabar went away smiling.

Yoseh said, "Fa'tad."

"Yes."

His stomach knotted. "Again."

"I'm thinking about gouging your eyes out, baby brother."

"Maybe I'll do it myself. Why does he have to see me?"

No one answered, not even to crack wise. Medjhah began

muttering about how the damned ingrate Qushmarrahan charity-case cooks were trying to poison their benefactors.

They downed what they could stomach, Yoseh drawing it out. Nogah told him, "Stalling won't help. You still got to go."

The compound was more crowded than it had been the night before. They edged around to one side and that took them past the cause of the increased crowding, the pen for the prisoners taken in the maze. "Look," Yoseh said. "Some of them are just kids."

Four children huddled in a corner of the pen, terrified. Yoseh was not good at guessing veydeen ages but figured them for five or six. Two yards from them lay a dead man. His skin had the waxy look that characterized all the prisoners except the children.

The dead man had a black arrow sticking out of his side. Nogah said, "He must have tried something on the kids."

Yoseh grunted. He looked at the rest of the captives and decided he did not want to find out what kind of hell existed deep in the Shu maze.

Yahada admitted them without bothering to announce them, indicating an out-of-the-way corner where they could squat. They did so. Yoseh was so awed he kept his gaze fixed upon his hands. His knuckles were bone-white.

Fa'tad's commanders were all crowded into his quarters. They were not discussing the arrival of the civil governor, as Yoseh expected, but what had been learned from several prisoners who had been interrogated already. Having arrived at the end, Yoseh did not follow it except to understand that during the next few days, while the Herodians were preoccupied, Fa'tad meant to scour the city hidden beneath the Shu.

Yoseh got no sense of why that was important to al-Akla—except that Fa'tad was now angry because two men had been killed and seven injured during the morning's invasion.

Fa'tad growled something about getting those damned kids out of that pen, he wanted them alive so he could parade them around in search of their parents. Somebody went to take care of it.

"Yoseh. Come here, youngster."

Shaking, Yoseh rose and approached Fa'tad.

"They tell me you saw your friend from the labyrinth again today."

"Yes sir. He was one of General Cado's bodyguards. The one who stood nearest him on his right."

"I pay little attention to the decorative people. Why didn't you say something at the time, when he was there for all to see?"

"I tried. I was told to keep quiet in ranks. I'm new at this. I have to trust the judgment of my elders. Silence seemed to be their highest priority."

Fa'tad grinned and snorted. Joab slapped his knee. Nogah looked like he would melt from embarrassment. Al-Akla said, "He's inherited his father's tongue." Several of the older men chuckled. "Well, young Yoseh. What do you think? Why would Cado have his bodyguards stealing children?"

"I don't know, sir. The ferrenghi are strange."

"They are indeed. I don't know why, either. It makes no sense. No matter how I look at it I can see nothing in it to profit Cado. And no way to find out."

"Maybe it's something the man does on his own, sir."

"Maybe. The ferrenghi are a cruel and corrupt race. You may go. If you see that man again, drop everything else and find out whatever you can. I'd surely like to talk with him."

"Yes sir." Yoseh retreated hurriedly.

Nogah was right behind him. "What the hell did you have to go mouthing off like that for?"

"Sometimes I just can't help myself."

"No one is going to hurt you," the Witch told the child, who could not stop crying. She could not keep the exasperation out of her voice. "You drink this and you'll go to sleep for a little while. That's all. When you wake up I'll ask you some questions. After that you can go home."

The child's sobs did not slacken, but he looked up at her, wanting to believe, unable to do so.

Torgo extended one huge hand, offering the boy a cup. The child refused it.

"You'll have to force him, Torgo." Always, they had to be compelled.

The eunuch did it.

The potion worked quickly. The child fought but soon drifted off. The Witch said, "I wish there was some other way to do this. Why do they fear so much? We don't mistreat them, do we?"

"We treat them better than they get treated at home, my lady. But they're too young to appreciate that."

"I don't need your sarcasm."

"Ma'am?"

"I know you don't approve of the way I've been doing this, Torgo. Too gentle-hearted, you think."

Torgo did not answer her.

"Come. Get him moved to the cataflique. And get the things ready. You're getting entirely too sloppy. Everything should have been ready before we started."

It was not as if Torgo did not have plenty of time. But he was growing lackadaisical, clearly becoming convinced that they were wasting their time. The same little fear had begun to gnaw at her heart. Failure after failure, and never a positive to encourage them to go on . . . Except the probability that every failure meant that they were a step nearer success.

It was hard to see failure in a positive light.

All was prepared to her satisfaction when the child began to show signs of recovering. She said, "Time for you to go, Torgo." And as he started to leave, "Has Azel been in today?"

"No, ma'am."

"He'll be back."

Torgo did not reply.

The Witch stepped inside the heavy green velvet tent that enclosed the child. She checked the charcoal to make sure it was burning properly, then began drinking water she drew from a jar with a tin cup. She drank till her stomach ached. She was going to be in that hot tent a long time.

This part was far harder on her than it was on the children. It would take her two days to recover.

She removed a lid covering a silver bowl, used a glistening

silver spoon to shake a little of the bowl's contents onto the coals. A sour, bitter smoke puffed up. She leaned back, trying not to inhale too much too soon.

She had to walk the saber's edge now, going into the twilight on the edge of sleep, where the wakening child would be held by the fumes, but remaining sufficiently in control to be able to lead the boy where she wanted him to go. It did not always work. Occasionally she had to do it over. She hated that.

It got no easier with practice.

She spooned more herb, delicately, waiting for the buzzing in her head to reach the right pitch. When it did she began groping for the boy's name. That part was always tricky.

This time she could not remember. "Damn," she said softly, and began feeling through her clothing. This time she had remembered to write it down but then had not remembered to leave the scrap of paper where she could see it.

She breathed shallowly, trying not to take in too much smoke.

Her fingers encountered the paper. She drew it out, frowned at it, wiped away the sweat that had begun to run into her eyes. Why couldn't she ever remember to wear a sweatband? She puzzled out the name.

"Histabel. Histabel, can you hear me?"

The boy did not respond.

"Histabel. If you hear me, answer me."

He made a sound.

"You must pay close attention to me, Histabel. This is very important. Say yes if you understand."

His "yes" was a sparrow's sigh.

"You are comfortable and relaxed and you feel very good now. Don't you, Histabel?"

"Yes."

"Good. That's good. I want you to feel comfortable and relaxed. Now I'm going to ask you some questions. Answer them the best you can. And I'm going to tell you some things. The things I tell you will all be true. Do you understand?"

"Yes."

"What is your name?"

"Histabel."

"Who is your father?" "Who is your mother?" "How many brothers and sisters do you have?" "How old are they?" And so forth, the boy answering every time, the answers being unimportant to the Witch except in that they set his mind in an answering mode.

"What I tell you is true, Histabel. You are four years old. In fact, today is your fourth birthday. Where are you?"

For a time the boy's mind resisted being loosened from its anchor in time. They always did, though with children the shaking loose was easier than it was with adults.

"It's your fourth birthday, Histabel. You're four years old today. Where are you?"

"At my grandmother Darragh's."

"What are you doing at your grandmother's house?" Cautiously, she led him through the details of a birthday celebration. When they were coming freely she jogged him back to his third birthday.

Third birthdays were very important to children of Qushmarrah. If a child lived that long it was likely to survive, so it received its real name on its third birthday. Whatever it had been called earlier was just a nickname. Fathers might pick names for their sons before they were born, but they would not reveal them till the exactly proper ceremonial moment. Premature disclosure would tempt fate too much.

Birthdays were good milemarks in tracing a young life. The Witch always used the fourth and third to establish her dominion. She had that now. She led the child backward into time, past recollections of people, places, and things, into a time when everything had been feeling and mood, and earlier still, into the closeness and warmth of the womb itself.

And back.

"What I tell you is true. It is a bright, sunny day, and one of the happiest you have ever known. Are you there? Do you see it?"

Confusion in the child's face. The Witch wiped sweat and sprinkled herbs onto the coals.

"Do you see it?"

"Yes." A little puzzled.

"Where are you?"

"Tel-Daghobeh, overlooking the Grey Reach." The child's voice had deepened subtly.

The Witch frowned. The answer did not make sense. "What is your name?"

"Shadid."

Ah. "You are Dartar, Shadid?"

"Yes."

Of course. Dartars had died that day, too. She had not considered that before, nor had she encountered one before.

She controlled her disappointment. Going in she had not expected much of this one. Slowly, she took him through the details of his happy day—the date Shadid's first son was born. She gained her hold upon the previous incarnation and in time brought it forward to the day she had examined from thirty points of view already.

"There is so much smoke we can't see twenty yards. They tell us if we want clean air we're going to have to take the top of the hill. But the stubborn damned veydeen won't stop fighting. We just fought off a band of old men and boys armed with tools and kitchen knives. What is the matter with the veydeen? Do we have to massacre every man, woman, and child?"

No, the Witch thought. *You have to slay one man, Nakar, my husband, and all the killing will stop. The smoke will clear and the rains fall and the fires die and the death and devastation prove to be less widespread than everyone imagined. But it will be terrible enough to leave everyone's thirst for murder slaked.*

She nudged the memory of the Dartar Shadid.

"The Herodians have begun to move. This part looks like it might get to be house-to-house. We are drawing random missile fire from the rooftops. It's more a nuisance than a danger. The snipers can't find their targets in the smoke. There is a smell of burnt flesh in it strong, now. Now . . . Now . . ."

The Witch did not press. This stutter was a warning that the end was near. The soul remembered and did not want to get any closer to the pain. She asked questions to fix the place and time.

She had no reason to believe that information might be useful, yet she recorded it all in hopes of charting a pattern.

Mostly, she found cause for ever-increasing fear.

A lot of people had died that day. Far more than there had been babies born. So far it looked like only the strongest souls had attached to new flesh immediately. But suppose that was an illusion? Suppose luck and proximity were equally crucial? In this instance the Dartar had died on the doorstep of a woman in labor.

She seldom knew enough, or unearthed enough, to see the transition so clearly.

Cautiously, she put Shadid to sleep and reawakened Histabel, restored him to his proper age, then told him to rest.

This had been an easy regression. Very little resistance. A pity all of them did not go as smoothly. A greater pity none of them ever turned up anyone more important than this.

If she could not unearth Nakar, her husband, then she wanted to find his murderer, Ala-eh-din Beyh.

"Torgo," she called weakly. "I'm done."

The eunuch appeared immediately. He had been outside the tent recording everything, in case her fragile, drug-sodden memory played pranks on her. "A Dartar," he said, disgusted.

"Yes."

"I suppose we can say we are a step closer to our goal, my lady. We knew it wouldn't be easy when we started."

For the first time she felt a spark of real resentment of the eunuch's ritual reassurances. "Get me out of here before I go mad. I got too much of the smoke again."

"Perhaps you should space the regressions more widely, my lady. So much concentrated exposure to the fumes cannot be healthy."

"I want him back, Torgo. I don't want to waste a minute I don't have to waste."

"And if a minute not taken now means having to pay with an hour or a day later on?"

His solicitude touched something deep. She flew into an instantaneous unreasoning fury. "You stop your fussing and nagging and do your damned job, Torgo! Let *me* worry about me. Get me to my bed. Bring me food and drink. Now!"

Inside the facade there was a very frightened woman.

The facade was starting to crack.

She ate and she drank and then she retreated into that place of warm sleep and pleasant dreams she found only after exposure to the drugged fumes. A still small but blossoming part of her fear was that she had begun to look forward to those hours of surcease.

"You sure favor that balcony these days," Meryel said.

Bel-Sidek turned, smiled. "It's a good place for thinking."

"For brooding, you mean. What is it tonight? The new civil governor?"

"Nothing so obvious and mundane. This morning I learned that there might be a traitor of relatively high station among the Living."

Meryel gasped.

"You're not at risk. We seem to have identified him. He's not in my organization. He's in the old man's."

"You're sure?"

"Not entirely. It's under examination, you might say. We've set it up so the man will betray himself if he's guilty. The ironic thing is, we found out on the very day he was to have been promoted to a level where he would know enough to pull the whole movement down. And we learned that he was suspect only because of a personal calamity that's befallen him already." Bel-Sidek decided not to go into that. "I almost feel sorry for the guy. Till yesterday everything was going perfectly for him. By tomorrow, probably, his whole world will have collapsed around him."

"You have to leave again?"

"Yes. I may have that to attend to, and the old man has a policy meeting set. I could come back afterward. If you want me to."

"So coy. So shy. So ingenuous. Of course. Now, I've had a

feast laid on especially for you. Why don't we see if we can't do that justice before we fuss ourselves about lesser things?"

Bel-Sidek seldom ate well, unless at Meryel's. "Let's have at it, then."

7

Aaron slid away, just leaving a hand lying upon Laella's breast. Their mingled sweat began to dry. He shivered with a sudden chill.

It had not been very good. They were both too distracted. And having Stafa waken in the middle of it and jump on his back and yell, "Giddap, Dad!" was not something to ignite uncontrollable passion. Neither was having the yell alert the rest of the household to what was going on.

Mish was particularly intrigued by what happened between men and women in the dark. Her interest disconcerted him, and at times touched him with thoughts and temptations that left him aghast at what could happen inside a man's mind. That left him so ashamed he could not face Laella for hours after he caught himself thinking them.

If she just wouldn't try to spy!

Laella got Stafa back to sleep. She moved in next to him, whispered, "I think I should tell Reyha."

"No. That would be too much of a burden for her. She'd end up calling him on it. Then how long would it take for him to find out where she got the idea?"

After a while, she said, "That could be dangerous, couldn't it?"

"Scared men are desperate and desperate men are dangerous. And unpredictable. He might get the idea he could cover up."

"Then why don't you tell bel-Sidek? Everybody says he has something to do with the Living."

"If he really does, then Reyha would be alone in the world."

"Maybe they wouldn't . . ."

"They'd kill him, Laella. They're hard men. They kill people every day for crimes less than Naszif's. For him it might be a very prolonged and unpleasant death."

"Then there's no way out, is there?"

"Not without choosing who gets hurt. And I don't want that on my conscience."

The old man watched bel-Sidek slip into the house, barely in time to get the stage set for the meeting. "Did you have an enjoyable dinner with our lady of the ships, Khadifa?"

"Yes sir. She was highly amused by what she called today's preposterous circumstances. Meaning her sense of irony got fat because the Living completed its biggest weapons-smuggling operation ever virtually without risk because of Herodian arrogance. If the new governor and his escorts hadn't bulled through the traffic waiting to enter the straits her ships would have come in first and we would have had to dodge and trick customs men all morning."

"Perhaps one of those very weapons will cut the pig's throat."

"You know him, sir?"

"I remember his father. They say this Sullo is identical to the beast that sired him. Your man is being watched. If the letter he received doesn't send him running to Bruda he's innocent."

"Yes sir. Did you eat, sir?"

"It can wait."

"You have to develop some regular eating habits, sir."

"I'm sure. Your mothering can wait, too. Answer the door."

Bel-Sidek had not heard the discreet knock. He went to the door expecting to find King early as usual. Instead, Salom Edgit greeted him. Bel-Sidek stepped aside. Edgit came in very

carefully. He looked awful. The news about Ortbal Sagdet must
have given him no peace.

Edgit went to his usual place and settled. Though he was early
he had nothing to say.

Hadribel arrived next. He exchanged looks and nods with the
old man. Guided by bel-Sidek he took the place usually occupied
by Sagdet. If Edgit noticed he showed no sign.

Then came King Dabdahd. He looked as ragged as Edgit.
Then the fanatics, together again and looking smug about recent
events.

The General surveyed the lot. "As stated previously, the
khadifa of the Hahr is with us tonight." He did not introduce
Hadribel. He and bel-Sidek were the only ones supposed to know
the names of everyone there—though, of course, everyone knew
everyone. They had all been officers together in the same small
army.

"New business. The arrival of a new civil governor. His advent
appears to have confounded and exasperated our oppressors as
much as it has surprised us. This intelligence should be of
interest to you all: he has in his train a sorceress of modest talent
named Annalaya. She hails from Petra or some such place on the
Allurican coast, where they make so many minor witches. Does
anyone have anything to tell us about the new governor?"

King said, "One of my men heard that Sullo refuses to stay in
the Residence." The Residence was the seat of the Herodian civil
governors. Like Government House, it was in the acropolis, just
a quarter mile away. Before the conquest it had been the main
temple of Aram the Flame. "He wants a place in the hills east of
the city. My man suspected him of a superstitious dread of a place
where so many villains met their fate."

"Keep an eye on that. Also under new business. Has anyone
got any idea what Fa'tad is up to, invading the Shu labyrinth,
other than tugging Cado's mustache?"

Headshakes.

"Salom? You have resources among those who work in the
Dartar compound. What do they have to tell us?"

"Nothing yet, sir. It's too soon. But I'll bet there'll be nothing.

Fa'tad is close. So close he doesn't tell his captains what he's doing half the time. Sometimes he doesn't know himself. Something catches his fancy, like a shiny coin fascinates a crow, and he plays with it. Sometimes he's like a kid pulling the strings on a knit garment. He just wants to see what will happen."

The old man ignored a pain that nipped at him like a malicious puppy. "We'll table that. Anything else new? No? Old business, then. We continue to become less apparent among the people of Qushmarrah. We lull the oppressor with the thought that time and frustration are disarming us. We begin a phase less active toward Herod but more attentive toward Qushmarrah."

He winced. The pain was particularly persistent. "Sometime soon an event will transpire which will make possible a serious attempt to reclaim our heritage. I have no control over when. It could be as soon as next week or as distant as six months from now. But the result will be very much in the hands of the movement to exploit. Comes that day we will launch the general uprising some of our brothers find so attractive.

"Your orders are these: reduce conflict with the oppressor and our own people. Expend the energies of your people in identifying the widest possible body of sympathizers. When the day comes we will be able to arm hundreds beyond our own number. I would prefer to offer those arms to men of known persuasion. The first hours, while the news spreads and the oppressor responds, will be critical. We must confuse and unbalance the enemy well enough and long enough for the insurrection to generalize. There will come a point where Cado and Fa'tad will not be able to cope."

Why am I making this speech? They had heard it till they were sick. "I am repeating myself. I apologize. The message is this. We are gathering our strength against an indefinite someday no longer. The date itself is not fixed but it is not likely to be more than six months away. You must prepare for it, and at the same time create the illusion that it is farther away than ever. One final word. You will tell no one the day is coming. No one. No exceptions. No excuses. He who speaks, and whoever hears him, will immediately join the former khadifa of the Hahr. Silence is that important to me. Do you understand?"

He did not get a chance to force acknowledgments. Someone knocked at the door, and yelled. Irritated, the old man waved at bel-Sidek, then gestured the others into the bedroom.

Bel-Sidek opened the door a crack and mumbled with someone. He closed up, came to the old man. "A boy, about ten, with this. For you, I assume."

The General looked at the folded paper with the sparrow on the outside. "Open it. Place it so I can read it." He willed his eyes to work well enough.

His correspondent had taken his disabilities into account. The message was written in large block print. He grunted and read it again, then found the shape he recognized as bel-Sidek. "Khadifa, you were right. Your man is visiting Government House right now." He offered the message to bel-Sidek. "Handle it as you see fit."

Bel-Sidek read the message twice himself, then remained contemplative for several minutes. It meant a great deal more than an enemy agent reaching a place of high trust within the movement. It could mean that all the guilt of those who had failed at Dak-es-Souetta, and the search for atonement and redemption implicit in their commitment to the movement, was moot, if not a prideful arrogance of false guilt. *Had* Qushmarrah fallen because an apprentice metalworker of no breeding or standing whatsoever had lost his nerve during the course of something that wasn't even a battle?

No. True or not, it wouldn't do. Too many great men and great families had too much emotion invested in the legends already in place. It had to stay quiet. But, even so, it had to be handled. The simple and final way would be to get rid of the man. But why discard a perfectly usable tool just because it had caused you injury? Why not retain it and use it with a little more caution?

"The khadifa of the Hahr has not yet assumed his new nor broken with his old district. If he could dip into that and loan me a dozen reliable soldiers who can be counted on to forget tonight's doings before tomorrow's dawn?"

Hadribel stared at him, almost smirking. "You want to borrow some men? Or are you practicing for a speech to the Senate?"

"I need men." He controlled his embarrassment and the anger that stalked behind it.

Hadribel looked at the old man. "Sir?"

"Right away, Khadifa. Time may be critical."

"Yes sir."

Hadribel waited for bel-Sidek at the door. After hesitating a moment, waiting for something more from the General, bel-Sidek went outside. In a moment he was laboring to keep pace with Hadribel.

The new khadifa of the Hahr pretended an epiphany. "Oh. I'm sorry. How is your leg?"

"It's been troublesome lately. But I've had to do a lot more getting around than I'm used to." Imply that he had done so because of his special relationship with the old man.

Hadribel forbore any expression of sympathy. "What's going on? I take it the old man knows all about it."

"He does."

"Big secret, eh?"

"Yes. Isn't everything?"

"You need me along on whatever this is?"

"That might not be wise. You'd figure it out. The old man thinks too many people know already. Meaning one more than him."

Hadribel laughed. "He does have that way about him." He went serious. "Honestly, how is he doing? Looked like he was having trouble tonight."

"He isn't getting any better. He won't slow down and let himself get better," bel-Sidek admitted. Then he lied, "On the other hand, he does seem to have stabilized."

"I worry. And I'm sure others do, too. If something happens suddenly, his passion for secrecy will leave us all in the dark."

"He claims he's made arrangements. How good I couldn't say. I live with him and don't know what he's doing most of the time."

"What's this big event he was talking about?"

"That's one of the things I don't know. He throws me out of the house when he even wants to *think* about it. You ask too many questions. That isn't a habit he encourages."

Hadribel accepted the rebuke sullenly. Bel-Sidek did not care. This was not a man whose good opinion concerned him. Politics. You had to get along with, mix with, people you wouldn't speak to in a lifetime otherwise.

He waited in the street while Hadribel and his sons assembled the crew he wanted. It took them only fifteen minutes. The Shu organization was efficiently managed.

Bel-Sidek took the men away from the Shu before he explained that they were going to capture a Herodian agent who would be coming out of Government House before long. He did not identify the spy. He told them the man was not to be harmed if at all possible.

"He should leave the door on the east side. He'll want to get out of sight quickly so he'll head for one of the streets that begin right across the plaza." He quizzed the men to make sure they knew the area. Most knew it as well as he did, which was all part of being a member of the movement. Knowledge was a weapon, too.

"You'll spread out, then, and let him get off the plaza. Then you'll herd him toward me. I'm sure you all know the drill. We've done it before. You don't have to get close enough for him to see you. He just has to know you're there and you're moving toward him."

Usually the tactic was employed when the Living did not want the hunters recognized afterward. This time bel-Sidek hoped to keep his quarry anonymous. Naszif would not survive long if he was recognized. These men did not concern themselves with the niceties of strategy or policy. For them traitor and dead were synonymous.

Hoping he was not too late, bel-Sidek dispersed his troops and began the wait.

On the harbor side the fog was drawing its mask over Qushmarrah. There on the east face of the hill the air was getting hazy, the haze catching a weird greenish tint from the just risen nail paring of a moon.

As he slipped out of Government House, Naszif, the son of bel-Abek, was in as fine a mood as ever he'd known. It had been a day of days; almost enough to counterbalance the misery of the day before. First, the promotion. Third in the Living in the Shu. And the rumor was, that was as good as being second because the khadifa of the Shu was reputed to be some pre-conquest lord who had gone into a coma years ago but was of such high family they dared not put him aside.

At last he had attained a position of power and influence—and, more important, of access. He would know what was going on inside the organization. He would know who was who. He would sit in on policy, planning, and strategy sessions.

Colonel Bruda and General Cado were as excited as he was. A long-ago investment had begun to pay dividends. They had doubled his good fortune immediately by promoting him to vice-colonel in the Herodian army. His being able to confirm the probability that Ortbal Sagdet had been khadifa of the Hahr had pleased General Cado, too.

He felt the forty gold double sudets that represented his promotion bonus. He smiled. He could now afford to get his family out of the Shu. But his mission prevented his doing so. Maybe a second household? Would his several masters accept that?

His mood darkened when he thought of Zouki. His family had been gutted . . .

He was too excited to pay proper attention to his surroundings, too thrilled to heed the old specter of guilt that had haunted him since that night at the Seven Towers. He did not feel the weight of fear that so often perched upon his shoulders. He missed completely the first couple of moves made by the men stalking him.

The scrape of a foot in the stillness, the flash of a garment in motion caught from the corner of his eye, and stark terror usurped his joy. It did not take a minute to understand what was happening. He had helped run Herodians when he was a ground-level man.

He fought the panic. Panic was the enemy's ally. If he refused to let it control him he might find a way out. Up to a rooftop. Down into a basement. They could not cover everything. He tried to remember how some victims had gotten away back when he was on the other end.

Then he realized that they must know who they were running. They had been waiting for him. They knew he had gone inside. The promotion . . . A ploy to send him scurrying to Cado, to betray himself?

Then it would not matter if he evaded them. They would catch him at home. They might tell Reyha . . .

He did panic then.

He ran.

All he could think of was getting back to General Cado. The Herodians took care of their own.

The soldiers of the Living were good. There came a moment when he was standing in the street, uncertain which way to go. A block behind, four vague shapes walked his way. Three men waited in each mouth of a cross street. Nothing lay ahead but haze lighted greenly by the moon. He went the direction they wanted him to go. And as he started a man stepped into his path, a limping silhouette. A man he knew.

"You can stop running now, Naszif. You have nowhere to go. Come. Walk with me. Quietly. Unless you'd rather I let those others know who you are."

"No! By Aram, don't." He giggled. How long since he had sworn by Aram and meant it? If secretly, he had adopted Herod, faceless god and all.

He was a vice-colonel, damn it. They would not murder him. They would ransom him. Trade him for somebody. He wished he had told Cado he thought the man Hadribel was going to take over in the Hahr instead of saving that for later. The Living would trade him and more to get a khadifa back.

"Come. Let's walk." The voice was harder now. "We'll go to my house and talk."

"Your father . . ."

"Is a harmless old man. He's nearly blind, and his hearing is what you would expect of someone his age. And he's dying. He's much too preoccupied with that to care about you."

Naszif glanced around.

"Yes. They're out there. Come. They're death. I'm life."

Resignation swept over Naszif. Almost, he felt relieved. There were no pressures now. No need to pretend. Everything was in other hands.

"You'll be watched. If you leave home, you'll be followed. If you move toward Government House you'll be killed. Good night." Bel-Sidek closed the door, leaned against it. A long night, not over yet, and he was supposed to return to Meryel's when it was done. "You heard, sir?"

"Every word. A vice-colonel in the Herodian army. The human animal never ceases to amaze me. We know traitors seldom act out of fear and less often out of greed. We seldom fathom what *does* motivate them."

Bel-Sidek muttered, "He never took anything but the salaries due him as a Herodian officer."

"A traitor for love. The triumph or defeat of Qushmarrah meant nothing to him when the struggle meant he had to be separated from his wife while she gave birth. He sold Qushmarrah for that. And that bastard Bruda really tried to get him here in time." The old man chuckled. "Those slimy bastards always keep their word. Damn them."

"He's really a vice-colonel? That commission isn't just a piece of paper they gave him?"

"It was real. Oh, if they pulled him out of here they wouldn't turn him loose with a field command. He isn't qualified. But something administrative, yes. A job like Bruda's, in Tuhn or Agadar."

"My hold on him is inadequate, then. I should have killed him."

"He'll remain controllable as long as he doesn't get near Cado. And for as long as it takes him to find the nerve to tell his wife that he's become a ranking Herodian officer. If his love is as strong as it seems, I suspect the depths of hers will reflect it and she'll be up to accepting what he is."

"Then I do have no choice."

"He's still vulnerable. Through his weakness. Love. You will tell him that we have his son and will hold him as a surety for his performance."

Startled, bel-Sidek asked, "Do we have him?"

"No. But I'll put that best man of mine on it and we will have him when the time comes. I'll have you take a message to Muma's in the morning. You can inform the man anytime afterward."

"Yes sir. How are you, sir? Do you need me?"

"Told the woman you'd be back to discuss shipping schedules, did you? Go ahead. I'm tougher than you like to think, Khadifa. I'll survive."

8

Aaron watched Laella carefully throughout breakfast. He could see no sign that sleep had worked any miracles and given her the answer that had eluded him for six years. Mish watched them both in that way she did when she knew what had happened between them in the dark, looking for he knew not what, but causing knots in his guts. Arif ate somberly and delicately while Stafa flew around the house chattering nonsense as he pursued some imaginary adventure, deaf to parental admonition. Raheb was closed in upon herself, maybe feeling her age.

Laella said, "I've got to do some marketing today." Thinking out loud.

Her mother said, "I'll go with you. I need to get some things."

Mish went into her pout immediately, for which Aaron was almost grateful.

Arif asked, "Can I go with you, Mom?"

"We'll see how you behave this morning."

Mish brightened some. She rose and started making Aaron a lunch.

Aaron said, "I won't need that today, Mish. We're only working half a day."

She looked like she could not make up her mind if she should be delighted or distraught.

Aaron yawned, caught Stafa on the fly, hugged him as he squealed and wriggled, trying to get loose. He extended a hand, inviting Arif. Arif looked unhappy for a moment, quietly jealous of his brother's facile way of getting attention. Then he plunged forward. Aaron let Stafa make good his escape—which amounted only to a furious dash in a circle which ended with a plunge onto his father's back—and took Arif into his arms.

That started the whole ritual of, "Do you have to go to work today, Dad?" and "Stay home, Dad," which finally ended with him bolting out the door.

He moved into the street feeling warm and content with his life and lot. Every man should be so loved and lucky.

Bemusedly, he reflected that he had not had a nightmare for two nights now.

"Aaron."

He looked up. "Bel-Sidek. Good morning. How is your father doing?"

"He's as busy as ever dying. He'll outlive us all. On your way to work?"

"Yes."

"Mind if I walk with you?"

"Of course not."

They walked in silence awhile, Aaron slackening his pace so his companion would not work so hard descending the hill. He could not help glancing over occasionally. He had been acquainted with bel-Sidek for years, and knew the man survived by scrounging odd jobs around the waterfront, but they'd never spent any time together.

After a while, bel-Sidek sort of sighed and said, "I guess there isn't any way to get at it but to go straight ahead."

"What?"

"You seem to be a fairly trustworthy man, Aaron. So I'm going to take a chance on you. I belong to the Living."

Aaron looked at him and frowned. "Everybody thinks that, anyway. Why are you telling me?"

"I am, in fact, a moderately important part of the command structure of the Living, Aaron. Mostly because I was a commander of a thousand at Dak-es-Souetta. Yesterday one of the men who fought for me there came to me for some advice. He doesn't know I'm with the Living and he wouldn't name names, but what he did say gave me enough to reason out the rest for myself."

Aaron stopped. He looked at his neighbor blankly. Inside he was in a complete state of confusion, panic fighting with wonder fighting with relief. He did not know what to say or what to do. He could not think. Aram!

"What I want from you, Aaron, is for you to forget all about this. All about what happened at the Seven Towers. It's been taken care of."

"Hell, man, he had a wife and kid." No way to stop it once it stuck its head out of his mouth. His tongue was a treacherous serpent. "You have to *think* before you go cutting throats. They didn't have anybody else in the world. What the hell are they going to do now? Your kind never think about that when . . ."

People were pausing to look at him before they hurried away. Bel-Sidek looked like he was in shock. But recovering. "Be quiet, Aaron! What's the matter with you?"

Aaron did manage to lower his voice. He let it all spill out.

Bel-Sidek interrupted. "I see I'm going to have to tell you more than I wanted. But trust you some, trust you all the way. Naszif isn't dead. We didn't kill him. Come. Walk. We're drawing too much attention."

And, Aaron noticed, Dartars were pouring into Char Street from the acropolis. He walked.

Bel-Sidek said, "You were right about Naszif. He betrayed your tower out in the hills. And he was still an agent of the Herodians. In fact, they had adopted him into their society and he had become a vice-colonel in their army."

"Naszif?"

"Yes. But now he's our man again. We've reclaimed him. He'll be working for Qushmarrah. His wife and son have lost nothing. And only you, outside the movement, know about this.

I want you to forget. Everything. Tell no one anything and go on living your life. Can you do that, Aaron?"

"I can. But you probably won't let me."

"What?"

Amazed at himself. Talking back to an officer. Serpent tongue letting anger six years old spew out. "It's people like you that can't leave anything alone. You can't as long as there are people like me whose lives you can spend." A strange, almost drugged feeling, like he was outside watching somebody else speak the unspeakable. "You go play your games with Fa'tad and General Cado. Just leave me and my family out of it. Leave us alone."

Bel-Sidek gulped air as he searched for something to say. "It's your struggle, too, Aaron."

Aaron spat into the dust. Then he laughed hoarsely. "Your ass. My struggle? The only people who aren't better off since the conquest are your class. And the monster who lived in the citadel. If I had any real sense I'd turn you in to the Herodians. But I'm an old dog and you people trained me too well when I was a pup. I can't turn on you now. Go away. Leave me the hell alone."

Aaron lengthened his stride. Bel-Sidek could not keep up.

As the anger evaporated, Aaron began to be afraid. Stupid. Stupid to let your mouth run away like that. Those were dangerous men. Crazy dangerous.

Bel-Sidek stopped. He could not keep up. He fought down the anger that nipped at him like a fire trying to get started. He had faced these blowups before. He did not like them. In part that was because he could not quite grasp the frustration that fueled them, in part because he heard enough truth in them to have his conscience wakened. He did not want to feel guilty about being true to his beliefs.

It would not be a good day. Like it or not he was going to spend it reexamining everything that he was, agonizing over his own goals and those of the movement.

When you looked at the situation the way an Aaron did there was no mystery why the movement had trouble attracting recruits. There went a man who had lost as much as any in the war, and he put at least as much of the blame for that on his own overlords as he did on the Herodians.

That kind of thinking—with its damnable core of truth—was an enemy more dangerous than all the spies Cado might have on his payroll. That kind of thinking might lead men to denounce the movement simply because they preferred Herodian order to the chance of a chaos that might interfere with commerce.

Bel-Sidek limped toward the waterfront, trying to shut out the pain in his leg and in his heart. Each hundred steps he glanced back to see how much the Dartars had gained upon him.

The Dartar column entering the Gate of Autumn seemed endless. The civilians awaiting their turn to get into Qushmarrah were sullen and growing more so.

Even to Yoseh it seemed that Fa'tad was sending in every man he had. And that just did not make any sense. What was so damned important about that Shu maze?

"Nothing, I'll bet," Nogah said. "Just Fa'tad tying to get Cado to think he thinks it's critical. Maybe so Cado will take it away and make a fool of himself looking for something that isn't there."

"What difference does it make?" Medjhah asked. "We get paid the same whether we dig around or we don't. Why worry about it?"

Somebody else said, "Yeah, kid. What you getting fussed for?"

Nogah: "He hopes we're on the job a month. You didn't see that veydeen slip he was making sheep's eyes at yesterday."

Medjhah: "Oh, she was tender, my brothers! Young and sweet. Her eyes were like almonds toasted and glazed with honey. Her lips were a bed of rose petals."

Yoseh snapped, "Knock it off, you guys."

Medjhah: "Best of all, she wasn't very bright. She was making calf eyes right back at him."

Nogah: "Sounds too good to be true. If she can cook I'm going to take her away from him."

Yoseh's protests only made the ribbing worse.

Veydeen in the streets paused to stare, startled by Dartar laughter. Yoseh said, "You're ruining our image."

He became tense as they passed through the acropolis, in the shadow of the Citadel. In an operation this size, how much chance Nogah's troop would end up where they had been posted yesterday?

Nogah must have arranged something. He broke off the column at the same alley. As Yoseh helped unload he kept glancing at that doorway down the street. Every glance provoked a wisecrack.

The house was closed up this morning. The crone was not in her usual place on the street. Had his daring yesterday raised her bile? Had she sealed up the fortress till the siege of the maze was over?

Nogah flailed his injured arm to work out some of the stiffness. Already some of his cousins were pushing into the alleyway. Another six men, assigned by Joab, arrived and dismounted, turned their animals over to Yoseh. Yoseh asked, "You're not going in there today, are you, Nogah?"

"Of course."

"But you're injured. Send me instead."

"I wouldn't do that. You'd miss your little veydeen doe." He laughed and marched into the shadows of the alley. Yoseh started after him.

"Hold it, little brother!" Medjhah snapped. "Come over here."

Yoseh went, reluctantly.

"You got a lot to learn about keeping yourself alive, kid. First rule of survival is don't ever volunteer for anything. Where volunteers get sent men get killed."

"Why does he keep me out of the maze?"

"He doesn't want you to get hurt."

"I'm not a child, Medjhah."

"You're no seasoned warrior, either. Qushmarrah isn't the mountains. Right now you're an apprentice. When Nogah is sure he can trust your judgment and ability to follow orders he'll find something exciting for you to do." Medjhah settled on a saddle he had pulled off one of the camels, leaned back against the wall.

Veydeen surged around the knot of animals, casting sullen glances at the Dartars impeding traffic. Medjhah ignored them till a trio of young wives came past, stealing glances at the mysterious nomads. He singsonged, "Come close, come closer, said the fox to the little hens. I cannot see you from here." It was a line from a popular Qushmarrahan fable.

The tallest woman lifted her nose and lengthened her step. The other two giggled and whispered behind their hands and hurried to catch up. As she was about to fade into the crowd the tall one paused to look back.

Medjhah tossed her a wave. "We'll see that haughty beauty again before the day is over."

"How do you know?"

"It's my irresistible charm. Veydeen women just can't stay away."

"More like they were carrying market baskets and they'll have to come back this way to get home."

"That, too. But I'll bet you right now she comes along this side of the street and gives me a chance to tell her more about the fox and the hens."

"You think so?"

"It's a game. Teasing game. Flirting game. She and I both know nothing would come of it even if that was what we wanted. No Dartar is going to introduce her to any mysteries. Can you see sneaking into a woman's home and bed dressed like this? Nobody would notice a Dartar who went calling while a woman's man was away?"

"Get veydeen clothing. Step back there in the alley and change. Once you're in the crowd nobody would notice you."

Medjhah looked at him oddly. "I never thought of that."

Yoseh shrugged. It seemed obvious to him.

Medjhah said, "We were talking about adventures before those hens came by flaunting themselves. Look at me, Yoseh. Perfectly content to sit here leaning against a wall, watching camels. You want to know why? Because Nogah has found me enough adventures already. Don't go looking for trouble. You might find it."

Yoseh nodded. There was sense in that.

They watched the women go to market for a while, Medjhah flirting whenever one would allow it.

The door down the street opened and the crone came out, followed closely by a woman whose face made Yoseh's heart jump. Then he saw that she was not the girl. Her mother, perhaps. At least her older sister. The look was there, but time had weathered it.

The women carried baskets. The crone eyed him narrowly as they passed. After a glance the other paid him no heed.

Medjhah did not exercise his charm upon her. When she was out of sight he laughed. "Heart going pitty-pat, little brother? Here's your big chance. Just walk over there and start talking. But what if her father is there? What if she has brothers? What if she spits in your face and screams for help?" Medjhah laughed again.

It was as if Medjhah could read his mind.

"Eh, don't worry about it, Yoseh. Come sit in the shade and watch the crazy veydeen. The parade is endlessly fascinating."

But the doorway down the street was open an inch. He could see the white of an eye pressed to the crack. Somehow, that shook the roots of the daydream, as though reality threatened to intrude and force him to live out the fantasy.

His spirit was restless. That communicated itself to his flesh. He began to pace.

Azel was plagued by an unaccustomed flux of the spirit. He was restless, uncomfortable, almost haunted as he moved through the Dartar infestation. What the hell were they doing? Why the hell couldn't they leave the labyrinth alone?

He fretted as he drifted through the press of Char Street. He did not like the feelings plaguing him. It was almost if he were suffering a premonition of disaster.

He slipped into the old man's house as quickly as he could. Almost too quickly to pay attention to safety. And that bothered him, too. A man dared not put caution aside.

The old man was in his bed. Azel said, "I'm here. Again. You seem determined to use me up."

He frowned. He did not like what he heard from his own lips. It was not like him to complain.

"Things have begun moving quickly. It cannot be helped."

"What is it this time?"

"The man you tracked to Government House. He turned out to be an officer of high standing among the Herodians. We want to turn him to our own advantage. We have him under control now but we don't expect our leverage to hold up."

"This is where I come in."

"The boy you took the other day is his son. We have informed him that we have the child in our control. I want you to convince him of that fact."

"How?"

"Take him there. Show him the boy. Then get the child into our hands as soon as possible. Have him be the next one examined."

"That's asking for trouble. If I take the man inside he might recognize something. And the woman isn't going to accept that without a squawk. Nor will she be pliant about who she takes for examination. It pleases her to imagine that she's the driving force behind everything and that we're parasitic hangers-on trying to profit from her researches. She tolerates us because she finds us useful occasionally."

"She has failed to see all the implications of her husband's death."

"She's lived a long time, General, and most of it completely out of touch with reality. She's surrounded by sycophants content to feed her fantasies."

"Then it's time she was awakened."

Azel listened as the old man told him what to do. He indicated his understanding and approval with a single nod. "There's one piece of news. Concerning the new civil governor, who seems eager to make enemies."

"Go ahead."

"He's chosen the villa of the widow of General Hanno

bel-Karba as his residence. A damn fool idea that can't have come to him overnight. He must have had people here ahead of time, looking for ways he can make trouble. Word is, he's already sent the General's widow a letter ordering her to vacate by sundown tonight."

The old man remained silent for a long time. Then he said, "I wanted the organization to stay out of sight and mind. But this cannot be tolerated. I suppose he's threatened to evict her?"

"Of course."

"The man is mad. He *wants* to get himself killed. But that is nothing to you. On about enduring your own travails."

General Cado was livid. He'd just heard from Sullo's own mouth a plan for confiscating the properties of the widow of General bel-Karba. Insanity! His pate was scarlet. He sputtered with rage.

Cado faced away from Sullo until he regained control. Then he faced around. "You come with a certain reputation, Marteo Sullo. I assumed that most of what I've heard was slander from the mouths of your enemies. But today I've learned that they have been too kind. Maybe they were ashamed to tell the whole truth about your arrogance, your vanity, your *stupidity*."

Now Sullo sputtered.

"You came here planning to embarrass me, eh? Stealing that old woman's house looks like an easy way, eh? Because she enjoys my favor? Maybe that's true. But did you bother to find out who she is and what she means to the people of Qushmarrah? The hell you did. You fool. You try to take that woman's home and the very least you'll do is end up dead. If you stay ahead of death for long it could mean the end of every Herodian in the city."

Sullo sneered, but beneath his sneer there was a hint of uncertainty, a varnish of fear.

Cado shifted to a gentler tone and pressed his advantage. "You saw the entire strength at my command yesterday afternoon. Twelve thousand Herodian troops not of the first quality or they would be out facing the Suldan of Aquira. Five thousand Dartar mercenaries commanded by an unpredictable madman who could turn on us any minute. With them I control Qush-marrah—just barely—because ninety-nine out of a hundred Qushmarrahans don't give a damn who runs things as long as certain precious institutions are left alone. That old woman is one of those institutions. Her husband never lost a battle in his life, whether single combat or massed armies. He is revered as a warrior demigod. These people believe he was struck down by assassins in Herodian pay.

"And that's true. And he won that fight, too. He killed them all. But he was injured so badly he could not participate in the battle at Dak-es-Souetta. He died of his wounds as we were taking possession of the city. Death was the only enemy ever to best him. Diehards hid the body and tried to convince the people that he was still alive, but they failed."

"Is this fable supposed to impress or intimidate me?"

"It's supposed to warm a sense of reasonable caution in that dried-up pea you use for a brain."

Sullo smiled nastily. "The masks are off now, aren't they?"

"They are."

"There is a strong party back home which feels that you have been criminally slack in bringing these people to heel and converting them."

"I suspected as much. Though I read my failing as not having stolen enough Qushmarrahan treasure to slake their greed."

"They've sent me here to make up for your deficiencies." Another nasty smile.

Cado smiled right back. "This little chat has been more useful than I suspected it would be. It's shown me my course of action. Which is to take no action at all. All I need do is back away and give you your head."

Sullo eyed him narrowly, distrusting the triumph.

"You'll be dead before the week is out."

"If you dare . . ."

"Not I, Governor. I won't lift a finger. You. Committing suicide. Your loving subjects, who're about as tamed and converted as they're going to let themselves get, are going to cut your throat. I'll wish you good day, sir. I'll even wish you good luck. You may make these people appreciate me much more than they do."

Sullo stalked out, not able to conceal his anger at being discounted.

General Cado relaxed, wondered how best to get convincing word to the Living that he and his had no part in Sullo's schemes, that he and the army of occupation would remain neutral in any dispute.

Medjhah was right. The tall and haughty woman came back, taller and haughtier than ever, but cutting a course much closer to the alley mouth. Medjhah renewed his invitation. The ice woman responded with a sway of body that said hips were moving in cruel mockery beneath her clothing. Her satellites giggled behind their hands and one who could not have been more than a year older than Yoseh flashed him a clumsy wink that scrunched up one whole side of her face. He winked back just to keep the game alive. He whispered, "They, too, were children when the rivers ran with blood."

Medjhah uncoiled. "I'm going to stretch my legs, kid."

"Be careful."

"Hey. What's my middle name? I'm not going to get near her. Them. I'm just going to see where they live." He drifted into traffic and disappeared. Yoseh sat and brooded on the meaning of life and death and decided he probably wouldn't live long enough to figure it all out.

The glare off the harbor was intense. Yoseh closed his eyes. He may have dozed for a few minutes. When he opened his eyes again he found a veydeen child staring at him. The boy seemed familiar . . . He looked some like the girl down the street. Of course! He had seen the boy with the old woman.

Something scaly and cold uncoiled and stretched inside his stomach. "Hello. What's your name?" He tried very hard to get his tongue around the odd shape of the Qushmarrahan dialect.

"Arif. What's yours? Are you really a Dartar soldier?"

"Good morning, Arif. I am Yoseh, the son of Melchesheydek. Yes, I am a Dartar warrior, though I am very new at it." Could the boy understand the difference between soldier and warrior? Probably not. Few adult veydeen could do that."

"How come you always wrap your face up in those black cloths?"

Yoseh could not answer that one. It was something you began doing when you became an adult. It was something the lesser tribes of the veydeen and the ferrenghi did not do, so that they stood apart, branded, uncouth and lascivious. It was something he did not ponder. It was something that *was*.

He countered with a question of his own. "What is your sister's name?"

The boy looked baffled.

Yoseh repeated himself slowly, carefully, thinking he had botched the dialect.

The glow of illumination lighted the kid's face. He said, "You must mean Mish. She's not my sister. She's my aunt. My mom's sister. Her real name is Tamisa but everybody calls her Mish. She's a real grouch."

Well. So.

Yoseh fell into a long conversation with Arif. He did most of the talking, answering questions about his native mountains and deserts and those great salt flats called the Takes, and about Dartar skirmishes with the Turok savages who lived beyond the Takes. He got in a few questions of his own, mostly defining Arif's family.

Another of those families decimated by the war. No close relatives left outside this house except some married aunts. The same sort of story you heard everywhere.

So where the hell did all the people come from? What had this crazy city been like before the fighting took so many? So crowded you couldn't breathe?

Their talk must have gone on half an hour. Medjhah came back, winked, went and sat in the shade and appeared to doze.

The girl came boiling out of the door down the way, looked around frantically, the back of one hand to her mouth. She was in a panic. Terror filled her eyes. She spotted Yoseh and Arif. She looked like she went limp with relief.

Yoseh stood as she bustled toward them. He could not help staring. The scaly thing in his stomach thrashed. She did not look at him at all. Her cheeks were red.

"Arif! What are you doing out here? You know the rules! You're going to get the spanking of your life when I tell your father what you did."

"Aw, Mish, I was just talking to Yoseh."

"He was perfectly safe here, Tamisa. When you tell his father will you mention that it took you a half hour to notice that Arif had left the house?"

Her color deepened. She faced him, mouth opening to snarl. But then her eyes met his. Nothing came out.

Down in Yoseh's stomach Old Scaly went into his death throes. Or something.

Medjhah chuckled into the silence that hung between them.

Mouth dry, Yoseh said, "My name is Yoseh."

Tamisa said, "My name is Tamisa."

"You are very beautiful, Tamisa."

The girl blushed.

Medjhah chuckled again.

Arif looked puzzled and displeased.

"Tamisa, don't you have another kid to watch, too?" Yoseh had just glimpsed a sturdy little one headed their way like he owned Char Street.

"Oh, Aram! Stafa! Mother is right. I'm a hopeless, irresponsible half-wit." She started to go. Too flustered to remember the older boy.

The younger one was there. The girl scooped him up as if that would save him from all the dangers he'd already evaded successfully.

Arif said, "Tell Mish about the time your father and Fa'tad ambushed the Turoks, Yoseh."

"I don't think girls are interested in those kinds of stories, Arif."

Tamisa put the younger boy down in front of her and held on. "I don't mind. At home all I hear is Mom grumbling about how her legs hurt."

Medjhah chuckled a third time.

Yoseh did not know what to say now. It was all in his lap. He was painfully aware of the disapproval of the passing veydeen who saw one of their virgin daughters speaking to a Dartar.

He just started talking. After a while the girl started talking back to him. They sat down. The boys began playing among the animals. Yoseh thought the camels were unnaturally tolerant of their behavior. The little one, the fearless one, climbed all over them. He got bumped down once when he planted a foot too painfully, but otherwise did as he pleased.

Nogah came out of the alley with a coffle of five pasty-looking prisoners and turned them over to Medjhah. His expression was unreadable as he drank from a waterskin. But he said nothing. He returned to the alley with the waterskin slung over his shoulder.

Medjhah got a javelin and perched himself where he could keep an eye on the prisoners. There wasn't a hint of laziness or sleepiness about him now.

Yoseh tried to keep talking to Tamisa, but the appearance of the prisoners had unsettled her. And the boys now clung close, frightened by the wild men out of the maze.

Medjhah whistled softly. "Hey, kid. Down the hill."

The smaller boy took off. "Daddy! Dad's home."

Old Scaly had a few convulsions left.

Azel leaned into the room where the eunuch was eating a late supper. "Hey, Torgo. We got a problem. I need to see the woman."

Torgo's eyes went tight and narrow. "I thought you walked out on us."

"Did I? I don't remember that. I remember saying I wouldn't commit suicide. Not the same thing." He kept his tone neutral. "I got to see her. Got an emergency request from the General. It's important."

Torgo rose, went to a sideboard. He washed his hands in a gold laving bowl, rinsed them in lilac water. "You're serious, eh? You would have stayed away otherwise. What is it?"

"I need to see her. She has to make the decisions on this."

"She can't."

"Can't?"

"Unfortunate, but true." The eunuch smirked. "She examined one of the children last night. She won't recover before tomorrow evening. At the earliest."

Azel spat a curse.

"I hope it's not a deadly emergency." The eunuch's smirk grew malicious.

"It could be. For all of us."

Torgo was amused by his effort to be polite. Azel knew he would protract this, make it a bully's game.

Azel gave details about the highly placed Herodian spy.

Torgo said, "I don't see a problem for us in here."

"The General wants to turn the spy around. He's dead set on it. His best leverage is here. The last kid I brought in was the spy's son."

Torgo was genuinely surprised.

"The General has two requests. First, he wants the spy brought in and shown the kid. Second, he wants the kid to be examined next so the Living can take possession."

Torgo nodded, grinned. "She won't allow the first. And her schedule of examinations is set."

Azel loosed his wickedest smile. "The old man anticipated that. I'd guess he figures this is a good time to define relationships more clearly."

"Eh?" Torgo looked uncomfortable.

"He understands the Witch. He knew her before Dak-es-Souetta and Ala-eh-din Beyh. He feels her desperation will lead her to bow to his superior wisdom."

"Or what?"

"Or he seals the Postern of Fate and pursues his war with Herod by other means."

Torgo snapped, "You get of a whore!"

"Not my idea, friend. I argued against it. But he's a stubborn old shit with nothing to lose and some right on his side. Her activities are a danger to the Living. There's a rumor the Living are behind the child-stealing. There've been too many kidnappings. People are getting upset. He wants her to back off. He wants to decide when, where, and how the children are taken."

"She won't agree."

"Her choice is agree or get no more children."

Azel watched closely. Torgo was angry but, like Azel himself, was restraining both anger and personal animosity. The stakes went beyond personalities. Torgo paced. He fiddled with things, flicked away specks of dust, made minute position adjustments. "I'll get hell for it but I'll go out on a limb. You can see the boy. The rest will have to wait on her."

"Thank you," Azel figured that would rattle Torgo.

"Bring him in blindfolded. Don't let him know where he's at or what we're doing."

"Don't worry about me. Worry about putting the kid somewhere where he can be seen without giving away where he's being held. I'll pay my respects to Nakar now. May he find Gorloch's favor again."

Torgo mumbled the formula sullenly. Azel grinned as he left. That ball-less wonder couldn't root for that because it would mean losing out on his fantasies.

Right now Torgo was as close as he was going to get to the woman he loved.

9

Aaron broke stride when he saw Mish with the Dartar. He glanced at the pasty-faced prisoners, the man watching them. That man looked back blandly.

Arif and Stafa arrived, whooping. Aaron settled the smaller boy on his left hip, took Arif's hand. He tried to keep his expression neutral as he looked at Mish and the younger Dartar. Arif babbled steadily as Aaron moved closer, telling him about the Dartar and his family.

As he came up, Mish said, "This is Yoseh, Aaron. He's the one who got hurt trying to catch the man that took Zouki."

The Dartar looked embarrassed. Mish looked frazzled.

"Why?" Aaron asked. He didn't know what else to say.

"What?" The Dartar looked perplexed.

"Why try to rescue the child?"

The Dartar looked more perplexed.

The other came to his rescue. "A quaint perversion of us barbarians, Qushmarrahan. We care for children. Not something you would understand, perhaps." He spoke carefully, making sure he did not lose his meaning by slipping into dialect. He underscored by staring at Arif and Stafa.

Aaron smiled. He looked at the younger Dartar. "Thank you.

150

The boy was the son of a friend. I hope you weren't too badly hurt."

"Failure hurt more."

Aaron did not know what else to say. He glanced around. There were eddies in the human river as people paused to watch what might be a confrontation. Uneasy, he looked at Mish, who was watching the Dartar boy in a kind of heated wonder. "How soon will your mother be home? Are you supposed to have something ready when they get here?"

"Oh! I forgot!" She ran for the door.

Arif said, "Yoseh, tell my dad about the time your father and Fa'tad . . ."

"He wouldn't be interested, Arif."

"My dad was a soldier. Weren't you, Dad?"

"In those days everybody was a soldier, Arif. It isn't anything to brag about."

Stafa was playing peekaboo with the other Dartar, looking round front of Aaron, then behind, while the man pretended to hide behind his face cloth. Stafa giggled.

Aaron wondered if he was losing his grasp on reality. That man had five prisoners at his feet and a spear in his other hand and he would stick them without compunction if they moved, but he was playing peekaboo with Stafa.

Yoseh did not know what to do or say. He was very uncomfortable. He wished the veydeen would go away. He wished he had snarled at the boy when he had come out. But then he would have had no chance to talk to the girl . . .

It did not occur to him that the man did not know how to break away gracefully.

The man said, "I suppose barracks food is pretty bad. It was when I . . ."

"It is bad," Yoseh admitted, surprised by the turn of conversation.

"Maybe Mish can bring something out. By way of thanks for what you tried to do. If she hasn't destroyed whatever she was trying to make."

Yoseh smiled, but the veydeen could not see that. He could think of nothing more to say.

He was spared the need to reply.

Mahdah and Kosuth came out carrying a corpse. It was not fresh enough to be one they had made. Its face had been obliterated by a beating. Entrails hung out through tatters that served as clothing. They dropped it amongst the prisoners.

The veydeen man—Aaron?—grabbed his older son's shoulder and said, "Come on, Arif." He moved out fast.

Mahdah and Kosuth watched him go. Mahdah asked, "What was that?"

Medjhah said, "Too complicated to explain. What's this?"

Kosuth was not in a good temper. "What the hell does it look like?"

Mahdah was less upset. "Came out of the same nest as these beauties. They must have been having some fun in there last night."

Medjhah dropped his lancehead toward the one prisoner who had a little spirit, who might have been the leader of the group. He slipped the tip under the man's nose and lifted, forcing him to look up or be cut. "You'll find us more imaginative but no less certain. Unless you care to help us?"

The man spat at Medjhah.

Medjhah drew the razor-sharp edge of his lancehead along the man's cheek.

Yoseh turned away from that casual cruelty—and let out a bark of astonishment. "Medjhah! That man! The one who took the boy . . . Hell! He's gone now."

Medjhah said something to Mahdah and Kosuth, came over. "The one Fa'tad wants?"

"Yes. I saw him up the street. But he disappeared in the crowd."

"Let's take a walk. See what we can see." He gave Yoseh a gentle push. "You go up the far side of the street."

They climbed halfway to the acropolis, saw nothing, gave it up. It was time, anyway. There were other things to do. The masons had arrived with their mud bricks and tools and somebody had to show them where Nogah wanted two maze passages sealed.

Too, Joab was working his way up the hill, stopping to give instructions to the watchers outside the alleys.

Tamisa's mother and sister returned from marketing. Yoseh watched, wondering if Tamisa would age as they had. He barely overheard Joab tell Medjhah to tell Nogah that he should leave three men in the alley overnight. Fa'tad had been running units in and out the Gate of Autumn all morning. The ferrenghi could not have kept track of how many were inside and how many were out.

Yoseh wondered if even Joab knew what Fa'tad had in mind.

Yoseh was amused when he heard Medjhah take his earlier notion and turn it into a suggestion that some men be clad as veydeen if they were going to be left in the city. Joab looked like that was about the craziest idea he'd ever heard.

Sadat Agmed had been stalking his quarry for six days, with no luck, and he was out of patience. It was not that the child was abnormally inaccessible. No more so than any daughter of a well-to-do family of the Astan. But she was inaccessible enough. He'd seen her only three times since he'd received the commission from the Witch.

He hated collecting girls. They were much more difficult.

He had spent too much time on this one already. People would remember seeing him around. He ought to report in, say he could not do the job, let her give it to somebody who could. But he had not failed a commission yet. There was pride at stake here.

A woman—the mother?—came out of the house, leading the little girl. They followed the same routine they had before, taking the uncrowded street uphill. Meaning they would walk about two hundred yards and be admitted to the home of another well-to-do family. They would stay three hours, then would return. Possibly it was something they were not supposed to do. Near as Sadat could tell, the woman and child left home only when no one else was there and they were certain no one would be aware that they had stepped out.

In this area women did not go out into public without a male companion. A conceit of the prosperous.

There was only one way to do it under the circumstances. And as far as Sadat could see, there was no opportunity to create more favorable circumstances.

He slouched after them, trying to look disinterested and innocuous, just somebody headed in the same direction and walking a little faster.

He had worked it out a dozen times. His timing was exact. He overtook them as they reached the mouth of the only alley and escape route leading off that part of the street. The woman glanced back just as he moved.

Her eyes widened and she tried to duck, but his blow put her down. He grabbed the girl.

The child screamed. Someone yelled. The woman wailed. Sadat charged into the alley carrying the girl. She was not heavy. As he went he fumbled out a wad of wet cotton. He forced that into her face.

A few blocks away he would be just some fellow carrying his sleeping daughter.

The blow to the mother had not fallen solidly. She staggered down the alley after him, wailing. Damn! And now a couple of men were with her, asking what had happened.

Sadat Agmed ran. But the child slowed him. He distanced the woman but not the men who took up the chase. Each time he glanced back there were more of them, shouting louder and looking meaner.

He became frightened. Frightened, he did not think ahead carefully enough. When he realized there would be no escape while he was burdened with the child, he abandoned her and took off toward the Hahr. But he misremembered a shortcut by one turn and ended up darting into a dead-end alleyway.

Dead end in more ways than one.

The mob pulled him off the wall he was trying to climb. Many were men who had small children, men who had become intimate with fear of child-stealers recently. They had no mercy in them, and no thought to ask questions. They were not armed, but that did not matter.

Sadat used two packs of flash and after each almost broke free. He flailed away with his knife till someone knocked it out of his hand. The slashes only enraged the men more. They punched and kicked and stomped him till he had been dead for several minutes.

Then, horrified by what the animal in them had made them do, they ran away and did not talk much about the affair.

A Dartar patrol reached the scene only after it was too late for anything but a cleanup.

Azel reported his conversation with Torgo to the General. The old man was more than ordinarily irritable. His aches and pains were piling up.

"He'll let you take the traitor to see the boy, at least?"

"He gave me that much."

"I presume you don't want to be recognized any more than he wants the citadel to be. Have you a way to handle that?"

"Have somebody deliver him blindfolded to the third alleyway south of Muma's Place. I'll pick him up after the delivery boys go. After I bring him out I'll walk him home."

"When?"

"As soon as it's dark. There's nobody up there after sundown."

"Be careful. The best men in the organization will be handling something else."

"I'm always careful."

"I know. Good day."

"Same to you." Azel eased out the door after a glance to make sure no one was watching. He was uneasy, suddenly. Like it was not a good time for . . .

He caught the tail end of a shout. Puzzled, he looked downhill. And saw a Dartar pointing at him.

Another Dartar appeared, looked, nodded, and started heading toward him.

Azel did not believe it for a moment. Why would they single

him out? Must be one of the ones he had run into in the maze. Damn the luck!

He bulled into the crowd, where they would have trouble spotting him because of his stature. He reviewed his choices, supposing they were serious enough actually to come after him. His favorite tool, the maze, was no good. A horde of those bastards were in there. He couldn't fight them all.

A horn sounded behind him. "Shit!" They had sounded an alarm. They were serious.

Why? What the hell was the matter with them? What did they have on him? Why the hell should they give a damn about a kidnapping? Unless Fa'tad had begun to sense a pattern?

He glanced back.

They had stolen his physical advantage. One man had mounted a camel and was keeping him in sight. Two more were pushing through the press on foot.

"All right, you treacherous sons of bitches." He pushed harder, edging toward the north side of the street, away from the maze and the Dartars uphill. In a conversational voice he said, "Make way for the Living, please," repeating it over and over, hoping it would not do more harm than good.

The horn sounded again. Answers came from uphill and down.

The crowd began to chatter and grumble. Somebody tripped one of the Dartars. That started a fight that threatened to become a free-for-all. The camel rider began laying about with the butt of his lance.

Azel chuckled. A long shot had come in.

An uphill Dartar pushed into his path, threatened him with a lance he held like a quarterstaff. Azel did not slow. When the Dartar swung the butt of the lance Azel grabbed it and yanked, kicked the man in the groin, punched his head, and pushed on. He reached the mouth of an alley running north.

He looked back again. The camel rider glared helplessly from a hundred feet away. Azel saluted him and entered the alleyway. As soon as he was sure no one was watching he climbed to a rooftop.

He continued to move warily there. Qushmarrah's rooftops, in the dense Old City, were another world, like the Shu maze, but one he did not know as well. He could not be sure he did not have enemies up there.

The crowd had begun to disperse by the time Aaron got out to see the cause of the uproar. Qushmarrahans did not want to be around when Dartars gathered in strength.

Two Dartars were lying in the street. One of them looked like the kid he'd been talking to a while ago. A man on a camel stood guard over them.

Aaron did not think. He just ran out, arriving as the camel rider brought his mount to her knees. That was the one who had watched over the prisoners while he had spoken with the younger one. Yoseh?

Aaron dropped to one knee. Both men were breathing. "What happened?"

The rider said, "Yoseh saw the child-stealer from the maze. We went after him. He said something to the crowd. They attacked us."

The boy opened his eyes. He tried to get up. Aaron offered a hand. The boy flinched away, then accepted. Aaron lifted him, slipped an arm around his waist, helped him stumble back to where he had started. He did not notice the Dartars gathering like ravens. He did not notice the scowls of Laella and her mother, watching from the doorway.

He set the boy down, looked back to see if the other needed help. That one was surrounded by Dartars. He looked at the boy again, intrigued by the scars and tattoos revealed when his face cloth was gone.

"Thank you," the boy said.

"Are you all right?"

"I'll have a lot of scrapes and bruises. Otherwise, yes."

Aaron assayed a weak sally. "You're going to have to quit chasing that man. You keep ending up . . ."

"We'll get him."

A one-sided row broke out at the house, Raheb so excited her voice squeaked. Aaron was surprised to see Mish headed his way with a bowl, rags, and what passed for medical supplies in their household. She settled on her knees before the boy, dipped a rag in the bowl, began cleaning the street dirt off his face.

Aaron settled on his haunches. He wondered what Mish thought of the boy's scars and tattoos. He smiled when she tried to scrub the latter away.

There was another feminine outburst, Laella this time, then Arif was there beside him, left hand on his right shoulder. Arif did not say anything. Aaron slipped his arm around his son's waist. In the background Stafa raised hell because his own break for freedom had been intercepted.

Aaron watched Mish and wondered why the crowd had turned ugly so suddenly. What had the child-taker said? They would have turned on *him*, probably, had they known what he was.

He realized that the shadow of a man on horseback had fallen upon them. He looked up. Into the wet grey eyes of an old hawk. Joab.

The thin shell cracked, somewhere there in the back. The poison of hatred boiled through.

Joab, whose horsemen had overridden a Qushmarrahan company on the Plain of Chordan, leaving Aaron's father and brothers among the dead.

Aaron's body refused to be controlled. He rose slowly, coiled to spring. His limbs began to shake. A sound like that made by a cat trying to cough up fur balls came from his throat.

Those grey eyes filled with surprise and maybe a touch of fright.

Aaron caught a glimpse of bel-Sidek standing on the far side of the street, watching him in amazement.

The dark fog parted. He shuddered, tore his gaze away from Joab, said, "Mish, come on," and gripped Arif's shoulder hard, headed him toward home. Mish came without protest, having heard something in his tone that silenced her penchant for contradiction.

Yoseh watched the girl walk away, saddened, puzzled.

"What the hell just happened?" Joab asked. "I thought he was going for my throat."

Medjhah said, "You offended him somehow. About six years ago."

Joab looked at the veydeen man, grunted. "What went on here? Are these men all right?"

"Just a little battered, sir," Yoseh said. He explained about spotting the child-stealer. Nogah came out of the maze and hovered nervously while he talked.

The General closed the door he had held open a crack throughout the excitement. He cursed softly, over and over. Azel had gotten away, but it had been a close thing and those bastards—Joab and Fa'tad, at least—were going to put in some time trying to find out why the man had been in the area.

Azel never made mistakes. Not to the old man's knowledge. Nor to his own, either, probably. But his stroke of tactical inspiration, invoking the name of the Living, just might turn into a strategic nightmare.

Not Azel's fault, really. His own, for overutilizing his best man. Had anyone noticed his frequent visits? Those had to stop, inconvenient as that would be. He dared not have a child-stealer connected with this house or the Living.

The Living would have to disavow him, condemn him, demand that he be punished for using the movement's name. Azel was deft. He would evade trouble. Whatever notoriety came of this would die out soon.

He looked across the room to his writing table, miles away. He had to scribble a note to Azel, warning him off, advising him that he would have to endure the name of outlaw for a time.

He started working his way along the wall, wishing there was someone he could bring in on what he was doing. He was too feeble to carry the whole burden. But did he dare inform his khadifas? Most would be appalled, even outraged, though not all for the same reasons.

Zenobel or Carza? Maybe. If it was presented carefully enough and he revealed the full scope of his duplicitous stratagem, so they would not be repelled by its unsavory immediate aspect.

The old man had spent too much strength getting to the door. He did not retain resources adequate to the return journey.

For once bel-Sidek was not sorry about the condition of his leg. Had he been healthy he would have arrived in the middle of things, while tempers burned their hottest and reason bent before a draft out of Chaos.

There was residual anger enough to trouble him as he questioned his neighbors. Inner, secret shame had left some defiant. They could not admit that they had been gulled by a thug. His reassurances were not well received.

He dared not pursue it too closely. He limped home irritated. Ortbal Sagdet had proven insiders could use the movement to their benefit. But who would have thought the baser sort of villain might use its name as a tool?

He burst in ready to treat the General to an angry monolog.

"Sir! Oh, Aram have mercy!" He dropped a squash he had bought for supper, fell to his knees. "Sir?"

The old man croaked, "Bel-Sidek?"

"Yes sir. I'm here, sir."

"The flesh betrays the spirit." The old man's words came one to the breath. "Get me to the writing table."

Bel-Sidek lifted him. He was so light! "What were you trying to do, sir?"

"Watched that uproar in the street. Bel-Sidek, a beast of a man, a child-stealer, used our name to escape Dartar justice. If there is such a thing. Where are you going? I said the writing table."

Bel-Sidek lowered the old man into his bed. "You talk too much, sir. Shut up and rest."

"The writing table. An order."

"So try me for mutiny. At least you'll have the pleasure of being alive to enjoy it."

"The word has to go out. That man has to be caught. People are too eager to think evil of us now."

"Dictate. I'll take care of it."

The old man worked his way around till he faced the wall.

Stubborn old bastard. What was he doing walking around without help? At the very least he could have broken brittle bones.

Bel-Sidek began his meal preparations, and worried. He was supposed to join Meryel again tonight. But it was obvious someone had to ride herd on the old man, whose reason was slipping. He could not leave. But it was imperative that he meet with Meryel and arrange for the disposition of the weapons in her warehouse. They could not be kept there in a mass. Too much to risk.

Hadribel. The new khadifa of the Hahr had not yet left the Shu. He would do anything to overcome the embarrassment of having allowed a Herodian agent to rise so high in his organization.

Yes. Hadribel. He would not have to be away from the house more than a few minutes to get Hadribel.

10

All the news came to Muma's first and fastest, Azel reflected sourly. Or, at least, all the news that was bad news.

A child-taker stomped to death in the Astan. He did not want to go, but he had no choice. If Agmed or Bel-Shaduk had got himself killed they would need to know in the citadel. Now.

He half hoped the man killed *was* one of those two. That was the sort of whack upside the head the Witch needed to wake her up.

Azel pushed away from his table and went out into the late afternoon. He headed east by alleyway and back street. The better streets all boasted Dartars headed for the Gate of Autumn and the compound beyond. He did not want to run into any more Dartars. He was in a mood to try to hurt them and that wouldn't be smart. They would only hurt him back.

He did not have to go rooting around the Astan to find out what he wanted to know.

Here and there along Goat Creek, in the open spaces before the Old Wall, were grounds designated for dumping. A Herodian conceit. They bred flies and rats by the million. But so had the pre-conquest custom—still followed west of the acropolis—of dumping anything unwanted out the nearest window, in hopes the rains would wash it away.

One of the bigger heaps served a grim purpose. It was there the corpses of criminals were thrown out for scavengers. It was next to the mound where unwanted babies were set out to die or be found by those who did want them. These days few were unwanted, few were exposed. Azel passed the place wondering if it might not have been better had he been exposed.

The body was there on Skull Heap. The day was failing but there was light enough. He turned back the way he had come.

Sadat Agmed, looking pretty harmless now.

Mo'atabar came almost before Yoseh settled himself to his supper. "Fa'tad wants him as soon as he's eaten," he told Medjhah, who was in charge because Nogah had stayed in the city with Faruk and another, hidden inside the Shu maze. "You, too."

Medjhah grunted. So did Yoseh.

Once Mo'atabar went, Medjhah said, "It didn't rattle you tonight, little brother."

"I hurt too much to worry about Fa'tad." He flinched, but not from the pain. They were questioning captives in the compound. Some needed convincing and were a little exuberant with their protests.

Yoseh did feel less uncomfortable crossing the compound. He supposed you could get used to anything. Yahada showed them inside and pointed out places to sit. Fa'tad was receiving reports from his captains.

He asked, "The man used the same powder we saw before?"

A man Yoseh did not know replied, "Twice, apparently. Our people weren't there to see it. He wasn't reluctant to use a knife, either. He cut a dozen men trying to get away. A couple probably won't live."

Fa'tad grunted.

"He was Dartar, Fa'tad."

Fa'tad looked up, grunted again, sourly. Yoseh wondered if he was having trouble with his digestion.

"One of the men recognized him. His name was Sadat Agmed. An outcast. From al-Hadid clan."

"I recall the man. A thief. And too quick with a blade. What did you find on the body?"

"Nothing. Except gold. Three pounds on each ankle and more on each arm."

"Child-stealing must be lucrative. So. Now we've run into two of them, armed with minor sorcery. Are there more? Who's buying the children they steal? What are they doing with them?"

No one had an answer. No one had a suggestion about how to find out, short of catching one of the child-takers.

"Tell me about the other one," Fa'tad told Yoseh. So Yoseh related events of the afternoon. Medjhah gave al-Akla the perspective from camelback.

"The important thing we learned," Joab interjected, "is that we're making no headway in the Shu. The man said he was an agent of the Living and the crowd turned on these boys."

Yoseh was surprised. He had not known that.

"The Living. We're not fighting them right now, Joab. We're trying to disarm them by example."

"Not fighting them? We're trying to take away the night. Their time."

"True."

"And how long before Cado gets wind of the fact we're leaving men in the city overnight?"

"Not long. But if we take the night from the wicked and Herod orders us to give it back, who gains in the eyes of Qushmarrah?"

"I still say you play the game too subtly," Joab grumbled. "Find the captains of the Living and come to an accommodation."

"We play for higher stakes, old friend." Al-Akla seemed to realize, suddenly, that he spoke before more than the inner circle. "Yoseh, Medjhah. You may go. Thank you. Your efforts will be remembered."

They rose. As he followed Medjhah out, Yoseh heard Joab say, "The one boy suggested we dress some men as veydeen."

"And how do we make their faces look veydeen?"

As they crossed the compound Yoseh mused, "I never thought how our faces would give us away."

"Maybe wisdom does come with age."

The old man heard the street door close and steps approach. Not bel-Sidek's familiar shuffle. He felt a moment of fright. Then he chuckled when Hadribel moved into the room.

"Are you all right, sir?"

"I'm fine."

"Bel-Sidek was very concerned. He said . . ."

"For all he's the man I've chosen to replace me when the time comes, bel-Sidek is a damned old woman when he starts fussing over me. The gods have been merciful tonight." He'd gotten worried about how he would get Naszif delivered to Azel.

"I have work for you, Hadribel. Work that *must* be done immediately, that bel-Sidek would have ignored even had his lapse meant the death of the movement. First, take me to my writing table."

Hadribel hesitated only a moment.

As he wrote his note to Azel, the General said, "I want you to go to Carza and tell him I have to see him immediately. If you both hurry he'll be with me most of the time you're running other errands. There'll be no cause for a nagging conscience."

"Other errands, sir?"

"After you've summoned Carza you must collect the traitor Naszif bar bel-Abek, blindfolded, and deliver him to an agent of the movement." The old man gave detailed instructions on how and where, with a strong caution against making any effort to get close enough to get a good look at the agent. "He's my most precious asset and I'll have no one know who he is lest he be betrayed even inadvertently.

"Once you've delivered the traitor you'll take this message to the hostel called Muma's Place." Hadribel needed special directions. He did not know the place. "Deliver the message only to Muma himself. Then return here. Knock. If Carza hasn't left he'll answer and you'll have to find some way to occupy yourself till he goes. If he doesn't answer then you're to come in and remain till bel-Sidek returns. Clear?"

"Perfectly, General."

"Good. Then help me to my bed and be on your way."

The old man sank into bed and collapsed into a deep, exhausted sleep, interrupted only when Carza entered, to be introduced to the ultimate secret of the Living.

Zouki came alert as sudden silence invaded the cage. It was a silence filled with terror. He looked around and saw the big man step through the cage doorway.

The big man came straight toward him.

His heart hammered. He wet himself. He whimpered. He wanted to get up and run but his body refused to obey.

The big man scooped him up and carried him out of the cage, through that huge place, into a large room lighted only by two candles at the far end. The big man set him down between the candles. "You stay there, boy. You don't move unless I tell you. Or you'll be sorry."

Zouki was too terrified to do anything else.

In the dusk a man leading an incongruously gaily decorated donkey cart came down the dusty country lane leading past the home of the widow of the Qushmarrahan hero, General Hanno bel-Karba. The man stopped before an old woman sitting by the roadside, weeping, watched over by several servants whose loyalty the Moretians had not been able to banish through threats or acts of terror. The man said, "Help her into the cart."

A servant, shaking, asked, "Who are you?"

"An old friend of her husband. I'm here to take you to safety."

The man's air of authority convinced the servants. They lifted the old woman into the cart, then followed the man when he turned and led his donkey back the way he had come.

Two miles up the road he turned off into a wood not yet devoured by the Herodian beast. He took them to a camp in a glen in the heart of the wood where they were received with great honor and solicitude by a band of men strangely garbed in black

camisards and pantaloons. The men were blackening one another's faces with charcoal.

They made the refugees comfortable and fed them well while
the cart man asked questions about the Moretians who had put
them out of their home. He changed to the strange clothing
himself and allowed his face to be blackened while he talked.

The old woman never spoke, never took her gaze from the fire.

The cart man asked, "Are we ready, Naik?"

"Yah, Khadifa."

"Then let's get to it."

Now the old woman looked up. "Are you the ones they call the
Living?"

The khadifa inclined his head slightly. He did not answer
directly. He said, "You will be back in your own home before the
sun rises, honored lady."

Azel was late to the rendezvous because Muma's sons were so
uncomfortable about the whole situation they had overscouted it.
But his man was there, head tucked up in a cloth bag, and his
escort was back where it was supposed to be. Good.

The man in the blindfold jumped when Azel touched him.
"Come," he whispered. The man came, saying nothing, coop-
erating even though he could have no certain idea what was
afoot. Azel kept an alert watch but saw nothing. No one moved
in the acropolis at night. Not even the Herodian sentries who
were supposed to be on duty. He led his charge in through the
Postern of Fate.

Torgo was waiting. He beckoned Azel to follow him. Azel
frowned. The eunuch showed none of his habitual impatience.

Torgo led him to a large room. The boy sat between two
candles at the far end, looking miserable.

Azel whispered, "I'm going to take off the hood and show you
your kid. You don't do nothing. You don't say nothing. You don't
turn around. You got that?"

The man nodded.

Azel removed the sack.

The man stiffened, took in a quick breath, restrained himself otherwise. Azel let him look as long as he wanted, till he nodded his head again to say he had seen enough. Then he replaced the sack, backed him out of the room.

Torgo closed the door. He whispered, "I woke her up. She wants to see you. I'll take care of him till you get back." Even in a whisper there was a hint of gloating.

"Good. I have a word for her, too. Where?"

"The altar."

Amused, Azel left the traitor to Torgo and went to see the Witch.

He found her standing by what remained of her husband. Her face glowed with a mad determination. It illuminated and made strange her beauty. But it did nothing to conceal the fatigue that weighted her down.

"I'm here, lady." No need to put her on the defensive. The news about Sadat Agmed was all the leverage he needed.

She turned, not removing her hand from the cold flesh of her husband. "Torgo tells me your General has threatened me."

"Not my General, lady. I'm just a bridge between you and him."

"By what right does he . . .?"

"By the right of good sense, first. Your haste has started to attract attention. And by the more primitive right of strength. We can't operate out there without his blessing."

"We shall see about that. Are you with me, Azel? Or have you truly deserted me?"

"I'm with you always, lady. Always. But I won't screw everything up by getting in too big a hurry."

"Damn you! You'll do what I tell you . . ."

"Lady! Sadat Agmed was killed today."

She looked at him hard. The color faded from her face. "How do you know that name?"

"I make it my business to know things. It's how I stay alive."

She stared for a moment, becoming just a tired woman as she did. "Tell me about it."

"He tried to take a kid in the Astan. He blew it. A mob got after him. He couldn't outrun them. They cornered him and beat him to death. Tomorrow the news will be all over Qushmarrah. It'll be ten times as hard to grab a kid."

The Witch sighed.

Time to drive it home. "I was in Char Street today, making arrangements about the traitor and trying to get the General to ease up on you. When I was leaving I was recognized by the Dartars I ran into the other day. I was luckier than Agmed, but a lot of people got a good look at me."

The Witch sighed again. "I guess you win, Azel. If the Fates will a thing, nothing we do will change it. Tell the General I'll do his boy next. Pick him up tomorrow night." She patted her dead husband the way a mother patted a colicky baby.

Azel bowed. "Thank you, lady." He backed out and returned to his charge, not convinced that he had been granted a triumph. "Come," he said, and led the traitor away.

He decided to take the man home through the maze. Less likely to be seen by anybody that mattered.

He was ten steps in when he realized they were not alone in the darkness. His nose warned him, catching a hint of camel and horse. He stopped, turned his charge, whispered, "We just walked into an ambush. When I take the hood off, you run like hell. Straight home. I'll hold them off." He lifted the sack and gave the man a shove.

The traitor ran.

The Dartars began to move.

Azel squeezed his eyes shut, placed a hand over them, faced away from the ambushers, threw a packet of flash.

They screamed.

He drew his knife and went after them.

As he stalked the last of the three he heard shouts from others approaching. He finished it, got the hell out, and headed for Muma's.

If they got in his way one more time, some night when he wasn't exhausted he was going to go in there and show them how to run the maze. They'd be picking up pieces of camel jockey for a week.

*   *   *

The night was still and the fire was banked. The children were snoring and the women were sound asleep. But Aaron was not. Each time he started to slip off, something brought him back.

He was conscious of the warmth of Laella beside him. That kept his filthy mind straying across to Mish . . . For a while he thought it was the ferocious guilt from thinking the unthinkable. That carried a speck of the blame, but only a speck. The main culprit was that business in the street, that reminder that the horror was out there still, waiting to pounce. He did not want to go to sleep because the nightmares were waiting on the other side.

He did not at first recognize the sound for what it was, someone tapping at the door. Then, more puzzled than frightened, he went and peeked.

"Reyha? What in the world?"

"I have to talk to Laella. I don't have anyone else."

"Come in." Aaron opened up. let her slip inside. He peered into the foggy street. "Where's Naszif?" He could not imagine a woman—especially timid Reyha—hazarding the Shu's night streets alone.

"Wake Laella. Please? I'll tell it all at once."

"I'm awake," Laella said, sitting up.

Aaron saw the stir had wakened Raheb, too, though she was pretending otherwise. He said, "Sshh!" and followed Laella to the hearth. They settled there. Aaron began stirring and feeding the coals, building up a small fire for the comfort. Reyha seemed troubled.

She said, "I don't know how to say this. It's so new to me. And so dangerous. But I have to talk to somebody. Promise me you won't say anything to anybody, ever. Please? Laella? Aaron?"

Laella nodded. "Of course."

Troubled, Aaron did not respond. He liked Reyha a good deal, but . . .

"Aaron?"

Laella gave him a look. "I'm sorry, Reyha. My mind wandered. Sure. Of course. But where's Naszif?"

"The kidnappers. They took him somewhere to show him they have Zouki. To make him do what they want."

"But . . ."

"I have to get home before they bring Naszif back. So let me tell it first. All right?"

"Of course we will," Laella told her.

"Sometimes I suspected but I never really believed it till he told me. Naszif is part of the Living. Very high up. They just promoted him to where he's the third or fourth highest man in the Shu. But he's in the Herodian army, too. They let him join right after the conquest. He's a colonel and he's been spying on the Living."

"He told you all this?" Aaron asked.

"Keep your voice down," Laella cautioned. "You'll wake the children."

"Yes. He did. This morning. He broke oaths to do it. But he said he had to tell me because of Zouki. He said the Living found out he was a Herodian and they took Zouki so they could make him do what they want, which is lie to General Cado and spy on the Herodians."

Aaron thought she was awfully calm about the whole thing. But Reyha was a sort of passive person, accepting of things that were beyond her control. He grunted. Laella said, "Why are you taking a chance, telling us? Aaron and I have no reason to love the Herodians."

"I'm too confused about my feelings. I need somebody to help me think."

Nobody said anything. Aaron could feel Reyha's pain. Nothing he could say would change that.

She finally observed, "You don't seem very surprised."

Laella rested her hand on Aaron's. "We suspected for a long time. Naszif did strange things sometimes."

"Oh."

"What do you want, Reyha?" Laella asked.

"I don't *know*! Except I want my baby back. If we had Zouki, Naszif says the Herodians would send us somewhere where we'd be safe and he wouldn't have to spy on people anymore."

Aaron wondered if they'd do that, really. Maybe. The tie that bound the Herodian empire together was its strange and bitter religion. If Naszif had adopted that, they might consider him one of their "confederates," with a citizenship only slightly more restricted than that of native-born Herodians.

He said, "I don't know how we could help, Reyha. Anything we did would put us in the middle between the Herodians and the Living. I won't speak for Laella, but I'd just as soon not have anything to do with any of them. I have my own family to worry about."

Laella said, "Aaron!"

"I don't know what you could do. I just wanted Laella to know because she always stays calm, no matter what, and I get rattlebrained, so maybe she could think of something when I couldn't. I wouldn't ever ask you to do something that would get you in trouble."

Laella told her, "We'll do whatever we can to help you, Reyha. You know that."

"Thank you. I'd better run home. Before Naszif gets back. He'd be very angry if he knew I told you anything."

"He won't know," Laella said. "Aaron, you'd better walk with her."

Aaron sighed. "Yes. I suppose I'd better."

Reyha had little to say during the walk. She had exhausted her reserves of courage and talk. When he got back home, Laella said, "Well? Something got to you while she was telling us. What was it?"

"Zouki was kidnapped before they found out about Naszif. So that couldn't be why he was grabbed. And bel-Sidek promised me the Living didn't have anything to do with it. Even Naszif didn't believe the Living would be involved in child-stealing. So how come all of a sudden they tell him they've got Zouki when they want to twist his arm?"

"Maybe they lied."

"But they're taking him to see Zouki."

"Don't bark at me, Aaron. I don't know who's doing what to

whom, or why. I'm not sure I care. Reyha and Zouki are what I care about. Do you understand?"

"Yes. There's no point fussing about it till we find out what they showed Naszif or did to him. I guess."

"What if he doesn't come home, Aaron?"

"Huh?"

"What if they . . . they did something with him: What would Reyha do?"

"We're getting ahead of things. When Reyha needs help—*if* she needs it—we'll do whatever we can. So let's not get fussed. Let's get back to bed. I have to work tomorrow."

Naszif burst out of the mouth of the Shu maze, turned left, lengthened his stride, ran all the way to the side door of Government House. He gave the password and his emergency code. To his amazement he was in to see Colonel Bruda before he got his wind back.

"What is it?" Bruda asked, knowing it would be dramatic if it had to be done this way.

"They've found me out. I can't take more than a few minutes or they'll know I came here. They're trying to force me to work against you."

"Damn!" Bruda punched the wall. "Just when we were getting close to them." He kissed a skinned knuckle. "You want us to take you out? I can send troops to get your wife."

"No. They have my son. He's their leverage. I'm going to stay in till I can get him out, too. And meanwhile try to learn enough to gut them. I just wanted you to know they're using me now. Whatever you hear from me will be what they want you to hear. I have to go. I don't want them to suspect I've slipped the leash. Tell the General."

"You've got more guts than I do. You find out where they're holding your son, let us know. We'll hit them and get him out. Then send you out of town."

Naszif nodded. "I will." He went downstairs, out the side door, and ran all the way home, where he found a shivering Reyha waiting in his bed.

"Did you see him, Naszif?"

"Yes."

"How was he? Was he all right?"

"He was clean and well dressed and looked well fed. He seemed healthy. They wouldn't let me talk to him. He didn't know I was there. He's all right except for being scared."

"What are we going to do, Naszif?"

"We're going to do whatever they tell us to do. For now."

The Witch waited only till Torgo told her that Azel and his companion had cleared the Postern of Fate. She told the eunuch, "I'm going to go have an unfriendly chat with our ally, General bel-Karba."

"My lady, I don't think . . ."

"That's right, Torgo. You don't. Because I don't want you to. You understand?"

"Yes, my lady."

"I won't be gone long. Get that child ready. I'll do him when I get back."

"But . . ."

"I'm strong enough, Torgo. I don't need to rest. Get on with your business and let me get on with mine."

She watched the eunuch depart, then gathered her skirts and headed for the Postern of Fate.

She had not been out into the city since the conquest. It seemed little changed, except that the night was more quiet. The Herodians had stilled the rowdy darknesses that had stemmed from the citadel and the mouth of Gorloch.

She slipped out of the naked openness of the acropolis and headed down Char Street, into the inevitable night fog. She made no more sound than the fog itself, and felt no more fear. There was nothing in Qushmarrah more dangerous than its Witch.

She came to the General's door. She paused. She sensed only the one enfeebled spirit within. The door was not barred.

Only someone supremely confident of his power would lie sleeping behind an unbarred door in the Shu.

She invited herself inside.

"Hadribel? Are you back already?"

A light sleeper. She stepped into the room where he lay. "No, General. Not Hadribel. Someone you don't want to see at all. Someone who did not want to come see you. But someone sufficiently tired of your lapses in regard to recognition of who is ruler and who is ruled that she felt compelled to come make the point clear."

The General met her gaze without flinching. He grunted. That grunt seemed to call her a damn fool woman.

"You had your creature Azel threaten me."

He looked at her a moment, then snorted. "*My* creature? Azel? Azel is nobody's creature but his own. He carried my message, yes, and it doesn't seem to have gotten garbled. He did his job. But if he were to surrender to his prejudices I suspect there's only one person who could touch his heart. That person is here and it isn't me, woman."

"You dared to presume to control me, General."

"I have a duty to Qushmarrah and my lord Nakar. Your obsessive behavior imperils the recovery of both. Go back to the citadel, woman. Examine the children already in your power and leave the city alone. If you press it too much it will turn on us all. None of us will get what we want."

"You don't understand. None of you do. You never have. I don't give a damn about Qushmarrah. I never have. I wouldn't care if it sank beneath the sea. I want my husband back. I'll do whatever it takes. And I won't let anyone get in my way. Not even you. Do you understand me?"

"I understand that Azel allowed his secret passion to cloud his reason, after all. His report on your obsession fell short of the truth. Go back to the citadel, woman. Be at peace with your heart. Be patient. Or you'll destroy us all."

"No. No. I'll destroy only those who try to hinder me." She smiled.

"What?" He tried to rise, suddenly, at last, aware that he was in danger.

"This is where the alliance ends, General." A web of dark

sorcery danced playfully on the fingers of her left hand. She laid her palm upon his chest and pressed down. He fell back with a little cry, body spasming. She turned and went out, pleased with herself.

She had taken only two steps uphill when she heard footsteps approaching. She turned and drifted downhill ahead of them.

The footsteps ended at the General's house.

She had cut it close.

She drifted downhill a little farther, meaning to cut across and head back uphill on the far side of the street, where the fog would hide her from any excitement that exploded from the General's household.

She froze, loosing a little bleat of surprise.

It was as faint as the breath of the sea a dozen miles in from the shore. But it was there and not forgotten, the faintest aroma of the misplaced soul. She could not help herself. She drifted to the street-side door, leaned her forehead and one forearm against it, and let the proximity of it wash over her.

Tears streaked her cheeks.

A door slammed up the street. Somebody ran into the fog cursing under his breath.

Nogah leaned against the wall of Tosh Alley, a few steps inside, and watched Char Street sleepily. He was not comfortable. There were few fogs like this at the Dartar compound. He did not like the clammy feel it gave the air, the way it limited visibility. It made this no decent place to be.

The scrapings and whispers and sometimes hints of far lights back in the maze did nothing to buoy a man's confidence, either.

Fifty warriors were not enough to hold anything. Fa'tad knew that as well as he did. They were a token, clinging to the dozen most important toeholds. They could be dislodged anytime the labyrinth creatures cared to make a concerted effort.

Fa'tad was convinced there was little concert among them, despite apocryphal tales of the maze being ruled by a sort of king of the underworld. If Fa'tad disbelieved that, did he also disbelieve the stories of great treasures collected by the people of the maze, of another labyrinth of natural caverns inside the hill that supported the Shu, with mouths deep in the heart of the builded maze?

Mo'atabar thought al-Akla was looking for those, thinking they would provide a way for him to sneak into the citadel and loot its reputed treasures. If those were half what was claimed, with them in hand the Dartar force could retire from the Herodian service and the tribes would never need fear the bite of the drought again.

Was that at the back of Fa'tad's mind? Nogah wondered. It did not seem quite the Eagle's style.

Something moved in the fog. He became alert. Then he gaped. He'd never seen such a woman. Her beauty hit him like a physical blow. He eased forward, to watch her on her way. As a barely discernible shape she paused several minutes at the door to the place where Yoseh's little doe lived, then vanished into the mist.

He wondered about his brother's injuries momentarily, then his thoughts returned to the woman. Had he seen a ghost? She had not made a sound. But gods, what a lovely spook, if ghost she was.

Hadribel sensed something amiss the moment he stepped through the doorway. He stopped.

There was a ghost of a hint of a scent on the air, vaguely feminine. He looked down. The apparently randomly distributed set of four dust bunnies, laid out according to bel-Sidek's instructions, had been disturbed. Oh. Of course. Carza.

But he had relayed the instructions. Carza was not the sort to forget.

He shut the door and hurried to the bedroom.

"Sir? Sir? Are you all right?" he asked, though he knew better the moment he laid eyes on the old man. He was a soldier. He knew death intimately, in all its guises.

The impossibility of it held him for a moment. Then the enormity of the disaster to the movement bore down on him.

The General gone! That indomitable will, that steadfast genius, lost forever.

Bel-Sidek was a proven field commander, a fine tactician, steady as a mountain in a storm, and the chosen successor, but the man lacked the magnetism, the ability to fire the heart and imagination, that had marked the life of Hanno bel-Karba.

Even so, bel-Sidek had to be made aware of the disaster immediately. Much had to be done, and fast, if the movement was not to stumble over this terrible moment. He forced leaden legs to take him out the door. Unaware that he was doing so, he cursed the Fates as he stamped along.

11

    Bel-Sidek felt the recriminations seethe inside him, along with the pain, the loss, the anger, the embarrassment over having been found where he had been found with Meryel. He restrained it all. He could not afford to yield at this most critical hour in the history of the Living. What he did this day would determine whether the struggle continued or the movement collapsed. He had to deal with issues, problems, and people entirely in the light of cold reason.

He paused before the door to the place he had shared for six years with a man who had meant far more to him than ever his own father had. "Send for Carza, then join me here," he told Hadribel. "Tell your messenger he is to accept no excuses or delays."

"What about the others?"

"After Carza gets here. I want to talk to him first." He pushed inside, left Hadribel to his assignment.

He sniffed. He did not catch the scent Hadribel had detected, but there had been time for it to fade.

In the interim between Hadribel's arrival and Carza's departure *could* a woman have come in? Absurd! But why not?

What woman? To what purpose?

179

He willed himself into the bedroom.

The old man seemed smaller and more frail in death. He looked as though he had died angry. No. Not angry. Bel-Sidek knew that look. He had died exasperated. Which suggested that the visitor, if visitor there had been, had been someone known to him.

The bedclothes were tousled as though he had wrestled his fate before succumbing. His nightshirt was partly open, revealing sickly yellow skin and . . . the edge of something black.

Bel-Sidek eased the dirty cloth back, using one finger.

A black handprint marked the old man's chest, over his heart. It was a dainty print, too big for a child but too small for a man. Bel-Sidek stared at it a long time.

It was a bad, bad omen. Because if it was what it looked like, the mark of a killer, they all had cause to be very, very troubled.

He had not seen this particular mark before, but he had seen its like. That recalled the killing touch of a sorcerer. Marks of that sort had been found on corpses often before the conquest, but not since. Cado and his henchmen had forbidden the practice of sorcery.

Bel-Sidek knew of no black magicians being in the city on the sly. He had heard of no witches but that one the new civil governor had brought along. Her? Unlikely. Had the Herodians known where to find the General they would not have chosen quiet murder. The end of the chieftain of the Living would have been a public spectacle a match for those of olden times, before the more peaceful Aram had dispelled the savage Gorloch.

He sat at the writing table while he awaited Carza, reviewing everything that would have to be done to ease the transition and keep the movement on its feet. His thoughts brushed the General's secret and special agent, passed on, came back again. If the man was half what the General had believed, he might become the Living's instrument of retribution in this.

But later. Vengeance had to await stability.

Carza entered without knocking. He had not slept and was not in a good mood. As he started to bitch, bel-Sidek pointed him toward the bedroom.

"Oh, I'll be damned," Carza said. "When?"

"Between the time you left and the time Hadribel came back. Assuming he was all right when you left."

"He was healthy and mean as a boar. Why?"

"Did you arrange the telltales the way Hadribel told you?"

"You know I did."

"I assumed. I had to hear it. They weren't arranged when Hadribel got here." Bel-Sidek pulled the old man's nightshirt open again. "Any ideas?"

Carza stared at the print. He shook his head, muttered, "Did he see it coming?"

"What?"

"He had me come over to tell me about this big operation he had going for Qushmarrah. Just in case. So there'd be somebody to keep it going."

"What was it?"

Carza shook his head. "I can't say. He was firm about that. Don't tell bel-Sidek anything. I'm supposed to take over that one thing and you the rest of the organization. He was right about it but the only way I could show you would be to tell you."

Bel-Sidek did not argue. No point. Instead, he decided to define the time gap in which the murder had taken place.

It could have been ten minutes or it could have been thirty. Carza could not be exact about when he had departed.

Hadribel arrived looking harassed. "I got messages off to the others," he said. "It's going to be light out soon."

"They can be grieving relatives," bel-Sidek said. "We've been setting it up that way."

Carza said, "You won't be able to get hold of Zenobel."

"Why not?"

"The old man sent him out . . . Hell. No need to keep it secret. You have to deal with the consequences."

Bel-Sidek asked, "What?"

"The new civil governor sent men to throw the widow out of her house so he could have it. The old man sent Zenobel to throw them out."

"Aram! Is that what he calls letting them think we're falling apart?"

"It had to be done."

"I realize that. But . . ."

Hadribel beckoned bel-Sidek. "Can I talk to you privately?"

Bel-Sidek left Carza scowling. He did not like being shut out, either. Near the hearth bel-Sidek asked, "What?" While he was there he started a fire for breakfast.

"While I was out rounding up messengers I got a few reports from the street. The Dartars left men in the maze overnight last night. And last night, while we had the traitor out on some sort of exercise, his wife left the house. The man on watch lost her in the fog. In this part of Char Street. A man brought her home later, a few minutes before the traitor returned."

"What the devil was he doing?"

"I don't know. The old man had me blindfold him and take him up to Scars Corner. Somebody else took him over there. I ran off on other errands."

"We'll talk to the woman. Though she wouldn't seem a likely candidate."

The Witch summoned Torgo from his repose. "I have to see Ishabal bel-Shaduk. Do you know how to reach him?"

"Yes, my lady. But why?"

"I have a commission for him."

"I suspect that Ishabal agrees with Azel. He just doesn't want to argue. He hasn't been around."

"Find him. Tell him he can name his price on this one. It'll be the last."

"My lady?"

"I found him, Torgo! I think. I stumbled right over him in Char Street, while I was out. It's almost over with, Torgo. We're almost there."

Torgo did not seem pleased.

"Three, four more days, Torgo. Things will be back to the way they were. Come. Why so glum?"

"I'm afraid we're doing too much to attract attention to ourselves."

"Foo! I'm surrounded by old women. Get your writing instruments. I'll give you the instructions you're to relay to Ishabal. Then we'll examine the boy the Living want, just to make sure he wasn't Ala-eh-din Beyh in his last incarnation."

"Why bother, my lady?"

"Azel will come for him. I don't want him or the Living to suspect what I've accomplished on my own. It'll take Ishabal a while, anyway, so I won't lose much time. And once we're sure we have what we need, we won't have any more use for Azel or the Living. Will we?"

She watched Torgo mull that over, begin to smile. "We won't at all. Not at all."

"So let's get to work. Get your writing materials."

Aaron left home groggy and distracted, unsure how he felt about Reyha's visit and revelations. He was concerned for Reyha and Zouki, yet resented this ominous certainty that a vortex of events, to which he was indifferent, was sucking him in, making him a blind player in a deadly game where there was no chance he could win or even get out unscarred.

What was all that up around bel-Sidek's place? Comings and goings like he'd never seen.

He turned uphill instead of heading for the harbor.

Bel-Sidek's door stood open. He paused on the threshold, not quite sure what he was doing there or if his interest would be welcome.

Bel-Sidek saw him and limped to the doorway. "Yes, Aaron?"

"I saw all the people. I thought . . . Is it your father?"

"Yes. During the night.

"I'm sorry. I really am."

"It isn't like it was a surprise. Maybe it was a blessing. He had to live with a lot of pain."

"Maybe. Is there anything I can do? Could Laella and her mother come up and help?"

"No. No, Aaron. We'll manage. Thanks for offering."

"I'm sorry," Aaron said again. "Well, I guess I'd better get to work."

"Yes. Thanks again. Oh. Aaron. Did Naszif's wife drop in on you last night?"

"No." He answered immediately, surprising himself. He walked away before there were any more questions, wondering if he had been protecting Reyha or himself. Only when he was halfway down the hill did he realize that he should have stood his ground long enough to find out why bel-Sidek had asked.

General Cado dressed while Colonel Bruda reported his midnight visit from Vice-Colonel bar bel-Abek. "Did he seem rational? I wouldn't want to waste him. Should we pull him out whether he wants it or not?"

"He was completely self-possessed. And quite determined. I don't think he's at risk as long as they think they control him. Leave him where he is. They might get overconfident and let him close to something they shouldn't."

Cado grunted. "Time to see Sullo off to his new country home. Let's talk on the way. Did you look into the kidnapping?"

"I did. If it weren't that it's being used against our man, it would be just another of a rash of similar crimes."

Cado descended a stair without speaking, headed toward his work office. "A rash? Of kidnappings?"

"More than thirty in the last six weeks."

"The Living twisting arms?"

"I doubt it. Hardly any of the children belonged to families who mean anything. However, there's a chance bel-Abek's child was taken before the Living found him out."

"Suggesting that the Living knew who took him? So they were able to recover him for their own purposes?"

"Yes."

Cado completed his office business, started moving again. "I smell something dirty, Bruda. Look into it. We can't allow a trade in stolen children. And I won't tolerate human sacrifice."

"I've started already, sir."

"Good. Are the guards down front?"

"Yes sir. They'll walk us over."

"Good. So. What's really bothering you this morning?"

"A messenger from Marcellino in Agadar. Just came in by boat. Says a force of Turok tribesmen, maybe two thousand strong, is pillaging east of Agadar, moving our way. They caught our troops in the open, by surprise, during an exercise, and slaughtered them. Marcellino barely has men enough left to guard Agadar's walls."

Cado stopped. "Turoks? Not Dartars or Dartars in disguise?"

"Turoks. Marcellino questioned a prisoner. They circled the Takes to the west, around Dartar territory. They think we're too slow and too weak to stop them."

Cado resumed walking. "Turoks, you say."

"Yes."

"I wonder. Did our comrade the Eagle have anything to do with them showing up?"

"I don't follow you. Dartars hate Turoks. And vice versa."

"Not always. Turoks sometimes visit Qushmarrah. They cross Dartar territory to do it, so there is some kind of understanding at some level. And they worked together in our grandfathers' time, during the first war. Qushmarrah employed auxiliaries from both tribes against Lepido's armies. Their fleet landed a mixed force in Tiguria that came within sight of Herod's walls twice. Fa'tad's father commanded that expedition."

"You sure you aren't seeing conspiracy where greed would explain things?"

"Probably. Still, the options the raiders leave us aren't attractive."

"So?"

"The obvious move is for us to loose our Dartars. But suppose they are working together? Fa'tad strips the country of livestock and valuables and retires to his mountains. We couldn't do anything, because to field enough men we'd have to strip Qushmarrah of every Herodian soldier.

"If we send one of our own legions instead, Fa'tad is a match for us here. He can attack us with every expectation of initiating

an uprising. He can then back off and let Qushmarrahans do his
dying while he saves his people to plunder whatever is left.

"If we don't do anything but wait for the Turoks to go home we
get unrest everywhere this side of the sea because we haven't kept
our promise to protect the people. Over on the other side we're
in hot water because we haven't protected their property."

They were outside now, moving through the dawn-splashed
acropolis. Ahead, a column of Dartars came out of the Hahr and
crossed the heights to the Shu. Cado wondered what they were
up to but did not ask. Bruda would tell him as soon as he found
out.

Bruda said, "It all depends on what's going on inside the head
of the one crazy old man, doesn't it?"

"We have to trust him. Whether he's trustworthy or not. And
hope he won't change his colors again without at least as much
provocation as he had last time."

They approached the Residence, practically passing through
the shadow of the citadel. Cado shuddered. The place still gave
him the creeps.

Bruda said, "Fa'tad started his herd moving south yesterday."

Cado watched Sullo's army of servants load a train of carts and
wagons. "It was time, wasn't it?" A flashy donkey cart, carrying a
large brown trunk, rolled up and worked its way into a gap in the
line. The boy driving dismounted and walked up the line to talk
to another driver.

"Yes," Bruda admitted.

"Then we can't account that an omen. Even if it is one."

"Not really."

"And here comes Sullo, timing his appearance perfectly."

Sullo did appear at the top of the Residence steps just as Cado
reached their base. The civil governor came down slowly, in all
his portly glory, beaming at everyone as though bestowing the
benediction of God. He greeted Cado effusively. Servants scurried, trying to impress with their diligence.

Sullo's eye fell on the donkey cart. "What's that?" he asked one
of his companions.

The man shrugged.

"General Cado. I assume those pigeon tracks on the banner on that cart pass for writing here. What does it say?"

Cado shrugged. "Colonel Bruda?" Cado did not read Qush-marrahan.

Bruda squinted, translated slowly. "'From the people of Qushmarrah, for the Governor Sullo, in appreciation, a gift.'"

Cado and Bruda frowned uncertainly. Sullo pranced over to the cart, shoved his bulk against its side, unlatched the trunk.

Colonel Bruda said, "Governor, you'd better let someone else . . ."

Too late. Sullo tossed the trunk lid back.

The fat man rose on his toes. He stiffened. A gargling, strangled sound ripped out of his throat. He turned, his face white with horror. He vomited, then ran for the Residency, pausing to vomit twice more before he disappeared.

Cado looked into the trunk. "The heads of the Moretians he sent to evict the old woman."

"Welcome to Qushmarrah, indeed."

"Try to find the boy who delivered the cart."

"Waste of time."

"I know. Make a showing. I'll go try to keep him from doing anything else stupid."

But Sullo was not on Cado's mind as he mounted the steps of the Residency. He thought he saw a way to ease the perils of responding to the Turok incursion.

Azel dozed in the shadows by the empty fireplace, not as unalert as he appeared. He cracked an eyelid when the limping man came in. The man talked to Muma instead of passing a message. Muma looked surprised. After an exchange the gimp nodded and hobbled outside.

Muma fished a son out of the kitchen, yakked at him, sent him out the back way. He poured himself a draft of hot tea, added a dollop of honey, came to join Azel.

"Another message?"

"A little off the usual."

"I saw you jump. What is it?"

"The palm sparrow has flown."

Azel sat up. "The old boy croaked?"

"That's what it means. That one wants to talk to you as soon as he can."

"I'd rather leave town. But I suppose I have to. He's the one the old man picked to take over."

"Maybe we all ought to leave town."

"Just when it's getting interesting?"

"Just when it's getting deadly."

Muma's son came back. He nodded. All clear. Azel rose, stretched, went out the back way. He caught up with the limping man. As he passed, he said, "At the Parrot's Beak," and went ahead.

He picked himself a good perch and waited, flipping pebbles at the morning pigeons grazing on the leavings of evening picnickers. When the shadow fell upon him he suggested, "Pull up a seat, Khadifa."

The cripple eased himself down.

"I'm Azel. I worked for the old man, special. I guess I work for you now. Them's his orders, anyway. So he finally went and did it, huh?"

"He did it, Azel. But he had help."

"What?" That caught him as much by surprise as had the pursuit of the Dartars in the labyrinth.

"We believe he was murdered. By witchcraft." The gimp gave him details. "I want you to view the body. See if you concur. Then I want you to find the woman who did it."

"A woman? You're sure?"

"No. Of course not. But once you come see the body you'll understand our presumption."

Azel shifted uneasily. "It's still in Char Street? I had word from the old man yesterday to stay out of Char Street. Dartars are up to something there, watching everybody like hawks, stirring things up. I been in and out too much lately, all the special jobs he wanted done. What you doing with the body? Moving it somewhere?"

"He had property in the country. His wife still lives out there. We're taking him there later."

"I know the place. I'll show up somewhere along the way. You going out yourself? We got a lot to talk about and this ain't the best place."

"You're right. It isn't. Maybe out there, day after tomorrow. I can get away with breaking routine today because my father died and there are things you have to do on a day like that. Unfortunately, I'll actually have to spend most of my time doing those things. Tomorrow I'll have to get back to my normal routine or there'll be questions."

"You ought to find some way to stop working," Azel said. "Ain't no way being boss of the whole damned outfit ought to be a part-time job."

"I have to eat."

Azel snorted. The man was a damned fool, seduced by the imaginary value of appearances. Who the hell was watching him? Bet he wasn't no hand-to-mouth day laborer before Dakes-Souetta. "You going to make any big changes? Or just go ahead the same old way?"

"No changes. That I foresee. Maybe after I'm more familiar with everything the organization is doing. I wasn't in on everything."

Azel snorted again. The guy was right there. The old man had thought him way too soft to follow through on some of the hard things that had to be done. But the best successor, anyway, overall. Go figure that.

The man asked, "How did you come to meet the General?"

"In temple. Long time ago. Look, I got stuff to do. Anything you want I should do right away? Besides try to find who did the old man?"

"I'd like to find out what the Dartars are up to in the Shu."

"You and half the world. I'll look you up if Fa'tad comes around and confesses." Azel rose, walked away before the new General could drag it out any more.

He seemed a little too passive to boss such a bloodthirsty outfit.

Azel strolled up toward the citadel, stroking the place with idle

but thoughtful glances. A woman killer, eh? And who might talk
herself into thinking she had a reason?

He was passing the Residence, where for some reason they had
a guard laid on that looked like half a legion, when by chance he
glanced back and in the distance saw someone who looked like
the eunuch Torgo. By the time he got back there without
attracting attention he was unable to pick the man up again.

Yoseh sighed when Nogah left the alley where he had spent the
night. Word had swept the column already: it had been a bad
night for those who had stayed in the city. As many as a dozen
might have been killed. More had been injured.

It would get worse, Yoseh was sure. He wished he knew what
Fa'tad was doing. Last night there had been talk about hidden
caverns, fabulous treasures, even a secret tunnel leading into the
citadel. Everybody knew about the wealth accumulated in the
citadel. If he could lay hands on that, Fa'tad could kiss Qushmarrah good-bye.

"Are you all right?" Yoseh asked as he dismounted.

"Just tired," Nogah said. "We were lucky here. It was quiet all
night—except when the most beautiful woman in the world
came past, on her way to visit your girlfriend's house."

"What?"

"No. She didn't actually visit. That was weird. She just stood
outside the door for a while."

"What are you talking about?"

"I don't know. I'm in love. I'm not supposed to make sense."

"You're doing a great job."

"There any special news?"

"No. Fa'tad started the herd south yesterday. He's going all out
against the maze today. That's it."

"You want to go in today?"

Yoseh glanced down the street. Right now that door was
closed.

"Don't want to miss a chance, eh? All right. I can understand
that. I'm in love myself. Going to sit out here today looking for
mine, too."

"That'll make Medjhah happy. He's got one picked out, too."

Nogah grunted, glanced around. "This crowd, we'll need more than two men to mind the animals." '

There *was* a crowd. Close to forty men today, to work this one access. And another dozen to go up and walk the rooftops in search of additional entrances to the maze. The street was pure chaos as Dartar numbers tried to move amidst normal morning traffic. The animals would create a choke point filling half the street. And it would get worse when the masons came later.

Dartars poured into the maze or clambered to the roofs. Nogah directed traffic. Medjhah planted himself in his usual spot and watched his brothers try to crowd the animals into a more compact arrangement. The camels were not inclined to cooperate. Qushmarrahans passing by cursed liberally but were careful to confine their invective to the hump-backed beasts.

"How are your scrapes and bruises?" Nogah asked.

"They ache. And I'm stiff all over."

"Good thing I didn't send you in there, then. It might get nasty today."

"I think Fa'tad is going to leave a whole gang in here tonight. Five hundred, maybe even a thousand."

"He's gone crazy. The ferrenghi will have convulsions."

"Maybe that's what he wants. If it's all some kind of game with General Cado."

Nogah grunted. Yoseh could see he did not, really, want to bother trying to figure it out.

Same with Medjhah. Hell. Medjhah did not care at all. He just lived from day to day and tried to enjoy what life handed him.

"Hell with these beasts. They won't crowd up any more." Nogah went and found himself a seat. After a while, he dozed.

Yoseh settled with the same intention, but remained too conscious of that door down the street. After a while, Medjhah began his singsing "Come closer." Yoseh noticed that the tall woman was alone this time and much more bold with her taunting hips.

A while later still, he noticed men across the street, watching.

Ferrenghi spies? Probably. Cado's men hanging around the edges to see what they could dig out of the shadows.

Then came the messengers, moving grimly down toward the harbor, and later all the captains heading uphill, faces blank, without a word to the men.

He heard it from the veydeen first. Overheard it as the news spread like flashfire. Turok raiders were pillaging the territories between Agadar and Qushmarrah. The Agadar garrison had been cut to pieces. The survivors were holed up in the city.

There were a few Dartar auxiliaries at Agadar. How had they fared?

The veydeen looked like they wanted to work themselves into a panic. Like they felt defenseless. He was willing to bet that they had not gotten this excited when they had heard that Herod's armies were approaching.

Then he began to get a glimmer. They feared chaos. They feared Cado would march out and leave the city open to destructive insurrection. An uprising by the few would bring reprisals down upon the many, sure as sundown.

He looked down the street at that door. Still nothing. Were they all dead in there? He glanced skyward. A few tall clouds lumbered toward the gulf. Would it ever rain again?

Even here on the coast it did not rain as much as once it had. And Qushmarrah needed a good rain, to sluice out the accumulated filth and stench.

The spies, or whatever, disappeared. The woman who interested Medjhah returned, flaunting herself again. The veydeen were blind, so preoccupied were they with gossip about Turoks.

"Watch this little pigeon fly away," Medjhah said, laughing. He strolled toward the tall woman, who did look alarmed and did hurry. Medjhah kept on walking after her.

For a while Yoseh amused himself by trying to kill a fly that had developed a determination to nest inside his nose. Once he had won that contest he did manage to doze.

"Hey! Yoseh! Wake up! Look what we got for you."

He jerked awake. The boy Arif stood before him, smiling shyly. His little brother was with him, holding his hand, which he dropped when Yoseh opened his eyes. The little one headed for the nearest camel.

The girl Tamisa was behind the boys, carrying something. Behind her, in the doorway, wearing a ferocious scowl, was the old woman. The other daughter, the older sister and mother of the boys, elbowed past her and carried a pot to the center of the street. She dumped it through a stone grate into the sewerage channel that ran there, went back into the house. She never looked at the Dartars at all.

"Good morning, Arif." Agan Yoseh worked hard on his dialect. He only glanced at the girl but his cheeks got hot. He was intensely aware of Nogah watching through scantly cracked eyelids. "How are you today?"

"Mish brought you dinner. She made it herself. Dad said it was all right." The boy plopped down beside him.

The girl stood there blushing. Yoseh wanted to tell her to do something but did not know what. He made an uncertain gesture. She took it as an invitation, settled onto a bundle at a very correct distance, sat formally upright with eyes on what she held in her lap.

The boy bubbled, "Did you hear about the Turoks, Yoseh? Are you going to go fight them?"

"Yes, I heard, Arif. I don't know if I'll have to go. I suppose someone will."

The girl said, "Mother thought you'd go. That's why she said I could bring this out now." She offered, so he had to take the bundle. "Are you all right? After the way they knocked you around yesterday . . ."

"I'm fine. Just a few bruises."

"That's good."

Yoseh glanced at the old woman. She had taken her place outside the door with her mending, daring traffic to trample her. All along Char Street the regulars were out, refusing to let the Dartar presence disturb ancient routine. He opened the bundle, saw nothing really familiar. He tried a few nibbles, found everything mouth-watering. "This is great. But there's way too much here for me. Mind if I share with my brother?"

"No. That's all right. Go ahead."

"Nogah. Come help me with this."

As Nogah approached, the girl realized he was not Medjhah. "How many brothers do you have?"

"Three. Medjhah and Nogah right here and Amar, who is a troop leader in Quadideh's company."

Nogah settled, went to tasting, nodded pleasantly. "This is excellent. What is your friend's name, Yoseh?"

"Tamisa."

"You're a very good cook, Tamisa."

She blushed. "I got a lot of help from Laella and my mother."

"Even so, yours was the hand in control." With nothing at risk Nogah could assume the burden of conversation. Yoseh mostly listened. So did Arif, with big, serious eyes, while the little one, Stafa, clambered all over a surprisingly patient camel. Yoseh saved him from a fall and set him on his feet. He marveled that these children of Qushmarrah were so well fed.

Dartar children, even now, were little more than bags of bones living on the edge of starvation.

Nogah got the girl to relax. Once she did, she turned into a chatterer. Some of her preoccupations seemed pretty shallow, though.

Arif grew bored. Looking disappointed in his new friend, he began wandering around looking at animals, weapons, and supplies.

Nogah asked Tamisa, "Who was the woman who came to your door during the night? I've never seen a woman so beautiful."

"Reyha? Beautiful?" Tamisa laughed. "She's an old hag. She must be at least thirty." Then her eyes grew big. She looked worried. She had said something she should not have.

"Maybe we're talking about different women. Come to think of it. The one I saw just stood outside your door for a few minutes."

Yoseh asked, "Is Reyha the one whose son was taken here?"

Tamisa nodded. "She and my sister have been friends all their lives. They even had Arif and Zouki the same day. She came because she was having trouble with her husband."

Yoseh said, "I've seen this Reyha, Nogah. If it's her you fell in love with last night you'd better worry about how fast you're going to go blind."

Nogah chuckled. "It doesn't matter who she was. She was that kind of woman you only see once, for a moment, and never again, but remember all your life."

"Ach! You're starting to sound like Father."

"I'm his son and heir. You two go ahead and talk." He got up and went and got his horse onto her feet. He hoisted the veydeen boys onto her back. Arif became frightened and wanted down. Stafa was as happy as a child his age could be.

Tamisa asked, "How does your brother know somebody came to our house last night, Yoseh?"

He reflected. It wasn't exactly a secret around here, was it? "He spent the night in the alley so nobody could get in or out of the maze."

"Oh."

"More of us are going to stay tonight. I know I am."

"Oh. Oh." Flustered. "I think I'd better get back to my chores. Before my mother . . . Arif. Stafa. Come on. It's time to go."

Yoseh sat there wondering if he'd said something wrong.

12

    Aaron had been distracted all morning. Not enough to make mistakes but enough to slow him down. Cullo had commented, not unkindly, expressing a genuine concern. Aaron had not been able to shake it.

Billygoat sat down beside him as he started on his lunch. "Think it'll rain? Looks like we got some clouds coming in."

Aaron grunted. It did not look like rain. Just clouds.

"City could use a good washdown."

Aaron grunted again.

"You ever notice the difference between men and dogs, Aaron? A dog comes to you begging, you give him the sorriest scrap, he's properly grateful. A man comes to you desperate, you try to give him a hand, four times out of five he turns on you. Makes the whole damned thing your fault. On the whole, I think I like dogs better than I like men."

His piece spoken, Billygoat got up to go.

"Wait," Aaron said. "Sit down. You're right. I'm sorry. I apologize."

Billygoat harumphed. "I reckon that means you got another problem to hit me with and be ungrateful about later."

"No! Look, I said I'm sorry. The problem I had—it got solved, all right, but then it didn't, either, really. It only made more problems."

"Yeah. That's the way she goes, most times. You hear about that child-stealer got caught over my way yesterday? Tried to grab a kid, got hisself chased down and stomped to death. That ought to ease your worries some."

"I heard. I also heard he used some kind of sorcery, same as the one who took the child where I live. And the Dartars were chasing that one up Char Street almost the same time the other was getting himself killed. If there're two of them maybe there're three or four or a hundred."

"I swear. You ain't going to be satisfied till your boy does get got. You live in Char Street. I come over Char Street this morning. You got two thousand Dartars packed in there asshole-to-elbow. Who you think would be dumb enough to try something with odds like that?"

"The Living might."

"Heh! We're getting around to something here, aren't we?"

Aaron told most of it, keeping the names out.

Billygoat listened. He thought. He said, "I figure they lied to him, not you. Handy way to twist his arm. Anyway, what you worrying about it for? Ain't your problem. You're starting to get silly, like some of these fools around here all in a panic because of some Turok bandits all the way around to the other side of the gulf."

Aaron had not heard that news yet. He had to have the story told.

Bel-Sidek glanced around as he left his home. "It gets any thicker out here people will be climbing over each other."

Hadribel's men began forcing a way through the press.

"Gently," bel-Sidek told them. "Let's not attract attention." They were already. Raheb Sayed had them fixed with her basilisk's eye.

"How will Cado respond?" Hadribel asked. The news about the Turoks had come only a moment before word that it was safe to approach the traitor's house. What Hadribel really wanted to know was if this was likely to become an opportunity for the movement.

"No telling. That son of a whore is as crafty as Fa'tad, in his way. Wouldn't surprise me if he made the whole thing up just to see how everybody jumps. We'll be very careful with General Cado."

"How can we get the old man out through this mess?"

"By investing heavily of patience, I suspect."

They crossed Char Street, entered an alleyway. Even there they faced foot traffic trying to beat the press on the artery. The walk took so long Hadribel felt compelled to scout their destination again.

"Still safe," he concluded.

"Let's get it done." Bel-Sidek was uncomfortable with this. But he had to know.

Hadribel hammered on the traitor's door. The woman responded. She looked at them without recognition, uneasy but not frightened, as though used to finding strange men at her door.

"My husband isn't here. You'll find him . . ."

"I know," bel-Sidek said. "It's you we want to see." He pushed forward. She had to retreat or be trampled. Bel-Sidek, Hadribel, and two of Hadribel's men were inside before she protested.

"Please relax," bel-Sidek said. "You're in no danger. We want to ask a few questions."

She looked for someplace to run. There was no place. They had taken all those away. "Who are you? What do you want?"

The questions were predictable. Bel-Sidek had decided to answer them honestly. "We are the Living. We want to know where you went last night."

She started shaking. She said nothing.

"One of our men was murdered last night. A very important man. My commander. It was done by a woman. You were out and in that area. If you felt you had a reason, if you suspected who the man really was . . ."

Her eyes grew huge. Her mouth hung. She swung her head

back and forth in little jerks. She tried to speak but could not force anything out.

"You didn't do it? How can we believe that? Where did you go?"

"I . . . can't . . . say."

"Why not?"

"Because you're evil, wicked men. You'd go terrorize people just because they're my friends."

"I don't intend debating relative morality or our duties to the city that nurtured us. We believe we're right. We're convinced our ends are just. A hero of Qushmarrah was murdered in his bed. We mean to find the woman responsible. If you're not guilty, show us."

The woman spat. "You haven't done enough to us already, have you? You overlooked one member of the family." She spat again. "To hell with you. Go ahead. Kill me. You've taken away everything I have to live for, anyway."

Hatred fouled the air. Bel-Sidek was startled by the fever of it. "I'm not going to kill anyone. I don't think you did anything but go to Char Street to visit your friend Laella. But my comrades want something more convincing than my guesses."

"What if I said I did go there?"

"I want to know what you told her and what or who you saw in the street, coming and going."

She sat down on the floor, against a wall. "You see? No matter what I tell you, you won't be satisfied. You'll want more. And there'll be nothing in it for me but pain. You want me to talk to you, give me my son back."

"I'd be tempted. If I had him. We don't make war on children. They aren't responsible for the crimes of their fathers."

The woman stared at him for half a minute, radiating hatred and disgust. She spat again, directly at him. "You want me to believe and trust you, telling me a bald-faced lie like that? After you dragged my husband out last night to show him that you do have Zouki?"

Bel-Sidek stepped back, told one of the men, "Don't mark her.

Hadribel." He took Hadribel aside. "Tell me what you did with the traitor again."

Hadribel repeated his story.

"Did he see the boy?"

"She thinks so."

"The General said we'd pretend. I think I smell something. The old man had a dark streak. It may have infected part of the movement. I want to know."

Hadribel scowled. He had worshipped the General, too. He did not want to think the old man had done something less than perfectly righteous. "I'll see what I can find out."

Bel-Sidek went to supervise the woman's interrogation.

She was damned stubborn. She would not talk.

Azel approached Government House reluctantly. He did not like having been summoned.

The mechanism had existed for years but the Herodians had not used it before. That disturbed him. Till he stepped inside Government House he thought about walking away from it.

He was especially uncomfortable with the news about the Turok pillagers. They were a random element that could destabilize an already rattled situation.

The doormen wasted no time conducting him to Colonel Bruda, who took him straight to General Cado. Cado said, "Thanks for coming. You heard about the Turok raiders at Agadar?"

"It's all anyone's talking about."

"Bad news gets around fast. How are people reacting?"

"Like they think the Turoks will ride in and sack the city."

Cado snorted. "In a moment I'll go downstairs to thrash out a plan for dealing with them. I want you to come along in case I need an opinion on how the Qushmarrahan people will react."

"I don't like that. I'm a spy, not . . ."

"You'll be a bodyguard again. No one there could compromise you. There'll be myself and Bruda, senior officers from the legions, the civil governor, Fa'tad and his top men. You're my only touchstone with the Qushmarrahan in the street."

"Crap. You take me into a big-time meeting, one of those guys—probably that nitwit lard-ass civil governor—will spot me on the street later and tell the world, 'There goes that guy that hangs around with Cado pretending to be a bodyguard.'"

"There's that risk. But indulge me, Rose. This will be tricky, balancing a response between Fa'tad, Sullo, and the Living. Have you heard what happened to Sullo?"

"I guess not."

"He sent twenty Moretians to take over Hanno bel-Karba's country house yesterday. Today the Living sent their heads back in a trunk."

"Really? A little last-gasp derring-do."

"I warned Sullo. He didn't listen. Watch him close. I may have to ask for a special favor soon. He's going to become an embarrassment."

Azel grunted.

"Watch Fa'tad, too. I have trouble reading him. Have any idea what he's up to in the Shu yet?"

Azel shrugged. "I've heard stories. I don't believe any of them."

"Tell me a few."

"There are caverns under the Shu. That's a fact. In some of the stories the bosses of the maze have filled those with stolen treasure and Fa'tad wants to grab that. In some other stories one of the caverns is a secret passage into the citadel, which Fa'tad plans to loot."

"Are these fantasies?"

"I lived in the maze when I was a kid. I never saw no treasure and never heard of no secret passage. Which don't mean they ain't there. Nobody tells a kid nothing."

"Fa'tad thinks he's on to something. He has half his men on it today. You think he's learned something from the prisoners he's taken?"

Azel shrugged.

"I hear he's executed most of them."

"They ain't model citizens."

Cado shook a little silver bell. Colonel Bruda came in. "Sir?"

"I need Rose in a bodyguard costume. Rose, I'd be very

grateful if you could find me even one of the men who did in Sullo's Moretians."

"They won't go around bragging."

"That's why there's still a group called the Living. But try."

The other children did not say much but they eyed Zouki in wonder. Some came to touch him quickly, lightly, as though hoping his luck would rub off.

Of all the children taken out of the cage he was the first to be returned.

But then the big man came again and Zouki knew that this time there would be no unexpected reprieve. This time they would do whatever it was they did with children.

Azel was in a foul mood when he entered Cado's meeting. He did not want to be there and he did not like holding his tongue the way he must. He thought a lot about getting out of town.

It was a nice fantasy but not one he took too seriously even though it seemed the most intelligent course to follow.

Cado nodded to the men who rose to greet him. There were fifty or sixty. They ranged to either side of a massive table six feet wide and twenty long topped by a colorful miniature of the north coast from Ocean's shore to Aquira in the east. Two thirds of the men were Herodian. They stood on the seaward side. Opposite, Fa'tad al-Akla stood with his captains. Sullo had assumed position at the far end of the table. He had an ugly female with him. She looked like she had gotten away from childhood just last week, but seemed less intimidated by her surroundings than did Sullo.

His pet witch?

She had the smell. A strong one. She'd be a bad one in another twenty years.

Cado said, "You've heard the bad news. You've had time to think. I have an idea of my own but I'm open to any strokes of genius you've suffered. Volunteers? No?"

Azel studied Sullo and his witch, uncomfortable because Fa'tad and several of his captains were eyeing him. He pretended not to notice, mimicking the sleepy indifference of his fellow guards while trying to catch everything he could.

Cado continued, "Colonel Bruda's people have put out markers on the map showing what we know, which is mainly that the Turoks are west of Agadar and moving our way, staying near the coast. Colonel Bruda has dispatched scouts by land and sea but we'll have been in the field several days before we have their reports. Fa'tad, you think they've grown bold enough to violate Dartar territory?"

One of the Dartars translated for the old warrior though he understood Herodian perfectly. All part of the game, as was Cado's having ignored Fa'tad's honorifics. He barked an answer translated as, "Not if they hope to get home with their booty."

"I thought not. I presume plunder to be the object of their exercise. They won't want a real fight. I'm not spoiling for one, either. So we'll march along the coast in easy stages and chase them back the way they came. Fa'tad, I'll need fifteen hundred horsemen. I've already told General Lucillo he'll be taking twenty-five hundred from the Twelfth. I want you on the road as soon as possible. As soon as naval vessels can be manned and loaded you'll have offshore support and supply.

"Four thousand plus naval support should be strength enough to chase the Turoks without us weakening ourselves here."

Right, Azel thought. Even left Cado a little stronger in respect to Fa'tad's gang, just in case. But what was he up to sending out troops from the Twelfth under orders from Lucillo, who commanded the Seventh Cadadasca? What was he saving Marco for? If he was going to use the general from the Seventh, why not its men?

He grinned. Old Fa'tad was all pruned up as he tried to untangle the same questions. And that pruning was probably the whole answer. A fillip to keep the Eagle wondering.

When the meeting broke up, Dartars would start scurrying around trying to find out if they had overlooked something about Lucillo.

Azel did not lead the sort of life that saw him sitting in on many military planning sessions. He found they were not very exciting. After Cado announced who was going to send how many men, it was all pounds of food and fodder, would the temporary span in the Cherico bridge stand up to the passage of an army, could soldiers who had been in garrison too long make the march from the Sahdri Well to Quadrat in one day or should they be issued an extra canteen? Should artillery be taken? One faction insisted. Another said it would only slow them down because the ox teams could not keep up a fast pace. And so forth.

Cado settled the artillery debate by saying he would load the engines aboard ship.

To Azel it seemed calm and professional and about as adventuresome as conversation amongst greengrocers. The Dartars did not say much, speaking only in response to direct questions, which Azel supposed was the way it was supposed to be, them being the hired hands.

Fa'tad kept an eye on him all the time.

The civil governor was all business, never saying a word. Azel did not learn anything about him.

He got the impression the ugly little witch was there doing what he was, sizing up the boss's enemies. She paid him no mind. Fa'tad made up for her indifference.

The man grew more obvious. Feeling for a reaction? Why? Had one of his gang recognized the stable boy who had busted a guy up for running off at the mouth about Qushmarrah?

Trouble with the whole thing was, Cado and Bruda were going to notice. No way to stop it, though. Just ride it out, like a ship in a storm.

Then the confab was over. Cado hadn't consulted him once. He was pissed. That risk for nothing.

Before sunset Joab and the Dartar elite, and Lucillo and his twenty-five hundred, would be off to stalk the ferocious Turok. Tension in the city would soar as everyone waited for the Living to try something because garrison strength was at low ebb.

Azel did not expect the Living to act. But a few fanatics might, and might set off the explosion the old man had feared from the moment he had made his deal with the Witch.

Qushmarrah might throw the yoke of Herod in a sudden

savage uprising but there could be no realistic hope of keeping its independence unless the flame of rebellion scorched the entire coast or the Living came up with a weapon more potent than the Herodian legions.

Nakar could be that weapon. Nakar the Abomination. Without Ala-eh-din Beyh to hold him in check.

He should not be thinking of that in Government House. Here he should remain the perfect Herodian agent in thought as well as appearance.

The military men had begun moving out. Sullo had gone with his shadow instrument. Cado and Bruda were whispering with Lucillo and Marco while Fa'tad eagle-eyed them from across the room. Cado suddenly bobbed his head and turned away, beckoned his bodyguards, stalked out of the room. He dismissed all of them but Azel immediately. "We didn't learn much from that, did we, Rose?"

"Found out the governor can keep his mouth shut when he wants."

"I guess you could call that a blessing. Yes."

"I need to get up on that balcony on the third level on the southwest corner. To see what direction somebody goes when he heads out."

"All right." Curious. He did not ask who or why.

Damned man trotted along with him, picking at this and that like he was maybe trying to circle in on something. Whatever it was, it had Sullo near the bull's-eye. And it wasn't like he was hinting that something should happen to the governor. He would come right out with that. No. It was like Cado's level of trust had suffered . . .

The damned Moretians! Of course. Cado had mentioned them to him. He had mentioned them to the General. The old man had had their heads chopped off. Cado was asking himself how the Living had found out so fast and he didn't like one of the possible answers.

He would have to give Bruda something that would ease Cado's mind.

The Dartars did not scatter the way they should have. They

paused out front, in a cluster, then moved into the streets west of Government House. The streets somebody exiting the side door would head for if he wanted to get out of sight quickly.

He could handle that. He'd just go out one of the public doors on the other side, maybe drift down and see what bel-Shaduk was up to before he went out for his look at what was left of the old man.

Meantime, Fa'tad deserved a tweak.

"One thing I did hear but didn't have a chance to check the rumor. Fa'tad supposedly left a couple hundred men in the city last night, in the Shu maze."

"That's useful. You didn't mention it before."

"Didn't know if it was worth it. It's just a rumor I never got a chance to check. You want I should go ahead and figure how to set Sullo up? Or do you reckon you're going to get along?"

That did for the moment. Cado said of course Rose should be ready if a move had to be made. Azel said he would do it and made his exit wishing Cado was not so interested in him. He'd rather deal with Bruda.

The sinkhole country looked better all the time. If there was a blowup, he was gone till the dust settled.

Yoseh realized he had been chattering for hours.

Actually, once she got over her initial shyness the girl did most of the talking. It was plain she did not get much chance to say what she thought at home. She offered him an ill-informed opinion on almost every subject imaginable. Yoseh found himself smiling and nodding in agreement just to keep her there.

Medjhah finally came back. He wore a look of awe. He sat down beside Nogah, shook his head, said, "You wouldn't believe it. I don't believe it. And I was there."

"Fortune smiled upon you?"

"Fortune crawled all over me. If I'd wished for gold I'd be the richest man in the world."

Nogah snorted derisively.

A pair of mason's helpers came out for more bricks. Yoseh wondered what was happening inside the labyrinth. It had been a quiet day. He had expected excitement but they had not brought out a single prisoner yet. Medjhah thought maybe most of the villains had slipped out during the night. Nogah grumbled that it was probably because the men he had sent in were loafing. Yoseh suspected the whole maze thing had been overrated and there had not been that many people in there to begin with.

Medjhah started playing catch with Arif, using an orange somebody had stolen from one of the groves beyond the compound. The boy was very inept, mostly because he was too afraid he would get hit. Yoseh thought his parents probably protected him too much. These veydeen all sheltered their children more than did Dartar parents.

Mo'atabar came down the hill alone. Nogah went to talk to him.

Stafa tried to get into the game with his brother and Medjhah. His idea of catch was to grab the orange and scurry around among the animals laughing till somebody ran him down. Medjhah caught up, started to lift him, thought better of it, set him down, and said, "Phew! This one needs to be changed."

Whereupon Stafa, still armed with the orange, headed for home yelling, "Mom! I'm pooped!" Like he had not known perfectly well and been too busy to be bothered.

Tamisa said, "I'd better go. Chores to do. Mother is going to be crabby enough as it is. Arif, come on."

Yoseh said his farewells and watched them go. He had disappointed Arif severely, he knew, being more interested in the girl than in him. But what could you do? How could you explain?

Mo'atabar went on down the hill. Nogah went back and sat down, preoccupied.

"What's up?" Medjhah asked.

"Joab. He's taking fifteen hundred men out to chase those Turoks."

That scaly thing inside Yoseh wakened and started wriggling.

"We going?"

"No. We're staying to play Fa'tad's game. He's taking all

horsemen. He wants to hurry and get between the Turoks and the herd. Just in case."

Yoseh tried not to show his relief. There was nothing dishonorable about it but he did not want to admit that he had no taste for fighting and glory and riding around in the weather.

There were a few more clouds now. The veydeen did not seem excited so it seemed unlikely they would turn to rain. He wished it would rain.

The city was a madhouse. Troops were on the move, headed south to assemble outside the Gate of Summer, whence they would march before sunrise. Azel was not pleased by the dislocations. They made it difficult to be as cautious as he liked.

What about tomorrow, when the garrison was reduced? Would the Living's crazies make themselves heard?

Something. From somewhere. He felt the first tingle of it. He did not like it because he had no idea from what direction disaster might strike.

He took position in sight of the place where Ishabal bel-Shaduk lived in the northern Shu. He watched for an hour. Several men visited. He recognized two as thugs. Guys who would do anything for money.

He had a notion what bel-Shaduk was doing. He did not like it.

He'd thought bel-Shaduk possessed of better sense.

Gold and women had their ways of dribbling blindness into even a wise man's eyes.

The day was getting on. If he wanted to get out the Gate of Autumn and back with plenty of time he'd better waste no more here.

He overtook the cavalcade moving the old man two miles east of the Dartar compound. The new gimp General told him to get up inside the covered wagon where the stiff lay.

One look at that black print and he knew his suspicions were fact.

The damn woman had gone mad! She would set the city on fire.

And she didn't care. That was the hell of it.

He climbed out of the wagon, drifted back to walk beside the gimp on his donkey. A comedown for him. He'd probably ridden a purebred stallion out to Dak-es-Souetta. "I got an idea where to start looking."

"Where? Who?"

"I'll let you know if it comes out sure. Meantime, I got a suggestion. Burn the old boy. Don't bury him."

"Immolation is a rite of Gorloch, not of Aram."

"How many people going to be involved in this, eh? All of them mourning the beloved General. What chance you figure there is all of them will keep their mouths shut about who, what, and where? Cado gets the word, he's going to have the old boy dug up and paraded around."

"I'll think about it."

Dumb shit. He was asking for it. "You put some time in on the new governor and his witch, too. There's something more there than meets the eye. Talk to you more when we get together. I got something else I got to do right now."

He turned and headed west.

There was a lot of traffic on the road. Too much. How much had to do with the funeral? He checked faces. A few were familiar. He remembered them all. It was a habit he had, one he followed unconsciously sometimes even when he was aware of no need. Thus he noticed two particular faces among the inevitable beggars and loafers inside the Gate of Autumn.

He had seen one for the first time not far from where Ishabal bel-Shaduk lived. He'd last seen the other in the halls of Government House.

So.

He did not lead them an interesting chase. He went to Muma's, where he spent the afternoon and early evening eating, thinking, and carefully, laboriously composing a long letter to General Cado. He entrusted that to Muma's youngest, a quick-witted urchin, and relaxed with some black-market beer before he went out for the night's work.

*   *   *

Meryel guided bel-Sidek to a mound of cushions. "You look awful tonight. If you'll pardon me saying so."

"I can pardon you anything if you can pardon me."

She looked at him curiously but did not pursue it while her servants came and went with the courses of their meal. Then she asked. He told her about his day.

"Murdered? You're sure?" She did not seem interested in his conduct while questioning the traitor's wife.

"It seems more likely all the time. The trouble is, I can't see who would have gained by getting him out of the way."

"One of the fanatics, getting impatient?"

"No. They honored him too much. Besides, getting him out of the way just puts me in the way. Tonight I intend to name another moderate as my successor so there's nothing to gain getting rid of me, either."

"Could it be the governor's witch getting even for what happened to his guards?"

"Not unless she's one hell of a diviner. I think he died before they did. Herodians would have taken him alive, anyway. Sullo laying hands on the mastermind of the Living so soon after getting here would have been a political deathblow for Cado. There are people in Herod who want his head. He survives because he's competent, he has several very powerful friends, and he has the indulgence of the Living."

"Hubris?"

"Fact. We could cause trouble enough to get him taken out. If a Herodian must rule here, we'd prefer General Cado. None of the likely replacements would be so kind to Qushmarrah. I'd better go. We have a lot to argue out."

Meryel rose with him. She said, "I have a few contacts among those who operate outside anybody's law. I'll ask them if they've heard anything that might have something to do with the old man's death."

Bel-Sidek paused at the door. "All right. Also find out what they know about a child-stealing ring. And about a man named Azel." He slipped out, not at all eager to face what lay ahead. But they did have to decide who should take over in the Shu and who should take over most of his own duties on the waterfront.

Too, he hoped to discover if there had been some dark side to the old man that, in his love, he had been unable to see.

The Witch moaned, twitched uncontrollably. Her flesh was beyond her command. All her will was bent upon the child, that stubborn brat.

Three times she had tried to breach the barrier of trauma. Three times she had been repelled. Never had she encountered such resistance. The previous life must have ended terribly.

She gathered her remaining reserves, feeble after half a day in trance. One last effort . . . No matter. This could not be the one she sought. Azel could have him and welcome.

Her thoughts were not that clear. They constituted more an instinctual flow than actual reasoning.

Once more she advanced upon the child's defenses. And this time found a tiny crack. She focused upon it, struck with all the remnants of her strength . . .

And screamed. And screamed.

Terror squeezed her heart.

The soul on the other side was that of Ala-eh-din Beyh. It was not lost. It was not bewildered. It had been lying in ambush.

Torgo did not think. Instinct drove him. He plunged inside the tent, fists flying. He knew what had happened without having to think it out.

He struck child and woman with powerful blows to the head. The shock broke the link. The devil in the child tumbled back into the abyss. But it did not vanish completely. Torgo felt the power there.

The Witch's screams waned. She lapsed into a deep sleep, maybe a coma. Torgo destroyed the tent, killed the fire in the braziers, fanned fumes away. Tears stained his cheeks.

Had he been fast enough?

She should have foreseen this. She should have trained him for this. In his ignorance all he could do now was watch and wait and hope that Gorloch would be merciful and permit her return from that far darkness into which she had fallen.

Power streamed from the child.

Outside, clouds began to gather.

13

Aaron entered the house and found the females all prickly and sullen. "Now what?" He was not in the mood for it. Things had not gone well at work that afternoon. The Herodians were sorting themselves out to line up behind the civil or military governors and were trying to frustrate one another by giving conflicting orders to their Qushmarrahan employees.

Arif said, "Nana's mad at Mish because she took Yoseh some food."

Mish said, "You *told* me to do it."

"A damn fool idea, Aaron," Raheb said. "And you didn't have to behave like a trull, Tamisa."

Laella snapped, "She did nothing of the sort, Mother. Tamisa, you shouldn't have spent all that time talking to him. It didn't look right."

"Maybe I just wanted to hear somebody talk who could say a whole sentence without cutting me down or bellyaching about something."

Point to Mish, Aaron thought.

Stafa said, "I ride horsy, Dad."

"You did? Arif, come here. Tell me what you and Stafa did today while Mom and Mish finish getting supper ready."

The women got the message.

It was not a world where women dared long exasperate even a man as gentle as Aaron.

He took Stafa into his lap and Arif under his right arm and they talked about camels and such till it was time to eat. The boys were exceptionally quiet during the meal. The women said nothing. He supposed he must be looking very fierce. Maybe they were all waiting for some giving of the law.

Let them stew. He could use the quiet.

It did not last, of course. But the women were not the instrument of its death.

There was, to his dismay, a tapping at the door. He was more dismayed when he opened it to find Reyha and Naszif outside. He stepped out of their way. They came in without saying anything. Both looked awful. Laella rose slowly, face pallid, as though some horror had come through the doorway with them.

Laella held Reyha for a moment, then helped her sit down. Naszif settled beside her, opposite Aaron. They looked one another in the eye, each knowing what the other knew. Mish moved the boys away.

Naszif said, "Reyha told you some things she would have been wiser to have kept to herself, as she learned today. She had a visit from the Living. Now you're in it, too, like it or not. The Living will be watching."

Reyha stared at her folded hands.

"She came to see you last night. This morning they came to see her. They knew she'd come into Char Street but not where she'd gone. They wanted to know that, and who she'd seen, and what she talked about. They were insistent. A very important man of theirs was murdered last night, here in Char Street, about the time she was out, and they think they have reason to believe a woman was responsible."

"Bel-Sidek's father!" Aaron blurted.

"Eh?"

"The old soldier who lives up the street."

"Khadifa," Raheb interjected.

Aaron scowled at her. "The old guy with the bad leg from

Dak-es-Souetta. When I was going out to work this morning there were people at his house. I got nosy and went up there. He told me his father died during the night. I wasn't surprised because the old man had been bedridden since they moved in."

"Bel-Sidek," Naszif mused. "That fits. He sounds like the man who visited Reyha. He had a bad leg. She'd seen him before but didn't recall who he was. He knew all of us. He didn't really believe Reyha had done anything. He thought she had come here to visit Laella. But he wanted to be sure."

Aaron was disturbed by the man opposite him. This was not the Naszif to whom he was accustomed. This Naszif was calm, collected, in complete control, and altogether too businesslike. He did not know what to make of the apparent change.

Naszif continued, "Reyha can be very stubborn. She refused to tell them anything till they gave Zouki back."

"Which they refuse to do because they'd lose their hold on you."

"No. According to the crippled man they can't do that because they don't have him in the first place."

"What?"

"Yes. Despite the fact that they took me to see Zouki last night, this morning one of them is denying that they have him. And I think he was sincere. If he'd had that advantage he would have used it. On the other hand, Reyha thinks she recognized the voice of one of the men with the cripple, subject to his orders, as that of one of the men who took me away last night."

Aaron had begun to get a bad feeling about this Naszif that he did not know. He was up to something.

"Is there something going on inside the Living? Are there factions operating without recourse to the established chain of command?"

"What are you doing, Naszif?"

"Thinking out loud. Consider. I'm sure the man who took me out last night, and who was with bel-Sidek today, is a character named Hadribel. Hadribel is the number two man of the Living in the Shu. He was taking orders from bel-Sidek. And bel-Sidek said, at least by implication, that the man who had died was more important than him. Who was that man, really? And who would dare murder him?"

"That's enough, Naszif. I've figured out what you're doing. I'm not going to let you use me. You had your one shot at getting me killed and got away with it. You don't get a second chance."

Naszif frowned, pretending he did not understand.

"Almost two hundred from our tower survived the Herodian prison camps, Naszif. Most of them came back to Qushmarrah. Some work down at the yard. You remember Big Turi? Bad Turi we called him sometimes. What do you think Turi would do if someone told him it was our buddy Naszif that opened that postern that night?"

Naszif looked troubled. Laella said, "Aaron! You stop that kind of talk."

"Be quiet. And use your head. What happens after he fills me up with everything he knows or guesses? The Herodians somehow get a sign, they grab me, and Naszif gets his message through. So what if old Aaron gets himself busted up some while they're getting him to tell them what he wants them to know? He gets rid of Aaron and he gets rid of one of the ways he's vulnerable."

Laella looked at Naszif, whose face was a blank, then at Reyha, who stared at her hands still, shaking as she shed silent tears. "Reyha?"

Reyha said nothing. She did not look up.

Straining her old bones till their creak sounded in the silence, Raheb moved to the hearth where she began adding wood to the fire.

Aaron's throat was so tight he was afraid he was squeaking when he said, "The guys who survived our outfit don't belong to the Living or anything, Naszif. But they've got it all planned out, what they're going to do when they find out who opened that postern. It's going to take them a long time to get that far, but the last thing they're going to do is send him out to run through the streets without his skin on."

He could not believe this was him talking. Never in his life, that he recalled, had he threatened anyone.

"I've kept quiet for six years, out of concern and respect for Reyha and Zouki. But now you've forfeited my silence by denying me and mine an equal concern and respect. Now you have to buy my silence. You will go out of my home and out of my life and forget I even exist. If you ever speak my name to anyone and I hear about it I'll see that yours is mentioned to those of our company who survived."

Naszif met his gaze briefly, saw that there was nothing more that could be said or done. He rose.

Raheb turned from the hearth. Clutching a large, greasy carving knife, she threw herself at Naszif. Aaron did not move fast enough to deflect her assault completely. The knife ripped a gash almost the length of Naszif's left arm.

It was eerie. Nobody made a sound. Faces pale, eyes filled with horror, they all watched in silence as Aaron disarmed the old woman, who stopped struggling the instant he did so. In a calm voice she said, "Sixty thousand murders blacken your soul, Naszif bar bel-Abek." She spat on him as Reyha, eyes still downcast, tried to look at his arm. "Sixty thousand curses upon your grave, may it be an early one."

Pale and terrified, Naszif backed toward the door. Reyha opened it for him. They went out. Aaron closed it behind them.

Still there was no sound except a soft sniffle from Laella. Raheb went back to her chores. The boys clung to Mish, frightened. In some symbolic gesture he did not understand himself, Aaron stabbed the carving knife into the door and left it quivering there as he went to comfort his sons.

He eased back from the boys and told them, "Go hug Mom. She needs you." They toddled right over, somewhat reassured.

Aaron watched, the fear snarling inside him.

"Aaron?" Mish said in a small voice.

"Uhm?"

"When I was talking to Yoseh . . . His brother Nogah said he stayed all night in Tosh Alley last night. In the middle of the night, he said, he saw the most beautiful woman he's ever seen. She came from up the hill. She came down and stopped in front of our door for a few minutes. Then she disappeared in the fog."

"Uhm?" The fear grew stronger.

"That man said they thought a woman k-killed Mr. bel-Sidek's father. If Nogah saw a beautiful woman, that couldn't have been Reyha."

"I suppose you're right."

Someone knocked.

Fear filled Aaron's home.

Bel-Sidek was just steps from his door when he saw the traitor and his woman leave the carpenter's home. What now? Didn't he have troubles enough? Now the traitor was going to go roaming around anywhere he felt like?

He eased into shadow and let them pass. They did not notice. They were engrossed in themselves. The woman moved with difficulty, still feeling the effects of her stubbornness this morning. The traitor carried his left arm oddly, as though it was injured.

The khadifas would begin arriving any moment. But this bore investigation. With a resigned sigh he limped to the carpenter's door. He knocked.

The door opened. The coldness that came into the man's face was so intense bel-Sidek retreated a step. "May I come in?"

"No."

Forthright and rude, that answer flustered him. What could he do?

But the carpenter surrendered some of his advantage. He stepped outside, closed the door behind him. "We aren't interested in the games being played around here, old man. By you or anybody else. Leave us alone."

"Qushmarrah . . ."

The carpenter spat at his feet. "You're not Qushmarrah. Thieves and extortioners, torturers of women and stealers of children, claiming they speak for Qushmarrah?" He spat again.

Bel-Sidek could not restrain his anger. It had been piling up all day. "Aaron, we've never touched a child!"

"If you believe that, you're a fool. A fool without an idea what those who owe him allegiance are doing in his name. And for that I fear you more than I fear you for all the knives you can send in the dark. A knife can kill a man but a fool can kill a city."

"Aaron . . ."

"Ask yourself, if you truly believe the Living aren't stealing children, how it is that they can *show* a man the child that was taken from him. When you have an answer, if you care to share it with me, you might find me more inclined toward conversation."

Bel-Sidek did not know what to say. The carpenter was behaving so far out of character, was so upset, that anything might make him do something crazy.

"Aaron . . ."

"Just stay away and leave us alone. You ignore me and I'll ignore you."

"All right, Aaron. I'm a reasonable man." And it was no time to press.

"I'm glad to hear that. If it's true. One thing I might owe you. A Dartar warrior who spent the night hiding in Tosh Alley saw a woman pass in the middle of the night. He didn't know her. He described her as the most beautiful woman he'd ever seen. Dartars are strange but I don't think they're strange enough to confuse my wife's friend Reyha with beauty. Good night."

Bel-Sidek stood there a minute after the door closed behind the carpenter, the only thought in his mind the certain fact that the Living were losing the war of the heart even where men had the most cause to hate the conqueror.

He turned away and began to labor uphill. This might be something instructional he might mention during his confrontation with the khadifas.

Azel left Muma's Place soon after sundown. A few experimental maneuvers showed him that Colonel Bruda's men were still on him. He spotted four. That big an effort suggested there might be more, less easily spotted. He must have stumbled good.

He took only the routine precautions of a man who did not expect to be followed. Let them get comfortable and confident. He would shake them later, when he needed to.

He drifted into the Blessed Way, a waterfront to acropolis avenue a quarter mile north of Char Street, but left it immediately. Herodian soldiers were busy there, questioning anyone who ventured into the street. He wondered what was up but had no time to find out.

The watchers tracked him through the narrow ways only because he did not care whether they stayed with him or not. They would not learn anything interesting.

Shortly before he reached the place where bel-Shaduk stayed, he did lose them simply by stepping around a corner, then scrambling to a rooftop. He scurried across the tops of several houses, to a point from which he could watch bel-Shaduk's place.

It leaked a lot of light.

Most Qushmarrahans went to sleep soon after nightfall, their working hours dictated by economics and the availability of natural light. Ishabal's place being so lighted suggested that all Azel's guesswork was adding up the way he expected.

"I thought he had better sense," Azel muttered.

The lights faded soon after he took his position. A man stuck his head outside. He saw nothing. He came out. A whole squad, seven more men, followed. They scattered but it looked like they had some common destination.

Azel thought he knew what that was. He set off across the rooftops, headed south. Easier to do that than try to follow somebody and maybe get spotted. As long as he'd guessed right about where they were going.

"The damn fool," he grumbled to himself. "She must have offered him a fortune."

He ran into no trouble. The lords of the roofs were lying low tonight. He wondered if that was an omen. He hoped it was just the weather. The drizzle made the footing troublesome.

He found himself a perfect position overlooking Char Street long before Ishabal's gang arrived. He even had time to scout his, and their, most likely avenues of retreat.

The damn fool was going to try it.

Ought to be interesting.

He settled down to watch. His vantage was perfect, tactically, but it was damned wet.

General Cado went over Rose's letter for the third time, almost character by character this time. Colonel Bruda stared out a window, toward the harbor, pleased that there was an overcast and an unseasonable chill. That would keep some people off the streets tonight. Maybe the troops could be moved without being noticed at all.

Cado asked, "How much of this do you buy?"

"All of it and none of it. I think Rose is telling us the truths he believes. That doesn't mean somebody hasn't been lying to him."

"I grow more curious about our Rose by the hour. He told me he learned to speak Herodian when he was a sailor, before the conquest. But how many merchants can read and write their native tongue, let alone a foreign one?"

"He's done great work for us."

"I know. I know. This is an example if only half is true." He tapped the letter, leaned forward, glared down at it. "General Hanno bel-Karba, presumed dead for six years, murdered, by witchcraft, the same night the Living slaughtered Sullo's Moretians on the estate of the woman who believed herself to be bel-Karba's widow. Our man Rose actually gets to see and identify the body because by lot he gets chosen to be a guard at the funeral. Do you buy that?"

"I can't refute it. His reported movements are consistent with his claims."

"But you didn't have him under observation every minute."

"No. He's a cautious man. He takes extensive precautions routinely."

"And he says he thinks somebody is watching him and if it's us would we kindly lay off and stop attracting attention because his bosses in the Living are never going to believe we think he's important enough to rate that much trouble."

Bruda smiled. "He's always been a brassy bastard."

"He's always been a bastard who doesn't add up."

"But useful."

"No matter how useful I'll never completely trust a man who won't accept a commission in the army. He's the only Qushmarrahan agent we have who hasn't enlisted and converted."

Bruda stared into the night.

"Keep watching him."

"I intend to. If only because I've never been able to find out who he is or where he came from. I have to satisfy my own curiosity."

Cado grunted. He let Bruda stare at the night while he read the letter again. "What's the implication here? Sullo had his witch avenge his Moretians?"

Bruda shook his head. "It would be something deeper. The acts don't balance. If Sullo had bel-Karba killed it wouldn't have been because of the Moretians. I don't think he knew about them till he opened that trunk."

"Uhm? Spin me a fable."

"I'll posit you a problem first. You know Sullo. He comes to Qushmarrah and right away stumbles onto the fact that Hanno bel-Karba is alive and running the Living. Even better, he finds out where to lay hands on the old man. What does he do?"

That was an easy one. "He snaps him up, whatever the cost, parades him around, and gets us laughed out of town as raging incompetents."

"He didn't."

"He didn't. Could he be playing for higher stakes?"

"Maybe." Bruda stared out the window, rehearsing his theory. He had given it a great deal of thought since first he had read Rose's letter. "You recall the death in the Hahr the other day? The reputed khadifa of the Hahr?"

Cado grunted.

"The public consensus in the Hahr now is that he was put away by the Living, not thieves. Because he had been using his position to enrich himself and his cronies, not to work against Herod. He was moving into all the usual underworld activities. His death was an example to the other khadifas, some of whom were involved in rackets in their own quarters. He was proof that nobody was immune to the law of the movement."

"You're going to spin me that fable now?"

"Yes. I think Marteo Sullo is an ambitious man. I think he harbors notions toward achieving the imperial honors. I think someone inside the Living offered him an alliance in return for removing that pesky old man. Access to an organization like the Living, which has contacts with malcontents everywhere, would be invaluable to an ambitious and unscrupulous man."

"Maybe so." General Cado read the letter for the fifth time. It contained other speculations of interest. "Suppose Sullo is up to something? How do we catch him?"

"We don't need to. I can manufacture evidence."

"What are you thinking?"

"Suppose we have Rose send Sullo away in imitation of a Living execution, then the story of a deal with a khadifa of the Living, who reneged, gets out?"

Cado laughed. He got up and joined Bruda at the window. Bruda watched tricklets of water slide down its outer face.

"You're more devious than I suspected."

"We'd be rid of Sullo, with the onus on the Living. They'd be discredited and chasing each other around trying to catch the villain."

"A double kill. I like it." Cado chuckled. "Give me a day to think about it and see what develops. You look for holes in it."

In the Dartar compound, with security verging on the absurd, Fa'tad al-Akla closeted himself with his ten most trusted captains, all of them men who had ridden with him twenty years or more. He had digested the day's reports from the Shu maze and was confident both that the myths he was feeding were groundless and that the denizens of the labyrinth were compressed just short of the point where desperation would overcome terror and they would fight back.

The Eagle told them what he intended.

They were appalled. They were aghast at his daring. They enthused. Their response delighted him. He was a mischievous old devil.

One of Joab's brothers, Bega, sometimes a too-practical sort, said, "I'm no mason. Will the mortar set up properly in this weather?" The rains were light but steady now.

Fa'tad did not know. It did not seem a critical question. All but a few exits from the maze had been sealed already. Tomorrow the masons would close the exits to the roofs. And that would be that, except for the final, critical few.

In the Shu, Yoseh retreated from the mouth of Tosh Alley, found Nogah. "You'd better come look," he whispered. "Something is getting ready to happen out there."

In the citadel, Zouki wakened for the first time since his encounter with the Witch. He was confused and frightened though he did not remember much. The memories he did have seemed half alien. Dreams awake. Places and events he never saw. Everything too elusive to grasp. Something worming around inside his brain. Someone else. Terror.

Thunder crashed outside.

Merciful sleep took him again a moment later.

In his quarters, Torgo paced. He was worried. He was frightened. Something unusual had happened. He did not understand. He needed the Witch to tell him what to do. And she could not be wakened.

Azel had not yet come for the boy. He was late. Way late. And it was almost time for Ishabal to show. Should he carry out his orders?

In his home in the Shu, Sisu bel-Sidek asked his khadifas to put forward the names of men they considered worthy of becoming their equals.

In Char Street, Ishabal bel-Shaduk gave his henchmen the agreed signal.

14

The boys were over the excitement and asleep. The women were not. Aaron doubted he could fall asleep easily, either. But it was time. He had to work tomorrow. Weather permitting.

One more day. Then his day off. By the time he went back, he hoped, the Herodian managers would have worked out their political differences and everybody could get back to building ships.

He reached out to snuff the candle.

Someone knocked on the door.

He cursed softly. Then thought the hell with them. Then realized that the knock was much firmer than those of Reyha or bel-Sidek. He felt a little twirl of fright.

The knock came again. Laella, her mother, and Mish all sat up and looked at him.

There had not been a major crime in Char Street since the Dartars had become interested in the maze. Nobody would be dumb enough to try something with a dozen of them watching from Tosh Alley.

He went to the door, glancing bemusedly at the carving knife. He had forgotten to remove it. The women were not about to

225

touch it. They were going to pretend he was lord and master for a day or two.

He slipped the latch, drew a breath to speak as he started to pull the door inward.

It slammed into him, knocking his breath out and hurling him back to land on his seat. Two men charged inside. One tripped over his outstretched leg and plunged headlong into the opposite wall. Two more charged in behind the first two. One stopped, held a knife at Aaron's throat. He gaped up at the man, lost.

The women started screaming.

A man in the doorway snapped, "Hurry up and grab him, damn it!"

One inside said, "Where the hell is he? Ho. There."

Laella shrieked, "Arif! No!"

Mish came flying across the room, landed on the back of the man threatening Aaron. Aaron staggered to his feet while he was distracted. He tried to slam the door. It smacked into the man standing in the doorway.

Old Raheb smashed a heavy crock down on the head of the man who had charged into the wall.

Aaron grabbed the carving knife and stuck it into the man who had threatened him. He did not remember anything they had taught him in the army. There were no thoughts in his head, just rage and terror. He stuck the knife in and it lodged between ribs.

One of the two still standing flung Laella across the room. The remaining man grabbed Arif, turned, kicked Raheb in the stomach, headed for the door while his companion tried to lift the man the old woman had crowned.

Aaron grabbed at the knife dropped by the man he had stuck. The man carrying Arif saw him blocking the way and in his eyes Aaron saw the dawning fear that he was not going to get out of this place.

The edge of the door slammed into Aaron's back. The man carrying Arif struck him in the side of the neck with a clumsy blow and bulled past. Outside, somebody yelled, "Ish! Trouble!"

The last man dumped his burden and charged. He kneed Aaron in the face, viciously, before going out.

After a moment, Aaron recovered himself, seized the knife. Bleeding from mouth and nose, he stumbled into the street, chasing the screams of a boy crying for his dad.

Yoseh and Nogah were near the mouth of the alley when the screaming started. They stepped out, looked down the street, saw what was happening. Nogah whirled and yelled, "Come on!" into the alley, then headed for the action.

A man popped out of shadow, yelled, "Ish! Trouble!" and tried to head them off.

Nogah cut him down with his saber.

Yoseh carried a javelin. He flung it a moment later, at a man who came into the street carrying Arif. He threw without worrying about the boy, a perfect cast that struck the man square in the center of the chest.

Another man grabbed the struggling child. Another came out the doorway. More charged out of the darkness downhill. Dartars poured out of the alley behind Yoseh.

The man with the child went to his belt in exactly the way that man in the alley had the other day. Yoseh threw his forearm across his eyes and tried to shout a warning to the others.

Intense light. Screams. Yoseh flung his arm down and ran forward. The man with the boy dropped his own arm, was astounded to find he was being rushed by a Dartar with a knife.

His hand went back to his belt.

Yoseh covered up again. The din rose to a ferocious level as Dartars from the alley, come out too late to be blinded, attacked anyone not wearing black. Men screamed. The child-stealers did not have weapons to fight swords and javelins. Nogah yelled, "Don't kill them all! Take some prisoners!"

There was no second blinding flash. Instead, Yoseh took a blow to the belly like the kick of a mule. He went down, gagging, unable to draw a breath. His stomach emptied. Even after there was nothing more to throw up the heaves continued.

He was vaguely aware of the villain moving away, of Medjhah arriving just in time to keep Kosuth from skewering Arif's father, of a quick passage at arms in which Medjhah and Kosuth

murdered another of the child-takers, then he was on his feet
again with the help of the boy's father.

The man who had Arif ducked into the first alley downhill, on
the north side of Char Street. Yoseh yanked his javelin out of the
man he had hit earlier. He and the boy's father took up the chase,
stumble-running like a couple of drunks in the direction of Arif's
screams.

Azel shook his head as the Dartars came piling out of Tosh
Alley. That dumb shit Ishabal did not know they were there.
Fool. Why hadn't he scouted the area again before he made his
move? Now he would pay.

Ishabal used some flash. Big deal. That wasn't going to change
anything now.

Whoa! What was this?

Four men charged into the chaos from up the street.

Azel chuckled. Those were Bruda's boys, come to see about
the ruckus. They must have followed Ishabal's men when they'd
lost him.

The Dartars didn't give a shit who they worked for. They
weren't wearing black. They piled on.

Ha! Ishabal had given up on flash and changed to punch. He'd
opened a clear path out, downhill, and he wasn't wasting it.

Azel prized himself up off the roof and bounded away,
muttering because his muscles had stiffened up in the few
minutes he had lain there in the cool and damp.

It was easy to figure what a man was going to do when you
knew what he had to do. Ishabal had to shut that kid up or he
wasn't going to get away. And he had to do it without hurting the
kid or the whole exercise was pointless. He would need a lead,
which he had, then a place where he could get his back to a wall
for a minute.

Azel knew a perfect place. If Ishabal had done his scouting
right, he would know it, too, and would be headed there right
now.

Azel took the shorter, straighter route over the rooftops.

The place was a cul-de-sac between buildings, three feet wide and ten deep, black as Nakar's heart inside, a deathtrap that would be avoided by anyone not armed with the confidence that came of having flash and punch and whatever else at hand.

Azel dropped into that place and folded himself up in a ball in the back, waited, wondered if he would stiffen up too soon.

Ishabal came, a vagueness moving in blackness. He faced out of the narrow place and went to work doing whatever he needed to do to quiet the brat down. Azel used the last of the racket to cover whatever sound he made unwinding and moving forward.

He did something to give himself away. The vagueness that was Ishabal stiffened, started to react an instant before Azel set the point of his knife against his spine and said, "Don't."

Ishabal froze. "Azel?"

"You really screwed it up, Ish. Going to have the whole city going crazy, trying to figure it out. And they're going to figure it once they start digging."

"I told them. They don't care. She says this kid is the one she wants. Look, we got to get out of here. They aren't that far behind me."

Ishabal was pretty good. Azel almost missed the minuscule warning hitch as he went to his belt. Almost.

Azel thrust. Ishabal bucked away from the killing blade. The flash packet flew from his fingers unopened, hit, spilled a few grains, began to burn slowly instead of exploding. Azel pushed the dying man away and squatted to collect the now unconscious boy.

A foot scraped. He looked up into the eyes of the same Dartar he'd run into twice before.

He clamped down on the rage that seized him, surged upward, flung the boy toward the sky, so that the upper half of his body landed on the roof and held him there. Then he faced the Dartar and his companion in the light of the smoldering flash.

So. He would leave them here with Ishabal. It would make a fine puzzle for whoever found them, the three of them all dead and the boy gone.

"You just got in my way one time too many, camel boy. This one is the last time." He moved forward.

In response the Dartar uncovered his face. Hell. He wasn't nothing but a kid. A shaky kid carrying a knife in his left hand, with his right hand tucked up behind him like he was wounded or something.

Azel moved in.

The Dartar's hand came out thrusting with a javelin.

Azel dodged and blocked just well enough to keep from getting killed. The head of the javelin sliced along his left cheek and ruined his ear. He grabbed the javelin's shaft and pulled.

The Dartar hung on and kicked violently with his left foot. Azel turned his hip to take the blow but it came higher than he anticipated, struck squarely on his right elbow, numbing his arm so badly he could not hang on to his knife. He kneed the Dartar and at the same time flailed the numb arm hard enough to knock the knife out of the boy's left hand. The Dartar pulled himself in and clung. Azel started to crush him in a bear hug.

The second man's knife came in and ripped along his ribs, a hairline of fire.

The kid was trying to hold him while the other man killed him.

He kneed the Dartar again and felt his grip go watery with the pain. Azel shoved him back into the other man, backed away, jumped.

First try, his still half-numb arm betrayed him. He slipped back. He jumped again. As he went up, the Dartar's companion buried a knife in his right calf and tried to pull him back down. He kicked the guy in the head with his right foot, pulled himself onto the roof. He yanked the knife out of his calf, dragged the brat all the way onto the roof so nobody could grab a leg and pull him back down.

Azel heard nothing stirring below. He lay there panting and hurting for a minute, till he heard cautious voices approaching in the darkness. Then he got himself up, picked up the brat, and started moving.

He ignored the fires in his cheek and ear, his calf and side. He told himself he was too good to let a little pain distract him.

* * *

When the uproar broke out outside, Zenobel growled, "What the hell?" and headed for the door.

"Hold it!" bel-Sidek snapped. "Kill the lamps. Whatever it is, we don't want it getting interested in us."

By the time the lamps were out and bel-Sidek had gotten to the door and had opened it a crack, the uproar was that of a battle. Bel-Sidek said, "It's a band of Dartars slaughtering a bunch of Qushmarrahans."

Carza asked, "Why?"

"How should I know?" bel-Sidek was troubled.

Zenobel asked, "What are Dartars doing in Char Street at this time of night?"

"Why don't you go ask?" bel-Sidek backed away so the others could take turns peeking. Zenobel ended up being the sentinel at the crack who reported to the rest, sitting there in darkness. "They've gotten a torch lit. Collecting up the dead and wounded. Looks like three prisoners and seven dead. None of them Dartars. Make that eight dead. They just brought in another one. Looks like they're getting ready to question the survivors. Some more around a doorway down there, talking. Funny. Nobody's come out to see what's going on."

Bel-Sidek said, "It isn't strange, here where the night belongs to the beasts of the maze. Close it. They aren't interested in us. Let's keep it that way. Light a lamp, King. Just one. Can't anybody think of an alternative to Hanno bel-Kaifa?"

Salom Edgit asked, "Why don't you trust him?"

"I trust him, Salom. That's not the problem. I don't like him. The dislike is so strong I think it would affect my ability to work with him."

Zenobel took another peek outside. He planned to sneak another in a minute. He held the door closed with his hand instead of latching it.

It exploded inward.

The Dartars helped Aaron out of the alley. By the time they reached Char Street he could move under his own power.

Mumbling, he invited them to bring Yoseh into his home so they would have light to look him over.

Aaron stopped in the doorway. A Dartar with bare saber stood guard inside. The fallen invaders had been removed. Laella, battered but apparently all right, knelt over her mother, in front of the hearth. Across the room Mish sat against the wall and held Stafa tight against her breast. She sobbed softly.

Laella looked up. Aaron shook his head. Her face turned to stone. She rose, came to examine his injuries. He moved aside so the Dartars could bring Yoseh in. They invited themselves to bring all their injured. Laella did not protest.

She touched his face. He winced, asked, "How is she?"

"I think she's hurt inside." There was an edge of hysteria in her voice.

"Take it easy. What about you? How about Stafa and Mish?"

"We're all right." She leaned against him. "What did we ever do to those men, Aaron? How could they do that?"

"I don't know. I'm going to find out." He pushed her away gently, went to his toolbox, and took out a heavy, bronze-headed maul.

"What are you going to do?"

"Go break bel-Sidek's other leg, then twist on it till he tells me the truth." And he actually meant it when he said it, though it sounded absurd a second later.

"Aaron . . ."

"They've got Arif, Laella. Just like they've got Zouki. I can't stand still."

He started for the doorway. On his way he tapped Yoseh's two brothers. "Come on."

Bel-Sidek was completely boggled by the apparition in the doorway. The carpenter looked like he had been beaten half to death. He looked incredibly ferocious with a huge hammer in his hand. "Aaron?"

"I want my son back, bel-Sidek. Your men took him, and killed his grandmother, and if you don't get him back to me I'm going to see that whatever is left of you when I get done hangs from a Herodian gibbet."

Bel-Sidek felt the bite of fear. He understood the threat. The carpenter knew or suspected enough to do the movement irreparable harm. "Calm down, Aaron. I don't know what you're talking about. I don't have your son."

"Just like you don't know anything about Naszif's son, Zouki, but you can show him to Naszif anytime you want to make him do something."

What would the General have done in this situation?

The carpenter was getting a little nervous, his crazy anger deserting him. He had not expected to break into a room full of hard-faced men. He did not know what to do next.

He stepped forward, raising the hammer threateningly.

Zenobel, Carza, and Dabdahd responded. Zenobel had murder in his eye. Bel-Sidek said, "Wait."

A Dartar stepped through the doorway, set the tip of a saber against Zenobel's throat. Another followed, threatened King and Carza. They backed away carefully.

The first Dartar asked, "Is the old one the man who knows, Aaron?"

"I think so. If not him, one of them."

Bel-Sidek started. The carpenter had guessed who they were. But he had not betrayed them. Yet. "Aaron, what do you want?"

"You know: I want my son back. And I want you and yours to leave me and mine alone. Forever."

Or he would tell the Dartars where they could scoop up the whole ruling council of the Living.

A voice from outside said, "Nogah! Troops are coming."

The Dartar with the saber pushed Zenobel back among the others. He looked bel-Sidek in the eye. "I see your face, old man. And I will remember it." He raised a hand, removed his face cloth, revealed a gruesomely mutilated visage. "You have till the fog rises this high tomorrow night. Then I come for you."

He turned, gently urged the carpenter out the door. The other Dartar backed out behind them, closing the door.

"Silence!" bel-Sidek snapped, before they could start. "Do any of you not understand what just happened?"

He got back a babble of outrage.

They did not understand, except for Carza.

"Quiet, please. So you're not as familiar with Dartar customs as you should be. But none of you ever served with them. When the man removed his face cloth he was doing what Dartars call 'showing the face of death.' Essentially he took a vow to hunt us down if the missing child isn't returned. I remind you that most of the Dartars outside are probably his brothers and cousins. Family will assume the vow as a matter of course. When word gets around, the rest will probably take it on, too. It's just romantic enough."

Zenobel made a sound of disgust. He was prejudiced.

Bel-Sidek rose. "I know nothing about child-stealing, by the movement or anyone else. But I suspect some of you might." He dragged his aching leg toward the door. "I want to be informed if you do. There is a growing public perception of us as responsible, or at least involved, and that could destroy us." He opened the door a crack.

The tramp-tramp-tramp he'd been hearing was what it sounded like, soldiers marching. "They got here fast." He noted the dread Colonel Bruda with them and shuddered.

There was too much interest in this part of the Shu.

He saw tendrils of fog just rising into view. It was that early still? It seemed it should be much later.

What a day. What a hellbiter of a day.

How come Bruda had had troops armed and ready to move at a moment's notice? Had the jaws of doom begun to close?

"The fog is coming," he said. "The man gave us a chance. As soon as it can cover us we get out of here. Hopefully before those Dartars have an attack of intuition and realize what they missed scooping up. Don't ever come back here. I'm moving out. I'll contact you later. Make your own arrangements to disappear, just in case."

He watched the soldiers. His small hope they would clash with the Dartars died. Tempers flared but never flew out of control.

"I want that boy, gentlemen. He's somewhere in Qushmarrah and we have the resources to find him. If he's not in my hands by sundown I'm going to want to know why not. And I'm not likely to be in a very pleasant mood. Do you understand?"

Azel had had a good many years in which to learn to carry on despite pain. He had been injured worse and had managed. But he had been younger then and, to be truthful, better motivated. He was losing his zest for the game. Tonight the sinkhole country looked like a lot more than a pleasant fantasy. It looked like the sanest bet for sliding out of this without getting carved up into little pieces.

But he had a mission. Spying on everybody, playing games with them, that could go to hell. Bruda having him watched proved he had worked those angles for as much as he could. A smart man got out while he was ahead.

He was out. As of now. Let Bruda and Cado stew and fuss because he was not there to be used. They could buy another knife. Always plenty of those around. Let that new General of the Living fume because he did not keep his appointments, because he did not pass along all his secrets.

In five minutes he would disappear from the face of the earth.

But the thing with Nakar still had to be played out.

In these new circumstances he would have to work on that idiot Torgo, who might be the only tool available.

He stayed on the rooftops till he ran out of houses to cross. He came down only when he had to, to cross gaps too wide to leap. His wounds nagged him, the leg the worst. He successfully evaded trouble though the Shu continued full of excitement.

He perched on that last rooftop and watched the acropolis. The kid lay on the tiles beside him, snoring. The precipitation had picked up a little but still could not be called a rain.

Awful lot of activity tonight. Especially around Government House. Looked like a lot of sneakery. A lot more than could be accounted for by the excitement in the Shu. Lot of soldiery slithering around . . .

Cado was sneaking a bunch of his men down to the waterfront

while there was a good chance their movement would not be noticed.

The boy showed no sign of coming around so Azel waited with the patience of a lizard, rubbing his wounded calf. Once a whole parade of soldiers, civilians, and Dartars came out of Char Street and headed for Government House. The seeing was not good enough to be sure but he thought Colonel Bruda was the man in charge.

One more reason to get out of the game *now*.

He'd have to get a message to Muma, give him the same option. The man had been the perfect and faithful partner for years. He deserved his shot at getting away clean. He had his arrangements made. All he needed was the warning word.

Azel saw his chance soon after the crowd passed. He got hold of the kid and dropped down . . . His leg buckled. He almost lost the brat.

He managed to walk only by keeping his leg completely rigid. That made moving through the pattern to unlock the Postern of Fate abnormally difficult but he got it right the first time.

He found Torgo dozing inside, having failed to respond to the alarm or, more likely, having failed to arm the damned spell. "Torgo."

The eunuch surged up, reached for a blade like an overgrown pirate's cutlass.

"Easy, boy."

"Azel. I gave up on you . . . What happened to you?"

"We got trouble, brother. You want to take this kid? Before I collapse?"

Torgo looked at the boy like he was a poisonous snake.

"Easy now. He's the one you wanted bel-Shaduk to grab so bad. Ended up he couldn't, so I finished the job for him."

The eunuch took the boy almost tenderly, looked at Azel suspiciously. "Why couldn't Ishabal bring him in? How come you even know anything about it?"

"He didn't bring the brat in because he's too dead to walk. Come on. I'll tell you about it while I'm getting myself patched up."

Torgo took the child to the cage first.

Azel told the thing exactly as it had happened, from his sighting of Torgo to the moment Bel-Shaduk fled Char Street with the boy. Invention came into play only when he described how Ishabal had been cornered and killed by his pursuers.

He did wish he had been able to finish those two. It wasn't likely Torgo would run into them, and it probably wouldn't matter if that part did get unraveled, but any loose end was an artistic flaw.

On the other hand, he was a practical man. He could not take risk just to make sure loose ends got snipped.

"What about the boy you were supposed to deliver to the Living? Something bad happened with him, Azel. She was hurt. I had to hit her . . . She could be days recovering."

Azel frowned. What now? "Tell me. Everything."

Torgo showed his teeth, ready to balk. Then he gave in, obviously at a loss and desperate for direction. He described events minutely.

Azel had watched some of Nakar's sorcery in the old days. He did not know, but he suspected what had happened. She had encountered a strong soul and had not been prepared. Perhaps even Ala-eh-din Beyh himself.

The eunuch stared at the new brat. The one, if the woman was right. Azel was grim now, thinking how diminished he would be when this one was opened. Time to start wooing Torgo, lest he come up with a crazy idea of his own. "Two days and today turns into yesterday again, eh? That don't excite me the way it used to, Torgo. The other brat can wait. The Living can make do without. I wouldn't go back out there now if I could."

Best to make a thing of his injuries. Never hurt to have them underestimate you. "Too many people out there looking for me now. Hell. If the Living can't control their traitor for two days they don't deserve to share the fruits of victory. Do they?"

Torgo grunted. Azel was sure he was thinking about what he would lose in a few days.

Good. Perfect. Feed his obsession. But don't underestimate him. They'd robbed him of his balls, not his brain.

"I need a big favor, Torgo."

The eunuch gave him a suspicious look.

"There's this guy who's been helping us since the beginning. He don't know what he's been doing, of course. But he's played square all the way. He deserves a break. And he does know a lot somebody would find interesting if they grabbed him and made him talk. I need you to take him a warning from me that it's time to disappear."

Torgo frowned. "Why?"

"Crap, man! Because I owe him and I can't go out there. In another hour I ain't going to be able to walk. You understand a debt of honor? Hell. I don't know. Look. You and me, we never got along good. We don't like each other. We never took no trouble to hide that. But we been working together. Getting the job done. We got the same friends and the same enemies. Despite we don't like each other we done each other straight. So if it was you out there that needed warning I'd see you got it. If only because I don't never want nobody else to wring your fat ugly neck before I get my shot."

The eunuch was not convinced. "Where?"

"Place called Muma's. Just off the hilltop. Wouldn't take you twenty minutes."

Torgo grunted, asked, "Why should I do anything for you?"

"What do you want most in the world, man? Never mind. I think I know already. And I think I know how you could get it. Without no complications. I think I might even tell you about it sometime was you to do me this favor."

Torgo studied him for half a minute. "All right. What's the message?"

"I got to write it. He don't see it in my hand he ain't going to believe it." Muma could not read but Torgo did not need to know that. The message would be for his benefit. He'd snoop, sure. The symbol on the outside would be warning enough for Muma.

"I'll get things to write with." Torgo slouched out, still suspicious.

This was not going to be an easy seduction.

15

Aaron recognized the man in the doorway because a few years ago he had come to the shipyard regularly, to interview workers, either hunting for a spy or trying to recruit one. Colonel Bruda, General Cado's chief spy and bully.

His heart went cold.

Bruda looked around at injured family and injured Dartars. He did not seem upset, only mildly perplexed. A harmless little man, going bald. Nogah rose from his brother Yoseh's side and went to face him. They exchanged words Aaron did not catch.

Mish moved over beside Yoseh, said something softly. Aaron wondered if the kick in the face had impaired his hearing. Stafa came and clung to his leg. He was confused and scared still. Aaron scooped him up and settled him on his hip. He patted the boy's back gently. Stafa held on like he was afraid he was going to drown.

Bruda came to Aaron. "This is your home? Your family?"

"Yes sir." His voice quavered.

Bruda took hold of his chin, made him turn his face right and left. "You look like hell but you're not too badly hurt, are you?"

"No sir."

"Anyone badly hurt? They try to do anything besides take your son?"

"The old woman. My mother-in-law. They kicked her in the stomach. Something's wrong inside. My wife thinks she's dying."

"I see." Bruda moved to Raheb, glancing at Mish and Yoseh. "You're lucky these Dartars were around. You resisted. They might have killed you for that." He squatted opposite Laella, looked at the old woman for a moment, met Laella's eye. "No improvement?"

Laella shook her head.

Bruda rose and strode to the door, barked something in rapid Herodian. Aaron recognized only the words for "sergeant" and "two men." He looked at Nogah. Nogah shrugged helplessly.

Bruda spoke to his sergeant a moment, then came back to Aaron. "Did they try to take the younger boy, too, or just the one?"

"Just Arif." Aaron began to shake.

"Try to hang on and bear with us. What's your name?"

"Aaron. Aaron Habid."

"Aramite? That sounds Aramite."

"Yes."

"Not to worry, Aaron. I don't care about your religion. I've seen you before, haven't I? Where would that have been?"

"The shipyard. A few years ago."

"Of course. Master carpenter. Right?"

"Yes sir."

"What did you do during the war, Aaron? Engineers?"

"Yes sir. The Seven Towers."

A flicker of something stirred behind Bruda's eyes.

The sergeant and two soldiers came inside with a stretcher rigged from two spears and several cloaks. Bruda indicated Raheb, spoke in rapid Herodian, then told Aaron, "We're all going up to Government House where we can give everyone proper medical attention and maybe put our heads together to unravel this."

Aaron's fear betrayed itself.

Bruda smiled. "No, you don't have to worry about the rack and thumbscrews. I think you'll help me because I'm going to help you. If I can. Is there a neighbor you can have watch your place while you're gone? Or shall I leave a couple of soldiers?"

Aaron had become flustered. He could think of no one to ask to watch his home. But he did not want Herodians hanging around attracting attention, either.

Bruda read him. "I'll have them stay inside."

The soldiers had Raheb on their stretcher and were awaiting orders. Bruda spoke to his sergeant. The man ordered two more soldiers inside. The place had become painfully crowded. The stretcher bearers worked toward the doorway. Laella took Stafa from Aaron before she followed. He was grateful. The boy had become a load.

Mish followed her sister, not trying to hide her fright. Aaron followed her. The Dartars came after him. Aaron noted that Bruda had only a few, the brothers and two more. The rest must have scurried back into Tosh Alley.

The fog had climbed the hill. It was as thick as ever Aaron had seen it. Drizzle fell through it. The air was cold for the time of year. He could not stop shaking.

He glanced back at his home, wondered if he would see it again. He moved closer to Laella.

General Cado was waiting when Colonel Bruda brought in his catch. Five Dartars. A Qushmarrahan family. One prisoner. Two of his own men the Dartars had mistaken for kidnappers. And a lot of bodies. "Is this the lot?"

"Not all the Dartars. I have their leader, though."

"Good. Release those soldiers so they can get to their ship." Cado had his own guards on hand.

"I left two guarding the house. They'll need to be relieved."

"We'll take care of it. I've sent for Fa'tad, Sullo and his witch, and Colonel bel-Abek. Anyone else you need?"

"A physician. And Rose. Rose was watching the child-stealing gang. They split up when they set out to do tonight's job. My men followed members of the gang when they lost Rose, figuring they would find him again. They walked into the action and got mistaken for gang members. Luckily only one got killed."

Cado scanned the disparate collection of corpses and frightened people, summoned an aide, rattled orders, then returned to Colonel Bruda. "Have you learned anything useful?"

"My man Taglio has command of both the Qushmarrahan and Dartar dialects. From what he saw and heard the family thinks the Living did the kidnapping. The Dartars think we did."

"Us? Why?"

Bruda shrugged. "They aren't talking."

Cado looked at the cluster of Dartars, all young and tattered, all scared and defiant. "You feel it, too, Bruda? That there's something very dark slithering around just out of sight?"

"Assuming Rose told the truth, I have to keep wondering who killed General bel-Karba. Somebody that daring has to be somebody convinced he can handle any reprisals. Anyone that strong, belonging neither to them nor to us, is someone we have to worry about. We have troubles enough without adding another complication."

Cado's staff physician came in and went to the injured woman without having to be told.

"Did you send men to look for bel-Karba's body?"

"Yes. We should hear from them in the morning."

"What about the child? His parents look ordinary. Anything unusual about him?"

"No. I talked to the father extensively. He didn't want to speak up because he's afraid of the Living, but he did let slip a few things. He was in the same unit as Colonel bel-Abek during the war."

"Significant connection?"

"I don't think so. I get the impression he has no use for bel-Abek. The connection between them is their wives. They've been friends since childhood. I can't see any reason why anyone would want to twist the arms of either parent of tonight's victim. He's a carpenter. Her relatives are all sisters married to nobodies. And that old woman who's trying to die from a kick in the stomach."

Sullo and his witch arrived. The civil governor was irked at having his repose disturbed yet was pleased that his political enemy felt the need to include him in what was afoot. Cado wondered if he would behave like a spoiled child if he learned that he had been summoned only because the military governor wanted to use his witch.

He had Bruda explain to them, then explain again when Colonel bel-Abek and his wife arrived, guarded by a dozen soldiers. He watched the interplay, or lack thereof, between the bereaved mothers. Bel-Abek's wife, a drab thing he'd never before seen, seemed to be melting from shame. The other woman ignored her existence.

Colonel bel-Abek asked, "Can I talk to Taglio?" He seemed excited.

"Are you on to something?"

"I think the kidnapping may have interrupted a meeting of the ruling council of the Living. The man who headed the movement lived right there on Char Street. I learned that just today."

A man came in to report his inability to make contact with Rose. He had left a message. Cado thanked him and dismissed him. "Go on, Colonel."

Puffing up, bel-Abek said. "He was murdered last night. Whoever he was."

"Hanno bel-Karba," Bruda said.

"Sir?"

"General Hanno bel-Karba was the mastermind of the Living. We knew who had been killed, but not where or when."

Cado saw Fa'tad, alone, looking like a great black crow, standing in a shadowed doorway, listening, studying everyone. Cado listened with only half an ear as bel-Abek reported what he had learned about the leading men of the Living. Fa'tad would be interesting tonight. He'd always held a grudge against Herod because of the assassination of Hanno bel-Karba.

He saw he had been noticed. He came across the room like he was some great lord and they his house servants. He stopped in front of Cado. "I'm here," he said in Herodian without a trace of accent.

"Did you overhear enough to understand the situation? Or should Colonel Bruda brief you?"

"I'd better hear it all."

While Bruda told it yet again Cado visited Sullo and asked if he would have his witch see what she could do for the old woman. The physician looked like he did not have much hope.

He stepped back to Bruda and Fa'tad as Bruda finished. Bruda said, "I want to send a squad to that house. They'll be too late to catch anybody but they might find something useful."

"Go ahead. Fa'tad, why would your men think these child-stealings a Herodian scheme?"

Fa'tad looked him in the eye for five seconds, then said, "Yoseh, come here," in the Dartar dialect.

Yoseh was sitting two feet from Tamisa, not looking at her, she not looking at him, yet he felt they were somehow in closer communion than ever they had been on Char Street. He was frightened. So was she. All that gobbling in Herodian did not help.

Then Fa'tad came and he was three times as frightened as before.

Fa'tad chattered with Cado awhile. Then, like a hammer blow to the heart, he said, "Yoseh, come here."

Panicky, he looked at Nogah and Medjhah. No help there. They just nodded.

He rose stiffly, went to stand at Fa'tad's left hand. He looked down at the shine atop Cado's head and wondered that these hairless runts had been able to conquer everyone who stood against them.

Fa'tad said, "Yoseh, tell the General everything you know about the man you caught in the alley the other day."

"The child-stealer? Everything?"

"Yes. Go ahead."

"But I don't have any Herodian."

"He'll understand you."

Yoseh closed his eyes, took a deep breath, told it all, right up to the moment the man had gotten away from him and Aaron with Arif. When he finished and opened his eyes he saw that the General's sidekick had returned. The two Herodians exchanged glances. Cado said, "Rose."

"Has to be Rose," the other said, in Dartar dialect. "That explains why he's been such a mystery. He isn't our man at all. But whose is he?"

"We talked of an unknown dark force earlier," Cado said.

"That will be all, Yoseh," Fa'tad said. "Thank you. You did well."

Yoseh retreated hastily.

Cado watched the Dartar boy go. He was angry with himself. Plainly, Rose had been using and manipulating him all along. Possibly he had been doing the same with the Living. He had made no secret of the fact that he was a member. The massacre of the Moretians almost certainly was his fault. The alacrity with which the Living had moved meant he had access to people in the movement at the same level as he had had here in Government House.

"Colonel Bruda, send men to that place where we make contact with Rose. Have them arrest everyone they find there."

"Yes sir."

Cado told Fa'tad, "This man Rose has played me for a fool, as he played others for me in my service." Who *did* Rose serve? Neither Sullo nor Fa'tad, for sure. The Living seemed just remotely possible, though no one in the movement would have authorized him to give up some of the information he had turned over.

A free agent? Absurd. It offended any sense of the natural order. No one man could have the arrogance to believe he could step between Herod and the Living and play them against one another for his own purposes.

Speaking of which. What might they be? On the information available Rose's purposes were completely shadowed. The man could not be after wealth. He'd never taken much in the way of pay. Just enough for a man to get by. The power to stand in the middle and exasperate everyone? That did not seem sufficiently sinister.

Bruda was back.

"Are they off?"

Bruda nodded.

"Then let's see how our guests can help us. Let's all drag chairs or cushions over and chat. Colonel bel-Abek, would you translate for Governor Sullo? We'll do this in Qushmarrahan. Informally."

People moved into position. The "guests" looked troubled. Cado spoke directly to the Qushmarrahan family when he shifted to their language. "Our purpose here is to unravel this child-stealing business. I hope we can come up with some valuable clues by pooling what we know. Your motive for participating will be the restoration of your son. Likewise, Colonel bel-Abek. Then, too, you might find you're grateful for the help given the old woman."

Sullo's witch had worked some sort of quiet miracle. The pain lines had fled Raheb's face and she was sleeping peacefully.

"We from Government House will begin. I'll go first. Colonel Bruda will follow, then Colonel bel-Abek. I'll then ask our Dartar friends to reiterate what they know, then we'll pass on to you. Some little detail somewhere, hopefully, will give us the beginning we need to make before we can take the first step toward understanding what's going on. If we know that, we'll probably know what we have to do about it. Colonel Bruda, would you ask Taliga to send in food and drink? We're going to be here a long time. Tell him to have those corpses removed and searched, too. They're a distraction."

Cado waited a moment, then started. He held nothing back, even when it had no apparent bearing on the subject at hand.

Despite what was being discussed Aaron could not concentrate. His mind kept straying to what to say when it came his turn to talk. Or he worried about maybe missing work tomorrow. His employers were not understanding about absences.

He was trying to hide the unbearable now behind fear of the future.

Even so, what the Herodians said was interesting. And so open you could not help wondering what they would do with him after they had divulged so many secrets in his presence.

The Dartars talked, too, even including Fa'tad al-Akla, who did not have much to contribute except the name of a child-stealer who had been killed in the Astan.

"A Dartar outcast?" General Cado asked.

"Yes. A man of no honor, disavowed by his own father."

"And the one tonight was Qushmarrahan?" General Cado spoke to Colonel Bruda, who was receiving reports from his agents as things went along.

"Yes. A known villain. Reasonably competent. Independent. Very quiet the past six months, apparently. Till this. He was identified by the prisoner, who also told us where he lived. A search turned up a cache of antique gold and nothing else. There was nothing useful on the body. The prisoner knows nothing else. He was hired for the one job."

Aaron glanced at the prisoner. The man was numb, sitting there waiting to be executed.

"We'll deal with him later. So these child-stealers are very careful about giving anything away, are well paid, and were known criminals before becoming involved. Except Rose, who does not fit the pattern. He's been our agent for five years and the Dartar testimony would suggest he was an occasional visitor to the place in Char Street we now believe to have housed General Hanno bel-Karba and his chief of staff, Colonel Sisu bel-Sidek. We seem to have conflicting possibilities if we look for a connection between the Living and the crimes. Mr. Habid, would you tell us your story?"

Aaron jumped. The inevitable had come and still he was not ready. He sat there like a lump, tongue-tied.

Laella took it for some benighted, romantic, patriotic refusal to betray Qushmarrah and the Living. "Aaron! You tell them what they want to know! You don't owe the Living anything!" She glanced at her mother.

He did so, wondering how he could have acted so positively and violently just a few hours ago, when he'd never committed such a violence in his life, and now he could not open his mouth.

He forced himself to croak, "I owe Herod. And so do you."

"Damn what happened six years ago! This is about tonight! This is about our son! The Herodians will pay for their crimes when they walk through the Flame."

He opened his mouth.

"And you tell all of it. Hear?"

The slight sneer on Naszif's face galvanized him.

He started clear back at the Seven Towers. Each time his story touched upon Naszif he spoke with the utmost contempt. Once he invoked a Dartar proverb, "Beware the man who betrays your enemy unto you, for he will betray you unto your enemy," but the bolt missed its mark entirely and fell among scowling Dartars. He went on through Colonel Bruda's arrival in his home.

Laella beamed at him, sort of.

General Cado frowned. "That's an interesting story. As an oral journal. But it sheds very little light on our problem." He was pensive for a moment. "Colonel Bruda will read you a list of names. Interrupt if you recognize any of them. You and your wife, too, Colonel bel-Abek. Colonel Bruda?"

Bruda read a long list.

Only Reyha interrupted. She mistook one of the women's names for someone she knew who had the same name.

"I was afraid of that," General Cado said. "Let me ask you this, Mr. Habid. Do you personally know anyone besides Colonel bel-Abek who has lost a child?"

Aaron shook his head.

"Do you, Colonel bel-Abek?"

"Only Mr. Habid, sir."

"I thought so. So. We have no obvious common denominator." He spoke directly to Aaron. "Those were the names of parents who have lost children over the past three months. There is nothing to tie them together. They come from a variety of classes and trades. They live all over the city. None have ever served the Herodian name. Only two have ever been suspected of dealing with the Living. None were at the Seven Towers though most bore arms during the conflict. Our man Rose is the only male Qushmarrahan I know who claims he didn't, which makes me doubt his veracity. You and your wife, and Colonel bel-Abek and his wife, are the only parents we can find with ties of any kind, however strained. That would seem to argue that the children themselves are indeed what the thing is all about. But we can't see that they have anything in common, either."

Aaron felt General Cado was looking at him as though he expected him to have the answer. All he could do was shrug.

A silence set in. Laella finally broke it. "They were born the same day."

"What?" General Cado asked.

"Arif and Zouki. They were born the same day. They have that in common." Laella did not look up at the Herodian.

"That's reaching for it. But . . . When were they born?"

"The last day of the fighting. The seventh day of the Moon of Ripening. Malach in the calendar of the Old Gods. I don't know what your people call it."

"We use a different calendar. What do you think, Colonel Bruda?"

Bruda was leafing through his documents. "I only have two dates of birth. They didn't seem much use at the time. But. One is down as seventh Malach, the other as the seventh day of the Moon of Ripening. Both children six years old. I only have four children on the list who aren't six. Those are all older. Ransom was demanded and paid. No ransom demands were made in any of the other cases though several of the children have been found and restored to their parents."

Colonel Bruda looked at General Cado. General Cado looked at Colonel Bruda. Everyone else looked at them. Cado said, "Get the dates of birth checked tomorrow. For now we'll assume they're the critical connection. But that just sets up a whole new puzzle. Why does being born that day make them important enough to round up?"

Naszif had been translating everything for Sullo's benefit. Sullo's witch had listened but with apparent scant attention.

She rattled a sudden question in Herodian.

General Cado said, "She wants to know what state the restored children were in. Colonel Bruda doesn't know."

Aaron recalled what Billygoat had told him. "I heard about a couple who were found wandering along Goat Creek. They had lost their memories of almost everything."

Fa'tad, in Qushmarrahan dialect, said, "My men found several such children this week. They were as the veydeen says, blank stretches of sand."

Aaron watched the witch as Naszif translated. She became increasingly agitated. Beads of sweat formed on her forehead. She asked a question when Naszif finished.

"She wants to know who died that day," Fa'tad said. "What great man."

Most everyone knew but no one spoke till Aaron, puzzled, said, "Ala-eh-din Beyh and Nakar the Abomination."

The witch moaned. For a moment it looked like she would faint. Then she pulled herself together and began rattling away in shaky Herodian.

Bel-Sidek had laid himself down certain he was too tense to sleep, but invidious slumber had slipped up and taken him unawares. The touch of a hand awakened him. He jerked up, flailing around after a weapon.

"Easy. It's Meryel."

He relaxed, searched her face in the wan light of the lone candle she had brought into the room. "Bad news?"

"It isn't good. The Herodians are rushing around everywhere. Colonel Bruda's men. They've been through your place on Char Street. They raided Hadribel's house. He got out a step ahead. They tore apart a place in Rhatiq Lane that was used by a criminal named Ishabal bel-Shaduk. They hit a hostel operated by a man named Muma and arrested everyone there, but Muma and his family had fled. They're still very busy in the Shu, rounding up suspected members of the movement."

"The traitor didn't stay in line. My fault. I shouldn't have pressed his wife so hard."

"They've arrested him, too. And everyone involved in the fight in Char Street. A child was stolen."

"I know."

"There's something big going on at Government House. Cado brought in Sullo and Fa'tad."

Bel-Sidek thought a moment. "It has to be the traitor. He's given them something to make them think they can break us. We'll have to fight back. I don't want to start a bloodbath but we can't stand still and take it." Zenobel would launch the counterattack. His men were the best prepared and his quarter held the greatest number of sympathizers ready to spring to arms.

That was the traditional plan. Let Zenobel begin, draw the Herodians, then loose Carza. While those two were embattled the men of the weaker quarters would massacre all Herodians, soldier or civilian, and sympathizers in their quarters before adding their weight to the forces of Zenobel and Carza.

"Did they actually put troops aboard their ships?"

"About twenty-five hundred. Including all their Herodian cavalry. Marco is in command. They sail with the morning tide."

Good. That left him facing only one legion and some odds and ends, plus the balance of the Dartars. "I'll move after the Dartars are back in their compound tonight."

If the thing was to start at night, as preferred, Zenobel's first objective would be to seize the Gate of Autumn so the Dartars could not become a factor in the fighting.

His one question was, had the traitor been able to betray the strategy?

Unlikely. Only the khadifas were completely informed. Only Carza and Zenobel had tactical roles so narrowly defined they had had to give their underlings some information about what ought to happen.

"I'll need writing materials and someone to carry messages. Damn! It has to come now, when the ruling council is in disarray and we're all on the run."

He could have Hadribel stay at the reins in the Shu and could cover the waterfront himself. That would leave the Hahr one big piece of unknown territory right in the middle of the city, and he could only hope the organization there would take flame and do its part.

"You're sure you want to do this?"

"No. I don't want to. But I don't see any alternative."

Meryel went for writing materials. She seemed sad that the hour had come. He got himself up and together. He was sad himself, though he'd always known that only fire and blood would loosen Herod's chokehold on the city he loved.

Meryel was a long time coming back. He raised a questioning eyebrow. She said, "One of my underworld contacts dropped by. I had to see him."

"And?"

"He knew of no organized child-stealing operation. But he knew the name Azel." She shivered.

"And?"

"Azel is a professional killer. The most dreaded in Qushmarrah. Nobody knows who he is. Azel probably isn't his real name since Azel is the name of one of the seven demons who spring forth from Gorloch's navel to work his will in the world. Azel the Destroyer."

Bel-Sidek nodded. "Like Nakar the Abomination." He knew the mythology, though he had been born to a family that followed Aram. By the time of the conquest most of the ruling class had, though they had kept the ancient names awarded them during the primacy of Gorloch to distinguish themselves from the masses.

Meryel said, "This Azel learned his trade working for Nakar. He may have committed as many as a hundred murders on Nakar's behalf. He survived the conquest. A year later he seems to have gone into business for himself, but doing only the biggest jobs. Some people think he killed most of the civil governors. But since nobody knows who he is and he seems to have no associates to talk, nobody knows who paid him. Opinion divides up between Cado and the Living. Except for the thing in the Hahr the other day, which may have been an imitation of his style, he's been quiet for the past six months."

Bel-Sidek sat quietly, thinking, for so long she finally snapped, "Well? Don't you have anything to say?"

"Yes. I want to go out on the balcony."

He did not notice her exasperated shrug, just followed her outside, stood above the fog staring at the black hulk of the citadel of Nakar the Abomination. After ten minutes of silence, he said, "The murder was no imitation. The man was working for the General. I actually met him this morning." He related the circumstances.

"Why are you so troubled?"

"Because now I think I see the General's great secret plan for delivering Qushmarrah. And it's a plan with both feet firmly planted in insanity. He meant to conjure Nakar, and restore him, so he could unleash his evil wrath upon the forces of Herod."

He saw Meryel looking at him like he was more than a little crazy himself.

"What do you know about sorcery?" he asked.

"Nothing. And I want to keep it that way."

"I'm no sorcerer. Never wanted to be one. But I've heard things here and there." He jerked off onto a different tack. "I knew the boy who was carried off tonight. He was born the day Nakar was killed. His mother always mentions that when she talks about him. Not coincidentally, the traitor's son was born the same day. I'd wager most of the children taken this summer were born that day."

Her look had not grown more understanding.

"They're looking for the traveling soul."

"The what?"

"In the agony of death the soul forgets and flees the dying flesh. After a time it seeks out flesh in the agony of birth and attaches itself to a baby being born. It has forgotten its past life, yet it carries within it memories of all previous lives forever. A skilled sorcerer can reawaken those memories and restore someone who has died."

Meryel shuddered. Her expression now was one of doubt.

"They're looking for the traveling soul of Nakar the Abomination up there."

"Who is?"

"His wife. The Witch. And Azel the Destroyer. They're stirring through the souls of children, looking for Nakar. And judging from the effort they mounted tonight they think they've found him. She must have had a bitter falling out with the General if it was enough to make her come out and kill him."

"I'll trust you, Sisu. I'll do what you think needs doing. But I don't believe all that."

"But don't you see? It's the only way it all hangs together."

"They're all dead up there, Sisu. And they have been for a long time."

"We don't know that at all. We don't know what happened that day except that Nakar and Ala-eh-din Beyh killed each other. I think the Witch survived. I think she's been biding her time till the moment was ripe."

"You may be right." She was going to humor him. "But you have more practical problems right now. You're going to war in eighteen hours. Remember?"

He remembered. He went inside and began composing messages. But his thoughts remained on Nakar and the General's mad scheme for freeing Qushmarrah.

And as he thought, he gradually became aware that he had come face-to-face with the great moral choice of his life.

The General had loved Qushmarrah completely, unreservedly, blindly, and no price had been too great to pay to rid its streets of the tread of foreign soldiers. Bel-Sidek had loved that old man as blindly, but did he love him so much that he would allow his nightmare dream to come true?

Aaron stood at General Cado's right on a balcony high on the face of Government House. Cado stared through the drizzle at the citadel. Naszif stood at Cado's left. No one else was there. Aaron was not sure why the Herodian had brought them up, into the rain.

"Are you a courageous man, Mr. Habid?"

Aaron had had that question in his own mind often since the attack on his household. "No. Not usually."

"Can you be brave for the sake of your son?"

"I'll do whatever I have to do." If he could, he thought. He was not sure he would not freeze when it mattered most. Even the Seven Towers had been no true test of his mettle. He'd never had any options there.

"You don't sound sure of yourself."

"I'm a carpenter, General."

"Yes. That's right. You see that over there, Mr. Carpenter? The citadel? Your son is in there. I have no idea how much time he has, but you can bet they won't wait any longer than they have to. We have to do whatever we can as fast as we can. Or we all lose. I, a city. You, a son. I've already put in motion all the machinery at my command."

Aaron wished Cado would get to the point. The more the man danced around it the more nervous he became.

"There's one avenue yet to be pursued. The Living."

"What?"

"I want to appeal to Colonel bel-Sidek directly."

Aaron stared at the man. He was mad!

"I want you to go home and wait. I'm confident bel-Sidek will try to contact you. He'll want to know what went on here tonight and how much you told us. We'll make it easy for him. We'll hang you out there without anybody watching or protecting you so there's the best chance you can deliver my message. Your only resource will be Colonel bel-Abek, who will accompany you as my representative. Because he has as much at stake as you do."

This was Naszif's first hint of what his role was to be. Aaron noted that he did not seem thrilled. But he did not protest, either.

Aaron himself was rattled and confused. All he could say was, "But I have to work tomorrow."

Cado looked at him directly, amazed. "I'll intercede with your employer. Are you going to help or not?"

"What do I have to do?"

"Just go home and wait till you're contacted. Colonel bel-Abek will make my representation for a personal meeting."

"What about my family?"

"Take them with you if that makes you more comfortable. Or leave them here if you think that would safer." Cado turned to Naszif and began giving instructions.

Aaron paid no attention. He stared at the citadel but did not see it. He did not think much, either.

He had frozen, as he'd always feared he would.

"Mr. Habid? What are you going to do?"

"Yes. All right. I'll do it."

He felt ashamed. He had said that for no high, holy, or heroic reason but just because he wanted no one, ever, to judge him in comparison with a despicable creature like Naszif.

Azel slept poorly, not just because of his wounds. He had no trust in his own safety, though he had holed up high in the citadel, in a cubicle difficult to approach and easy to defend. Torgo had come once, to report his message delivered and maybe to be seduced a little more. He did not trust the eunuch not to return with a knife.

He wakened to the sort of spine tingle he got when danger was near, but a quick survey showed him it must be his imagination. Unless . . .

He watched out the small, glassless window for half a minute. A woman came into view, walking slowly, studying the citadel.

Sullo's witch. No wonder he had the nerves.

They had it figured out. Their countermoves had begun. Those would be animated by total desperation. They were in a race against a deadline they could not determine, so they would come hard and fast, from every angle and with everything they had.

How good was she? Could she find the Postern of Fate? Could she unravel its pattern, traps, and alarms? How lucky was she? Ala-eh-din Beyh had succeeded as much through luck as through talent.

As desperate as they would be, they would make their own luck.

It would be a race against time from this end, too.

* * *

Arif did not sleep at all. He sat in the great cage and cried, a slave to bewilderment and terror.

The Witch slept a deeper sleep than ever she had slept. She had spent too lavishly of her physical resources. She would be longer than usual coming back.

16

Aaron did nothing but trudge along silently, heading home, head bent in the rain. Rainwater trickled down the back of his neck and carried the salt of nervous sweat into the abrasions on his face. Naszif seemed content to carry on without conversation. They had a job to do, they knew what it was, and there was no need to belabor it with false chatter or to burden it with insincere camaraderie.

This was an alliance of necessity, not of love.

The rainfall was still something short of a full drizzle but it had been falling long enough to wash away the city's patina of dust and get started on the layers of grime underneath. Char Street was thoroughly wet and slick. Aaron heard the occasional gurgle from the sewer. Some water had begun to accumulate in the channel.

Much more would be needed to cleanse it. This little bit would just stir things up and make the stench riper.

Much more would be needed to fill the reservoirs and rain barrels of Qushmarrah, all of which were low. There was talk about a public works project to recover more of the water from the springs that fed Goat Creek.

Aaron would have said these things to another companion, or another might have said them to him.

Two Herodian soldiers remained on guard inside Aaron's home. They had not been frugal with his candles, which exasperated him, but neither had they robbed him, so he supposed he could count himself lucky.

Naszif dismissed them.

Aaron latched the door, lay down with hopes of getting some rest.

That was impossible, and not just because Naszif's pacing bothered him. Goblins of fear pranced and wrestled and giggled through the caverns of his mind. No matter where he turned his thoughts, he encountered a haunted shadow.

It was like those nights in the pass six years ago when he had not been able to sleep nights for fear of the events of the following day.

Naszif's restlessness did not help.

Aaron gave it up after a while, got up, tried to put some of his nervous energy to work. For years he had been meaning to take the sensible precaution of installing a peephole in the door. Putting one in now seemed an appropriate act of self-flagellation.

He was surprised to find that it had started getting light out, that the fog had begun to retreat despite continued rainfall, that Char Street had begun to come to life.

Before he finished his chore a dozen nosy neighbors had dropped by to ask what had happened during the night. The daily incursion of the Dartar horde occurred, and they proceeded with their siege of the Shu maze and the sealing of its exits as if for them there was no higher purpose. Elsewhere, he knew, soldiers and horsemen were marching out to meet the Turoks, and the Herodian war fleet was making preparations to catch the morning tide. And ambitious and evil men were scheming schemes. As always.

He was exhausted when he finished. His eyes burned with fatigue. He lay down again, and this time he slipped off despite the riot in his mind.

* * *

"I feel like I ought to be doing something more active," bel-Sidek told Meryel, topping off a belly already overly stuffed. He muttered, "I've been eating my own cooking too long," then reverted to the subject. "I've always led from the front."

"Which explains why you've only got one leg that works."

"Guarantees you won't see me running from a fight."

"You done stuffing yourself?"

"Yes. Enough is more than enough."

"Good. I have news for you. Your neighbor in the Shu is home. You said you wanted to talk to him."

"I'd like to do a lot more than that. Nobody talks to a khadifa the way he talked to me."

She laughed at him. "Politics and observation of the proprieties of social status have to take precedence over stress and family and personal relationships. Right?"

He glared. "Don't you go sensible on me. I'm in no mood for reasonable. What's the situation?" At that moment it occurred to him he had the solution to his command problem right there. Meryel would make a perfect khadifa of the waterfront. He knew of no one more competent.

Be impossible to get her accepted, though. Not only was she a woman, she was no veteran of Dak-es-Souetta.

How had that come to be so critical a qualification?

He listened with half an ear and plucked salient points out of the report she had gotten from people who worked for her, not for the movement. "He didn't bring his family home? He didn't go to work? That's not like him."

"He had a family disaster, dolt! You didn't work yesterday, did you?"

Only yesterday! It seemed like a year already. The General in the ground less than a day. And the whole movement in disarray already. "All right. Call it a basic character flaw. Go on."

"There is something going on. If I was Cado I'd have an army of spies watching to see if somebody tried to make contact. Best my men can see, the nearest Herodian is in Government House.

I think they want you to have a clean chance at him. I think he has a message."

Bel-Sidek felt queasy. A message? From Cado? "Send some people to round him up. Drag him up here."

"Hold your horses, Mr. Khadifa. I'm a sympathizer, not a soldier. My people don't give a damn one way or the other about the Living. They'll do some things for me but they have their limits. And I have mine."

Maybe he should have gone to ground somewhere else.

"Besides," she said, "Char Street is full of Dartars again. You said Dartars backed him up last night. You try the usual heavy-handed Living move and they'll eat you up. Right?"

"I suppose. Forget it, then. Let Cado go whistle."

"You've become a living exasperation, you know that? I'm beginning to wonder if the General didn't pick the wrong man to take over. You don't want to be bothered thinking, or even with doing much of anything. But you've given orders that will start a war in about twelve hours. You need to know what's going on. You for Aram's sake need to set up a command headquarters and get lines of communication opened to your khadifas. Or your great rebellion isn't going to be much more than a glorified riot."

He glared at her, unaccustomed to take that from anyone but Herodian functionaries on the waterfront. Taking it there was part of the holy mission.

"I'll go myself, then."

"No. You don't think those Dartars will recognize you in the daylight? I'll go. You're going to the Hahr with a couple of my men. I own some empty buildings there. Some of the weapons are hidden there. They'll do you for a hideout and headquarters. My men will run a few messages for you so you can get started. Then they're out of it.

Bel-Sidek sighed and rose. He wasn't going to win a point.

Meryel said, "You have to stop nursing hurt feelings because the old man pulled a fast one on you. Get up on your hind legs and let's go."

Yoseh was restless. His injuries ached mercilessly but he could not remain still. That doorway down there . . .

They had managed a few whispered words before Cado had
run the Dartar contingent out of Government House, Fa'tad and
all. He never said a word about their having been in the city after
curfew. Nor had he asked a question about what they were up to
in the Shu. Fa'tad seemed disappointed.

The Eagle walked them back to their post in Char Street.
Yoseh figured he'd had something to discuss but he'd never said
a word. He'd just prowled around in the fog, taking in the site of
the excitement, then he had gone off up the hill, still leading the
mount he had ridden into the city, like an old man had nothing
to fear from the night in this nest of killers and thieves.

Maybe, if you were Fa'tad and favored of the gods, you did
have nothing to fear.

Now the old man was back. He was in the alley with Nogah
and some of his old cronies, including Mo'atabar. Doing what,
Yoseh did not know.

"You're going to wear your boots out, little brother," Medjhah
said. "Why don't you plant yourself and take a nap?"

He couldn't. Despite the night. He shook his head.

"You'll be sorry you didn't."

"Why? What's up?"

"I don't know. That's just the voice of experience. You skip a
chance to snooze you're always sorry."

Yoseh grunted. "I'm going up to see what's up there on top."
He had not yet seen anything of the upbuild or the underneath
of the Shu. The upbuild was supposed to be a wonder if you saw
it from the sea or some eminence where you could view it as a
whole. From the cobblestones of Char Street you could not see
anything more interesting looking south than you could by
looking north.

He lined up behind several mason's helpers waiting to carry
materials up a narrow stair built into what once had been a
breezeway between buildings. Traffic headed up was waiting for
several helpers who were coming down. Once he did get up top
all he saw was what looked like more of the same.

The buildings fronting on Char Street were mostly one level
high, their roofs a hardened and painted whitish stucco material

just like their fronts, slightly sloped and rounded so water would run off. Foot traffic mostly kept to a four-foot-wide pathway of planking. Pathways meandered here and there and more stairways climbed in front of or between places set back about as far as the cross alleyway in which Yoseh had met the child-stealer. Only a very few residents were out in the weather, watching Dartars and masonry people trudge back and forth.

Yoseh went up to the next level. It was much like the one before, except that here and there, there were narrow ways like streets two storeys above the original streets, leading not only to doorways but to some ladders and stairways going down. Some of those were being blocked by the masons, working under tents that kept the rain off. Most legitimate stairs and ladders were inside, where many generations might live in the same vertical stack.

Back in the heart of the quarter there were places accessible only by descending as many as five flights.

The third level was the highest with any access to the maze.

Yoseh had trouble imagining what it must be like when all the people were moving around up there. Be like a swarm of bees pouring out of their hives.

Higher up there were places rounded in shape that did resemble big hives. Other than at the center of the quarter most of the fourth-level places stood free.

He wondered what the quarter might have become in another hundred years if the Herodians had not forbidden this endless piling on. Six or seven levels, so complicated nobody from outside could find his way around?

Though the sprinkle was not heavy he came across several low places where accumulated drainage ran in tiny brooks, into catch basins and on. At each pool there were women filling jars. Not a lot of the water would go to waste.

One of the runoffs, though, ran into a ladder well. He imagined it must get pretty damp down in the maze when there was a lot of rain.

At the highest levels even the wooden pathways were painted white. White and white and white, and he the only body moving. The misty drizzle made it difficult to see far. He felt lost in some strangely weathered desert.

He turned back, his nervous energy not diminished. But he was soggy now and getting miserable.

What the hell was going on in Qushmarrah? Everyone seemed to be up to something. He could not understand his place in the middle of it all. He wished he had stayed in the mountains—except when he thought of Tamisa.

An impossible dream, of course, but his heart quickened, anyway. Maybe the impossibility was half the attraction.

He was thinking about asking Nogah to let him go inside the maze to explore but there was something going on when he got back, Fa'tad digging men out of the alleyway and hurrying them off. Yoseh was astonished. Some had exchanged their Dartar black for Qushmarrahan-style clothing. Wrapped in cloaks against the wet, keeping their heads down, they did not give themselves away.

"What's happening?" he asked Medjhah.

"Someone came to see your girlfriend's brother-in-law. Fa'tad wants to know where they go."

Naszif shook his shoulder. Aaron grumbled, "What?"

"Somebody at the door. I think this is it."

A thrill of fear. Aaron tried to bounce up but he was too sore. He had stiffened up terribly while he slept.

He put the peephole to its first use.

He closed it, whispered, "A woman. Alone. Ugly."

An almost smile from Naszif. "Let her in." He stepped over where he would be out of sight behind the door when it opened.

Aaron opened up. "May I help you?" He did not look at the woman, glancing up and down the street instead. He saw nothing but Dartars and normal traffic. No one appeared interested.

The woman said, "I'm the one you're waiting for." She sounded amused.

"Come inside." He stepped aside. "You woke me up. What do you mean, you're the one I'm waiting for?"

"You have a message from one General for another, don't you?" she asked as she pushed past.

"Not me. They just figured I'd be watched. Naszif has the message." He closed the door.

The woman eyed Naszif, surprised but not uneasy. "They didn't mention you. I'll tell them to pay closer attention."

Aaron was uncomfortable. The woman talked and acted like a man. "Shall I stir up the fire and heat some water?"

"I won't be here that long. Thank you, anyway. All right, Mr. Naszif. What's the message?"

"General Cado would like to speak to Colonel bel-Sidek concerning Nakar the Abomination and possible destinies of Qushmarrah. That's all I'm authorized to tell one of his agents. I could say more to his face. On my own, I'll say the General seems ready to offer whatever guarantees the Colonel feels are necessary to maintain his safety during their talks. The General thinks we've reached a crossroads. He thinks the interests of Herod and the Living may be allied at the moment."

Aaron gawked at Naszif. The man always had had a tendency to be pompous, but nothing like this. Had he taken lessons when he became a Herodian?

He grinned.

So did the woman. "Interesting. He might go for it out of plain curiosity. That's all of it?"

"For the moment. Unless you wish to take me to Colonel bel-Sidek."

"I don't think so. I'll see what he thinks and let you know." She turned to the door.

"I urge you to waste no time. The General feels we're up against a lethal deadline. Minutes may be critical."

"I'll tell him not to fart around."

She left them aghast.

"Now what?" Aaron asked.

"Now we wait some more."

Aaron started digging around trying to find something to eat.

"There she goes," Medjhah whispered "Give her a minute, then tell Nogah."

Yoseh looked at the woman frankly. "Walks like a man."

"They can't all be young and graceful. Unfortunately. Now. Go." Medjhah got up and strolled toward one of the wagons used by the masons. It was a large four-wheeler, covered, and the driver was huddled inside.

"Nogah?" Yoseh said into the darkness in the alley.

"We saw her. Go get in the wagon with Medjhah."

Puzzled, Yoseh walked toward the wagon. Medjhah had disappeared. The driver was outside, checking the harness on his oxen. Yoseh looked inside the wagon. It was empty except for Medjhah.

"Come in, little brother."

Yoseh clambered over the tailgate. "What are we doing?"

"We're going to follow the woman."

"Why?"

"Fa'tad thinks she can lead us to the chief of the Living."

Yoseh tried to reconcile that with what he understood of what had happened last night. He could not. "Why does he want to do that?"

Medjhah shrugged. "Not now." The wagon rocked.

Nogah climbed inside. Kosuth followed him, then Fa'tad and two of his old-time cronies, then Juba from their own bunch. Juba was not a relative but always had been a sort of adoptive cousin.

"Tell him to get moving," Fa'tad said. He nodded to Yoseh and Medjhah.

Medjhah said something out the front of the wagon. The Qushmarrahan clambered up onto the driver's seat and yelled at his oxen.

The wagon lurched forward. "Real racing chariot here," Nogah cracked. Nobody laughed. Yoseh thought Fa'tad looked more sour than usual. Hard to tell, though. He was wearing his face cloth, which he did not often do.

As they passed each of the other stations occupied by Dartars someone came to report to al-Akla. Each told him the woman had continued uphill. He received their remarks with sullen grunts.

Yoseh began to suspect the old man's problem was much like his own. He did not know what the hell he was doing. Maybe circumstances had conspired to abort this master plan, or had thrown other possibilities into his path, so that he was unsure how to proceed.

The wagon reached the head of Char Street, squeaked and rumbled through the acropolis, and began to descend into the Hahr. The men who came to report now wore Qushmarrahan garb and were more circumspect.

Finally, the wagon halted in a narrow, quiet street. The driver spoke for everyone when he asked, "What you want to do now, chief?"

Bel-Sidek listened to Meryel carefully, but puzzled. He could see no percentage in meeting the Herodian, unless just to put him off his guard. The man wouldn't expect an uprising while they were talking. "Why should I go to the trouble? Just to get rid of my curiosity?"

"It's the child-stealing thing," Meryel guessed. "The man I saw specifically mentioned Nakar. I'd say Cado is in a panic about that business."

"Think he knows something we don't?"

"Either he thinks he does or he wants you to think he does. He's conversant with current events inside the movement. He directed his message to you specifically."

"He had the traitor and the carpenter to advise him. I want to talk to the carpenter more than I did before. Tell Cado's runner I'm giving a meeting serious consideration. I'll send a messenger to Colonel Bruda with instructions if I decide it's in my interest to meet. After Cado's man leaves talk the carpenter into coming to see me."

"Just like that?"

"You're a persuasive woman."

She harumphed. "I'm going to be an exhausted woman if this back-and-forth keeps on." She turned around and marched out.

"Got to do something to show her I appreciate her." Bel-Sidek settled, leaned back, closed his eyes, let his thoughts run with the problem of the citadel. In moments he felt frustrated and powerless.

He must have dozed. When a soft sound startled him awake he found the room full of Dartars. Where had they come from? He scanned them quickly, careful to show no fear. They were like dogs that way. They could smell it on you.

One asked, "Have you got the boy back yet?"

He shook his head. He had forgotten that one and his threats.

"You have only nine more hours."

Bel-Sidek smiled thinly. When the fog came in no Dartar would be in a position to cause him any grief.

Another sat down in front of him. "He suffers from youthful idealism still. When he is as old as you and I he will see the inconsequence of someone else's child when matters of policy are at hand."

Fa'tad! And still armed with that gently nasty sarcasm with which he commented on things Qushmarrahan.

"You're surprised, Colonel bel-Sidek."

"Yes."

"I'm somewhat surprised myself. I've come here with no specific objective in mind."

Liar, bel-Sidek thought. Fa'tad was the last man on earth to make a move without knowing exactly what he was doing.

"Perhaps I'm squandering the treasure that is the knowing of how to find you. Maybe I had a hunch you might have something to say to me, knowing these hands hold the balance of power in this factious city."

Bel-Sidek looked the old warrior in the eye, spied a twinkle there. "Do my ears deceive me? Do I hear an offer to change sides again?"

"Change sides? No. You didn't hear that. We don't change sides. We're completely faithful to the cause of the Dartar tribes. But there have been times when we have been deceived and deserted by those who styled themselves our friends."

"I can't debate that with you. Nakar himself decided that the drought had hurt Qushmarrahan agriculture too much to allow sending any of its product away from the city. Cado can pay your hire only because so many thousands of stomachs were quieted during the war."

"Yet there were ways Nakar could have shown gratitude for services past and have ensured those services in the future had he been less miserly. But at that moment he had no need of our savage lances. He had not yet sensed the gathering Herodian storm. When he did he whistled, expecting us to come running like dogs. Treacherous curs that we are, we answered maltreatment with maltreatment."

"Stipulated," bel-Sidek said, pleased that he had found a sarcasm to match Fa'tad's. But the Dartars were not amused.

Fa'tad observed, "This thing with Nakar is most inopportunely timed. Given another three days, possibly four, we would have had what we came for and would have begun our preparations to leave the Herodian standard. We came so close. But that's the story of our generation."

Bel-Sidek eyed Fa'tad narrowly. The man was up to something for sure.

He would bite. For the moment. Maybe he would learn something. "What did you come for?"

"The treasures of the citadel. We've made no secret of that. They were promised us by the Herodians. They never meant to keep their promise, of course. They knew we couldn't get inside. But we persevered, and finally found the way, and it turns out we can't get into the citadel till probably two days after the citadel comes to get us."

"The rumors are true? There's a tunnel from the Shu maze?"

"There is a passage. But like the citadel itself it's sealed off by unbreakable spells. There is, however, nothing to keep determined men from bypassing the blockage by cutting through the rock and going around. But that is going to take too long."

Bel-Sidek leaned back, unafraid now, confident he had a handle on the situation. The old man wanted to trade horses. And he was sneaking up on the point rather quickly for a Dartar. "Why are you telling me this?"

"You would like us to leave Qushmarrah. You know the circumstances under which we would blow away like milkweed seed. Are you wedded to the strategy of your predecessor, who never abandoned his allegiance to the dark gods?"

That allegation startled bel-Sidek . . . Azel had claimed he had met the General in temple. And Azel had been Nakar's private assassin. "I'm not married to the concept."

"Ah. I feared the entire ruling council of your movement was guilty of a cynical manipulation aimed at effecting the restoration of Nakar. We have a basis for discussion."

"Uhm?" Let him lead. Let him lead.

"There *is* another way into the citadel."

"If you're going to suggest that I know it you're sniffing the wrong trail. I'd have used it to clean the place out long ago. That wealth would buy a lot of weapons."

Fa'tad eyed him. "That has a certain plausibility. Nevertheless, the information exists within your organization. Those children have to be delivered somehow. Hanno bel-Karba was a careful planner. He would have made arrangements to ensure that such a critical piece of information did not get lost if misadventure overtook him . . . Ah! I see you've thought of a name."

The Dartars stirred. Fa'tad gestured. They were still.

Bel-Sidek had thought of Carza. And now knew why Cado wanted to see him. Cado wanted that name. He was holding a trump he hadn't known he had. Why shouldn't he play it himself?

Fa'tad said, "You're wondering why you should give these dogs of Dartars anything. The immediate answer is simple. We have you in our power. And Nogah here has sworn to kill you when the fog comes in. Your successor will face either Nakar the Abomination or, if he is smart enough and quick enough to abort that, the implacable hostility of five thousand Dartars that would keep him from ousting Herod forever. Your cause is dying. In a few years it will expire from old age. On the other hand, if we were to get into the citadel you might find us grateful enough to aid your cause. And you'll have gained an unvanquishable fortress from which to strike at Herod. Perhaps even through the Shu maze. Is that treasure, that you never had, suddenly more important than the goals of your movement?"

A central point, bel-Sidek reflected. If the treasures of the citadel would buy independence, wasn't he bound to pay? It was a cheaper fee than any they had considered paying before.

"One question. Suppose that treasure is just as much an illusion as the supposed treasure of the king of the Shu maze?"

"Then I'll have made a great fool of myself. I'll have given Qushmarrah away and will have done nothing but return a few frightened children to grieving parents. I'm confident of the wealth, however. I visited the citadel occasionally in older times."

"As did I. Can we state this as a clearly defined undertaking? So I'll know exactly where we stand."

Fa'tad reflected. "Given the secret of entry into the citadel, which exists somewhere within your organization, my forces will penetrate the fortress. They will deliver the children held captive there. To you, if you like. They will terminate any possibility of the resurrection of Nakar. They will take of the treasure of the citadel as they desire. They will hand the fortress over to your forces. They will leave the city to you and the Herodians."

"A good deal, on the face of it," bel-Sidek said. And he believed that. But he wondered what lay behind the smiling face. It seemed too simple, too straightforward, and maybe too small for Fa'tad al-Akla.

Unless he was under a lot of pressure from home and would have to leave soon, anyway.

That was a good possibility.

"Any my part? Other than learning how you can enter the citadel?"

"Don't make Cado a deal when he comes looking for one."

One of the Dartars, who was watching the street through a crack in a boarded window, said, "The woman is coming."

Fa'tad nodded. "I've been a little slow. It's your move, Colonel bel-Sidek."

"Can you keep your man away?"

Fa'tad seemed amused. "I think I can restrain his ardor so long as he and I are certain he will have the chance to deliver the boy. Still, the deadline he set seems to me a sound one. Why wait for

Nakar? The deal stands if you deliver the information before the fog comes in. I can be reached in the alley below the place you formerly occupied."

"And if I can't get the information?"

"We'll find you again."

Meryel burst in. "Sisu, what the hell are you doing? You've got twenty men sitting around . . . Shit."

Fa'tad bowed slightly and walked out. His men followed. Bel-Sidek watched thoughtfully.

"What the hell? That was al-Akla."

"He followed you here." Bel-Sidek told her the story.

"What're you going to do?"

"First I'll see if my conscience says I have to go through with the General's plan."

"You *want* Nakar back? If you think you owe somebody that, you're crazier than the old man was. You even consider it, you can kiss me good-bye."

"There are those who would approve."

"So?"

"I merely state that for the record."

"You think al-Akla would keep his bargain?"

"Possibly. He certainly handed me ammunition to spend against him. I'm tempted to give him what he wants, then tell Cado he's looting the citadel. Let them get into it. Let the Living deal with the survivors."

"Will you?"

"I don't know. Right now I'll call off my own war, then get Carza where I can talk to him. If anybody knows the way in there, he does."

"The carpenter refused to come," Meryel said.

"So I suspected. Probably doesn't much matter now."

Yoseh settled into the bed of the wagon, glad to be out of the rain. He huddled up, pondered the incomprehensible ways of the mighty. The others piled inside. Somebody growled at the driver. The driver growled back, unimpressed. The wagon lurched forward.

One of Fa'tad's cronies asked, "Think he'll try to screw us?"

"It's the Qushmarrahan way. On the other hand, I made him a tempting offer. An inspired improvisation, if I say so myself." Al-Akla chuckled. "Driver! Turn left and stop. Nogah, Medjhah, Juba, I have a job for you."

17

Aaron slipped into the main shed at the shipyard. Those who could were there, working out of the rain. The rest had been sent home. He found Billygoat caulking a small boat. There was always work for a caulker.

Billygoat gave him a strange look. "You coming in?"

"No. I just wanted to talk. You heard?"

"Yes. It's around. How are you doing? How's your family handling it?"

"I'm all right now. They're taking it about like you'd expect. But we aren't without hope. The Herodians know who did it. Can we talk?"

"Sure." Billygoat wiped his hands on his clothing. He was not fastidious. "But this isn't the place. Unless you don't care who listens."

The others had slowed work and were watching. Cullo and another Herodian were drifting their way. Aaron wondered if this made any sense, after all. "Part I don't want anybody to hear."

"Let's go for a walk."

"You'll get soaked." He was already.

Billygoat shrugged. "As long as it isn't pouring. I find rain

274

relaxing." The old man shoved his tools toward his helper. "Clean them up."

Neither foreman stopped Billygoat. None of the workmen spoke to Aaron, though some eyed him with pity.

"You have friends in high places," Billygoat said after they stepped into the damp. "Never saw anybody excused from work by order of the military governor."

"Really?"

"Messenger was waiting when we came in. Had a letter saying you was to be let off as long as you needed, without prejudice, the way they say. Signed by Bruda and Cado, according to Cullo. He was impressed."

"Trying to back me into a corner, I guess."

They went in beneath the scaffolding on the lee side of the ship they were building. Not much moisture reached them. Billygoat sat on one timber balk, leaned against another. "Talk to me."

Aaron told his story. Billygoat did not interrupt. When Aaron finished, he said, "It's a grim tale. If it's advice you're after, all I can say is, you got to do whatever you got to do to help your boy."

"I understand that. That's no problem. But all those people are pushing me into the middle of their plots and politics. I don't give a damn about any of that. I just want my son back. But whatever I do, somebody will claim I betrayed him. They could take it out on my family. How can I get out from under that?"

Billygoat picked up some sodden wood chips, pitched them at an invisible target. "I don't know, Aaron. I wish I did. I wish I could give you some magic formula. But all I can say is I'm sorry. You got yourself in the classic trap that gets the little guy. Not your fault, but there you are. When the big guys go to butting heads they always figure if you aren't with them you got to be against them. There's anything practical I can do, I'll help."

"I don't want to get you into it."

Billygoat did not argue.

"There is one thing. Wouldn't put you at any risk." The real reason he had come.

"What's that?" Billygoat kept throwing chips.

"Sort of an extra hammer."

"Well?"

"You hear something's happened to me or my family, ask around for somebody who was at the Seven Towers, in Four. Like Big Turi. Tell them I said it was Naszif that opened the door. They'll know what that means. Would you do that?"

"Sure, Aaron."

"Thanks. I'd better get back, see if there's any news."

Sullo and Cado watched while Annalaya tried reaching through the corpse of Ishabal bel-Shaduk in an effort to summon his spirit. The governors had set animosity aside for the moment, in the face of a greater threat.

The woman backed away from the cadaver. Cado thought she looked troubled. She shrugged, defeated. "Too late."

Sullo took her into his arms, patted her back. "You did the best you could."

Cado concealed amazement. What was this? *She* did not appear pleased. "I so wanted to please you, my lord."

Cado thought her tone lacked sincerity. Who was using whom? Cado asked, "What's our approach now?" Calling up the child-taker's ghost had been a long shot but he had hoped.

The witch disengaged herself from Sullo. "We will have to find the way by trial and error. As Ala-eh-din Beyh must have." And there was more hidden in her voice when she mentioned that name.

Mystery on mystery. "There's a way? *Is* Fa'tad on to something?" That would not do. Let Fa'tad plunder the citadel and the Dartars would melt away faster than summer snow.

"The entrance appears to be a pattern gate," the witch said. She had an odd accent, maybe atop a mild speech impediment. "It appears to be a complicated construct. Possibly a double pattern. Probably with inbuilt traps. The first steps seem too obvious for a sorcerer of Nakar's attainment." Again an oddity of voice, a chilliness, at mention of the name.

"A trap?" Cado had only the vaguest notion what she meant. He was of the old school: no commerce with sorcery.

"There are certain to be several, some obvious, some subtle, all deadly. That is the nature of a pattern. You create a pattern gate to keep people out."

"Be careful, then. Colonel Bruda will give you whatever support you need."

Sullo donned a smirk. "My people can handle this."

"Perhaps." Cado left them, perplexed by the woman, thinking Sullo needed watching. If—when!—they penetrated the citadel the man would go for the treasure like a shark to blood.

The big man brought a child into the cage. The other children whispered excitedly. There was something special about this one . . . He had been brought back once before. Apparently those who went out did not come back at all.

Arif lifted his gaze.

"Zouki!" He jumped up, then got scared all over again. The big man gave him such a funny look. Almost like he hated him . . . The big man backed outside and locked the cage but stayed outside staring. He was scary.

Arif edged toward Zouki. "Zouki?"

The other boy just sat there. There was something creepy about him. Something scary. Arif wanted to move away, to hide. "Zouki?"

Zouki looked up. There was no recognition in his eyes. For a moment. Then something stirred. He seemed suddenly old and dangerous and much more scary. Arif backed away, frightened.

"What did you do to him?" Arif shouted. "You're a bad man." He kept backing away, crying, terrified.

Thunder crashed outside the citadel. The rain fell harder.

Azel watched the soldiers from his eyrie. They had the place surrounded, the Postern of Fate covered. There would be no getting out. If the kid they needed wasn't the one he'd brought in, the siege would turn ugly. There weren't many stores laid in. Of course, if they busted in, things would get even uglier.

He should have done something about Sullo's witch. She was

the only tool they had. But he'd had no time, even had the notion occurred while it was practical.

When she woke, the Witch would see why he'd nagged her. This was what he'd wanted to prevent.

Torgo showed up for a little more seducing. "What are you doing?"

"Watching the show and wondering if I'm too old to learn to fly. How's she doing?"

The eunuch looked worried. "Not good. She extended herself way too much."

Azel spat out the window. That figured. She'd keep right on being more trouble than help. Just like a woman. "She better wake up before they figure out how to get in here."

Aaron had not yet gotten the door closed when Naszif demanded, "Where the hell have you been?" Like he was some child who had wandered without permission.

"I arranged for someone to tell Big Turi who opened that postern if anything happens to me or mine." He felt soaked to the bone. He started shedding wet clothing.

Naszif glared, angry, none too afraid, maybe with a touch of hatred.

"There's nothing else to say," Aaron said. "Did you see General Cado?"

"Him and the ugly woman both. Things are moving." Implied, the suggestion that Aaron stick a little closer, in case.

He hung his clothes up, dressed dry, settled down with cheese, bread, and water. He did not offer to share. After a while, he asked, "What's next?"

"Bel-Sidek wants General Cado to come to him if they're going to meet. If that's what bel-Sidek decides to do he'll send a guide here. I'll take him to the General. So we just sit."

Sit around and wait for something to happen. As they had done at the Seven Towers.

He wished he had brought his family home. He was feeling as alone as he had in those bad old days. How soon could he get away from here? How soon would they be able to come back?

He thought about Arif up there in the citadel, so young, so much more alone than he, so surely terrified by the collapse of his safe little world. "Naszif?"

"Yeah?"

"Suppose we let everything else go and just worry about getting the boys back?"

Naszif grunted. He wanted to nap.

Nothing to do but sit there and think.

The rain was steady now, though not yet heavy. The clouds seemed to be stirring over the citadel. Yoseh paid no attention. He was soaked to the marrow, miserable, and only marginally grateful that it was no colder. The breeze was steady and merciless. And Medjhah had been right about snatching sleep while the chance was there—damn him!

Yoseh was on the street supposedly pretending to doze while he watched the animals and kept an eye on Tamisa's place. But he was only supposed to pretend. His eyes kept crossing and his vision kept blurring. And Faruk, like he was psychic, kept coming out to plant a boot in his bottom whenever he started to nod.

There was not that much to see. A few people came and went at Tamisa's but Fa'tad did not seem interested.

This life in the city of gold was just one breathless adventure after another.

Bel-Sidek was thoroughly irritated by the time Carza deigned to make his appearance. He was tired and the weather had awakened a pernicious ache in his leg. Neither improved his temper. More, several of his men from the waterfront, though told their help was essential, had begged off reporting because they did not want to miss work. That was not something to put a captain into a positive, optimistic frame of mind. What was he running here, some kind of social club?

He had moved across the street and up the hill a few doors from the place where Fa'tad had found him. He had gotten men in to replace Meryel's workers but not enough to put out watchers adequate to his needs. He worried. He was surviving by the grace of Aram here.

Those of his own who *had* shown were his best, men who had stood with him at Dak-es-Souetta, willing to storm the gates of Hell if he gave the order. The five hardest were with him when Carza showed.

"I hope I haven't inconvenienced you too much," bel-Sidek said, not bothering to smother his anger.

"You have. You know damned well you have. Are you having trouble making up your mind? Or did you just chicken out on bringing down the storm?"

"Sit down." Bel-Sidek nodded to two of his men. They sat Carza down. "No. I didn't chicken out. I found another way."

"Get your hands off . . ."

"Be quiet, Carza. I'll tell you when to speak. Here it is. I know what the old man planned. And Cado knows. And so does al-Akla. They aren't happy. Luckily they're preoccupied with the citadel. It's surrounded by Herodian troops. There'll be no communication with the Witch. Additionally, I, personally, am categorically, adamantly, inalterably opposed to resurrecting Nakar."

"You're going to chuck the movement because you don't like the way he worked?"

"I didn't say that. I also suggested you keep quiet. I said I'd found another way. It has more to recommend it, in my estimation."

"I'm listening."

"Being intentionally abrasive won't help."

Carza made a sour face but kept his mouth shut.

"Al-Akla has offered to abandon the Herodian standard. He's offered to leave Qushmarrah and return to his mountains. He suggested he might be persuaded to help clear the city of Herodians. I think it can be arranged so Dartars do most of the clearing."

Carza got more sour by the second.

"To facilitate that sequence the Living need only deliver on a promise made al-Akla by Cado, six years ago, which he did not fulfill."

"I'll bite. What's the payoff?"

"The contents of the citadel."

Carza looked at him like *he* was the crazy one.

"Which would constitute no loss whatever because we've never had control of whatever's in there."

"You're kidding."

"Not even a little."

"How are you going to get him in so he can steal our city's treasures?"

Bel-Sidek smiled a smile in which all the pain in his leg smoldered. "That's why you're here, old comrade."

Carza pretended he did not understand.

"I served the General a long time, Carza. I knew him better than his wife did. But there were things he hid from me, just as there were things he concealed from her, because he valued our good opinion. For all his foibles and crotchets I loved him, though it's obvious that at the end he'd become crazier than a troop of drunken rock apes. I don't think you can convince me he wasn't the sort who would ensure that his knowledge survived him."

"Crazy? Why crazy?"

"What sane man would voluntarily resurrect Nakar the Abomination?"

"More than you suspect, evidently. Though that wasn't the meat of the old man's plan. What do you want from me?"

Bel-Sidek paced, giving Carza time to reflect. Then, "I want the key to the citadel. I want it badly."

"And I can't give it to you. I don't know what it is."

Bel-Sidek stepped to the door. "Sheed." The man came in. "Go to the Minisia. Find Homena bel-Barca. Tell him Carza will be tied up for a while. He's to act as khadifa till Carza comes back."

Homena bel-Barca was an old friend. Despite being Carza's second his ties were with the moderates.

"You can't do this, bel-Sidek."

"I'm doing it. You rejected my authority by refusing my request."

"You push me, you'd better kill me."

"I don't want it that way, Carza. You're valuable to the movement. But if you insist."

Carza gave him a searching look, suspecting he might be serious.

He was, at the moment.

Meryel was right. He had to take charge. He had to show that he was in charge.

"Tell me what I need to know, Carza."

General Cado was extremely uncomfortable clad Qushmarra-han and bundled against the rain. No one gave him a second glance but he could not shake a feeling that they all knew what he was and were snickering to themselves. All part of the Herodian curse. Everywhere but in the home provinces Herodi-ans were out of place, stubby little bald men.

He'd never articulated the curse concept to anyone.

Hell. They were by damn in charge, short or not. They were masters by right of conquest.

He glanced at the guide Colonel bel-Sidek had sent, sniffing for the taint of treachery. This was the biggest risk he had taken since he had accepted battle at Dak-es-Souetta, counting on unproven Dartars to give him the day. For all he had known, Fa'tad's offer had been just a ploy.

He could tell nothing. His companion was as bundled up as he, hunched over as he marched into the slanting rain. Just a brother in misery.

It was not weather to inspire flights of fancy leading to sudden treachery. It was weather for plodding straight ahead, for mud-dling through. The afternoon was leaden grey, depressing. The citadel, as they skirted it, was a lump of wet dark stone, filled with menace, an awakening viper coiled beneath twisting clouds.

Cado was concerned about his fleet. If the weather was no worse at sea, wonderful. The breeze would push the ships across the Gulf of Tuhn at six to eight knots. They should reach the far shore sometime tomorrow. The troops should be ashore and astride the coast road, behind the Turok raiders, before nightfall.

He hoped for a great and bloody success, the impact of which would strike Turoks and Dartars, the peoples of the coastal provinces and his detractors in the mother city. A few thousand Turoks taken unaware would make a potent statement.

From the acropolis they descended into the narrow streets of the Hahr. He wondered how much longer, how much more runaround to confuse him about where he was . . .

He caught a flash of motion from the corner of his eye. His companion grunted and pitched forward. Something hit him in the back of the head and on the shoulders. Darkness descended.

He awakened with his hands and feet bound and his head tied into a sack. He was in a wagon. And he was frightened—more for his troops than for himself. He had sent both generals into the field.

Bruda was good at what he did. But could he cope with a Sullo? Could he manage if things started falling apart?

It looked like Colonel bel-Sidek had decided it was time the Living moved.

He wondered if anyone would bother ransoming him. Taliga might not want to bother. His sister would profit if her husband fell to an enemy blade.

He developed a tormenting itch in his bladder.

18

Naszif had gone to Government House with the Living's guide, it seemed forever ago. He had thought Aaron ought to stay, just in case. Now Aaron wished he had asserted himself and had insisted he go, too. Or at least had told Naszif to tell General Cado to send his family home. He was painfully alone here.

Would Naszif return now he had played out the part General Cado had given him? He hoped not, but feared that was a futile hope. He had caught the eyes of the mighty and they were not going to let him slip away.

Someone tapped on the door.

His heartbeat doubled. He started to sweat. He went to peek through the peephole.

It was the Dartar Yoseh.

He opened up. "Yes?" He smiled. He liked the boy despite himself.

"Fa'tad wants to talk to you."

Aaron did not respond. He stared into the street. It was almost dark out. The rain was not yet a downpour but it was a real rain now, and steady. What they called a soaking rain. The sewer channel was alive, snorting and gurgling. When the weather cleared, Qushmarrah would have a newly scrubbed look and a fresh, clean smell.

"Sir, Fa'tad wants to know if he can come talk to you."

Sir? Better keep an eye on this boy. "Fa'tad al-Akla?"

"Yes sir." The Dartar was amused. "I understand, sir. He scares me, too."

Aaron snorted, a predictable response from a man whose courage had been questioned. "He can come. As long as he doesn't blow trumpets and make a Dartar carnival out of it."

"He'll be here in a minute." The boy hurried away.

What now? Aaron wondered. He did not retreat from the doorway. The street was as vacant as ever he'd seen it, barring the presence of the Dartars. Tonight, at least in this area, they had made no pretense of leaving for their compound.

Fa'tad had on his polite face when he arrived with Yoseh and the boy's older brother. Nogah? To make him feel more comfortable, having someone around he knew at least vaguely?

"I'm sorry I can offer no hospitality," Aaron said. "But welcome to my home, anyway."

Fa'tad looked around, comparing the actuality to reports he had received. "Thank you. That you have received me is hospitality enough."

"To what do I owe the honor of your presence?"

"Ha!" Fa'tad snorted. "You do that almost as well as a Dartar."

Aaron was puzzled. The man must have heard something he had not said. He was just trying to be courteous.

Fa'tad said, "I am hoping you will help me carry off something that should get your boy back. If we move fast."

Aaron was not so naive as to assume Arif's well-being meant anything to Fa'tad al-Akla. The old nomad wanted to use him. But that was all right. He would play if it looked like Fa'tad could deliver.

"Tell me about it." He hoped he could separate fact from tall tales. He accounted himself a little too gullible. Look what bel-Sidek had told him. "I won't guarantee anything."

"Well spoken! Always examine the horse's teeth. Very well. I will tell you everything."

When dogs fly, Aaron thought. "Go ahead."

"When I chose to follow the standard of Herod I was promised the treasures of the citadel, which would be of great help to my people. Six years have passed. I have not yet glimpsed those treasures. General Cado has made no effort to breach the citadel. A few days ago, curiosity sparked by the kidnapping, I began investigating the Shu labyrinth. From criminals captured inside I learned of a legend about a secret entrance to the citadel. I searched for it. I found it. But it is sealed by spells as potent as those protecting the citadel above. I thought to best the spell by tunneling around the blockage. But then we all learned what the kidnappings are about. It was evident that my method of attack would be too slow. You follow so far?"

"I follow." Aaron smiled weakly. "I don't necessarily believe, but I follow." He felt wildly daring, talking that way to Fa'tad al-Akla.

Fa'tad smiled back. His raptor's face seemed to fall into a smile naturally, which was astonishing. "A skeptic. Good. A man does well to be skeptical in times like these. So. The nature of the game, and the stakes, changed last night. And then again this afternoon."

Startled, Aaron asked, "This afternoon? What now?"

"General Cado has disappeared. Rumor says the Living have taken him captive. I presume to prevent him from interfering with their effort to resurrect Nakar the Abomination."

That was a blow to the heart. And he had heard enough around Government House to suspect General Cado's disappearance would throw the garrison into chaos.

Al-Akla continued, "Governor Sullo will try to assume Cado's responsibilities. It's one of the promises he made to the people who sent him here. I do not want him in control. Another promise he made was that he would, once he obtained the power, abrogate Cado's treaties and begin looting Qushmarrah's treasures—especially those of the citadel, which grow more fabulous with every telling."

Aaron suddenly feared for his family, caught in a squabble between the Residence and Government House. He demanded,

"How can you know what Sullo promised anybody before he left Herod?"

"We may be savages, carpenter, but we do have our friends across the great shining water." Fa'tad's voice was edged with sarcasm.

Aaron began pacing. If this was even half true he had to get his family out of harm's way. And what about Arif? His gut feeling about Governor Sullo was that the man did not give a damn what happened to Qushmarrah's children.

"What do you want?"

"I want to divert Sullo. I want to appeal to his greed and so distract him while I find General Cado and steal Sullo's witch. Without her he cannot go anywhere. What I need from you is for you to run breathless to Sullo to report that the Dartars are only a few hours short of breaking into the citadel from the maze. I hope he will chase us off and waste a few days hunting for the way. We won't tell him where it is."

It did not add up. Aaron said so. And he asked, "How does this get you into the citadel?"

Fa'tad thought a moment, as though trying to decide if he ought to say more. "Uhn. I intend to use his witch. She's our only hope of getting in there in time."

"But . . ."

"No more answers. No more questions. You know enough already to destroy me if you develop a sudden sympathy for Governor Sullo. I am going to return to my alley now, leaving you to reflect. Leaving you with the assurance that the first thing we will do once we break through is find your son. In fact, if you wish, you may go with us when we storm the citadel. Nogah. Yoseh. Come."

Out they went.

Aaron snuffed the one candle he had had burning, sat in the dark thinking. Arif haunted every moment.

The nightmares were real now.

Yoseh asked, "Did you mean that about going after his son before anything else, sir?"

"Hell, yes. If the boy was unfortunate enough to inherit the soul of Nakar the Abomination, then he is the key to our survival. He has to be gotten away from the Witch. At whatever the cost."

Yoseh did not like the tone of that but he had exhausted his store of daring.

Medjhah heard them stirring, came to meet them. He whispered something to Fa'tad that Yoseh did not catch. Fa'tad grunted and hurried toward the alleyway.

The darkness was crowded. The troop had a stranger under guard there.

"Colonel bel-Sidek," Fa'tad said. "I had begun to fear we wouldn't see you again."

"But I had to come," the veydeen replied. "It's almost time for the fog to roll in." He sounded amused. "Though I doubt there'll be any fog tonight, in this."

Yoseh thought al-Akla sounded like he was trying to suppress excitement when he asked, "Did you get me what I need?"

"No. Unfortunately. The man I thought might know has proven stubborn. He insists he doesn't know. I've come to suspect the chances are at least even that he's telling the truth."

Fa'tad did not say anything for a minute. No one else said a thing. Then, "Give him to us. We'd find the truth in an hour."

"No doubt. And then be dead before morning."

"Eh?"

"No. I've alienated half my organization already. Basically, I've bet my life on you as the alternative to the restoration of Nakar. I won't push the hard-liners any farther."

Several men growled. A few made threats. The Qushmarrahan said, "Do as you will. But if I'm not back soon the hard-liners will take control. Before dawn the streets will be red with blood. You'll recall that some misguided Qushmarrahans would rather spill Dartar blood than Herodian."

Fa'tad grunted. Men stirred angrily. The Eagle said, "Go back to your men. Remember that the sands are running through the glass. A minute of delay may be the minute Nakar needs. Go."

The Qushmarrahan went, limping.

Someone asked, "How come you turned him loose?"

"He was telling the truth. And I have no wish to leave your body on a Qushmarrahan street, to be torn by dogs and abused by children."

No one argued with that.

"We aren't in a position to deal with rebellion. Too much is happening."

Yoseh was puzzled. But Fa'tad was not going to explain. Fa'tad was being Fa'tad, whose thoughts were known to none.

Yoseh wondered why he did not, at least, have the veydeen followed.

Azel pried himself away from the window. What the hell was he watching for? He couldn't do anything if he did see something coming.

He needed to move around. His body was going to petrify.

"Getting too damned old," he muttered, feeling his wounds far more than he would have years ago.

His stomach was a knot. He had not eaten. He had just plain forgot.

He headed downstairs.

He stopped off to mix and gulp an analgesic draft, went on to the kitchen. He ate what was available without complaining. He learned that the stores situation was not as grim as he feared, though there would be nothing fresh for a while.

After eating he limped down to look at Nakar and Ala-eh-din Beyh. Nothing had changed. Unless the darkness was a little deeper.

He stood there a long time, letting silence surround, enfold, enter him. He wondered if the General's scheme would have worked. Nakar always had possessed a keen sense for danger.

Might still find out if the Witch came around in time.

Yes. It could work out. It could.

"There you are. I heard you were roaming around."

Startled, Azel faced Torgo. He turned a retort into a grunt. "Catching up on my worrying. Any improvement in her?"

"Not yet." The eunuch was troubled. "I've never seen her sleep so deep so long."

"She wouldn't listen." Azel moved toward the doorway. "But maybe we're not so pressed. I been watching the Herodians. If they're trying to get in they're doing a good job of hiding it."

"That's good to hear." Torgo had something on his mind but could not quite get to it. "I'm going to eat now. Want to come along?"

What the hell? Just as polite, Azel replied, "Sorry. I just ate. Going to go back up and watch now."

"Later."

"Sure."

Azel watched the eunuch out of sight. Maybe he would be easy, after all. The General's scheme might get its test yet.

With Torgo safely in the kitchen Azel sneaked into the Witch's bedchamber.

No woman looked her best in the midst of sleep but she looked worse than he expected. She seemed aged a decade since he had seen her last.

He left in a hurry, unsettled, pained.

Colonel Bruda scowled at his visitor. "Don't press me, Governor. I spent the day in the mud and rain, prospecting for a body I never found. I'll have more of the same tomorrow if General Cado's disappearance is a false alarm. If it isn't, I have my orders. They're very specific when it comes to dealing with the civil authority."

Sullo smiled and nodded. He had not yet spoken.

"I've been back a half hour and haven't sat down yet, let alone cleaned up or fed myself. I'm in a bad mood. I won't play power games. I'll stick to my orders regardless. Am I clear?"

"Perfectly clear, Colonel. Perfectly. I'll keep that in mind. Meantime, might I broach the matter which brought me here?"

"Certainly, Governor." He doubted Sullo would. "Though I'd appreciate brevity. I want to get after this supposed disappearance." He had Colonel bel-Abek waiting in the next room.

"Of course. I came to express my support and to inquire if the military have prisoners we might use in experiments meant to help penetrate the citadel gate."

Bruda looked at the man, wondered how he could, without Rose's knife, put him out of the way neatly, with no kickbacks. Keeping the reins on Qushmarrah would be hard enough without Sullo intriguing and interfering. "I'll find you some volunteers. How soon do you need them?"

"Annalaya expects to start about midnight."

Bruda grunted. "I'll get you started. Now. If you'll excuse me?"

Sullo smirked. "Of course, Colonel. Of course."

Bruda turned his back, headed for the next room, determined to find out what had happened. Bel-Abek had been in the middle of it . . .

Bel-Sidek had not yet wrung himself dry when Zenobel arrived. The man stamped in, stared at him like he did not know whether to be angry or conciliatory.

"You have a problem, Khadifa?" Bel-Sidek could not help being envious of Zenobel. The man remained untouched by the disasters of the war. He was healthy, youthful, virile, handsome, energetic, and his family fortunes had suffered no insurmountable setbacks.

"I may have several. I'm not sure. Is is true you have Carza under arrest?"

That was getting around? How the hell did you get people to keep their mouths shut? "In a manner of speaking. He refuses to respond to an order so I've relieved him of the Minisia. I'm holding him here till I get what I want."

Zenobel eyed him. He met the man's gaze. Zenobel said, "What's the problem? Maybe I can talk to him."

"Maybe." Bel-Sidek did not think it was likely. Carza did not like Zenobel. On the other hand, they were the same kind of fanatic. Carza might enlist Zenobel in his scheme.

Bel-Sidek began probing Zenobel's attitude toward the dark gods. Zenobel did not put up with it long. "What're you doing? I'm as religious as a turnip."

"Carza was involved with the citadel in a scheme that, through sorcery, would've resurrected Nakar."

Zenobel stared. And kept staring till Bel-Sidek asked, "Are you all right?"

"Why would he want that?"

"Would a resurrected Nakar not deliver Qushmarrah from the Herodian yoke?"

"Let me think for a minute. Hell. How about you fill in a little? Maybe I can get him to see straight. We talk the same language."

They did that, Bel-Sidek reflected. Why not risk it? The worst would be that he would have to restrain Zenobel, too.

He told the story as he knew it.

Zenobel did not comment for a long time. Finally, he said, "I'll see what I can do with him. I like the idea of getting the Herodians and Dartars at each other's throats. That might set the fur flying all along the coast. But don't you think taking Cado out gives Fa'tad too great an advantage?"

"What do you mean?"

"Ha! Don't be coy. It's all over the city. The Living have taken Cado captive. That's the other reason I came. Bruda has put all Herodian troops on alert. He has patrols in Herodian residential areas to warn Herodian citizens that there may be trouble. The guard on the Gate of Autumn has been trebled. The Dartar compound has been warned to be prepared for civil unrest."

"That snake!" Bel-Sidek muttered. "That bloody damned snake!" Al-Akla had grabbed Cado and was handing the credit to the Living. Had to be. There was no other explanation.

Though that one did not make much sense.

"What?"

"Nothing. Go see Brother Carza. I have to do some thinking."

He did a lot of thinking but did not get anywhere. He was not sure where he wanted to go now. He could make no strategic choices because he had no idea what Fa'tad or the Herodians hoped to accomplish, beyond the obvious.

There were tactical steps he could take. He did so, beginning with patrols meant to sweep the neighborhood of watchers.

One possibility nagged: suppose al-Akla had *not* grabbed Cado? Suppose some of his own people, in sympathy with those in the citadel, had?

He was a troubled and beleaguered captain, was Sisu bel-Sidek.

19

Aaron hunched against the wind whipping the rain in under the portico of the Residence. This was not going to work. They would just give him the runaround and not let him see anyone. And right now he was so miserable it was hard to care. Had the citadel not been right there, so close he could sense its evil, he would have gone home.

But it was there, a pitiless reminder that Arif was imprisoned, at the mercy of evil, and he was out here, able to do nothing but this to help.

The man he had spoken to earlier finally returned, seemed surprised to find him still waiting. "The governor will see you, Mr. Habid." That seemed to surprise him, too. "If you will come with me?" He led the way past blank-faced Moretians. They made Aaron's skin crawl. He had heard that they ate human flesh.

His guide's Qushmarrahan was atrocious. Other than native staff, though, who were part of the furniture of the place, and beneath notice by official occupants, he was the one man in the Residence who spoke the language at all.

The man led him to a poorly lighted room where Governor Sullo was watching his witch. She was seated at a table, bent over a chart, using draftsman's tools, working out something Aaron did not understand.

Governor Sullo greeted him with a limp handclasp and an insincere smile. He jabbered at the man. Aaron caught a few words, though not enough to make sense. He waited for the translation.

Putting it more politely than the governor, the interpreter asked what he wanted.

"I went to Government House but they told me General Cado was unavailable and Colonel Bruda didn't have time for me and nobody else was authorized to deal with me, so I came here."

"But what do you want?"

"I want to visit my family. I want to take them home."

Governor Sullo was impatient with all that and barely pretended that he was not. "Yes. Yes. I understand. We'll take care of it. You had something to tell us about Fa'tad."

"Oh. Yes sir. I don't know if it's important or not . . ."

"Will you tell it?" Exasperated.

Good. "Yes sir. Sir, all afternoon and evening Fa'tad and his captains have been in the Shu, especially in my part of Char Street, dashing in and out of the maze." It came easier than he had expected. He might get through it without freezing up. If the witch did not catch on. She had given him one odd glance but seemed preoccupied, uninterested. "They were excited. After a while I overheard enough to find out why. They found out how to get into the citadel from the maze. When I left to come here they were talking about how they were almost through and pretty soon it would be too late for anybody to keep them from grabbing the treasure. They were asking each other what they were going to do with their shares."

Was he feeding it to the governor too fast? No. Not with the translation slowing it, keeping Sullo impatient to hear what came next.

"How long?" Sullo demanded, apparently conversant with the myth al-Akla had been spreading. "How long before they penetrate the citadel basements?"

Aaron tried to look bewildered by Sullo's intensity. Never had a fish been so eager to take the hook. If only the witch didn't come out of her reverie . . . "Just before I left, one of them was talking about five more hours."

"Five hours," Sullo muttered. "Before dawn. By damn! Carpenter, how long ago was that?"

"I don't know." Aaron scratched the back of his neck. "At least two hours, I guess. I went to Government House first. Then I came here. I don't know how long I was out in the rain, trying to get somebody to talk to me."

"Two hours? Damn! There might not be time. Thank him and get him out of here."

As the translator tried to move him out Aaron protested, "What about my family?" He threatened to get stubborn.

Governor Sullo cursed, snatched pen and paper from his witch. She frowned at him momentarily, faded into her thoughts again. He scrawled something, sanded the message, thrust it at Aaron. "Go on! I'm busy." He turned his back.

Aaron placed the note inside his clothing, safe from moisture, as he allowed himself to be steered toward an exit.

From the Residence he headed straight toward Government House. Along the way a voice from the darkness asked, "How did it go?"

"He swallowed the bait whole. He hardly asked any questions."

"Excellent." Footsteps hurried away.

Aaron kept walking toward Government House.

Sullo very nearly did a jig. "Fortune is grinning at me," he said. "First Cado sends both generals out of the city, then he lets himself get grabbed by these pathetic Qushmarrahan rebels. There's no one between me and complete control but that fool Bruda. And now this. The citadel on a platter. If I move fast enough to take it before the savages."

Without looking up Annalaya cautioned, "Fortune wears many faces. Some are deceitful masks."

"I need Bruda put out of my way."

She looked up then, her ugly young face empty of expression. "I know. I know. You don't want to hurt anybody. So don't hurt him. Do something that will make it look like he's had a stroke. I'll only need a day. That's time enough to get hold of all the reins. After that if he wants to stay a colonel he'll do what I tell him."

Annalaya sighed, pushed back from the table, went to where she stored her tools.

Half an hour later she told Sullo, "It's done." The Governor was dressed for the weather, waiting. She went back to her table.

"Aren't you coming?"

"No. I'll continue my research. In case your miracle doesn't work out."

"What are you saying?"

"I'm not saying anything but what I said. You don't need me over there. If I stay here working we won't have lost any time if we do have to go in the front door, after all."

Sullo was not satisfied with that answer but he did not have time to cajole or beat the truth out of her. He joined his surviving Moretians and launched himself into the rain.

They were pleased to see him at Government House, almost. It had been a day of disasters. With Bruda suffering a seizure the entire city, for the moment, rested on the shoulders of ensigns and appointive tribunes who still had all their hair. They did not want the liabilities and responsibilities of directing more-senior professionals elsewhere in the city.

Sullo became impassioned with a malicious glee. Welcomed as a savior! How much better could it get?

"Let me see where the troops are," he said. "Tell me what they're doing now."

They showed him and told him.

Bruda's priorities had been protection of Herodian life and property, then reinforcement of strongpoints. He had put the garrison on alert but had kept the mass of troops out of sight for fear of provoking something.

"Assemble runners," Sullo ordered. When those had been gathered he sent them off with orders that would strip the barracks of men and arms and would send four thousand soldiers into the

Shu. He wanted to overawe the Dartars there with everything he had.

The military staff were astounded and baffled. When they asked what he was doing he told them, "What brought me here was a report, from a reliable agent, that al-Akla is about to shift sides and rebel with the natives. At the moment he's in the Shu maze, attempting to penetrate the citadel through secret passages. If he succeeds—and he expects to do so before dawn—the citadel is to become the headquarters for his Dartars and the native rebels. We weren't supposed to discover his treachery till the Dartar standard appeared atop the citadel, which would be the signal for a general uprising.

"Thanks to my agent we have an opportunity to abort this treachery. And to claim a conqueror's share of the citadel treasures."

He could not tell if they believed him. He did not care. They went to work as though they believed.

An hour later he was out in the rain at the head of Char Street, telling an improved version of his story to field officers while soldiers cursed the weather and hurried to surround the Shu maze. This audience was more skeptical than that at Government House. But recent events made convincing evidence for Sullo's contentions.

Sullo believed none of his story himself. He could not picture Qushmarrahans or Dartar savages as posing a serious threat.

Nogah came sliding out of the darkness to report, "The carpenter was right. Sullo swallowed the bait whole. He has messengers running everywhere, calling out the troops. Looks like he's going to send every man he can scrape up."

"Excellent." Fa'tad called men out of the alley, sent messenger after messenger scurrying off. Yoseh paid no attention. Nobody but Fa'tad knew what Fa'tad was up to. Trying to figure it out just confused him. And everyone else, too. Even Nogah had stopped asking questions and just went ahead and did what he was told.

Anyway, he was distracted. Tamisa had come home a few minutes ago and he could not keep his mind off that place down the street. Foolish, he knew. But he felt crazy enough to just walk down there and knock and ask to see her, to find out how she was.

Men were slipping away, climbing quietly to the upper level above the alley or crossing Char Street to disappear into the nearest alleys over there. Fa'tad hurried up top to "check on masonry stores," whatever that meant. When he returned, he said, "Yoseh, come here a minute."

Yoseh went, with a sinking feeling. Nogah and Medjhah closed in. They looked grim, what he could see of them. He did not think he was going to like this.

Fa'tad said, "The ferrenghi will be here soon. When they come those of us left here will scatter like we've been taken off guard. Yoseh, I have a role for you to play."

Yoseh groaned. The soft sound vanished in the patter of falling rain and chuckle of water running in the street.

"When we scatter I want you to run around like a mouse in a panic. You're young and you do a good job of looking confused. They shouldn't be suspicious when they catch you."

Nogah and Medjhah protested.

"Quiet." Fa'tad told Yoseh the story he wanted related to the ferrenghi soldiers. "You stick to that, don't resist, and pretend to be scared and you'll be all right."

Yoseh knew he would not have to pretend. He did not announce that, though.

Fa'tad said, "Just to make sure, and to give you a little added confidence . . . Come along." He marched straight down to Tamisa's door.

Yoseh followed, bent against the rain, suddenly conscious of the massive loom of his surroundings, warrens filled with terrified rabbits. How many thousands were in there, praying that no one out here remembered they existed?

The carpenter looked out his peephole. Al-Akla said, "Fa'tad." He never called himself the Eagle. "A word, if you please."

The veydeen opened the door and beckoned them inside.

Yoseh found Tamisa immediately. She was changing Stafa. Her sister was tending the old woman. He and the girl locked gazes. She lost track of what she was doing.

Fa'tad was saying something to the carpenter about leaving his door unlatched so Yoseh could use it as a bolt-hole if he got the chance, after the ferrenghi captured and questioned him.

Yoseh took a step forward. He kept looking at the girl but spoke to the older sister. "How is she doing?"

"She's going to be all right."

"That's good." After an uncomfortable pause, "We should have Arif out soon."

The older sister glanced up. There was moisture in her eyes but her voice was cool and even. "Thank you."

"Yoseh. Come along."

He stepped into the rain hoping he had not lied.

"Did you hear what we said in there?"

"Yes sir."

"Try to keep it in mind. The ferrenghi are coming." Fa'tad faded into the darkness.

A clangor wakened Azel.

Soldiers! Masses of soldiery. There was no racket like that made by masses of armed men in a hurry.

He bounded to the window, his wounds sending bolts of pain through his flesh.

Rain and darkness. Not a lot to see but scores of lanterns, like swarming fireflies, moving into the Shu.

What now? There were thousands of men down there.

He made himself as comfortable as he could. This would be a long and troubled vigil.

Naszif returned to Government House after a prolonged and thankless round of inspections for Colonel Bruda. Government House was as still as a tomb.

Bruda should be pleased. The Gate of Autumn was untouchable. The soldiers there were ready for anything.

Control of that gate would be crucial, whatever happened.

He entered Government House enrapt in his own misery. He was in Herodian harness for the first time ever. And Herodian uniforms were not suited for the rain. Until he neared Bruda's offices he did not realize that something was wrong.

The moment the silence struck home he grabbed an ensign and asked what had happened.

Worse than he could have imagined in a nightmare. Bruda laid low. Sullo in control. "The fool! The damned fool!" This was madness. "It's a trap! It has to be a trap!" And it was too late to keep the trap from closing.

Nothing to do now but try to survive.

The sentries assigned to patrol the wall north of the Gate of Autumn were not. They huddled inside, out of the rain. Their officers were more guilty than they. Because the sentries were not in an area considered critical no one had informed them that there was high excitement in Qushmarrah tonight.

The wall did not remain naked. Nomads came and dropped rope ladders. Silent men came up from outside, moved into the city, steady as trails of ants.

Who would believe it? Dartars did not go toward possible battle without their mounts. Everyone knew that who knew nothing about life and history in the Khadatqa Mountains.

No Herodian saw them but they were not overlooked by the eyes of the Living.

Governor Sullo moved down Char Street toward where Fa'tad al-Akla had had his command post. His Moretians formed a tight screen around him. A tribune by his side said, "The men are moving into the maze through all the entrances the Dartars left open."

"What about the savages? Any resistance?"

"No. They've scattered like startled mice. We've only caught one so far. Just a kid. Didn't know which way to run. Ended up plowing right into our men. They scared hell out of him. Had him talking in five minutes."

"Good. I'll have a few questions for him. Can we do something about these animals?" Char Street was filled with nervous horses and camels.

"They'll wander away when they get hungry enough, sir."

Sullo gave the tribune a sharp look. Another one of those, performing his duties with an absolute rectitude that masked a contempt for the civil authority.

They would by damned get that whipped out of them before he was finished with Qushmarrah.

Momentarily, he wondered what reliable hulls were available, in harbor. He would have a treasure fleet to form as soon as the weather cleared.

"This is where al-Akla was set up." A file of soldiers with unhappy faces, carrying lanterns, moved into an alleyway steadily.

"They look like they know where they're going."

"The routes in are marked out with ropes and, I gather, the false branches have been blocked off. So it's just a matter of following ropes to the area where the Dartars are mining."

"Good of them to do the work for us."

"Yes sir."

"Is that the prisoner?" He indicated a Dartar standing against a wall, unguarded, apparently too scared to run.

"Yes sir."

"Let's look at him."

The savage shrank away as Sullo approached. The tribune was right. He was just a kid. "You," Sullo said. "You were with al-Akla?"

The boy looked at him blankly. Of course. He did not speak Herodian. Another of Cado's failings. He should have made them learn.

"Can you talk to him?"

"Yes sir."

"Ask him where al-Akla is."

The tribune asked. The boy gulped, looked around for help that was not there, started chattering.

"He says al-Akla is in the labyrinth, directing the mining. Most of his captains are with him. Fa'tad expects trouble when he gets into the citadel. Big trouble, apparently."

Sullo asked questions. The boy answered with apparent

forthrightness, shaking. He did not know much that was useful except that Fa'tad was so sure he faced a fight he had taken a thousand men into the maze with him.

"The boy is a dolt. Al-Akla didn't take a mob in there to storm the citadel, he took them to hold it after he gets inside."

The last soldiers had disappeared into the alley. Sullo walked over and looked inside, the tribune and Moretians staying with him. He stared into the darkness. His feet felt cooler than they ought. A quarter-inch-deep flow of water came from the alley.

He glanced to one side . . . "What happened to the boy?"

The prisoner had vanished.

Sullo felt a sudden hollow develop in the pit of his stomach. Something was wrong here . . .

But that could not be.

He recalled Annalaya's cryptic remark about the faces of fortune.

The arrows began to fall with the rain, hissing like quarrelsome snakes. Moretians began to drop. Lanterns fell and broke. Tricklets of burning oil slithered across wet stone.

Sullo grabbed the only chance he had. He flung his fat bulk into the darkness before him.

When the door slammed shut Aaron bent, fed the wick of a candle to a coal in the hearth, coaxed a flame to life. He held the candle high.

The Dartar boy stood with his back against the door. His face cloth was gone. He looked terrible, as though he had just peered down the throat of Hell.

Aaron got up and went toward him.

"Don't. Don't look out there."

"I was going to bar the door." He took hold of the boy's arm and urged him toward the hearth, sat him down.

Laella and Mish were wide awake, watching. Aaron nodded to Mish. "Make some tea." He went back and barred the door.

Mish settled onto her knees before the hearth, fed in a few precious pieces of fuel. She did not look at the boy directly when she asked, "What's wrong, Yoseh? Did they scare you that bad? Did they hurt you?"

"No. Yes. They scared me. But it's not that. It's what's going to happen now. Fa'tad is going to kill them."

Faintly, through the heavy door, Aaron heard cries.

From her position against the back wall Laella said, "Aaron, this wall is damp again. You've really got to do something."

Each time there was a heavy rain the wall passed water. He thought it came down from a bad spot in the roof. But nothing he tried did any good. He took a look mainly to keep peace in the household.

This time there were beads of water on the bottom foot of the wall, forming and dribbling down like drops of sweat.

The ferrenghi witch glanced up when Fa'tad made his entrance. She did not seem surprised. "So. Fortune did wear a false mask." Maybe nothing could surprise a sorceress.

"What?"

"I cautioned him that his luck might not be as good as it appeared."

"He was a small man, fat with greed, easily led."

"Yes. Was? You killed him?"

Fa'tad smiled, a little sadly, a little wearily. He *was* an old man and age had taken its toll of everything but will. "No. He's underground but he isn't yet dead."

"I see. And you come to me because you want into the citadel."

"Yes." No point hiding it.

"There was no hidden way in then, through the maze?"

"No."

"What will you do about Nakar? Are you one of those who want to restore him?" Suddenly, she seemed intense.

Fa'tad chuckled. "I'd be the first devoured if Nakar were resurrected. I value these old bones too much to permit that."

She studied him briefly, assessing his honesty. "I'll help you, then. The ancient doom must be discharged. Nakar must be destroyed, whoever helps complete the task."

Al-Akla frowned, surprised and puzzled. "I expected to work for that." He did not question his good fortune. "How close are you to finding the path?" He would not argue with fortune but he would keep a sharp eye on it.

"An hour or an eternity. This is sorcery. No gate pattern can be defined completely from outside. Each is unique. Each must be opened by steps. I have been eliminating those possibilities made impossible by this pattern's needs and what we know of its specifics. I have reached my limit from this vantage, though. Now I have to have someone actually walk the pattern. Colonel Bruda offered me prisoners to use. His promise is no longer of value."

Fa'tad responded to the hint by grunting. "I'll find you someone." He told his men to take care of her wants and to guard her well. They understood. He moved to another part of the Residence. He meant to adopt it as his headquarters.

Reports from his captains looked promising. The ferrenghi, taken from their blind side, had collapsed everywhere but at the Gate of Autumn and at Government House. About the Gate of Autumn he was indifferent. Time would take care there. But who would have thought those soft Government House functionaries would turn stubborn and defy his worst?

He inquired about the progress of the masonry work and learned that the remaining entrances to the labyrinth had been sealed. Excellent.

Four thousand ferrenghi veterans out of the way with hardly a blow struck.

He remained unsettled, though. The Living had manifested their interest and existence in no tangible way. Yet they were out there watching, waiting, invisible and unpredictable. The longer they did nothing the more dangerous they would become.

Azel was not an introspective man, not one to look inward for the meaning of what moved him. But time weighed heavily. His thoughts kept turning to the meaning of his own behavior.

And shied away. It almost seemed there were a few soft spots in there. He backed away lest he get so close he'd have to face them.

He wanted to admit no weaknesses. He was like a natural force. He acted . . .

A clash of arms rose outside. He looked, could tell little in the darkness and rain. No evidence to show who was doing what to whom. But something strange was afoot in Qushmarrah. None of those soldiers who had charged into the Shu had shown again.

When there *was* light enough to make out details he discovered that the soldiers besieging the citadel had been replaced by Dartars. A few corpses in Herodian white lay on the pavement like bundles of clothing cast off by refugees too hurried to be burdened by possessions. Though the image that crept into his mind was dead kittens.

Dartars? What the hell?

The world had gone crazy.

One by one the lanterns consumed the last of their fuel. As each died the world underground became a little darker, a little smaller, tighter, and a little more fearful. The clash of metals and cries of wounded echoed up from deeper in the maze. Some of the soldiers were having trouble with those who haunted the labyrinth. Those ghouls seemed desperate to reach the surface. What drove them so?

Governor Sullo was incapacitated by terror, one fright short of voiding his bowels. His Moretians kept him moving as they sought a way out. They also kept him quiet, knowing the soldiers he had gotten into this fix would need little provocation to turn on their self-appointed commander.

Going downhill within the maze—toward the harbor, not toward the heart of the labyrinth—proved a bad idea. In places water stood waist-deep. In others it was as deep but not standing, it was running toward the heart of the maze.

No wonder the vermin were trying for the light. The deep places were filling. They were being forced out of their fastnesses. People were not the only thing being trapped by al-Akla's masonry.

Sullo grew more terrified. He was going to drown . . .

The Moretians reversed course and sought salvation upward,

growing ever more impatient with their employer's wheezing, whining efforts to keep up.

The last lantern gave up.

Raw panic filled Sullo's throat with a shriek that could not tear its way free. He managed only a soft, "Don't leave me! Please?"

Soon afterward a big outcry ran through the maze. It took a while to sort out into any sense because of the legions of echoes.

General Cado had been found and liberated.

That small part of Sullo's brain still capable of reason recognized the exclamation point marking the end of his brief and disastrous reign as master of Qushmarrah.

20

Aaron peered through the peephole into a Char Street empty of life. It was Saabat, the holy day, the day of rest, and it continued to rain, but neither accounted for the absence of traffic. No matter what, Char Street bustled with people who had places to go and things to do. Except today.

Aaron did not like it. He had a feeling it was, somehow, a little bit his fault.

He turned away. Mish and Laella were putting the final touches on a bedraggled make-do breakfast. Eating would be grim for a while.

None of the markets were open. If the rain persisted they would not be providing much that was fresh tomorrow, either. Country people would not be eager to slog the muddy roads, even though they could be sure of good sales if they did.

The Dartar boy ate sparingly, aware that his hosts were short of supplies. A good one, Aaron thought. For a Dartar. But a Dartar even so. He bore watching.

Aaron accepted a bowl of mushy stuff from Laella, lighted near his mother-in-law, foreseeing many similar meals. "How do you feel this morning?"

Raheb grunted noncommittally. She had not yet come to

terms with the fact that she owed her life to a Herodian witch. The foundations of her certainties had been cracked and chipped and it would take her a while to mend then.

Mish and the Dartar were comfortable now, but Mish still did most of the talking, chattering without letup. Aaron wondered if he had been as empty-headed and naive at that age.

"Yoseh. When do you think al-Akla will try to break into the citadel?"

Mish shut up. The women listened intently.

"Today sometime, sir. As soon as possible. He has to do it fast if he wants it all to work out."

The boy had, so far, shown no inclination to rejoin his brothers. Aaron wondered what special instructions he had received concerning the Habid family. "After we eat I think we should go find out what's happening."

The boy nodded though he did not seem taken with the idea.

Stafa asked, "Arif coming home, Dad?"

"I hope so, pretty soon, Stafa." Stafa had proven more resilient than his elders, except in the heart of the night, when he had been terrified that bad men would come take him away from his mother.

Aaron said, "Laella, if this doesn't work out we're going to have to move."

"I know." She said it with a conviction she usually reserved for Aram's law. She had something to add, too, but a knock on the door interrupted.

Aaron went, carrying a knife. He looked through the peephole. "Yoseh, it's your brother." He opened the door.

Yoseh watched Nogah come in, uneasy. He had been given no specific orders about what to do after he ducked into the carpenter's house but he was sure they had not planned for him to stay till they came to get him.

Nogah looked at him a moment, shook his head, asked, "You moving in here, kid? Come on. We have work to do."

Yoseh was too embarrassed to reply.

Tamisa got even for him, sort of. She filled a chipped cup with the pale tea her family drank, went to Nogah and offered it in such a sweet, polite, gentle manner that he could not refuse without looking an ass.

She came away smiling wickedly. She winked at Yoseh. She had begun to sense her power.

Yoseh waited nervously while Nogah sipped, Mish bustled around, and the carpenter got himself ready for the rain. Nogah scowled but did not say anything. He had become defensively uncomfortable under the scrutiny of the two older women.

Out of nowhere it occurred to Yoseh to wonder if this rain had reached far enough south to spread some moisture across the mountains. He could imagine the women and children bustling around trying to salvage every possible drop. He could see the old men and stay-at-homes trying to reinforce embankments meant to channel streams into shaded and hidden pools. Precious, precious, the rain.

Maybe this would be the turning they had been awaiting since he was a child.

Stafa went to Nogah and asked, "I ride horsy?"

"Not today. The horses are all inside. It's raining."

The boy pouted for a moment, then got interested in something else.

"Are you ready?" Yoseh asked the carpenter.

"Yes."

Yoseh recalled examples of his father's flowery oratory, thanked the women of the house for their hospitality. Nogah stared at him slack-jawed. He opened the door, let the veydeen precede him, then told Nogah, "Thank Tamisa for the tea and let's go, big brother." He was amused. Service with Fa'tad al-Akla did not permit many chances to practice the social graces.

The street was deserted. Mounts and gear had been removed. Fa'tad had no more interest in the Shu, except to leave a handful of men there to intimidate the veydeen. The exits from the labyrinth were no worry. They had been sealed with far too many thicknesses of brick to be opened by the men trapped inside.

Yoseh asked, "Where are we headed?"

"The Residence. Fa'tad's made that his headquarters. And us

guys have to keep an eye on the ferrenghi witch. She's almost ready to have a crack at getting into the citadel."

Yoseh frowned. The carpenter asked, "The witch Governor Sullo brought? She's helping you now?"

Nogah said, "She doesn't care who she lets inside as long as they finish what Ala-eh-din Beyh started. I get the feeling it's personal." He sounded like he had trouble believing the woman could be as pliable as she had proven.

They entered the Residence, shook the rain off. Yoseh wondered what they would do with the carpenter. Fa'tad would not want him tagging along everywhere. Nogah said, "Go up those steps there and down the hall to the left. I'll report in."

"Come on," Yoseh told the veydeen. "Let's see this witch. If we're going to be watching her we're going to be right in the middle whenever whatever happens." He was not excited about that. He had a Dartar's dread of sorcery.

The carpenter followed, gawking at their surroundings as much as he did. "They say the citadel is a hundred times as rich as this."

"I know," the carpenter said. He seemed too awed for thought or conversation.

They found Medjhah and the others in a large and poorly lighted room where a homely woman leaned over a table, frowning, oblivious to their presence. Medjhah, Mahdah, Faruk, and the others surrounded Yoseh, chattering, teasing, obviously pleased that he was unharmed.

That warmed him inside.

They were less effusive than they might have been without an audience. They were Dartar and veydeen, and ferrenghi were present.

The carpenter smiled uncomfortably. The woman ignored them so thoroughly they might not have been there—till she rose suddenly, said, "I'm ready to begin my experiments," in accented ferrenghi. Yoseh caught only the fact of her readiness.

Medjhah fumbled out a few clumsy phrases to the effect that they had to wait for Nogah. She was not pleased. Like the rest of them she had had no sleep and wanted to get on and get it over.

Nogah showed a minute later. He said, "Fa'tad wants to know how much longer we're going to stall around up here." He shoved a captured knife and sword at the carpenter, who took them but looked at them like he had been presented with a fistful of snakes.

Medjhah replied, "Yon beauty is waiting for you, big brother, her little heart going pitty-pat."

Nogah gave him an ugly look. "Then let's move out." He communicated with the witch using signs, though Yoseh knew he could have stumbled around and made himself clear with his crippled ferrenghi.

Azel was talking to himself, he was so tired and hurt so much. Torgo did not help. The eunuch was getting as nervous as an old woman.

Time was sliding by. Whatever they were going to try out there, they were getting close to trying it.

He could not see much because of the rain but he suspected the Dartars were busy. Damned few were watching the citadel. Al-Akla probably had every man he could plundering. It looked like a "grab everything quick and get out before the Herodians send relief forces" deal.

Fa'tad had chosen his moment well, hadn't he? The camel-loving bastard. The coast west of Qushmarrah in chaos because of Turok raiders. The east facing the threat of war. Beyond Caldera the legions faced Chorhkni, Saldun of Aquira, and his allies. That standoff had persisted for years. It was sure to be tested before summer's end. Would be tested instantly if troops were withdrawn to deal with an uprising elsewhere.

A scuffle behind him. Torgo. Again. "Azel, I think she's coming out of the deep sleep, into normal sleep."

Azel grunted. "Good. How soon can we wake her up?"

"She should get a normal amount of regular sleep if she can. At least. As much as we can let her have, for sure. Her weariness has gone deeper than the flesh and the mind. The soul needs time to recover, too. Or she could stumble during the final rite and destroy us all."

"You know how long the resurrection rite ought to take?"

"No. A while, though. It won't be like twisting a love charm. What are they doing out there?"

"Nothing yet. Still." Azel turned back to the window. "Wait. Here comes their witch."

Torgo crowded up beside him. He had to work to hide his true feelings about the eunuch's proximity. Torgo said, "I thought she belonged to the Herodians." She was surrounded by Dartars who looked ready for trouble.

"Maybe they got something she can't do without." Azel regretted the remark instantly but its cruelty went right past Torgo. Azel shrugged, paid attention to what was happening down there. He laughed suddenly, a near roar of tension flooding away.

"What?" Torgo demanded. "Why are you howling like a hyena?"

"Look! We got all the time we're ever going to need. She ain't working on the Postern of Fate, she's pecking on the fake pattern Nakar put in front of the main gate. She can mess with that forever and not get anywhere because there ain't nowhere to go."

Torgo looked. He was grinning when he pulled back.

Azel went to work. This was a good time to let Torgo get a solid idea that he might have help if he decided it would not be a good plan for Nakar to hang around after he kicked ass on the Herodians.

Azel chuckled. Let Torgo take care of old Nakar and set it up so the Witch saw the eunuch do it, and who did that leave to pick up the pieces and comfort the widow and help straighten out Qushmarrah?

It was a long chance. But it sure as hell wasn't as long as it had been when he'd begun playing the game.

He leaned forward again. This time he spotted the father of the chosen brat with the sorceress and Dartars. Bastard was in for some heartbreak, wasn't he?

Azel pulled back. "Why don't we go down, get us something to eat and maybe get drunk while those idiots are pounding their heads bald on the wrong stone wall?"

* * *

Bel-Sidek eased back from the edge of the flat roof when he heard someone coming up. He sat up in a puddle, already wetter than a fish. Zenobel and Carza appeared. Carza was still angry. Zenobel nodded wearily. He had gotten through at last.

Bel-Sidek said, "We're all here now," needlessly, to the other khadifas, who had been with him for some time, without enthusiasm. "You look like you have something to tell us, Zenobel."

"Just the latest. They have the whole wall except around the Gate of Autumn. They're ignoring that. They have patrols all over the city, keeping people off the streets. They're only looting Herodian property."

"So far," King Dabdahd grumbled.

"So far," Zenobel agreed. "They don't get into the citadel pretty soon, I think they'll grab whatever they can get. They'll want to be long gone when Nakar comes around."

"But Nakar isn't. We're not going to let him."

"Fa'tad doesn't know that."

"Yes, he does," bel-Sidek said. He was unsure what to think about Fa'tad's actions. The notion that he meant to loot Qush-marrah and head for his native mountains, where he would be safe from retribution, seemed too direct and simple. "In the sense that he knows I'll do everything I can to stop it."

Gold, silver, and jewels were as valuable to Dartars as to anyone and Fa'tad had said he wanted the treasures of the citadel for his people, so they could buy their way out of the grip of famine. But if he plundered Qushmarrah and left an angry coast behind, where would he spend his treasure?

The others looked at bel-Sidek, less than honoring, waiting for him to drop some pearl of wisdom they could condemn or contradict. He said nothing. He preferred to let someone else start the inevitable argument.

Salom Edgit obliged. "What're we going to do?" His tone implied that someone was ducking hard choices. This Salom Edgit who, a few days ago, had had no faith in the future or movement.

"We're not going to do anything. For now."

"What?" They looked at him with varying expressions. Carza was furious.

"Is there any sensible reason to get our men killed while Fa'tad isn't bothering anyone but Herodians? If he turns on our people we'll respond. Meantime, let his men take the brunt. We'll conserve strength and trickle it into areas where concentrations will be useful if we do have to fight."

Zenobel protested. "But honor . . ."

"Honor hasn't got a damned thing to do with it. And never has. All right. Say we try to get even for Dak-es-Souetta. Our men are poorly armed and out of training and not all of them are anxious to fight, anyway. Win or lose, we'd suffer badly. Say we did smash Fa'tad. Then with whatever we had left we'd had to deal with the surviving Herodians, then with the expeditions Cado sent out when they return, then with whatever Herod sends to restore order."

"You have a negative outlook, bel-Sidek."

"Would you say it's unrealistic?"

"Damn it, no! I hate it, but you're right."

Carza snapped, "Yet with Nakar restored we'd suffer none of those weaknesses."

King said, "I'd sooner swear allegiance to Herod."

Carza seemed baffled.

Smugly, bel-Sidek asked, "Have you forgotten what it was like when Nakar was alive?"

"No," Carza snapped back. "I haven't forgotten." His anger was in check by the strength of a whisker.

Carza's family had been favored under the old order. So some there were who would welcome a restoration, not having had to bear the weight of the sorcerer's previous incarnation.

For some reason bel-Sidek thought of the carpenter Aaron with his powerful resentments of those who had ruled before the conquest. There were tens of thousands of Aarons in Qushmarrah and they could well represent an additional factor in the already confused power equation.

Only Nakar the Abomination had been strong enough to rule without some degree of consent from the ruled.

The argument sputtered on without bel-Sidek contributing, reason gradually conquering passion. Carza's view won no support. Bel-Sidek watched the Dartars move around in front of the citadel.

Speak of the devil! There the carpenter was, right in the middle of things.

But would he not be at that gate himself if it was his son imprisoned and scheduled for sacrifice? Hell, yes. And damned be the politics.

He could find nothing in his heart with which to condemn the man. "Carza. Will you come look at those people and see if you can tell what they're doing?"

Carza did as he was told, with poor grace.

What kind of rule could they provide, should they come to power, when they could not manage courtesy, or even civility, among themselves?

A nasty thought tracked across his mind. If Herod and Fa'tad were pushed out, there might be a bloody period till a strongman emerged. And that man was unlikely to be Colonel Sisu bel-Sidek. He did not have the backing. Pressed, he would have to bet on Zenobel.

It was something to consider in his spare moments. His companions would be thinking about it, not that the possibility of independence actually existed.

Carza snorted, then laughed softly. "The fools are going at it from the wrong direction. They can't get in through the main gate."

Bel-Sidek's stomach knotted suddenly. No! So much time had fled already. For all anyone knew they were bringing Nakar around right now . . .

He wished to hell he had some idea what was going on in there.

He tried to put that out of mind. Too much fear came with those thoughts. His stated attitudes condemned him as surely as any Dartar or Herodian should Nakar make his return.

King Dabdahd crept up beside him. "You were always the genius staffer, bel-Sidek. The strategist the old man counted on. What would you do with the citadel if you grabbed it? You think Fa'tad might?"

It was not like King to dither and flutter around the edges of something but it was not like him to have an original thought, either. Clearly, he had had one. He did not want to state it plainly because someone might laugh.

Bel-Sidek saw it clearly enough. "You could be right."

Fa'tad might want the citadel itself as much as the treasures inside it. From within its impenetrable walls he could scour the city of every valuable before he left for his mountains—or he could stay and rule, harvesting Qushmarrah's wealth slowly and more certainly. He might even rule with a certain benevolence, restricting his predations to Herodians and those who declared themselves his enemies.

He'd then have a place to spend treasures for the benefit of his people.

At last bel-Sidek thought he saw the true face of Fa'tad's ambition. An ambition that would live or die according to whether or not he took the citadel before Nakar quickened.

"You're right, King. Thanks for making me see it. I'll give it some thought." What it meant, though, he feared, was that the Living would have to try to prevent it—with all that implied in lives wasted and new vulnerabilities.

Salom Edgit asked, "Do we all have to be up here for this? I could use a chance to dry out."

"I can go along with that," Carza said.

Bel-Sidek nodded. Still, someone had to keep an eye on the Dartars. He asked for a volunteer, got King Dabdahd. The rest headed for shelter and continued debate.

The fleet from Qushmarrah reached the far shore of the Gulf of Tuhn sooner than anticipated. The weather was more hospitable there. The troops were ashore and ready to greet the Turoks before nightfall. Whatever happened elsewhere, those raiders would be numbered among General Lentello Cado's triumphs.

Not a soul witnessed the Herodian landing.

Zouki followed Arif wherever he went, whatever he did. Arif fled, dismayed by the look in Zouki's eyes, a terrible but unreasoning look. A beast look.

What did it mean? His young mind could not make sense of it. It was merely another fright among many.

The big man and another came to the cage. Arif was terrified. Something about the shorter man . . . Zouki was frightened, too. He ran to hide with the rock apes, though he remembered nothing directly.

The two men stared at Arif and spoke too softly to be overheard. Arif was sure they were talking about him. He wanted to run and hide, too, but was petrified. He did not want to get closer to Zouki, either. And there was nowhere else to run.

One of the girls came to Arif after the men left. She just stared at him. That made him uncomfortable. He said, "My dad will get me out." He wanted to believe that so badly he had convinced himself it was true.

Belief made the terror almost bearable

21

Aaron felt like a clown, carrying a knife and a sword. He could not help thinking his Dartar companions found him amusing. What did he know about swords? He had not had one in hand for six years and even back then all he'd done was keep his blade clean and sharp and oiled. That night in his own home was the only time he'd seriously tried to kill somebody.

Then he looked at the Dartars more closely. It was unlikely many were more experienced than he. They were too young. Fa'tad would have his veterans placed where the chances of real fighting were greatest. The advantage these boys had was that they had grown up in a harsher environment and fiercer culture.

The Herodian sorceress chattered steadily. Even Nogah could make no sense of what she said. He sent for someone to interpret.

The man who came was an older Dartar who made the youngsters nervous, obviously someone whose good opinion meant a lot to them.

"Mo'atabar," Yoseh told Aaron. "Our captain's second and a friend of our father. Having him here is like having Father's ghost watching over our shoulders." The boy was determinedly on his best behavior.

Mo'atabar translated as the sorceress rattled on. At first it seemed she was just talking to herself, thinking out loud, making little sense. Then she said something about men watching them. Everyone responded as though to an unexpected thunderclap. It took Mo'atabar a minute to stop her and back her up.

"Two men watching from the citadel, in the top of that tower." She pointed with her nose. "Another half dozen on the roof of the red and white three-storey building with the balconies, there on the edge of the square."

Aaron tried to appear unconcerned as he glanced that way. She meant the home of that crazy woman who owned the ships. He spied the silhouette of a head. The light was too poor and the distance too great to make out any features.

Mo'atabar said it. "The Living. They have been quiet as mice but you know they're out there watching. Faruk, come here." Mo'atabar whispered to the younger Dartar, who then ambled off toward the Residence.

The sorceress was on to something else now, muttering about the job at hand. "Something wrong with this pattern. Doesn't feel like it goes anywhere. Almost like it folds in on itself. When am I going to get someone I can experiment with?"

"Soon," Mo'atabar promised. "I just sent a man to find out."

Liar, Aaron thought, catching enough of that to understand. Whatever message Faruk had carried, it had had to do with the Living. No one ever told the truth. Everyone was maneuvering and trying to manipulate everyone else. Which said what about his place in the middle of things?

He did not see how he could be any use to anyone anymore. The Dartars were paying him off by letting him tag along. Unless they used him as a symbol, a banner to be trotted out and pointed at as an inspiration for a noble cause.

He tried not to think of Arif, or of Arif's proximity, maybe no more than a stone's throw away. He had to keep his head.

A troop of Dartar horsemen passed, coming from the direction of the Residence, looking like they were headed for trouble. Mo'atabar hailed their captain, who said they were headed into the Shu where some of the trapped Herodians had broken through a third-level closure and were trying to fight their way

out of the maze. The outbreak had been contained but it needed
to be pushed back and the breach sealed again. Right now there
was fierce fighting on the tiers above the place where Aaron lived.

A moment of panic.

Then reason returned, accompanied by the realization that
most of any bloodletting would take place in the Shu because
most of Herod's men were there.

"Yoseh, I need to get my family out of that. They'll be in the
middle of it."

The boy looked at him like he wondered why he was wasting
time. "I'll tell Mo'atabar."

Mo'atabar summoned Aaron and tied a piece of colored cord
around his left arm, at the elbow. "So you'll be known as a friend.
But don't push your luck."

"I'll be back." Aaron started walking, expecting a challenge
before he got out of sight of the citadel. Though he did not run
he wasted no time.

Yoseh watched the carpenter hurry away. He tried not to worry
about Tamisa. Not his place. No reason to trouble himself. She
was as far beyond his reach now as she was before he met her.

Nogah asked, "What's he up to?"

Yoseh explained.

"Good idea. I'm starting to think our witch is as useful as
udders on a bull. When's she going to do something besides talk
to herself?"

Nogah was frightened! Damn! He was sure they would not
break through in time.

Yoseh saw the same fear everywhere—and in the witch most of
all. The citadel had given them a lot of time. Maybe they were
playing games in there. Maybe they were just letting the invaders
torment themselves.

Yoseh had not been tense till he began thinking about what a
deadly race this was. The pressure had begun to mount. Now he
wondered why he had talked himself into coming to this mad
city. Mo'atabar was right. It was the city of lead and gold. Only

the gold was imaginary and lead was what became of your dreams.

Men leading a string of ten prisoners came out of the rain—not Herodian prisoners of war, as Yoseh had expected, but Qush-marrahans with the ratty look of petty criminals. Mo'atabar lined them up in a sad parody of a formation.

"What we're doing here is trying to get into the citadel," Mo'atabar told them. "There's a sorcery on the gate. We have to penetrate it. I won't tell you your part isn't dangerous but I won't risk you unreasonably, either. Your chances of getting through are good. And once we've found our way inside you'll be released."

Yoseh knew he would have jumped at the chance had he been stuffed into a cell waiting to be chained to an oar in a Herodian galley.

"We got a choice here?" one man asked. He looked more hardened than his fellows.

"Of course. We won't force anyone. If you don't want to volunteer let me know. I'll cut your throat and the rest of us can get on with our work."

"'Bout the way I thought it'd be."

Mo'atabar told the sorceress, "They're all yours. Tell me what you want to have them do."

In the beginning Yoseh thought what the witch was doing was a lot of foolishness. She picked a prisoner, lined him up just so, had Mo'atabar tell him to take four baby steps forward. He was to remain motionless there till he received instructions otherwise. Then she had another man repeat that and take a couple of side steps, then three forward.

By the time the fifth went through his routine unharmed the others began to relax. And Yoseh realized there was something happening, after all.

That fifth man looked a little like he was behind the heat shimmer that rose off the Takes. And the sixth, once he got where he had been told to go, was only a vague discoloration except when Yoseh looked at him sort of sideways and indirectly.

The seventh man disappeared completely. There was no evidence he existed at all—except for his screams.

Aaron thought he was clever to move his family into Naszif's home. With no one in the streets, with every door and window barred so no one could see trouble coming, none of Naszif's neighbors would know who was staying inside.

He got them in unnoticed, with everything they could carry. Then Laella accompanied him to the door. There was a look in her eyes he had not seen since the day his company had left for the Seven Towers. She avoided touching the weapons he carried so clumsily. "Be careful, Aaron," and the way she said it made it more than a parting caution. It was a prayer.

He kissed her forehead. "I will. Believe me, I will. I'm no hero."

"Don't say that. Yes, you are."

He looked at each of them in turn, and Stafa the longest, then he went.

Aram had to be guiding him. Going home, down Char Street, he had run into no one, though he had been sure he would encounter Dartars who would not believe the cord around his arm. He had not. And it looked like his luck would continue now.

It did not occur to him to wonder what had become of all those horses and men who had hurried into Char Street supposedly to keep the Herodians from escaping.

"Aaron."

He was so startled he almost drew his sword. He looked around—and there, in the mouth of an alley, was bel-Sidek. He looked around again, hastily, suspiciously, fearfully.

"I'm alone, Aaron. And unarmed."

"What do you want?"

"I have a message for your Dartar friends."

"What? Why?"

"Occasionally even our enemies do something we favor. We—my faction among the Living—have no desire for Nakar's return. I've told Fa'tad I'd accept the looting of the citadel if that's his price for leaving Qushmarrah."

"So what's the message?" Aaron did not believe a word the man said, but neither did he disbelieve. The captains of the factions all created their own truths. Parts of some might actually dovetail with reality.

"It's direct and basic, Aaron. They're trying to get into the citadel through the wrong door. The sorcery protecting the main gate is a fake and a decoy. The real entrance is a postern around to the south. The pattern guarding it has been in place two centuries, which is why no one knows about it. It leaves the wall looking unbroken. I'm told there are alarms built into the pattern. You won't surprise anyone."

"They know what we're doing. They've been watching all morning."

"Ah? Pass that along, then. Quickly. They've had too much time already." Bel-Sidek glanced up and down the street, retreated into his alley.

Aaron looked around, too. He saw nothing but frowning buildings and falling rain. He shrugged and hurried uphill.

The Dartars seemed surprised to see him. He went straight to Mo'atabar with his story.

Mo'atabar seemed disinclined to credit it but Nogah butted in. "Let the witch decide. She's the one who knows this stuff. And she sure isn't getting anywhere going at it the way she is."

Yoseh told Aaron, "She's hit a dead end. She's lost three prisoners in there and still can't find the way."

Mo'atabar scowled. He did not like being taught to suck eggs by his grandchildren. But he relayed the message, anyway.

The Herodian woman brightened. She began chattering more fervently than she had earlier. She dropped what she was doing and hastened around to the south face of the citadel. After a few back-and-forths she froze and stared. Her chatter became vehement.

Mo'atabar said, "You were right, carpenter. She's cussing herself out for not having seen it. And answering herself, saying she missed it because it was so cunningly hidden."

"She's arguing with herself?"

"All Herodians are mad," Mo'atabar declared.

Reyha had nothing to do and teetered at the brink of terror, so Naszif had her accompany him on his endless rounds of the barricades. He found her chores to occupy her hands and mind. She went along because she needed the distraction desperately.

Naszif himself was, in a sense, pleased to be caught in a desperate siege. Fending off those Dartar traitors left him no time to brood about Zouki.

The fending had grown easier. They no longer seemed interested in conquering Government House, only in keeping him confined, out of touch.

He cursed his inability to discover what was happening elsewhere. He cursed the rain. In better weather the siege would not have cut communications. The whole sprawl of Qushmarrah could be seen from the heights of Government House. Information could come and go via signal lights or semaphore.

Reason said Herodian arms had suffered a disaster. Else the nomads would have been driven from the acropolis by now.

That *idiot* Sullo!

An ensign came running. He was little more than a child and did not belong here where his story might be cut short before it began. "Sir, the physician said to tell you Colonel Bruda is coming around and it looks like he'll be in control of his faculties."

"Very well. I'll be along in a minute." He checked one more post, stalling while he composed himself. He told Reyha, "So ends Naszif bar bel-Abek's day of glory, with nothing accomplished."

Reyha did not reply. She did not speak unless he made that necessary. Her last voluntary statement had been a generalized expression of gratitude for the help given Raheb Sayed.

Bruda had, indeed, made a dramatic recovery. He was sitting up, working on a heavy breakfast, when Naszif arrived. "It as bad as they're telling me?" he asked through a mouth full of apricot.

"Probably worse. I don't know. We're cut off. I expect they

control the city. No one has tried to relieve us or even to reach us. I've had all I can do just to hold on."

"Did a good job, too, for only having kids and superannuated veterans. Might as well tell me everything. Don't worry about repeating something these kids might have told me. They probably got it wrong."

Naszif told it as he knew it.

"That's Fa'tad al-Akla. Pick the moment to perfection, then strike like lightning. Having Sullo take over must have been a sweet that made him drool."

"What should we do?"

"What we can do and what those old farts in Herod will tell us we should have done, in retrospect, are two different things. If *any* of us get out of here they'll want to know why we didn't fight to the last man. You and your wife light somewhere, have something to eat while I give this a think."

Bruda pondered for fifteen minutes. Then, "Our problem is that we don't know what's happening. Take a white flag and go find out what al-Akla has in mind."

Naszif's heart tripped. "Yes sir."

Colonel Bruda had spoken in Herodian. Reyha did not understand till Naszif told her.

The labyrinth could have passed for one of the hells that awaited those who rejected Herod's nameless god. Terror and madness were the twin regents of the subterranean dark. The crazies from down deep continued their insane push toward the surface, attacking anyone they encountered. In turn, the Herodian troops had taken to attacking anyone who approached them.

The flooding continued to worsen.

Nonetheless, General Cado had gained a measure of control in his own vicinity. He guessed that as many as two thousand of his men had been killed, wounded, or drowned already.

He forbore swearing a mighty oath of vengeance only because the passion might rule him when he broke free at last and the effort to requite Fa'tad might prove suicidal. Who knew what disasters had transpired in the rest of the city?

Had the Living come out of hiding?

Had Nakar returned to grind everyone beneath his iron boot?

He would know in a few hours, he hoped. His tribunes thought they had found a way out through one of the drains carrying runoff water down from the third level. But it would take a lot of work yet to widen the passage enough using only weapons for tools, the soldiers wedging themselves into the drain with their bodies, working blind, under a continuous fall of water.

An officer came to report, "They've found Governor Sullo, sir."

"Yes?"

"He's dead. Murdered by his own bodyguards."

Cado grunted. Another political complication. "Stupidity is one capital crime for which there's never a pardon."

Would he, too, be found guilty and have to pay the supreme penalty?

Aaron had grown so accustomed to the rain that his only accommodation to it was to keep his head bowed so the drops would not hit him in the eyes. Yoseh muttered, "We'll all catch our death of cold."

Aaron agreed. "At least she seems more optimistic on this side." In two hours of probing, the witch had not lost another prisoner and only twice had her explorers encountered any obvious danger.

His stomach wound ever tighter. The sorceress had whispered a long time. Now Mo'atabar had Faruk aside for instruction . . .

Mo'atabar slapped Faruk on the behind. He scooted off around the citadel. Aaron shaded his eyes and studied the place, sensing its awareness of their presence, feeling something more, something like a great dread, or a great storm, slowly wakening. He thought he recognized that feeling Qushmarrah had lived with all the time till six years ago.

He looked at Yoseh. The boy felt it, too. They all did.

His heart plummeted. But he refused to believe that anything had happened to Arif. His son was all right. He had to be.

Yoseh's brother Medjhah came trotting around the side of the citadel. "Company coming, Mo'atabar. Ferrenghi officer with a white flag."

A moment later Naszif and Reyha appeared. Naszif was decked out as a Herodian. He exchanged looks with Aaron, sneering mildly at the company Aaron was keeping. He asked, "Who's in charge?"

Aaron indicated Mo'atabar.

Naszif approached the Dartar, who looked at him curiously, surprised to encounter a Herodian officer who had his hair and looked Qushmarrahan.

Reyha stayed a step from Aaron, staring at the wet pavement. She glanced up, then down again quickly. Softly, Aaron told her, "We're going in there pretty soon. We've found the way. We're just waiting for reinforcements."

"Oh." No more than a whisper. She peered at the citadel.

"Are you all right?"

"I'm fine." In a voice like a mouse, defeated and embarrassed.

"It's all right, Reyha. Nobody blames you for anything. It's not your fault."

She just shook her head, stared at the pavement. After a moment, she said, "I want to stay here, Aaron. I want to get Zouki when you go in there."

He wanted to say that was impossible, that there was no place for a woman among men storming a fortress, but said instead, "It'll be dangerous." He knew her desperation for her son better than he knew the few men he called his friends.

"I know. But I want to be there. And if he's not all right . . . If something's happened . . . Then the danger won't matter."

"I don't like the way you're talking, Reyha."

"Zouki is the only thing I have to live for, Aaron." She had scary stuff going on in her head, barely edging her words.

He did not know what to say so he said nothing.

Mo'atabar was telling Naszif something about the Herodians getting out of Qushmarrah.

For the first time, suddenly, Aaron realized that when dawn broke tomorrow and the workweek began he might be unemployed.

Azel clumped downstairs, ignoring his pain. He roared, "Torgo! Torgo! Where the hell are you, you ball-less bastard? We just ran the hell out of time!" He stampeded toward the Witch's chambers, roaring all the way.

Torgo popped out, pallid.

"We're out of time!" Azel yelled. "They're going to come. Wake her up."

"What happened? I thought . . ."

"I don't know what happened. You think I can read their minds? All of a sudden they're around working on the Postern of Fate. Won't take them long to work through the pattern. So let's hit it!"

Trouble was, though they had talked about it, they had no plan for meeting this challenge. Decisions were the province of the Witch. Even to Azel it had seemed there would be time enough to get organized after she woke up.

"Take care of her. Get her moving. I'll go try to arrange something to slow them down."

Torgo just stood there, mouth open, face pale, eyes dull.

"Move it, Torgo! Or we're all dead!"

Torgo drifted back into the Witch's chambers.

Azel limped on down to the main floor. He found the staff assembled already, terrified, alerted by his bellowing earlier. Here were all of Gorloch's surviving believers, eight men and twelve women. Not much to brag on. Azel told the men, "You guys get out some weapons. They're going to come through the Postern of Fate. Nakar left a hundred tricks and traps. Set them up. Turn them loose. We got to buy time till she can get down here to help."

They responded with no enthusiasm.

"Hey! You think about this. You remember this. They ain't

going to leave nobody alive if they get in here. Not you, not me, not nobody." He eyed the women. What the hell was he going to do with them? "Any of you want to help the men, grab a weapon and go." Surprising him, four chose that course. "All right. The rest of you go upstairs and see what Torgo has for you." He had a nasty idea. "Wait! You. You. Go keep an eye on those kids. Be ready to move them if I tell you."

The last two hurried off. Azel grabbed a lighted lamp and went down to visit Nakar and Ala-eh-din Beyh, only once he got there he ignored them. He stepped around one and over the other, carried the lamp into the darkness behind the image of Gorloch. He passed through a doorway closed by dusty black curtains, entered a suite of rooms that had been used by priests before and after ceremonies. Those chambers had remained inviolate since Nakar had stepped out shortly before the arrival of Ala-eh-din Beyh. The Witch had been forbidden trespass.

He hadn't forgotten his way around. He made several minor arrangements, then went to a wardrobe cabinet where sacerdotal robes and accessories still hung. He eased between hangings, used a knife to probe a seam in the cabinet's back.

Something clicked.

The cabinet back swung away into darkness. Azel followed it into a hidden room eight feet by eight. He lighted three lamps from his own, inventoried the room's contents.

Everything was there, as it had been when one of his duties had been to maintain the bolt-hole.

There were three ways out. One tight crawlway wormed through the citadel walls to debouch near the Postern of Fate. A vertical shaft climbed the citadel's tallest tower, the top of which was the highest point in Qushmarrah and could be seen from nowhere else. It could be reached only from this room.

The third exit lay beneath the floor. It burrowed deep into the earth.

He was satisfied. The escape option was covered. He topped off the oil in the three lamps, left one burning. There would be no time to piddle away lighting one if a retreat became necessary. He closed up and went to find out how Torgo was doing with the Witch.

He muttered all the way, cursing his wounds.

Bel-Sidek sensed something amiss the moment the soldier let him into Meryel's house. Something had changed. He could not lay a finger on it immediately . . .

He had left one of his own men on the door when he had slipped out. The man who let him in was not one of his own.

The khadifas were waiting where he had left them with orders to compare their resources in case it became necessary to take action. Hadribel was all puffed up with anger. King was red with embarrassment. Salom Edgit would not meet his eye. Carza was smiling like a cat with feathers in its whiskers.

So.

Bel-Sidek faced Zenobel, who showed him nothing. "Surprise. You made your move before the fact."

"What?" Startled.

"I'd thought you'd make your play later. I'd forgotten you tend toward overconfidence."

Zenobel did not look confident now.

King said, "We took a vote . . ."

"I know. Four to one to overthrow the overly cautious General, with Hadribel casting the dissenting vote and miffed enough to withhold the strength of the Shu at a time when the organization is enfeebled already by its loss of control in the Hahr. Which now owes allegiance to the khadifa of the Shu. So what do we have here? Shall I become a prophet and foretell the future?"

"By all means," Zenobel said, with less composure than he had possessed a moment ago.

"The movement will fall into two factions, the smaller loyal to the General's picked successor, the other the more successful. Once the invaders evacuate the city the war faction will split again when you and Carza try to shake off nuisances named King Dabdahd and Salom Edgit. We may see Living blood shed by the

Living. Then the final act, as you and Carza struggle for the right to shape Qushmarrah's destiny.

"About the time you get it sorted out Herodian legions will come to reclaim a city which has been too busy playing faction to prepare for their return."

He looked them all in the eye. Even Zenobel flinched.

He pushed out the door, to where four of Zenobel's men waited. "Take me wherever you're supposed to keep me confined."

The carpenter's conversation with the veydeen woman seemed personal, deserving of privacy. Yoseh drifted nearer Mo'atabar and the envoy.

The envoy wanted to speak ferrenghi. Mo'atabar refused. He was not going to let the man hide from witnesses.

The man gave in. "Colonel Bruda sent me to find out what terms Fa'tad might offer."

"Go over to the Residence and talk to Fa'tad, then."

"I stopped there. No one was there. Your group are the only Dartars I can find."

"Is that so?" Mo'atabar smiled nastily. "Then I'll have to tell you for him. He wants all ferrenghi, military or civilian, and all veydeen with the ferrenghi allegiance, to leave the city. You're to go on foot, taking only the clothing and shoes you're wearing, carrying only a small amount of food. You're to go out the Gate of Autumn and march eastward. The deadline for compliance is dawn tomorrow. Ferrenghi not on their way by then will be killed or sold as slaves."

The envoy wanted to argue but he knew finality when he heard it. "I'll relay that to Colonel Bruda."

"Do that. I'm sure he'll want to spread the word and find out how desperate his situation is. He can send messengers through the streets so long as they go in uniform, unarmed, alone, with a red cloth tied around their left arms."

The veydeen ferrenghi struggled to keep his temper.

Mo'atabar smiled again.

The envoy spun around, stalked toward his wife. Mo'atabar

pointed, indicating that Yoseh should stay near him. The man snapped at his woman, "Let's go!"

The mouse growled back. "I'm staying here. I'm going in there with them."

The man started to shout, froze, slammed his jaw shut, and whirled again. He glowered at the citadel. "I'll be right back. I'll go with you." He ran off.

The carpenter said, "His son is in there, too."

"I was there," Yoseh reminded him. He faced the citadel himself. That child-taker was in there, probably. That short, wide killer to whom he had shown the Face of Death . . . But only the carpenter knew. Right? And he would not know the significance of the act.

Yoseh was afraid. And felt guilty about his fear, though he knew if he asked, his brothers and cousins would admit they were frightened, too. But that was different, somehow.

Oh, did he wish that he had not come to Qushmarrah.

Mo'atabar and the ferrenghi sorceress were whispering up a storm, the woman's gestures growing more animated by the moment. They were ready.

A score of Fa'tad's picked veterans, armed and armored as heavily as ferrenghi heavy infantry, trotted around from the far side of the citadel.

She could not get her mind to function. She felt like she had been drugged. Nothing made sense. Torgo was begging her to get herself together. She could not. She could not remember why it was important that she wake up, though Torgo had told her several times.

Azel bulled his way into her bedchamber. "What the hell is this? I told you to get her up and get her down there."

"She's awake. She's just having trouble getting her bearings."

"What the hell are you being so delicate for? You going to curtsey your way to the gallows?"

Azel's abrasive voice began to draw her out of the fog. She watched him storm toward where she sat on the edge of her bed, his hand rising. She willed her body to move but it did not respond before the blow fell.

Pain shot through her, reached into that hidden place where anger slept, wakening it. Her surroundings came into focus.

Torgo hurled himself at Azel. Azel stepped aside. She snapped, "Torgo! That's enough! Azel, I shan't forget this."

"I hope not. I probably just saved your life. Candyass here would've dicked around till they were in here chopping you up for dog meat."

"Who? What are you talking about?"

"Damn you!" he bellowed at Torgo. "You didn't tell her?"

"I told her." Torgo sulked.

"He told me but the message didn't get through. I would appreciate it if you'd calm down and get to the point."

Azel said, "We got Dartars pounding on the door, woman. They're going to be inside any minute." He had a smug I-told-you-so look.

Some residual mental fog stalled her momentarily. Then she asked, "How can that be? Nobody has found the Postern of Fate before."

"They got their own witch and she unraveled the way in. Are you going to do something or are you going to sit there and just let things happen?"

The fear hit like a blast of steam. Nakar! If she did not do something she would lose him—and everything else. Just when she had found the right child.

She lunged forward. The women who had been standing around, silent and helpless and embarrassed, tried to stop her, insisted they dress her. She shook them off. There was no time. Her dream was under attack. Her love was in peril. For even entertaining that idea she would see those savages lose their souls.

Torgo and Azel and the women swept after her. The men muttered at each other angrily. She paid them no heed.

As she marched downstairs she asked what steps had been taken. Azel told her and made a few suggestions. Torgo sulked some more, a gigantic infant with feelings easily bruised.

"You take charge of stalling the attack, Azel. Do whatever you have to, to buy time."

"What I need is a little help from you. You bloody their noses and they'll back off."

She did not bother answering. "Torgo, stay with me. I want two women to light the lamps in the temple. The rest go with Azel."

She caught an exchange of looks between the killer and the eunuch. Azel was disappointed in her again. He seemed, almost, to despair.

Arif knew something had happened, and that something dreadful was going to happen, when all the people ran into the big room where the cage was. They came straight to the cage. The big man opened the door. They all came inside.

Zouki peeked out of the vegetation. He saw the woman. The beautiful woman. He went into a fit of tears. Arif thought he looked puzzled, like he was terrified and did not know why he should be.

The woman pointed. "That one, too."

Arif wanted to run away. He thought he could get away from them if he got in there with the rock apes. The apes hated the big man . . . But Zouki was there and something would not let him run. He hesitated a moment too long, anyway. One of the adults was between him and the vegetation, running after Zouki. Then the big man caught him up as he started to run the other way.

Thunder shook the citadel.

"Torgo!" the woman snapped. "Hurry!"

The big man said nothing, just snatched Arif up and set out after the beautiful woman. Behind them, Zouki squealed, caught. The other adults began rounding up the remaining children. The short, wide man yelled at them to hurry.

Aaron had stomach cramps. He had trouble hearing the Herodian sorceress, who had gathered everyone around. As soon as she stopped talking about it they were going to do it. The

Dartar boy Yoseh stood to his right, shaking. Reyha pressed against him from the left, strangely calm.

Mo'atabar translated from the Herodian, loosely. "She says that right inside the gateway we should run into a narrow, straight passageway about forty feet long. That's all she can tell about it from here. She says it should be the hardest part. We get through, the place should be ours. She says get through fast, don't stop for anything. She has to get in to the anchor for the pattern so she can kill its traps. Questions? No? Then let's get lined up."

They would pass through the pattern single file, follow-the-leader, so each man could repeat exactly the steps taken by the man ahead. Traps could be evaded but not disarmed except from within.

The surviving prisoners drew straws. Three would win immediate release. Four would lead the column. The winners cheered and the losers wept. Mo'atabar issued captured Herodian short-swords to the latter.

Aaron eyed the equipment carried by the shock troops. In addition to heavy shields, helmets, armor, javelins, and pikes, many had coils of rope wrapped around them, rope ladders, bundles of javelins and arrows and bows, or stuffed packs on their backs.

The line began moving.

His place was toward the end, behind Yoseh. Only Reyha, Mo'atabar, and the sorceress followed him.

He heard the screaming before he caught sight of the breach. He nearly voided himself. But the line kept moving and he thought of Arif in there and he kept moving, too.

Yoseh wanted to yell at the carpenter to stop stepping on his heels. He was moving as fast as he could. He had to concentrate on what Mahdah was doing so he would not misstep.

Sweat poured out of him, mixed with the sweat of the sky. He'd never been so thoroughly scared. Never before had he been given so much time to work himself into a panic . . .

He heard the screaming as the entrance wavered into existence, alive with flashes of pink and lemon light. As that dreadful maw welcomed him the momentum of the line faltered, but only for a moment. He skipped over two of the veydeen prisoners, then three of the warriors Fa'tad had sent to lead the attack.

Halfway along the passage there was a small guardroom the sorceress had not mentioned. Two men and a woman lay dead there. Blood covered everything, looking like shiny black paint in the feeble light of a single lamp. One of the men had been disemboweled. Yoseh gagged at the stench.

"Keep moving!" Mo'atabar yelled. "This tunnel is a death-trap."

It was. Yoseh stumbled over another five bodies before he reached its end. Three were his own people, one was a prisoner, and one was a woman with a javelin protruding from her back.

The passage ended in a large space divided into stall-like compartments by partitions of rough boards. The pink and yellow lights still played there. A fire burned in a corner. There was a lot of screaming. Dartars chased people through the maze and got caught as often as they caught someone.

"Stop!" Mo'atabar yelled. "Nogah! Get the bodies out of the passage. Find out if any of them are still alive. See if you can find lamps or lanterns or torches."

"Enemy bodies, too?"

"All of them."

Nogah assigned Yoseh, Mahdah, Faruk, and two others.

It was not pleasant work, nor was it easy, but it did not take long, either. Yoseh was pleased when he discovered that two of the Dartars were not dead.

Mo'atabar told the surviving prisoner he was free to leave.

The ferrenghi sorceress set up in the guardroom, began disarming the pattern gate.

Mo'atabar tried to convince the carpenter and veydeen woman they should stay with the sorceress. They refused. They wanted to run with the hunters.

Mo'atabar shrugged. "Your lives," he told them. "Your risk."

"Our children," the woman countered. She did not say much.

The look in her eye made Yoseh's flesh crawl. It was the look he imagined shone in the eyes of cannibals.

The battle of the storeroom ended, a Dartar victory but not cheap. Another five of the shock force had been slain. The losses concerned Mo'atabar though he tried to hide it. "Nogah, you and your bunch collect up the stuff these men were carrying." Yoseh ended up with a coil of rope, a bow, and arrows. What was he going to do with those?

The fire went out of its own accord. Beyond lay the only apparent exit.

Offered a bow, the carpenter refused. "I'd probably hit myself in the foot. Give me a javelin if I have to take anything." He accepted a shield, too. He said he had learned to use both in younger days.

The veydeen woman asked for a javelin, too. Handed one, she held it away like it was a poisonous snake.

Mo'atabar herded everyone together near where the fire had died. He said, "I asked the witch what next and she says the next area is kitchens and stuff. Once past those we should be past the worst."

Nogah muttered, "That's what you said about the passage coming in."

Mo'atabar scowled. "Look out for booby traps and ambushes." He added other cautions.

Yoseh did not listen closely. This was not the Dartar way of war, mounted, sweeping across the desert. This was like fighting through the caverns of the underworld. He stared at the dead defenders. Men and women both, all far too old to fight. Old as Tamisa's grandmother. He did not like what that implied.

Those ancients had sacrificed themselves. Though their efforts had not been fanatical or terribly courageous. It seemed a desperate attempt to buy time. Which had to mean there was something to buy time for.

Nakar the Abomination.

Yoseh's fear deepened.

He glanced at the carpenter and felt sorry for the man.

Mo'atabar read the same story from the same signs. He

admonished everyone to hurry. "Ready?" Like a good Dartar chieftain he led the charge.

The nothing of the opening hurled him back into the men behind him.

"It's blocked!" someone yelled.

"But there isn't anything there!"

Mo'atabar cursed and probed with a javelin snatched from someone's hand. "Blocked," he admitted. "Some damned witchery. Break through a wall or something. I'll drag the ferrenghi witch up here."

Men dropped their packs, began unlimbering tools.

The Witch paused at the doorway to the place of worship. She told the women who had accompanied her, "Go help Azel. Tell him I will be watching over you. Torgo, you stay with me. Keep control of the children."

Thunder shook the citadel. Torgo said, "It's like if they get too close together . . ."

"Maybe. Zouki, come here."

The frightened women left. The Witch dragged the boy Zouki through the doorway. "Close it up, Torgo. I'll seal it so it can never be opened. The same with the other entrances."

"But . . . Azel . . ."

"He has served his purpose. I have grown tired of him. I am going to let him die a hero's death defending his lord." She settled the boy Zouki by the altar, took the other from the eunuch. "Go on, Torgo. Get busy."

Torgo followed his orders but he was uneasy. He was not a genius and not an astute judge of men but he did feel sure that when Azel died he would not do so for the sake of the High Priest. Azel was a complex man who had concealed himself inside so many masks and lies he did not now know himself but he had given himself away in his conspiratorial whispers. There was one tiny hole in his emotional armor.

Torgo pursed his lips, feelings mixed. Because of that, and so much else, he wished Azel an evil end—but he feared that Azel might be their only hope for salvation.

* * *

"Here they come!" Azel roared. The stall trick had been good for an hour. He hoped the damned woman hadn't wasted the time, that she'd laid on a whole troop of tricks and barriers. He shoved his sack of provisions out of the way, let fly with a throwing spear. It stopped the first Dartar dead. "All right! Now! Run them in now."

The women whipped the terrified children into the battlefield of the kitchens. They did not go far, mostly stood around screaming while the adults pelted the Dartars with missiles from behind them.

The Dartars looked at that mob of brats, for a moment did not know what to do. That cost them. Azel laughed.

Their captain pushed them out behind their shields, formed a miniature turtle, advanced toward the brats. Archers began spraying arrows around. The turtle gobbled half a dozen kids, delivered them to cover behind the bakers' ovens.

When the turtle advanced again Azel flung a pair of lanterns toward the bowmen. The lanterns smashed. Flames leaped up. While the archers were occupied he grabbed a woman and used her as a shield. He charged into the turtle, laid about him with a meat cleaver, put three of the damned camel lovers down before he ducked back, still laughing.

The violence tore one of his wounds enough that it began to bleed again.

He could have held the bastards there and picked them off as they stampeded around trying to save the brats—if the citadel staff had not gone squeamish about the kids. The women ran off. That left him and two men to hold four exits.

He hurled his cleaver at the Dartar kid who had shown him the Face of Death but the boy moved. Azel grabbed his provisions and fled toward the great chamber where the cage stood. He wished he had a bow. He could give those Dartar bastards fits, sniping from the shadows there.

The staff would retreat from there toward the Witch's chambers, leading the chase the wrong way, buying more time.

He laughed again.

He had lied to them. He had told them the Witch had fortified her quarters with spells that would keep them safe once they closed the doors behind them. They would flee there thinking they need do nothing but lock up and wait for Nakar.

Hell. Maybe he hadn't lied. Who knew? The woman might have come to her senses. She'd put out a few other barriers, hadn't she?

General Cado sighed. The water chute was packed with soldiers. Nothing else but to try it. He gave the order to go.

The first man out was waist-high into the drain when three arrows hit him. He fell back on the men below him.

The Dartar watchers sped a dozen arrows down the drain, began filling it with whatever they found lying around loose.

A third of the way up the hill from the waterfront, in a second-level home in the center of the Shu complex, a woman wholly insignificant otherwise noted a trickle of water running down a wall, starting at eye level. She was baffled. Nothing like that had happened before.

Naszif stopped so violently he slipped on the wet paving stones and fell. Two hundred men surrounded the entrance to the citadel. Qushmarrahans. Armed. He recognized several, including his former commander, Hadribel.

The Living! Out of the shadows now.

They meant to take the citadel from its conquerors as soon as they felt the Dartars had done all the killing for them.

All he could do here was get killed himself. He got his feet under him and took off. The Living noticed him too late to stop him.

22

Aaron looked around frantically, yelled for Arif. Beside him, on her knees, Reyha held a terrified little girl to her breast, rocked and crooned softly, gently tried to quiz the child about Zouki. She got no answers. Ahead, the Dartar boy Yoseh stood in a doorway looking back, hesitant to leave them.

"Arif!"

His son did not answer. He was not here with the others. Zouki was not here.

Fear and horror redoubled. Several children had been hurt in the fighting, despite all efforts to avoid that . . . The Herodian sorceress jabbered at him and pointed. She wanted him to move along. He determined to stand his ground.

"Aaron." Yoseh beckoned him. "Come on. The children are not here. The Witch has them."

"How do you know that?"

"I asked these kids. They told me she came and got them and took them somewhere with her."

The bottom fell out of Aaron's stomach. A little hope died.

Yoseh led the way into the largest room he had ever seen, trying to stay alert enough for himself and the carpenter and veydeen woman, too. He had heard of this place. It was as awe-inspiring as the stories said. But there was no time to gawk. It was a madhouse. Rock apes and more children were screeching and running around. Mo'atabar and the others were trying to fight their way up a stairwell off to his left. They were up against another invisible wall. It let missiles come down but would not let them go up. Mo'atabar was ready to tear the place down to get around it.

Then Yoseh glimpsed the child-taker flitting through far shadows. He yelled, sped an arrow, and charged. When he reached the spot he found nothing but a snarling rock ape.

The ferrenghi sorceress shouted a warning that no one but, perhaps, Mo'atabar understood.

Brilliant light. A blow like the sudden impact of a hundred fists . . .

He did not know how much time had passed. When he came to he found his vision and hearing both impaired. He could barely hear Mo'atabar and the ferrenghi sorceress arguing bitterly at the foot of the stairwell. Mo'atabar wanted to carry the attack upward. The witch wanted to go another direction. She insisted the upward retreat was a diversion. Somehow, she carried her argument—and that left old Mo'atabar looking very frightened.

What now? Yoseh wondered as he staggered to his feet and went to see to the carpenter.

Bel-Sidek stood near the doorway to Meryel's balcony, listening. Meryel asked, "What in the world are you doing?" She had arrived home and instantly been arrested and put in with him by Zenobel's men.

"I'm listening for Dartar trumpets."

"What?"

"Anytime now my self-appointed successor is going to be forced to drink deeply of a dark and bitter wine called Fa'tad al-Akla."

Azel drifted through dark and silent corridors, cautiously. Had he been anyone else his mood might have been called sad. He hadn't done nearly as well with the camel jockeys as he'd hoped. Of course, if the woman had bothered to take time to do something besides just throw up a few barriers . . .

He had given them the slip. They should be headed upward now. That should hold them awhile. Maybe long enough for him to bash a hole through the woman's obsession and get her to fight. She could've cleaned the place out in the time she'd had since the bastards broke in. If she'd bothered to take it. But no. A little paint on the surface, a sop to keep him off her back, maybe, and right back to Nakar.

Damn Nakar . . . Well, might not be long left in that story. Depended on Torgo. The big idiot was primed. Set to go. If he didn't fade at the end.

He reached the temple door.

It was closed. For the first time in memory. "What the hell?" He tried it gently. It did not yield. A slight buzzing sensation tickled the tips of his fingers.

For a fraction of a second hurt flickered across his face.

Suspicion became conviction when he tried a side entrance and found it sealed, too. The same tingle teased his sense of touch.

Was *he* the object of her fortification?

That flicker of hurt came and went.

Maybe there had been some foreshadowing. Maybe he had felt it. Maybe that was why he had prepared the temple.

Or could it just be that Torgo had, at last, managed to get a knife into his back? He turned more grim than ever. The eunuch's payoff wasn't far off now. He was tempted not to wait on Nakar.

There were other ways to enter the temple. Ways of which even the High Priest's woman was unaware.

Azel the Destroyer had not been the messenger of Nakar the Abomination for nothing.

Three minutes later Azel slipped into the sacristy. He placed his provision pack in the hidden room, closed that up again, then crept up behind the image of Gorloch. He settled to watch Torgo and the Witch.

They had the brat whose taking had caused his first encounter with the Dartars tied into a chair. The kid was calm, attentive, almost eager. Azel was troubled. There was something wrong there. The boy seemed old beyond time.

Torgo and the Witch had the other kid strapped down on the altar, damned near in touching distance of Nakar. The kid carried on, screaming, fighting them. The Witch got set to go into her trance. Torgo fluttered around like an old woman, doing three things at once while trying to settle the kid down. Dumb ass. The kid was scared shitless. He wasn't going to calm down for anything.

Double scared?

Azel eyed the time-locked corpses of Nakar and Ala-eh-din Beyh, the brats, considered events of six years ago as heard secondhand. He considered knowledge picked up at Nakar's left hand. He hadn't a whit of that talent himself but he understood theory and mechanics.

Damn! The mad bitch could bring the whole world down around their ears. "Hold it!"

They jumped. The Witch squeaked. Azel cursed the look in her eye, pushed the pain aside. No time for that now. "You can't do this, woman. Not this way."

Torgo looked like he might drizzle down his leg. "How did you get in?"

"I walk through walls. Don't worry about me. Worry about what will happen if you jump into this the way you're going."

The Witch turned her back. Only Torgo showed interest. Irked, Azel demanded, "How did we get into this mess in the first damned place?"

The Witch ignored him. Torgo glanced at her, stared at the floor as he continued work.

Azel spat, "You put them in that damned time trance because Nakar would've got stomped dead if you didn't, woman. Remember? Ain't nothing changed, neither. You wake them up now they're going to go right on from where they left off." He eyed the Zouki brat. The kid looked back. Damned if the brat didn't look like he understood. Was the Ala-eh-din Beyh soul awake?

Somebody tried the main door. Torgo glanced at it, frowned. Azel slipped off his perch. "They're here."

Torgo watched him warily. "Worry about them, Torgo. Not about me. Want to bet they find a way in?" The damned woman hadn't stopped her preparations. Now she was lying beside the kid on the altar, working on her trance.

Torgo looked at her, at Azel, a rat caught in the open, dogs closing in. "What can we do?"

"Probably not a damned thing. Unless you can make her hear sense. Know how to do that?"

"I don't think so."

"Shit. Do your job, then. And hope Gorloch smiles." Azel drifted toward the door as though considering some rude greeting. But as he passed the Zouki kid, he punched the brat so hard he almost broke the boy's neck. "That'll put him out for a while. Get on with it."

The Witch began to murmur. Near as Azel could tell, her whole plan was to waken Nakar and ask him what to do next. Damned moron. Shit for brains. How did anybody let somebody get so much control they turned into a soul slave, stripped of even the sense to harken to survival instinct?

Something turned over inside Azel. For a moment he had the uncomfortable feeling that he'd glimpsed his true self. As though some impartial observer had asked what *he* was doing trapped like a rat.

The sounds of scraping and pounding came from the wall. Them damned camel jockeys knew they couldn't bust the door down so they were going after the wall.

"How long?" Torgo asked, looking that way.

Azel shrugged. He looked at the Witch. "How long you going to be, woman?" The kid was whispering back, stammering, resisting. Maybe the Nakar soul didn't want to come out and risk Ala-eh-din Beyh's final vengeance.

He never understood what that was about. Nakar hadn't talked about his enemies, back when. But a long time ago he'd offended somebody bad and there'd been a cabal out to get him ever since. A new assassin-wizard had turned up every few years, each cleverer than the last. Maybe the gods themselves contended against Nakar. If there was ever a guy who could get the gods down on him, Nakar had been him.

Azel glanced at the time-locked Nakar, at the Witch. What the hell did she ever see in him? "Torgo. You thought about what we discussed?"

The eunuch paused, glanced at the besieged wall, at Azel, at the woman, looked ashamed. He nodded.

"You in?"

Torgo nodded again.

"Good. Maybe we'll get out of this yet." If the ball-less wonder really could stick a knife in Nakar's back. "Looks like she's getting through." The kid was stirring, reluctantly.

A stone fell from yon wall. Dust puffed away. "About out of time, Torgo. Can you wake her up so she can take care of them?" The Witch hadn't responded to his earlier question.

"I don't think so." Another stone fell. A hand reached through, felt around. "I'll try."

"You do that." Azel stalked over and drove a knife through the hand.

Torgo tried. Azel gave him that. But the Witch wouldn't wake up. Azel suspected she didn't want to leave the trance's comfort.

The hole in the wall grew. Azel discouraged the Dartars with a spear till he noticed the Zouki brat stirring.

Thunder shook the citadel when the kid raised his gaze to the Witch.

Azel clouted him in the back of the head. "That's enough, Torgo. We can't force her. Pick her up. Follow me."

"What?"

"You want to just sit here and wait for those assholes? Or you want to move someplace safe?"

"Where?"

"Trust old Azel. He was Nakar's number one buddy. I know stuff about this place even she don't. There's a place he put in before any of us was born. They'll never find it." He didn't believe that but it wouldn't hurt if Torgo did. "We'll have everything we need to finish up." He grabbed the Witch's things.

Torgo looked like a condemned man given an unexpected reprieve.

The pounding on the wall continued. A head poked through, ducked back.

Azel limped to the wardrobe, dropped the stuff he carried, opened the panel, tossed the junk through, helped Torgo ease the Witch into the hidden room. "Let's get the rest." He rubbed his leg. It ached badly. His hand came away spotted with blood.

They rounded Gorloch's flank as a slim Dartar slithered through the wall. Azel chuckled. "I'd say their timing is about perfect." Torgo gave him a puzzled look. Azel chuckled again. He was going to find out real soon now. "You're stronger. You lug Nakar. I'll get the kid." He slashed the straps binding the boy to the altar.

The skinny Dartar stayed where he was, helped make the hole in the wall larger.

The boy opened his eyes. His face had changed, darkening somehow. Nakar was there. He had heard the Witch's call but hadn't come into this world quite yet.

Thunder boomed.

Azel grinned as he hoisted the brat. Some lord of Hell was favoring him today. He stepped to the other kid, lashed out, meaning to break the brat's neck. He glanced at the Dartars. Four were through the hole now, getting brave, getting set to charge. He gave them a grin, a wave, said, "Good-bye, assholes," and took off.

Torgo was lifting Nakar as Azel passed him. Azel clipped him behind one knee. He collapsed. Azel chuckled again as he rounded Gorloch's image, listening to the Dartars roar toward the eunuch. One of them howled, "Arif!"

Fa'tad peeped through a crack in the shutters of a second-storey window of a commandeered house. The Living's soldiers had entered the citadel. Finally. They had dithered forever. "Excellent. Give the signal."

One blast from a horn, taken up at a distance. Black figures, like sodden crows, raced toward the citadel. A wagon appeared. It carried bricks.

At least four of the Living's top men had been sucked in. And Fa'tad knew where to grab their commander. Once the citadel was sealed up the Living would be nothing but a nuisance anymore.

"Collect Colonel bel-Sidek," he ordered. He remained rooted, staring out, troubled. Mo'atabar should have reached the top of that tower by now. But there had been no signal.

Where was he?

Would Nakar have to be paid, after all?

Dartars scrambled through the hole like rats in flight. Aaron scrambled with them, clambering atop men, feeling elbows and fists and knees dig into his flesh as others climbed on him. He tumbled to the floor, glimpsed Arif bouncing on the shoulder of a fleeing man. He yelled, "Arif!"

The Dartars charged a man who was floundering around trying to disengage himself from a stiff corpse. Aaron froze. That was Nakar! Terror held him rooted.

The man shook loose and rose. He was huge. He hurled Nakar at the Dartars. Several went down. The rest hit him. He grabbed a javelin from one and a sword from another and struck out like a lioness beset by hounds. For a moment it seemed he might overcome them all.

Bellowing, Mo'atabar got his men to back off. The big man began to retreat.

Arrows and javelins hit him. He made no sound. He just looked puzzled, like he could not believe it.

Reyha brushed past Aaron, keening. "Zouki!" The boy's head hung at an odd angle. She dropped to her knees by the chair where Zouki was tied.

Yoseh grabbed Aaron's arm. "Come on!" He hardly glanced at the idol as he flew past, into the darkness beyond.

Aaron stumbled after him, averting his eyes from Reyha's pain, from the scarlet ruin of the big man and those he had slain, from the ugliness of the monster god who still had the power to torment Qushmarrah. He went numbly, without hope, unable to restrain a moan when Reyha started wailing.

The Herodian witch yammered at Mo'atabar. Mo'atabar yelled at his men. Some paid attention. Nogah's bunch wolfed after Yoseh and Aaron. One had enough sense to bring a lamp.

Ten minutes whirled away, time flown on the wings of vultures. They found no sign of Arif. Hopeless, Aaron trudged back when Yoseh and Nogah went to consult Mo'atabar.

The sergeant and sorceress were shouting at one another. Mo'atabar stopped long enough to order the hole through the wall plugged.

"What's going on?" Aaron asked.

Nogah said, "It seems that if everything has gone Fa'tad's way we have several hundred of the Living in here with us now. Nice of Mo'atabar to tell us the plan. We were supposed to go up instead of down. They say a fortress's defenders always retreat upward. We were supposed to go to the top of the high tower, then climb down outside. That's why all the ropes and stuff." Nogah cursed in dialect. "That's the Eagle. We'd have the Living's captains and best men trapped like we have the Herodians caught in the maze."

"Why?" Aaron asked.

"Fa'tad knows." Nogah shrugged. "Ask him when you see him. In Hell. It didn't work. We came down. We prevented Nakar's restoration but got caught in our own trap."

"I don't want to make you cry, boy," Mo'atabar said. "But we haven't prevented anything." He kicked Nakar's corpse. "The sorceress says they can manage without this. If they can waken Nakar inside the boy."

Aaron groaned, began to weep, his calm proving more fragile than he had thought. He went to stand beside Reyha, as though somehow two miseries might cancel one another, a little.

The Herodian sorceress edged him aside, knelt before Zouki, studied him for a long time. Finally, she grunted.

"What?" Aaron and Reyha asked together.

The Dartar racket had faded. Azel levered himself up from

where he'd been sitting. He cursed softly. Damn, his leg hurt. It was stiffening up, too. And still seeping a little. He drew his knife.

He kicked the Witch a good one. She did not respond. "I hope you didn't kill us, you crazy bitch." Damn her. He couldn't stay mad at her. Easier to stay mad at himself for having been weak enough to get sucked in.

The kid wasn't unconscious but neither was he alert. He seemed caught on a cusp between today and yesterday, Nakar there but shy. Maybe unwilling to come forward while there was a chance that might mean final victory for Ala-eh-din Beyh. Fine. Let him float. He needed time to work out how to use Nakar without him getting loose completely.

He slipped out of hiding, knife poised. There weren't many of those Dartar bastards. He knew the secret ways. He could pick them off, make them wish they'd never heard of Qushmarrah. Get shut of them and he could concentrate on the Witch and the brat and doing what had to be done.

Pity Torgo couldn't be here to do the dirty deed and pay the final price. Now working it so he came out looking good was going to be tricky.

He slid into the shadows of Gorloch's image, eavesdropped on the Dartars. Some were muttering because their sorceress said Nakar could be restored outside his body. She was doing something with the other brat. Some were plugging the hole they'd busted through the wall. A few were breaking up stuff for the wood. What the hell?

Ah! Now wasn't that amusing? The Living had come in behind them. And that pile of wood was so they could roast Nakar and Ala-eh-din Beyh.

Azel grinned wickedly. Hell and damnation! Yes! If the Witch's only choice was to bring Nakar back in the kid, instead of shoving him back into his own body . . . All kinds of possibilities there. No way Nakar could manage a child's body like it was a grown one. And it should be a whole lot easier for the woman to get over a kid.

Hell with hunting Dartars. Wasn't any point with the Living in the citadel. Let those bastards wear each other down. He'd work on the survivors.

He retreated to the hidden room.

The Dartars would look for the brat again. That sorceress. Didn't look like shit but she was the same stripe as Ala-eh-din Beyh. She knew. She'd whip them into looking. If she put her mind to it she'd find the room despite Nakar's spells of concealment. She'd been good enough to get through the Postern of Fate.

He checked his leg. Not good. Still oozing. Had he left a trail? He checked. No sign. His clothes were absorbing it. He needed to get off the leg and stay off. But he couldn't. Not yet. He made a rude bandage and bound it tightly. That would have to do.

The room was a deathtrap. Better move to the top of the tower. Their sorceress couldn't do them much good if he got the Witch and the kid forted up there. All he'd have to do would be to sit on the trapdoor. They couldn't get the leverage to push him off.

He rifled his pack, found analgesic powder, washed it down with water from a small canteen. Bitterness remained in his mouth. He relaxed five minutes, hoping it would start to work fast. He almost drifted off.

He jerked awake. None of that! They wouldn't get him by default.

He checked the boy's pulse, afraid he might have whacked the brat too hard. The kid hadn't stirred. He was all right.

Better get on with it. He could nap afterward.

He took the boy up first. The ladder seemed a mile high. His leg was killing him when he got back down, the pain powder doing nothing at all. He recalled his impulse toward the sinkhole country. Why hadn't he had the plain damned sense? He had no more brains than that idiot Torgo.

That one cut was leaking again. It wanted rest badly. There was no time. He adjusted his bandages.

He took the Witch up next, limp as a fish. Why the hell couldn't she help out a little? Dumb bitch wasn't worth all this.

One more trip to go, his supplies and the stuff she'd need to finish up. He rubbed his leg and again told himself he could lie down afterward.

He did not think he would complete that final climb. He suffered leg cramps. His shoulder muscles tightened into rocky knots. The bleeding worsened. He tore others of his wounds open. He suffered vertigo. He was sure he had done himself permanent damage. But he couldn't quit. He was what he was, ridden and driven.

The force within triumphed. As always. He completed his climb, dropped his load, closed the trapdoor, for a moment faced into the rain. It hadn't wakened the woman or boy. He covered the Witch the best he could, though that was only a gesture. Thunder cracked as he settled on the trap. He'd rest and let the analgesic work before he tried to waken the woman.

He glanced up. Hard to tell through the rain but it seemed the clouds were low and moving fast, swirling around the tower.

He lowered his head and closed his eyes. Ten minutes ought to be enough rest.

Zenobel stared at the cage in the great hall. He recalled the place as it had been before Dak-es-Souetta. It had gone to seed. Become shabby. That was sad. Say whatever about Nakar, he had made the citadel Qushmarrah's glorious crown.

King Dabdahd hustled up. He had the citadel staff besieged in the Witch's quarters. He said, "They won't surrender. They won't even talk."

"Is she up there?"

"I don't know. We tried breaking through the wall to get around the spells on the door. I lost two men. They didn't see her. That doesn't mean anything."

Zenobel grunted. "What about those damned Dartars? Any sign of them?"

"None but their dead."

Zenobel considered the children he had had rounded up. Were they settled down enough to talk sense? He rose from his seat.

Carza trotted up. "We found the Dartars. They're barricaded

in the temple. They broke through a wall to get inside. Should I finish them?"

"You want Fa'tad to kill *us*?"

"Huh?"

He did not know. Neither did King. They had been busy when the news had come. "He sealed the gateway behind us. Bricked it up. Only way we can get out is through the windows. If the drop doesn't kill us his archers will."

King went pale. Carza looked bewildered.

"You don't get it? Al-Akla has done it again, this time to Herod and us both. Bel-Sidek wouldn't laugh at fools but he's sure won the right. He warned us."

Carza just frowned. It surpassed him. "We have a mission, Zenobel. A holy mission. If you won't carry it out I will."

"Go ahead. Waste all the lives you want. I don't care anymore. Nothing we do will change anything now."

Bel-Sidek did not look around when the Dartar arrived. The nomad was polite. "Fa'tad would like to see you, sir." The steel wore a velvet mask.

Bel-Sidek took Meryel's hand. "If I'm to be executed let it be done here where I've known my only happiness."

"Fa'tad has no wish to slay anyone, sir. He said only that he wishes to speak with you."

Meryel squeezed bel-Sidek's hand gently. "Go, Sisu. Maybe you can do something yet."

Bel-Sidek nodded, though he doubted it. Wearily, he followed the Dartar out into the rain. Maybe Fa'tad did just want to talk. He had sent only the one man.

The day was nearly gone. Very little light remained. The clouds hung low above the citadel, turning and churning. He could not get interested. It had been a day as long as forever piled on a week a hundred times as long as that. The end was in sight now. At last.

Qushmarrah was passing into a new age—not that which he and the General had envisioned. "Warrior. Have they finished Nakar yet?"

His companion drew in upon himself. "I can't say, sir. There's been no word from our men inside the citadel." Later, he added, "Nor any from yours."

"Oh." That did not sound good. Bel-Sidek eyed those busy clouds for as long as he could take the rain in his face. Nakar's last hour had come during a ferocious rain, with clouds whirling around the citadel. He had been a prisoner elsewhere then, but . . . Hadn't it been something like this? Was this precursive of the resurrection of the Abomination?

Bel-Sidek and the Dartar passed through and walked parallel to a file of bedraggled Herodians being escorted from the Shu. Fa'tad was accepting the surrender of those he had entombed in the labyrinth. Maybe the Eagle was not interested in a total blood baptism.

Bel-Sidek spied General Cado among the captives. Ha. Now the man would know how it had felt for the vanquished after Dak-es-Souetta.

Cado met his eye, recognized him, smiled wanly, winked as though they were fellow conspirators. Bel-Sidek snorted. Co-conspirators in defeat. Pawns who had let themselves be manipulated by the old genius of the Khadatqa Mountains. The gulled and downcast.

Whatever else, he thought, you had to admire the Eagle's daring.

Yoseh was scared again. They had looked everywhere, over and over, and had found no sign of the Witch or child-taker or Arif, no hint of a hidden exit. Every minute fled meant a greater danger.

Nogah observed, "The sorceress probably could find it but she's too busy making like udders on a bull." She could not be diverted from the corpses she was cooking. The stench was enough to gag a vulture.

Yoseh said, "Maybe she knows what she's doing."

"Like hell. She's riding with her eyes shut same as the rest of us. What's keeping the damned veydeen?" The Qushmarrahans had not yet tried to get in.

Mo'atabar made periodic sallies toward the bonfire, to remind the sorceress that she had said the Witch could recall Nakar without his body. She showed no real interest. Yoseh hoped she knew what she was doing.

"They're here," said the man posted where they had broken in.

Mo'atabar hustled over, listened, said, "They're not in any hurry."

Once they got the carpenter calmed down Nogah decided to stop waiting on the woman. "Aaron. What would you do if you were going to put in a secret exit?"

"Eh?"

"You're a carpenter. Think like a carpenter. A carpenter probably did the building. Wouldn't you think?"

The man thought. "I'd use a cabinetmaker. I'd put it where it wasn't obvious and I'd demand the finest possible joins so nothing would show."

Yoseh said, "Tamisa told me that's the kind of stuff you do."

The carpenter nodded.

Impatient, Nogah snapped, "So prowl around. Think like a cabinetmaker. Show us where some other carpenter might have put a hidden door. The fix we're in it won't matter if we tear things up."

It took only minutes. "Got to be this wardrobe," the carpenter said. "Best place for it."

Medjhah ripped the wardrobe apart. Nogah went after Mo'atabar. Mo'atabar came and crawled through the wreckage. "There's a room back here, all right. But there isn't anybody in it."

"There would be a way out," the carpenter said. "The room is just to buy time."

The sorceress appeared. She exchanged words with Mo'atabar. Mo'atabar said, "She tells me there are three ways out. One is in the floor, here." He stomped. "One is in the wall, here." Thump went a fist. "The other one is in this wall, here. Open them up."

Medjhah tried brute force again, without luck this time.

"Let me," the carpenter said. He had pulled himself together. Other than thunder nothing had happened for so long he was starting to hope again. Maybe the sorceress's lack of haste encouraged him.

It took him just a minute to open the secret doors.

"Good." Mo'atabar studied the openings. "Kosuth, down you go. Medjhah, you take this one. Yoseh, you take that one. Be careful but don't waste time. The Living have started in on that wall."

The sorceress said something, went away. Yoseh hoped she was going to delay the veydeen. He could not worry about them, though. He stared at that little doorway, scared stiff. It barely seemed big enough . . . Mo'atabar kept talking, did such a good job making it sound routine that he felt shamed by his reluctance. He swallowed, crawled into the hole.

It became an upward shaft immediately, that had to go all the way to the sky, up and up and up, into silence, into darkness like Nakar's own heart.

It got scarier. After he climbed so far he lost count of rungs, thunder shook the citadel. He felt the vibrations. For a moment he was afraid the place would fall down around him.

He climbed more slowly, conserving his strength. The ringing cleared from his ears—and what at first seemed imagination proved to be a genuine whisper that frightened him more till he realized it had to be rain falling on a surface overhead.

He paused, rested, marshaled his courage, resumed his climb. Three rungs higher his hand closed on slick moisture. It remained sticky when he pulled it away.

The crown of his head bumped something hard and cold. He felt around. Rusty iron? The rain drummed away. It would be thick and heavy.

This was the final test. He could retreat and report and suffer no questions but he would always wonder, was he a Dartar warrior or some cringing veydeen mouse?

He pushed with his head, increased the pressure till the metal gave. Nothing happened. He pushed again, slowly, steadily, till his eyes rose above the edge—and he was face-to-face with someone just a foot away.

He nearly let go. He did squeak. That was the child-taker,

lying dead or sleeping in the rain. Nobody could sleep in the rain, could they?

He pushed till his shoulders reached roof level. He saw Arif and the Witch, sprawled in the rain, dead or sleeping, too.

What now?

He reached for his knife, to make sure of the child-taker, then changed his mind and reached for Arif's ankle. If he could drag the boy over and carry him down . . .

Something hit him so fast he never saw it coming. He slammed back against the side of the shaft, then fell.

Squeak. Azel remained motionless only because of the watery state of his flesh. Weak as a newborn, he couldn't betray himself when he wakened.

He cracked an eyelid, saw the Dartar kid from the Shu. That little bastard was everywhere. Haunting him. How the hell had he gotten up here? Azel realized he had rolled off the trapdoor after he'd fallen asleep.

Gorloch or luck gave him the moment he needed and the energy to capitalize. The Dartar turned, reached for the Arif brat, got him by the foot. Azel put everything he had into his punch. The Dartar flew backward, fell, the brat's shoe flipping after him. "Hope you land on your head, asshole."

He didn't have energy enough to stand. The rainwater where he'd lain was red. Clots of blood floated there. Damn! He was bleeding to death. Wouldn't that be ironic? He rolled into a sitting position atop the trapdoor. Thank Gorloch it had fallen shut. He would not have had the strength to close it had it fallen the other way.

He fiddled with his bandages till he got the bleeding stopped. One more small effort, then he would put down roots.

He eased over to the Witch. "Wake up, woman." No response. *Whap!* He cracked her cheek with his palm, rocked her head halfway around. "Come on, damn it! This is it. You get on the stick and call up Nakar or kiss your ass good-bye. They know where we're at and we got nowhere else to hide." He popped her again. This time he glimpsed a flash of eyeball.

That was it. That was all he had, except an ounce of iron will that let him guide himself as he collapsed, so his torso sprawled across a corner of the trapdoor.

The first blow reached her but the drug held her. The second sent alarums of pain coursing through her. She opened one eye far enough to see her tormentor.

Azel? But how . . . ? She was soaked. She lay in a pool of water. Rain fell upon her still. Thunder stalked overhead. The chill followed the pain inside her, opening channels through which thought and sense began to flow. She gained control as Azel fell as if he had melted.

She shoved her upper body up to the length of her arms, turned her head slowly. Her thoughts did not run crisply but she could reason. And she could remember some of what had been happening around her while the drug ruled her. She understood where she was and why and how she had come to be there and for one moment she actually appreciated Azel and his stubbornness.

She had yielded to weakness, perhaps to defeatism, and had permitted herself too much of the drug. Fool. Maybe she was as crazy as Azel claimed. Maybe she didn't deserve Nakar back. Maybe she was too weak.

Her body would not support itself. She collapsed. But she resisted the allure of sleep, of escape. The hour had come. Time had run out. Azel had said they knew where she was . . . Her gaze fell on the boy.

He was asleep. More than asleep. Unconscious. She felt Nakar in there, quiescent, in a twilight of near-awareness, reluctant to come nearer the light.

Ala-eh-din Beyh.

Of course! That was it, as Azel had insisted. Nakar dared not come forward. To do so meant facing the consequences of total defeat. He *had* lost that struggle . . . Her fault. Her fault completely.

But . . . Vaguely, as though recalling a fading dream, she

recaptured tenuous memories from below. Azel hitting the other child. Azel had broken his neck. Ala-eh-din Beyh would not be there now. That vicious soul had traveled on.

It was here for the taking. All she had lived and suffered for. If she kept her wits and conquered her flesh and found the strength to draw forth her beloved's soul.

She wept a single tear, though. Never again would her man be the man she had known. The body was still down below. That Herodian sorceress, that bitch from the same kennel as Ala-eh-din Beyh, would have wasted no time destroying it.

She looked at the boy and laughed madly, picturing herself mothering the new young Nakar. Then she turned to the things Azel had brought up. What she needed would be there. Azel always did whatever had to be done.

She was slow, so slow, but soon she was ready, soon she was reaching into the darkness, calling her love.

Arif was lost in a nightmare. He could not wake up. He was terrified but not as much now as he had been. This was so unreal he could not believe it completely. He seemed to hear his mother reassuring him, "It's only a dream, Arif. It's only a dream."

Something alien was there in the darkness with him, frightened and wary, too, but big and dangerous and patient, like a giant, poisonous toad waiting in the dark for prey. That thing moved seldom. So far he had fought it off each time it had. He had begun to gain confidence there.

Then the voice came, remote at first, a woman calling. "Mother?" The voice called, compelling and reassuring. He seemed to turn toward it and move that way. The voice grew louder. He moved eagerly—till he recognized it as the voice of the beautiful, evil woman who stole children.

He tried to stop moving toward the light, could not.

The thing in the darkness shifted, turned its invisible eye upon him. He felt its amusement, its iron, wicked intent.

He tried to scream.

That thing swam up toward the light, gaining fast.

* * *

Instinct made Yoseh flail out. He was not conscious enough to think. One hand dragged over several rungs. He felt fingernails rip and break. He got a solid hold. His arm wrenched violently. He screamed.

He grabbed with his other hand before the first gave way. He stopped his plunge. He clung there shaking and whimpering with pain, afraid to move.

The child-taker had not been dead. Had not been sleeping. Now the man would take steps.

He had to get word to Nogah and Mo'atabar and the Herodian sorceress *now*. But he could not move. His muscles had locked, refused to let him. His fear of falling would not respond to his will.

He could not yell again, either. His tight, dry throat would let him do nothing but croak.

Tears flowed. A coward. He had feared he was, always. And now, when all depended upon him acting, he could not. He burned, thinking of the shame upon his father.

23

Aaron had himself under control now. Outwardly he portrayed quiet calmness. But could it last? His mind was a hornet's nest of terrible thoughts and fears.

The hidden room was crowded beyond enduring. They were packed in there belly-to-back, shoulder-to-shoulder, breathing into one another's faces, smelling one another's fear. The sorceress had not been able to prevent the Living from breaching the temple wall. She had had to spend too much attention on Zouki. Aaron could hear the Qushmarrahan rebels cursing outside the wardrobe. The wardrobe that would hide nothing if opened because Medjhah had demolished the concealed opening.

There was no sound in the little room. Most of them were holding their breaths. Only the sorceress was doing anything. Something to shield them, to hide them, to baffle the Living, he prayed.

He called upon Aram's love and mercy repeatedly, silently, in his heart.

In time Kosuth and Medjhah returned from their quests. In whispers they delivered negative reports. The bolt-hole in the floor just led down and down to water. The other ran to a hidden exit inside the guardroom behind the postern—inside the brick wall Fa'tad had installed.

"Even so," Mo'atabar murmured. "Even so." He began indicating men. "Crawl in there. Hide. It's too crowded in here."

Despite the maddening crowding no one wanted to go into the crawlway. Aaron thought only a second and knew he would fight if they tried to send him. He could not endure the closeness.

How much worse for these men, reared in the wide expanses of the mountains and Takes, beneath sprawling desert skies?

Something landed at the bottom of the third bolt-hole, *plop!* Aaron was right beside that, pressed up against Nogah and Medjhah, more pressured now that the latter had returned. He recognized the object immediately. He retained barely enough caution to confine himself to a whisper. "That's Arif's shoe." It was so wet it had splattered water.

Medjhah said, "It must have come from outside. Up there. In the rain. Yoseh must have . . . They must be on top of the tower. We must be right under it here."

Mo'atabar forced his way through the press. Aaron watched his passage spark unreasoning rage in the eyes of the Dartars he brushed. Those men barely controlled themselves.

As Mo'atabar arrived a second object fell down the shaft, hit, *ping!* metallically. Nogah squeaked, "That's Yoseh's ring. The one Father gave him."

Medjhah whispered, "He can't come down. That has to mean he can't come down. He wants us to come up."

Nogah had a counter remark. Mo'atabar scowled. He was suspicious. He wanted to think and talk about it before he did anything.

Aaron could not control himself. His muscles seemed to act of their own accord, compelling him to enter the shaft and start climbing.

Nogah and Medjhah followed immediately. Before Aaron climbed fifty feet he heard Mo'atabar and the sorceress arguing over which should go first.

Soon he ached in every muscle. He was no ape or sailor

accustomed to climbing. His body had suffered already. But fear for Arif drove him.

He bumped into someone. *Someone!* A soft whimper came from above. "Yoseh?"

A grunt. An inarticulate sound filled with pain and fear and humiliation.

"It's Aaron, Yoseh. Are you all right?"

Another whimpering sound. Not a positive sign.

Nogah forced his way up beside Aaron, so that they clung to the unseen rungs side by side, so crowded in the shaft that they might not have fallen had they let go. Nogah whispered to his brother. He could get no sense from the boy. He began making soothing, comforting sounds. Aaron clung to the rungs and wondered how long he could keep that up before his body betrayed him.

After a while Medjhah asked, "What's the story?"

Nogah replied, "He fell. He caught himself. He got hurt doing it. He'll be all right. I'm tying him to the rungs till we can lift him out."

"Going to be a bitch getting past him."

"Uhm. Where's Mo'atabar?"

Aaron intuited the import of the question. Mo'atabar was a sizable man. He would not be able to force his way past Yoseh. Whatever waited above, there would be no help from Mo'atabar or anyone below him.

Medjhah said, "Mahdah is behind me, then the sorceress. Then Mo'atabar."

Mo'atabar growled a question. No one responded to his impatience.

Nogah said, "Yoseh says there's an iron trapdoor lying flat up there. It's heavy. It opens on the floor of the parapet. The Witch and the child-taker are up there with Arif. He thought they were out cold or dead but the child-taker surprised him and knocked him back down when he was trying to sneak Arif into the shaft."

Oh, Aaron thought. Maybe that explained the shoe.

"How about now?"

"Who knows? The child-taker will be waiting, I guess."

Medjhah grumbled something about Yoseh should have made sure of them up there while he had had the chance. In a strained voice, Nogah said, "There's no choice now. We have to do it. Let's go."

Never in his wildest boyhood fantasies had Aaron pictured himself in anything like this. He never had had the stuff of heroes. Charging up a ladder into the teeth of death, in defiance of doom and the dark old gods . . . Aram! Send down the flame of love and mercy. He squirmed past Yoseh, who continued to make sounds of pain.

Above, Nogah stopped. "I'm there," he whispered. "The trap." Yoseh had not fallen too far, after all. Not more than fifteen feet.

"Now what?"

"Medjhah? You past Yoseh?"

"Almost. As far as I can get."

"Aaron?" Nogah's voice broke. The warrior was as frightened as anyone, Aaron realized. He knew just how poor his chances were.

Aaron looked inside himself. He was terrified but he had it under control. Arif was up there, maybe no more than ten feet away. "I can do it." Despite muscles of water. Despite being unarmed. He could not recall what had become of any of the weapons they had given him during the course of the day.

"Medjhah?"

"Ready."

"Tell them to get their tails moving down there, as soon as we go. Tell Mo'atabar to carry Yoseh up if he has to."

Medjhah relayed the message. Nogah said, "Now!" Aaron heard his bones and sinews creak as he pushed up against the iron door.

Azel felt the trapdoor pushing up against him. He couldn't do a damned thing. Everything he had left, it seemed, he needed just to keep his eyes open.

The Witch was doing it. Somehow, despite the circumstances, she had reached Nakar and was luring him forth. He saw the shadow growing in the brat's face. Maybe Nakar sensed the passing of Ala-eh-din Beyh. Good thing he'd broken that other brat's neck.

He managed a warning grunt. The Witch was alert enough to catch it. "A moment longer, Azel. Only a moment more. Don't let them come."

Don't let them come. How the hell was he supposed to stop them? All he was now was dead weight. If they managed enough upward force they would tumble him off and all he could do was lie there and watch them climb out.

The shadow in the kid's face darkened quickly. The clouds overhead grew more excited. Thunder hammered.

And Azel wondered not about Nakar's advent but about the exit he needed to make after he had outlived his usefulness. He was in no condition to end the story of the Abomination.

"He's coming," the Witch breathed. "He's almost here. We're going to do it, Azel. We're going to do it."

Aaron slithered up next to Nogah. Chest-to-chest, scarcely able to breathe, they took what room they could and heaved together.

The trap remained stubborn . . . then gave.

As it began moving Nogah grunted, "First!" and sprang with it, as though the climb and all before it had taken nothing out of his body.

Nogah's feet were not yet clear when Aaron followed. Nogah threw himself at the child-taker, who had toppled off the trap. And the child-taker took him out.

What kind of man was he, Aaron wondered as the stubby man, on his back, moved jerkily in lightning flashes and sent Nogah plunging headlong into the battlement surrounding the parapet. Nogah went limp.

Aaron nearly gagged doing it, was astounded that he could, but found what it took to kick the child-taker in the head. He whirled on the Witch and his son as Medjhah clambered into sight.

Arif's eyes were open and watching but that was not Arif looking out. That was something hideous, dark, and evil.

He could not move, looking at that.

Medjhah staggered forward, knife falling toward the Witch. She made a feeble gesture, barely in time. The knife turned to flame in the Dartar's hand, sizzled through the rain. He screamed, flung it from him, fell forward into the woman, bowling her over. A knife appeared in her hand. She stabbed him once, weakly, before Aaron recovered and kicked again, striking her wrist more by luck than design. Mahdah came up, circled to the side, to put the woman between himself and Aaron.

Aaron looked at Arif again. The darkness within him was growing still but had an unfocused quality, as though the thing surfacing was confused and far from being in control. For an instant, even, it seemed that Arif himself looked out of those eyes, begging help defeating his devil.

The Herodian sorceress rose from the chute.

Fa'tad stepped onto the portico of the Residence. His most senior prisoners accompanied him. Witchfires pranced atop the citadel tower. He recognized the veydeen carpenter. "Finally."

General Cado observed, "You have done it."

Fa'tad chuckled. "So it would seem. Fatig, get the carpenter's family. However it went they should be there for him when he comes down."

A messenger left immediately.

"Don't count your chickens."

Fa'tad turned to Colonel bel-Sidek. "Sir?"

"That's a witch's game. Two against one and no one alive can match either of the two."

Thunder and lightning hammered the night like the crackling bacon of the gods. Clouds spun madly overhead. Rain fell in ever greater torrents.

Fa'tad al-Akla lost his smile.

The Witch had regained her feet. She held the boy before her. His face darkened ever more as the thunder bellowed ever more fiercely. "Too late!" she crowed at the Herodian sorceress. "You're too late, meddler. You can't stop it now. I can withstand you all till he comes." She threw back her head, shrieked into the teeth of the lightning. "He comes!" Let Qushmarrah know. Let all the world know. Nakar was coming. The hour of vengeance was at hand.

In response the Herodian witch knelt beside the ladder well, reached down. Then she rose, helping a child climb onto the parapet.

The other one . . . But Azel had broken his neck. Hadn't he?

The Witch almost collapsed in her terror.

Azel cracked an eyelid, considered his surroundings through vision gone fuzzy, listened with hearing gone as feeble as an old man's. He shut out his pain and fear, examined the situation. As that Herodian bitch brought the other brat onto the parapet.

He was not deceived. Not for an instant. The sorceress had saved the brat by her art but Ala-eh-din Beyh wasn't in him now. Had he been there the storm would have ripped the tower apart. But the Witch believed, if only for a moment. Believed and surrendered to the doom she saw as her punishment for having failed her husband.

Damned fool woman.

Damn fool man, he. Lying there with both legs and one arm past death's door and for what? For her? What damnable fool hid down deep inside him, gulling him all along, so that he'd thought he had some chance of making her his own? He was an idiot. As big a fool as anybody he'd gulled during his idiot's quest.

He eyed them all, women, boys, father, Dartars. He had no regrets, felt no remorse. But he was alive still. Alive, he had to make decisions.

The carpenter shouted, "Easy," at the Witch. He had to shout to be heard above the storm. "Take it easy. Don't . . ."

A fool to the last, that woman. Not thinking with her brain. Deceived by a rustic sorceress from beyond the sea.

Instead of fighting on, going down swinging, making them pay for whatever they won, she chose the easy way out again.

She shook the carpenter off, stumbled backward, looked out over the city she hated, then leaped from the parapet.

Live a fool, die one, Azel thought. She'd defeated herself. She'd lost to herself.

No one was watching him. It was an effort of herculean proportion but he managed to move one hand from his waist to his mouth. He began to chew.

He could've stopped her, he thought as the shadows closed in. He could've shouted. They would've killed him but he could've warned her before she took that step. He could've given her Nakar . . . The last thing in his sight was the boy. Nakar was looking out of those young eyes, looking at him, and Nakar knew. By holding his tongue he had destroyed them both, Witch and wizard alike.

Azel used his last ounce of strength to force a mocking smile and a farewell wink.

Aaron tried to grab the Witch as she backed off the parapet. In the last instant she changed her mind, reached for his out-stretched hand. But the distance separating them was too great. Down she plunged, vanishing in the darkness, trailing a scream in which he heard Nakar's name and a curse upon Qushmarrah.

Chance? Curse? Whim of the gods? At the moment the Witch struck stone the earth shook. The tremor was barely discernible but it was enough.

A lightning crack appeared in the leaky wall in the home of that otherwise insignificant woman in the Shu. Plaster chipped away. A hair of water squirted through. The stream expanded swiftly.

The wall came apart.

The surge destroyed the next wall it encountered.

In minutes the hundreds of thousands of cubic yards of water trapped in the maze were in motion.

It would have been an awesome sight from the harbor had anyone been out there to watch the avalanche of water and rubble and bodies roar down and hit the bay.

They got Yoseh up out of the shaft. Mo'atabar and the others followed. Soon they had ropes over the side. Fa'tad had men waiting below.

They lowered the Herodian sorceress first, so she would be down there when Arif and the injured arrived. Already she had done something to put Arif asleep. Already Aaron understood that when Arif awakened he would not recall the threat that had come so close to devouring him. He would not forget his imprisonment completely but the worst horrors would be cleansed from his mind. He would remember that his father had, indeed, come to his rescue.

They lowered Aaron right after Yoseh. When he reached the cobblestones he found Laella and Mish and Stafa and even old Raheb waiting. Only Mish had glances to spare for anyone but him and Arif. She had a few for Yoseh, who seemed more embarrassed than pained now that the sorceress had seen to him. His brothers had proclaimed him a hero.

Laella clung to Aaron and Arif and wept as she had not done since the day he had come home from the Herodian captivity, releasing all her fears and tensions in the form of tears.

Aaron said, "It's all right now. It's all right. It's all over now." He glanced at the sky. Once frenzied clouds had gone drowsy already.

"What about this one?" Medjhah asked Mo'atabar, kicking the child-taker.

"What about him? He's dead, isn't he?"

"Bled to death, looks like."

"Leave him lie. Fa'tad will send a cleanup gang in tomorrow. Let them worry about it. I'm too damned tired. All I want to do is get down and lie down."

Medjhah shrugged. He nudged the dead man with his toe. "He was a tough bastard. For a veydeen."

"Wonderful epitaph, Medjhah. A real Dartar eulogy. It's your turn on the rope. Mind the slick."

Those who were sent into the citadel to take prisoners and loot and dispose of the dead failed to find a corpse atop the tower. The disappearance was a great puzzle but no one worried it long.

Aaron had said it was over. That was not quite true. History is the whole loaf, not just a slice. History is a river flowing, events its tributaries. The end of Aaron Habid's tale was but an event in other stories.

Epilog One:

Immediate Events

Six days after the fall of the citadel Cretius Marco met the Turok raiders in battle. He slew or captured all but a handful. The same day, a hundred miles east, Diro Lucillo received word of events in Qushmarrah. He turned on his Dartar auxiliaries. Joab extricated his men, fled eastward, seized control of the fortified bridges behind the expeditionary force. Four days later, in a lightning strike, his men captured the Seven Towers. Qushmarrah could not be approached from the west.

Earlier, the Herodian fleet had made harbor in Qushmarrah and been captured intact.

Eight days after the fall, after intense discussions with Colonel Sisu bel-Sidek, Fa'tad al-Akla proclaimed the Dartar kingdom of Qushmarrah. Bel-Sidek served as his grand vizier the rest of his days.

Several senior officers of the Living did not survive to see the founding of the new estate.

Fa'tad sent to the Khadatqa Mountains for the rest of his people. Thus did he overcome the relentless drought.

Eighteen days after the fall, encouraged by the Herodian disaster to the west, Chorhkni of Aquira marched. He and his allies scored several early successes, but one too many when they captured the commanding Herodian general. The refugee general Lentello Cado replaced him. He ruined Aquiran ambitions at Algedo, where, when the allies withdrew, Chorhkni and all his sons remained dead upon the field.

Epilog Two:

A Longer View

The Dartar Kings of Qushmarrah were five: Fa'tad, who ruled eighteen years; Joab, who reigned six months; Moamar, who lived three years; Faruk, who survived nine; and Juba. Juba ruled for twenty-nine years and was at war every minute of the final twenty-eight.

Aaron Habid remained a shipbuilder all his days. From his yard came the swift galleys that held Herod's fleets at bay. His son Arif followed in his footsteps. But his son Stafa became a famous privateer, one of those fearless shipmasters whose predations so incensed Herod that the Imperial Senate declared the Third Qushmarrahan War. His sister-in-law, Tamisa, dedicated herself to Aram and so died childless.

Naszif bar bel-Abek pursued a distinguished career in Herodian service, attaining the proconsular rank and governing three different eastern provinces before his retirement to a villa in

Carenia. His son, Zouki (Succo), became a famous jurist and philosopher. A grandson, Probio, elevated the family to senatorial rank.

Lentello Cado died an old and bitter man, still in exile on the nether shore. None of his magnificent efforts to illustrate the Herodian name earned the forgiveness of his enemies in Herod.

The brothers Nogah, Medjhah, and Yoseh inherited the wild mantle of Fa'tad al-Akla. On land and sea they harried the Herodian lion wherever it appeared.

In the fourth year of the Third Qushmarrahan War, Yoseh led a fleet into the harbor of Utium, the port of Herod. He burned the city and the unprepared Herodian fleet, then ravaged the suburbs of Herod itself but failed to penetrate the city wall.

In the eleventh year of the war the brothers landed an army in Edria, north of Herod, and sustained it there fourteen years, devouring everything Herod sent against them, twice besieging Herod itself. They fought boldly and valiantly but in the end the superior stubbornness and vaster resources of Herod prevailed.

The Third Qushmarrahan War lasted twenty-eight years. Qushmarrah won every major battle but the last, before the city wall.

Herod's legions razed Qushmarrah to the last stone. Two centuries later the emperor Petia Magna ordered a new city built upon the site. It took the name Qushmarrah but was Herodian to the bone.

Qushmarrah fell in Yoseh's seventy-fourth year. He survived thirteen more, an active pirate till the day he succumbed to a stray arrow sped by a Herodian marine.

An old hermit in the sinkhole country lived nearly as long, hunting and fishing and occasionally visiting one of the nearer villages to amuse himself with news of the latest foibles of the world. He never looked back, never had any regrets.

THE DRAGON REBORN

Sequel to *The Great Hunt*

Book Three
ᘑᘈof~ᔱ
The Wheel of Time

by

Robert Jordan

Praise for *Eye of the World*

"A powerful vision of good and evil...fascinating people moving through a rich and interesting world."   —*Orson Scott Card*

"Richly detailed...fully realized, complex adventure."
                                                    —*Library Journal*

"A combination of Robin Hood and Stephen King that is hard to resist...Jordan makes the reader care about these characters as though they were old friends."   —*Milwaukee Sentinel*

Praise for *The Great Hunt*

"Jordan can spin as rich a world and as event-filled a tale as [Tolkien]...will not be easy to put down."   —*ALA Booklist*

"Worth re-reading a time or two."   —*Locus*

"This is good stuff...Splendidly characterized and cleverly plotted...The Great Hunt is a good book which will always be a good book. I shall certainly [line up] for the third volume."
                                                    —*Interzone*

The Dragon Reborn
coming in hardcover in August, 1991

Robert Jordan's
THE EYE OF THE WORLD

The acclaimed first volume of
The Wheel of Time

"This one is as solid as a steel blade, and glowing with the true magic. Robert Jordan deserves congratulations." —Fred Saberhagen

"The next major fantasy epic!" —Piers Anthony

"A splendid epic of heroic fantasy, vast in scope, colorful in detail, and convincing in its presentation of human character and personality."

—L. Sprague de Camp

☐
☐ 51181-6 $5.95
Canada $6.95

FANTASY ADVENTURE
FROM GLEN COOK

☐ ☐	50389-9	THE BLACK COMPANY	$3.95 Canada $4.95
☐ ☐	50210-8	DREAMS OF STEEL	$3.95 Canada $4.95
☐ ☐	53379-8	AN ILL FATE MARSHALLING	$3.50 Canada $4.50
☐ ☐	53376-3	REAP THE EAST WIND	$2.95 Canada $3.95
☐ ☐	53382-8	SHADOW GAMES	$3.95 Canada $4.95
☐ ☐	50842-4	SHADOWS LINGER	$3.95 Canada $4.95
☐ ☐	50220-5	THE SILVER SPIKE	$3.95 Canada $4.95
☐ ☐	50307-4	THE SWORDBEARER	$3.95 Canada $4.95
☐ ☐	50929-3	THE TOWER OF FEAR	$3.95 Canada $4.95
☐ ☐	50844-0	THE WHITE ROSE	$3.95 Canada $4.95

Buy them at your local bookstore or use this handy coupon:
Clip and mail this page with your order.

Publishers Book and Audio Mailing Service
P.O. Box 120159, Staten Island, NY 10312-0004

Please send me the book(s) I have checked above. I am enclosing $ _____
(please add $1.25 for the first book, and $.25 for each additional book to cover postage and handling.
Send check or money order only—no CODs).

Name _____
Address _____
City _____ State/Zip _____
Please allow six weeks for delivery. Prices subject to change without notice.

FANTASY ADVENTURE
FROM FRED SABERHAGEN

FANTASY BESTSELLERS
FROM TOR

☐	55852-9	ARIOSTO	$3.95
☐	55853-7	*Chelsea Quinn Yarbro*	Canada $4.95
☐	53671-1	THE DOOR INTO FIRE	$2.95
☐	53672-X	*Diane Duane*	Canada $3.50
☐	53673-8	THE DOOR INTO SHADOW	$2.95
☐	53674-6	*Diane Duane*	Canada $3.50
☐	55750-6	ECHOES OF VALOR	$2.95
☐	55751-4	*edited by Karl Edward Wagner*	Canada $3.95
☐	51181-6	THE EYE OF THE WORLD	$5.95
☐		*Robert Jordan*	Canada $6.95
☐	53388-7	THE HIDDEN TEMPLE	$3.95
☐	53389-5	*Catherine Cooke*	Canada $4.95
☐	55446-9	MOONSINGER'S FRIENDS	$3.50
☐	55447-7	*edited by Susan Shwartz*	Canada $4.50
☐	55515-5	THE SHATTERED HORSE	$3.95
☐	55516-3	*S.P. Somtow*	Canada $4.95
☐	50249-3	SISTER LIGHT, SISTER DARK	$3.95
☐	50250-7	*Jane Yolen*	Canada $4.95
☐	54348-3	SWORDSPOINT	$3.95
☐	54349-1	*Ellen Kushner*	Canada $4.95
☐	53293-7	THE VAMPIRE TAPESTRY	$2.95
☐	53294-5	*Suzie McKee Charnas*	Canada $3.95

Buy them at your local bookstore or use this handy coupon:
Clip and mail this page with your order.

Publishers Book and Audio Mailing Service
P.O. Box 120159, Staten Island, NY 10312-0004

Please send me the book(s) I have checked above. I am enclosing $ _____
(Please add $1.25 for the first book, and $.25 for each additional book to cover postage and handling.
Send check or money order only—no CODs.)

Name _____
Address _____
City _____ State/Zip _____
Please allow six weeks for delivery. Prices subject to change without notice.